D0724883

Also by Lauren Accardo

Forever Adirondacks Novels

WILD LOVE
SWEET LOVE

bold love

LAUREN ACCARDO

JOVE
New York

A JOVE BOOK
Published by Berkley
An imprint of Penguin Random House LLC
penguinrandomhouse.com

ISBN: 9780593200339

First Edition: January 2022

Printed in the United States of America
1 3 5 7 9 10 8 6 4 2

Book design by George Towne

Dedicated to my in-laws—
the Porlas, Wright, and Accardo families—
and everyone connected to these wild,
crazy, big-hearted people.
Thank you for the inspiration.

chapter **one**

Bethany Jones closed her eyes as the sunshine melted into her skin, tugged at the corners of her matte-pink lips, and seeped into her soul, warming her from the inside out. She breathed in, tasting the scent of freshly printed books and a tangy orange blossom candle on her tongue.

"Told you summer in Pine Ridge was nice." Sydney's voice broke through Bee's thoughts like a pebble on a pond.

"I never doubted you," Bee said. She turned away from the big front window of the Loving Page bookstore where she'd erected the base of a small-scale sailboat for the last of the summer displays.

Sydney artfully arranged a basket of delicate scented soaps—ocean breeze and fresh linen—next to the cash register before stepping back to admire her work. "Does anyone use bar soap anymore?"

Bee placed a hand on her hip. "If nothing else, people give them as gifts. And they make the cash wrap smell nice. Seriously, Syd, you've got the incredible smells in here down to a science."

Sydney grinned, gazing around the bookstore she'd single-handedly transformed from dusty old shop to town jewel. "We sell so many candles. Obviously, the romance novels are still our bread and butter, but profits have completely shifted since I expanded our candle section."

A brief but distinct pang of jealousy hit Bee in the chest. Her dreams didn't reside in a tiny mountain town or a romance-themed bookstore, but she filled with longing as she watched Sydney flourish in a business she worked for and helped make thrive. They'd met at a discount gym during Bee's first year living in New York City and bonded over the subpar equipment and their favorite Zumba instructor. Sydney quickly became Bee's closest, most trusted female friend, and despite their paths drifting over the past few years, they'd never lost touch. And when either of them needed the other, she was always there.

"I pulled a specific box of titles I want featured in the window," Sydney said.

"If they don't work with my color scheme, I'm vetoing them." Bee winked.

With a roll of her eyes and a smirk, Syd turned over her shoulder, disappeared into the back office, and emerged carrying a box the size of a small child.

"Here." She dropped the box next to the front door and brushed off her hands. "I think you'll be pleasantly surprised."

Bee peered into the box of books with spines in shades of pale blue, creamy white, and dusty pink. "*The Prince Problem*," Bee read. "*Heart of Stone. Josh and Odie: A Love Story.*"

She lifted her gaze to where Sydney stood adjusting the soaps for the third time.

"Male-male romances?" Bee asked.

Without turning her attention, Syd said, "Yeah. I mean,

some. Queer romance. They cover the whole spectrum. Well . . . you know, not the *whole* spectrum. But that's my goal."

Bee turned back to the box, gazing at the spines with new affection. "Wow. Didn't realize a small town would be so accepting of such inclusive content."

"You have a lot of misconceptions about this place," Sydney said. "Of course, we have the requisite bigot, the handful of misogynists, the old folks using terminology that makes your skin crawl. But the majority welcome diversity and inclusion. It's really refreshing."

Bee raised a single, skeptical eyebrow. *No one town could be that perfect, could it?*

"Okay," Sydney said. "So it's not Club Trade on a Thursday night. But it's not Mayberry, either."

Club Trade on a Thursday night rivaled Mardi Gras. Bee grinned. She'd worked hard to promote the gay nightclub where she'd worked for the last five years, starting as a bartender and working her way up to assistant manager and event host.

But as quickly as the warm memories surfaced, doubt and anxiety crept in to taint them. She loved the life she'd created in New York; loved the people, loved the work Club Trade did behind the scenes for the LGBTQ+ community. Loved being surrounded by supportive, like-minded allies, but lately the schedule and demands had begun to weigh on her.

The club scene wore her down. She knew she couldn't continue kissing cheeks and hustling bodies in the door for much longer. Every morning, as the sun peeked over the New York City skyline, Bee crept into bed with aching feet and a nagging question in her mind: *How long can I keep doing this?*

She'd saved every penny she'd made over the years, only indulging in the occasional vacation with her best friends, Abe and Jamie, and then a few weeks back, the day after she

gave her notice at the club in anticipation of attending design school in London in the fall, her brother, Isaac, called.

"Those books will fit with your window aesthetic,
right?" Sydney asked.

Bee's brain catapulted back to the present. She didn't
have the mental wherewithal to dive into her younger brother's issues, or how, because of him, she'd deferred enroll-
ment at the London School of Arts and Design and settled
on a weekend in Pine Ridge instead of moving to the United
Kingdom. She loved Sydney and missed her since she'd
moved from New York, but Taylor's bar didn't have quite
the same vibe as the dives and pubs of East London.

"Absolutely," Bee asked. "They're perfect. And did you
say you have white fabric?"

"Yep." Sydney turned toward the tiny back office.
"White tulle from a Christmas display. Will that work?"

Bee envisioned billowing sails on her boat behind a
hand-painted sign that read, **SAIL AWAY WITH ROMANCE.**
Just because she'd describe her current relationship status
as hopelessly single didn't mean she had stopped believing
in love.

At least, not altogether.

She followed Sydney into the back office.

"Ugh," Sydney said. "Crap."

Bee followed Sydney's gaze to a shelf at least four feet
above both their heads. "Ladder?"

"I only have a stepladder," Sydney said. "My old extension ladder busted, and I haven't had a chance to get a new
one yet."

"There's a hardware store just down the street, right?
Let's go get you a new one."

"Hey, I have an idea!" Sydney turned toward Bee with
bright, shining brown eyes. "I know someone who can
help us."

Bee's gaze narrowed. "But don't you need the extension
ladder?"

"It's not really in my budget at the moment." Sydney brushed past her with a toss of her hand. "Come on, I could use a break anyway."

Bee stepped out into the summer sun and soaked it in again, delighting in the brief, quiet moment of small-town life. Downtown was quiet, peaceful, serene. She'd been in town only two days, but already, the charm of Pine Ridge had made its mark.

"Don't fight it," Sydney said.

Bee opened her eyes to find Sydney grinning smugly. She flipped the sign in the front window to **BE BACK SOON**, locked the door, and joined Bee on the sun-dappled sidewalk.

"I dunno why," Bee said, "but when I think of the Adirondacks, I think snow. Summer up here is very different."

Sydney beamed as if she'd designed the season herself, before unlocking the passenger-side door of her pickup truck. "I've only told you this a thousand times. Can't believe how long it's taken me to get you up here."

Bee bit her lip, the typical excuses hot on her tongue. The demands of her life in New York City consumed her, and for most of her adult life, she'd welcomed those demands with open arms: friends who requested advice, friends of friends who needed a couch to crash on, cousins of friends of friends who heard she had the best vintage-shop recommendations, hosted the best parties, knew the coolest drag queens. *Call my friend Bee; she's amazing, and she knows everyone.*

Everything about her carefully curated life felt safe and controlled and planned. Everything except for her family.

Isaac's phone call found her heading to work from the apartment above the club that she rented at a great discount. *Ugh, okay, listen. Don't hate me. And don't panic. I'm in the hospital. I'm a little banged up, but I'm gonna be fine. I just . . . need some money.*

She'd emptied her bank account for him, and all at once her whole world felt like a prison.

Enter Pine Ridge.

"I'm a terrible friend," Bee said as they climbed into the truck. "Just don't forget, in another lifetime you'd also have dragged your feet on spending a whole weekend in the mountains."

A smile spread across Sydney's face as the truck roared to life. "Yep," Sydney said. "Another lifetime."

They pulled away from the Loving Page and drove through downtown, Sydney maneuvering the narrow roads with ease. She wore New Balance sneakers caked with mud and gray sweat shorts with a big white T-shirt Bee was sure belonged to her hunky mechanic husband, Sam.

Another lifetime. Pine Ridge, New York, certainly had the vibe of a different era. But something about it had lured Sydney, caught her, reeled her in. Perhaps the hot husband she'd met the first night she arrived in town a few years back? Bee gazed out the window as the jasmine-colored forest blurred by and wondered if it might have been something else.

"You're sure this person can help us?" Bee said.

"Absolutely. He's tall, and he's usually got nothing to do but roam around town and bother people who actually have jobs."

Bee snorted a laugh. She'd worked nonstop since she turned sixteen years old. Aimless drifting didn't often find its way into her vocabulary.

"Plus," Sydney said, grinning at Bee with stars in her eyes. "He's supercute."

Bee laughed louder. "Oh God, please. I've had enough big-city drifters in my lifetime. I don't need a small-town drifter for comparison."

The devious smile sat on Sydney's lips as they made their way around sharp turns and meandering bends in the country roads, eventually turning onto an unpaved drive laden with potholes and dips that forced the pickup truck to amble and rock.

"Tell me he lives in a tent," Bee said as the trees around them grew more densely packed.

Sydney remained silent, her grin speaking volumes. One last turn and the massive home appeared before them.

"Wow," Bee said. "Okay, so. Not a tent."

Mountain dream home was more like it. Soaring, dark wood beams and towering windows from ground to sky displayed a glittering lake beyond, which anyone approaching could see clear from the other side of the house. The whole scene belonged on the cover of *Log Cabin Monthly*.

Bee forced her mouth shut as she climbed out of the truck and hurried after Sydney to the looming front door. "This place is insane," she whispered. "Is this guy a reclusive billionaire or something?"

"Former football player," Sydney said. "And he's not a recluse. Remember I told you about that annual bake-off? The one Jared's fiancée entered? The guy who lives here was a judge, and after spending a few weeks in Pine Ridge, he loved it so much he decided to stay."

Bee tilted her head, waiting for Sydney to acknowledge the familiar story. "Someone happened to find themselves in Pine Ridge and ended up loving it so much they moved here? Gee, where've I heard that one before?"

"I'm telling you," Sydney said. She raised her hand and knocked on the door. "This place has something special."

Around them, birds chirped merrily, the trees rustled in the breeze, and tiny, hidden creatures snapped twigs in the distance. But inside the house, nothing stirred. Sydney knocked again.

Silence.

"Hm," she said. "His car's here."

"Forget it," Bee offered. "There's gotta be somebody in town who has an extension ladder, right? Or someone taller than five foot four?"

Sydney worried her bottom lip and peered through the

towering front windows into the exposed living room. "Yeah, but . . ."

A sneaking suspicion crept into Bee's brain. "This isn't a setup, is it, Sydney darling?"

Syd's cheeks bloomed with color. She avoided Bee's stare.

"Because," Bee continued, "you can put the juiciest slab of Pine Ridge man meat in front of me, and I'm not biting."

"Ew." Sydney grimaced. "Was that intentionally off-putting?"

"Oh, come on. You stock nothing but romance novels in your store. I thought you'd have heard everything by now."

Sydney rolled her eyes and meandered off the front porch. "I stock the *best* romance. None of my authors would dare write anything so nasty. Come on, maybe he's out back."

They circumvented the house and picked their way down a sloping green lawn toward the lake, glorious and sparkling in the midday summer sun. Maybe Bee would never move to the tiny mountain town, but she began to see why other people did.

Thirty feet from a rickety dock floated a barn-red canoe, untethered and drifting lazily on the placid surface of the lake.

"That sucks," Bee said.

"What?"

"His boat came untied, right? He's gonna have to . . . I dunno. Swim out there and get it?" Bee's legs trembled at the thought.

Sydney placed two fingers in her mouth and whistled, the shrill bleat slicing across the water. Like a prairie dog rustled from his hole, a shirtless, tousle-haired man popped up from the boat.

"Hey!" Sydney waved an arm over her head. "Got a sec?"

Shirtless ran a hand through his dark hair, snagged a paddle from the depths of the boat, and crossed the water in one swift, sharp line. The closer he got, the drier Bee's mouth became.

The man was cut. Tight abs twisted and flexed as he dipped the paddle into the water—left and right and back again—drawing her gaze to the smooth planes of his chest and shoulders. The guy had muscles she didn't know existed. An elaborate, tribal turtle tattoo covered his smooth, brown skin from shoulder to elbow.

The boat sped toward the dock, and Bee's heart crawled into her throat as she envisioned the old heap splintering into a thousand pieces as it slammed against the shore. But in one swift motion, Shirtless leaped out of the canoe and onto the dock, pausing the forward motion and sending the vessel bobbing back into the body of the lake.

"What's up?" He lumbered toward them, a crooked smile hanging on his curvy lips. Black mesh gym shorts hung on his muscular frame, and it took everything in Bee not to gawk. She'd been around all kinds of beautiful men in her life, but Shirtless tickled something different inside of her.

"Denny, this is my friend Bee. Bee, Denny."

His dark eyes lighted on her, flickered across her chest and back up to her face. Despite the fact that she wore a crew-neck tank top and loose-fitting, tie-dyed lounge pants, her skin prickled as if he saw clear through her clothes. He, on the other hand, showed no signs of any such shame despite being distinctly more naked.

"How's it going?" he said. As his smile grew, the angles of his cheekbones sharpened.

"Nice to meet you," Bee answered. "Your house is absolutely ridiculous."

A rich laugh, warm as chocolate, danced across his lips. "It is, right? I probably don't need all that. Syd's brother-in-law is a master salesman. He totally suckered me into buying it."

A touch of California surfer dude tinged his speech.

"Someday he'll get furniture in there," Sydney said. "It's the epitome of a bachelor pad right now."

"I keep telling you I need help," he said. "I start clicking around furniture websites, and I can feel my brain power down."

"Speaking of help," Syd said. "Can we borrow you for a few minutes, tall man? Bee's helping me with some ideas for the store window, and there's a bunch of stuff in the storage space at the bookshop we can't reach."

"Of course," he said. "Let's go."

He ran a hand through his silky dark hair and motioned toward Sydney's truck.

Bee didn't move.

"Do you um . . ." She motioned to his outfit. Or lack thereof. "You wanna maybe grab some shoes or a shirt?"

"Didn't realize the bookstore had a dress code." A warm smile lit his face as the golden rays of the midday sun enhanced the glow. "I guess if I *have* to."

Denny sauntered toward the house, his eyes and smile lingering on Bee just a bit too long before he fully turned. Her sun-warmed skin turned prickly and hot.

"Well," Bee said. "He'll definitely be able to reach the storage space."

She didn't have to look at Sydney to know a victorious smile graced her lips; her singsong voice said it all. "Told you you'd like it here."

chapter **two**

Denny shifted, pressing himself against the passenger door but still unable to completely physically distance himself from Bee. Her soft skin brushed against his elbow every time Sydney's pickup truck hit a bump in the road, and the fresh air whipping through the cab carried a hint of her perfume. Something like freshly cut grass warmed in the summer sun.

He cleared his throat. He wanted to glare at Sydney, let her know he knew *exactly* what she was trying to do here. She'd mentioned her "gorgeous, smart, funny, authentic, warmhearted" friend Bee a million times. He may have been knocked around in the NFL, but his cognitive skills remained sharply intact.

This was a setup.

While he'd never shied away from beautiful women in the past, he didn't want a weekend distraction. He'd settled in Pine Ridge because he needed something different, something permanent. Something stable.

What was that exactly?

He ran a hand over his mouth and peered out the window as the sun broke through the trees and turned his line of vision a kaleidoscope of greens and yellows and browns.

Well, hell. He didn't know what permanent and stable meant. But he had plenty of time to find out.

Sydney's truck pulled up to the Loving Page, and Denny breathed in Bee's summery scent one last time before he climbed out. His old life may have included canoodling in clubs and flirting with every gorgeous woman who crossed his path, but Denny 2.0 had to erase "one-night stand" from his vocabulary.

No matter how intriguing Bee's black rose tattoos were or how delicately they wove around the curve of her shoulder and disappeared under the thin white fabric of her T-shirt.

"You coming?" Sydney called.

He blinked and ran a hand through his increasingly unmanageable hair. He still kept a to-do list—a habit instilled in him by his parents and reiterated during his days in the league—but these days, it read more like a suggestion list. *Power-wash the deck. Sweep out the guesthouse. Order more vitamins.* He'd have to add: *Get a haircut.*

He followed Bee and Sydney into the sunny, welcoming little shop and stopped just inside. The last time he'd been in, Sydney had rearranged a few tables to feature summer romance novels. Today, the shop sparkled and radiated with fresh energy.

"Wow," he said. "It looks very cool in here."

"It's all Bee," Sydney said.

Paper flowers in every color of the rainbow hung from the ceiling and danced lazily in the gentle breeze of the ceiling fan, while gauzy white curtains covered the windows and billowed and swayed to a different rhythm. Books arranged by color and size fanned out over tabletops and perched in stacks like carefully designed buildings along the wall shelves. The entire room moved.

"I feel like I'm on a boat or something," Denny said. "Like . . ."

He held his hands up, waving them around in circles and trying to demonstrate the sense of motion he couldn't put into words.

Bee smiled and a lilting, melodic laugh escaped her throat. "Exactly. I'm flattered, actually. That's what I was going for."

"She's good, right?" Sydney said, innuendo beaming from her smile.

Denny scoffed, desperate to avoid any further match-making from the town's resident romance expert. "You got a folding chair or a stepstool or something? I can grab that stuff for you from the back."

Under Sydney's direction, he sifted around on a shelf in the tiny office, retrieved a large box labeled **White Fabric**, and carried it to the front of the shop.

"Just leave it there," Bee said. "I'll figure out what I want to do with it."

Denny crossed his arms across his chest and glanced around. "What else can I do for you while I'm here? Anything else requiring height or raw, brute strength?"

He flashed a smile, and he swore Bee's cheeks tinted pink, making her icy-blue eyes seem to glow. Even when he tried not to flirt, he couldn't help it. She was cute. Really cute. Why shouldn't he try to make her smile?

"Nah," Bee said. "We do have a couple of things that require raw, brute strength, but nothing you can help with."

He laughed, the faint taste of a challenge whetting his appetite. "Touché."

"Actually," Sydney said. "It's almost one o'clock, and I'm starving. Can we pay you for your time with lunch at the diner?"

Denny's phone buzzed in his back pocket, and he

quickly checked the screen. **Coach M**. He didn't have to add *Call Coach* to the to-do list. It had been there for weeks.

"Yeah," he said, replacing his phone and ignoring his old friend for the moment. "I could eat."

A flash of worry crossed Bee's face as she tucked a loose strand of silky blond hair behind her ear. Maybe she wanted time alone with her friend?

"Unless," he said, "you don't want a strange dude infringing on your friend time?"

Bee smirked. "Nah, I'm actually more comfortable with strange dudes present. Makes me feel at home."

Denny followed Sydney and Bee outside and across the street to the Black Bear Diner. He'd slowly made his way through the menu in the year and a half he'd lived in Pine Ridge, but he'd recently discovered one of the line cooks had a knack for French food. If asked nicely, he'd whip up a croque monsieur or coq au vin that made Denny's head spin. Pine Ridge continued to surprise him.

They found a booth near the back, weaving around the small clusters of locals dining in for lunch, and Denny inhaled, savoring the sweet scent of warm maple syrup lacing the air. A young waitress he'd never seen before dropped menus and three full mugs of coffee on the table before hurrying away on a snap of gum.

"Bee," Sydney said. "Have you heard from Isaac today? How's he doing?"

Denny retrieved a coffee mug and sipped as Bee's face darkened. *Isaac*. Of course she had a boyfriend. Every one of her friends had probably tried to set her up with their one straight, single guy friend.

"He's okay," she said.

"Any updates on when he might be out of the hospital?"

Bee lowered her gaze to the dingy white Formica tabletop as a tense silence hovered over the group.

"Not yet." Her magenta-painted fingernails trailed over the intricate black rose tattoo covering her right shoulder.

"Boyfriend?" Denny said.

Bee looked up sharply, her mysterious azure eyes narrowing as they fell on his face.

"Brother," Sydney filled in. "Bee's brother got into a nasty motorcycle accident a few weeks ago. His medical bills were through the roof because he's got no insurance, and Bee's in the process of bailing him out. Their parents could've helped him without putting so much as a dent in their bank account, and she'd been saving that money for years so she could enroll in this interior design program at a school in London—"

"Um, hello?" The words lashed off Bee's lips, cutting Sydney short. "Can we drop it? I thought we were gonna have a nice, pleasant lunch during which we discussed controversial topics like who's the messiest Real Housewife and what's the deal with the gift shop at the end of the street that only sells novelty underwear?"

A curious smile tugged at Denny's mouth. The girl was sharp. Dodgy, but sharp.

Bee pursed her lips and stared at Denny, the weight of her gaze pulling him in. "You do what you have to do for family, you know? I have the money, he needs it—end of story. Now. The underwear shop. Please. I have to know."

Sydney explained the origins of the Pine Ridge Panty Palace, as it had been so affectionately dubbed years ago, but Denny couldn't tear his eyes off Bee. Her lightly tanned skin shimmered in the fluorescent diner lights, and every few minutes they'd catch eyes and his heart would beat a little bit faster. He wanted to know what her ink meant. He wanted to know where else she had it.

Conversation turned toward the town and Bee's work in New York at clubs and drag shows, and over the course of an hour, he learned she loved anything glittery and over-the-top, including her friends, and while she enjoyed the club scene, the weariness in her brow told him she might be ready for a change.

"All right, friends," Sydney said as the empty lunch plates were cleared and the last sips of coffee downed. "I have to wrap up stuff at the shop so I can get home and start prepping for tonight."

"The one night I actually have plans," Denny grumbled. A hobby shop in Utica had gotten wind of his presence in upstate New York and begged him to do a signing. He agreed, as long as they donated his fee to the closest Boys & Girls Club.

"What's tonight?" Bee asked.

"I told you," Sydney said. "Preseason game."

"Oh, right," Bee said, rolling her eyes. "Football."

"I take it you're not a fan," Denny said. *If she didn't follow the sport closely, could it be possible she didn't know who he was? How much had Sydney told her?*

He prayed he wouldn't have to explain his sharp transition from four-time Pro Bowler and reliable defensive back Denny Torres to family embarrassment and league outcast for retiring in the prime of his career.

"I'm always working on Sundays," Bee said. "Also, I guess I just don't understand it."

"Like, downs and penalties and play calling?" Denny said.

"No." The all-knowing smirk graced her lips again. "It's a modern-day gladiator arena. Thousands of people paying good money to watch men kill each other on a field for sport."

A tremble ran through his arms. He understood better than most. The casual disregard for players' health had certainly pushed him toward retirement. With every game, he lost a little more of his focus and dedication, trying and failing to see the point of it all beyond lining the owners' pockets with more cash than they knew what to do with.

"They're not *killing* each other," Sydney said. "They're playing a game. A game they love. A game most of them would probably play for free if asked."

Denny laughed. A lot of people felt the way Sydney did, but until a person poured their blood and sweat into the field day after day, year after year, their opinion didn't hold water.

Bee's eyebrows slowly raised as she studied him, and something about the look told him she knew he had a lot more to say on the subject. He'd love to sit down and explain it to her. Maybe she would be the one woman he'd encountered in his life who understood.

"Would you have played for free?"

The question knocked the wind from his lungs. "I, uh . . ."

He sipped his cold coffee and dropped his gaze to the ceramic cup between his thick fingers. At eighteen years old, he would've payed to play. In the last years of his career, the contracts became so lucrative, he couldn't figure out how to say no. The business end of football became a web he couldn't escape from.

"Sorry," Bee said. "That wasn't fair. I should've just flat out asked how much you're worth."

Her eyebrow quirked, and once more she graced him with a glittery smile. The girl had a lot to say, even when nothing came out of her mouth.

"I just remembered I have a really important appointment to get to," Denny joked, matching her smile. "We'll have to continue this conversation another day."

"Ah, I leave tomorrow," Bee said. "I'll let Sydney tie up this loose end for me on her own time and report back."

A whisper of disappointment floated across his skin. He didn't want the conversation to end over cold coffee amid the scent of fried cheese and bacon grease, Bee concluding he was some kind of money-hungry idiot athlete with nothing else going for him.

Or am I?

Bee and Sydney stood from the table and moved toward the exit, leaving him no additional time to wonder.

chapter **three**

one week later . . .

Grocery bags weighed Bee and Jamie down as they entered her apartment, dropping the haul next to the kitchen island. A sheen of sweat broke out on Bee's forehead. She snagged two bottles of water from the fridge, handed one to Jamie, and gulped hers down.

"I cannot wait," she said, "until one of us can afford a summer share in the Hamptons. Ten years living in this city and I'm still not used to the summer heat."

"I wouldn't be caught dead in the Hamptons," Jamie said. "Why don't you just come to Fire Island with us?"

Bee sucked on her bottom lip and tried to formulate an answer that wouldn't insult her friend. How could she explain that she was over Fire Island? The incessant partying, the casual drugs, the constant judgment of status and income. Every night out felt like a fashion show, every brunch an episode of *The View*. Fire Island wasn't a break. It was the city on uppers. A millennial version of the life she'd abandoned back home.

"Maybe next summer," Bee said. Despite her lack of funds, she still hoped to be living in London by next year, enrolled in the London School of Arts and Design BA Interior Design course. The school had allowed her to defer acceptance for one year, but it had taken her five years to save up what she'd given Isaac in the span of a phone call. Fire Island seemed a more likely destination, no matter how much she didn't want to admit it.

"What can I do?" Bee asked as Jamie began unpacking groceries.

"Open the wine and go sit in the living room until I tell you dinner is ready."

"No way," she begged. "Let me help."

"Girl, don't even try to get in my way." She and Jamie had started working at Club Trade around the same time and became fast friends. He'd watched her stumble through too many burnt late-night grilled cheese sandwiches to trust her with anything beyond wine. He smacked her butt and handed her the chilled rosé they'd picked up at the liquor store. "You're the most help if you get the hell out of here."

A wry smile curled on her lips as she accepted the wine. Cooking wasn't exactly a time-honored tradition in the Jones household, instead assigned to a housekeeper and the occasional private chef. Bee's culinary skill began and ended with Easy Mac and cinnamon toast, her younger brother's preferred after-school snack.

She poured each of them a glass of rosé before sinking into her plush velvet sofa with the latest issue of *Harper's Bazaar*. A cologne sample in the magazine pages triggered a memory of the beefy football player she'd met the previous weekend. She couldn't imagine how he smelled so delicious after coming directly from a boat on the lake.

And he was cute. Good Lord, he was cute. Black hair, smoldering mahogany eyes, and cheekbones so sharp anyone who kissed him would have to be careful. The intricate tattoo she glimpsed earlier would need further inspecting, too.

She shook her head, erasing the lusty thoughts. There would be no further inspecting tattoos. Before her mind wandered any further over mental images of Denny's chiseled abs and spectacularly broad shoulders, her phone rang. She checked the screen, but the number read **Unknown Caller**.

Her phone rang more than most, and she always answered, never knowing who was on the other end or what disaster someone might need assistance with. For a moment, she wondered if her mother might call from a hidden number.

But why?

She ignored the tiny hope tickling her gut and hit the Accept button.

"Hello?"

"Hey, Bee, this is Denny."

Bee grinned. Much better than her mother and the Jones family drama.

"Denny Torres," he said. Deep laughter. "Tall man? Pine Ridge?"

She didn't need Denny's name, much less the qualifier. His voice had burned into her memory like a brand. When he'd said goodbye to her after their lunch with Sydney in Pine Ridge, he'd laughed and said, *Next time you're in town and you can't reach the top shelf, you know who to call.*

The wider his smile grew, the more asymmetrical his face became, as if God gave him one tiny physical flaw to keep him from being too perfect. She'd thought about that smile more than she cared to admit in the last seven days.

"I remember," she said. "Hi. How are you?"

"Good!" he said. "I hope you don't mind, but Sydney gave me your number."

Sydney. Bee shook her head. The romance novels Syd-

ney peddled at her bookstore had obviously gone to her
head. One quick lunch and Sydney was shipping her two
friends from three hundred miles away.

"It's fine," Bee said.

"I thought about texting, but it seemed kinda imper-
sonal."

Bee clenched her teeth together to keep from laughing.
Had this guy consulted her mother before he'd called? She
heard Fran Jones's voice in her head. *Texting is for teenagers and crack dealers.*

"You're a rare breed," Bee said. "I don't know many
guys your age who prefer calling over text."

"I'm a rare breed in a lot of ways." He laughed, and she
found herself smiling. He had an awkward confidence about
him, as if he knew he lacked couth but didn't care. Sydney
had told her earlier that he had a ton of baggage, and she'd
seen the subtle lines of tension at his eyes when she'd joked
about playing for free. Maybe his confidence covered deeper
issues.

"So," Bee said after a pause. "What's up?"

"I know this is sort of out there, but I wanted to ask you
something."

She waited. "Okay . . . ?"

He cleared his throat, and a single goofy laugh followed.
"Syd mentioned my house needs decorating. I mean, more
than decorating. I've got bare-bones furniture, just enough
to get by on. A couple of lamps, a mattress, a shitty couch.
It's sad."

"Okay."

"You've got such great taste. And Sydney said you're in
design school? Or planning to go to design school? She told
me about how you've helped a couple of friends in the city
redecorate their apartments and that you're really good
at it."

Another long pause. "Are you going to ask me what you
want to ask me, or am I going to have to guess?"

"Sorry." He laughed again. "Would you decorate my house for me? If you could make this place look half as good as the Loving Page, I'd be seriously grateful."

She caught her own stare in the mirror hanging amid her gallery wall opposite the couch. Her face twisted up in confusion. "Listen, I know Syd told you I'd emptied my bank account for my brother, but I don't need the handout. Design school in London was sort of a pipe dream."

A pipe dream she'd saved years for. A pipe dream that would finally allow her to separate from the life she'd fallen into in New York and create her own world someplace where her needy brother didn't call every thirty minutes to ask for her advice, or a couple hundred bucks, or the name of that guy she knew in the Berkshires with the Fendi discount. She'd been Isaac's one true family since he was born, and after she moved away from Long Island, she'd become the responsible "older sister" to plenty of other people. She needed to get out. And she needed the means to do it.

"It's not a handout," he said. "Sure, I thought maybe you could use the money based on what I heard at lunch, but I could also really use the help."

She breathed deep, gazing down at the fashion magazine in her lap, a pair of black snakeskin heels staring up at her. At least she wouldn't be tempted to shop in Pine Ridge.

"What's so important about decorating your house?" she asked.

"It's kind of a long story."

"I've got time."

He laughed and groaned all in one breath. "My parents are coming in October."

Again, she waited. "Okay . . . ?"

"My parents are two of the scariest people you've ever met in your life." His voice grew weary. "They expect a lot. Always have. Football was the one thing I was good at, and they supported it in their own way, I guess. But it was sort of my whole identity in my family. The jock in a bunch of brains. So now that I'm not playing anymore, I'd like to show them I've got more to offer, you know? That I've got my shit together. Or that I'm at least on my way."

Connecting with parents. Or attempting to, anyway. She knew something about that.

"A well-decorated home is the way to show them you've got your shit together?" she said.

"It's a step in the right direction."

She tapped her teeth together. When she'd given her notice at the club, she'd also forfeited the upstairs apartment Gerald, the club's owner, allowed her to rent at a discount. With the lease on Jamie's roach-infested studio ending, he planned to move in and told her she could crash as long as she needed, but she knew the situation was temporary. Gerald had already replaced her position at Club Trade. And Bee needed somewhere to go.

"I'm interested."

"Oh man, that's amazing." His voice flooded with relief. "I didn't even tell you how much I'd pay you."

"That's because I'm going to tell you how much I'll charge."

"You . . ." He laughed. "Okay."

"How big is the house?"

"It's four bedrooms, four and a half baths. About four thousand square feet."

She twisted her necklace and did some mental math. She could use the opportunity to replenish her bank account, throw some money to Isaac so that he could get by without working for a while, and start living the life she'd always planned for instead of the life she'd been stuck with.

"Exclusive of room and board, three thousand."

"Uh . . . dollars?" he stammered.

"No, rupees."

He coughed out another laugh. "Bee. No. There's no way."

"Well, that's what I need to make it worth it for me."

"No," he said. "I mean, that's ridiculously low. I'll give you ten."

She sat straight up on the couch, the magazine page slicing her ring finger as she went.

"Damn it!" she yelped.

"Okay, fine! Twelve?"

"Denny." She laughed. "You're a trip, you know that?"

"Fifteen?"

"Stop." She tossed the magazine on the coffee table, sucked on her stinging finger, and breathed deeply. "That's too much."

"It's what anybody else would charge."

"Well, I'm not anybody else."

"That's for damn sure. It's fifteen. Keep arguing with me, and I'll make it twenty."

She ran a hand over her face and envisioned fifteen thousand dollars. It was enough to get her to Europe and then some, enough to share with Isaac—set him up for independence and possibly curb his propensity for death wishes. She could finally leave the exhausting club world, add a huge job to her portfolio, and start putting her skills to good use. She could finally get out from under the umbrella of what she should do and get down to what she was meant to do. The road she'd been waylaid from her entire adult life.

"This is really important to me," Denny said. His voice careened on the edge of sadness. "I know it might not make total sense to you, and I know it's not a conventional request from a near stranger, but I promise, you won't regret it."

Jamie's curious stare caught her eye from across the apartment. She didn't often stop to consider others' opinions when making life decisions, but something in Jamie's concerned gaze gave her pause.

"Where would I stay?" she said.

"I have a guesthouse. You'd be more than welcome to

stay there. Or if you feel more comfortable, I can put you up somewhere. There's this great new hotel—"

"I can find my own place," she said. The idea of a man putting her up at a hotel brushed a little too close to *Pretty Woman* territory for Bee's liking.

"Right," he said. "Sure. I mean, you're Sydney's friend so she can probably steer you in the right direction if you need it."

She breathed deep, sniffing out pros and cons like a hunting dog. But the prospect of doing creative work and being paid for it proved incredibly tempting. Add to that a break from New York and her chaotic city life, and she struggled to find reasons to say no.

"Can I think about it?" she asked.

"Of course! Absolutely. For sure."

She grinned, the image of his lopsided smile appearing in her mind. "Cool. So I'll call you tomorrow and let you know what I've decided."

"Perfect. And if you need any more information or the money doesn't work for you anymore, just shoot me a text. Or call me. Whatever."

She smiled again. "I will. Thanks."

"Have a good one, Bee."

She ended the call and immediately looked up to meet Jamie's stare. He paused with a wooden spoon poised over her stockpot, sticky red liquid dripping down in a regular rhythm.

"Do I even want to ask what that was about?" Jamie said. He sipped his rosé and raised a perfectly manicured eyebrow.

As she explained Denny's pitch, Jamie's eyebrow rose higher and higher in his forehead until she feared it might pop clear off his face like a cartoon.

"Sweetheart," Jamie said. With slow, purposeful move-ments, he set the wooden spoon down, covered the pot, and joined her on the couch. He placed a cool hand over hers and lowered his pointed chin. "You're sure about this?"

"At this point, what are my options?"

"You know everybody in the drag world, everybody on the club scene." He closed his fingers around hers. "Somebody has a job for you. Somebody owes you a favor, I'm sure of it."

Bee's neck prickled. She stood up from the couch and sauntered into the kitchen to refill her wineglass. "I'm not sure that's what I want anymore."

"I just don't want to see you abandoning everything you know and everything you've worked for just because Isaac needs help again."

She set the rosé bottle down on the counter and turned back toward him, a knot forming beneath her ribs. "I'm not doing this *for* Isaac."

Jamie's eyebrows continued to inch higher toward his hairline. "He doesn't factor into your decision at all? Make a little money for yourself and set him up, too?"

Damn, he knew her so well. Of course Isaac had factored into her decision. But just this one last time.

"Am I supposed to let him just live on the streets?" she said. "He has to recover from his injuries. He can't work right now."

"Oh, Bee, come on."

"What?" She pierced Jamie with a glare.

"You've been down this road with him a thousand times." He tucked his chin as if to challenge her into a rebuttal. "And even if, for a moment, we pretend like you're not *kinda sorta* still making decisions with your hapless brother in mind, is this really the next best step for you? Going up to the mountains for a couple of months because a cute boy wants help? Troubled puppy without a friend in the world needs the help of a good woman to make his mommy and daddy proud? Where have I heard this story before?"

She scoffed. "So I have a type."

"Girl." His eyes widened. "A type is preferring blondes over brunettes. You have supersonic radar for people who need help. Sticking by Robbie during his ninety days in rehab? Bailing on your own birthday party because Caleb called crying for you to go out to deep Queens after his cat died? How about that guy you dated whose name I can't even remember who let you pay his electric bill for three months and then went on a two-week vacation to the South of France? *Without you.*"

The words stabbed her in the chest, her cheeks heating with a thousand fires. Hearing her past vocalized was like walking through a relationship haunted house. "We can't all be emotionally unavailable serial daters who bail on relationships three months in."

He released a deep breath and joined her in the kitchen, his lips pursed all-knowingly. "Bee."

"I'm sorry," she said. Shame flooded her chest. "I'm an asshole."

"It would only be cruel if it wasn't true." He grinned and pulled her into a hug, wrapping her in the clean, sharp scent of Tom Ford Tobacco Vanille. "I just want you to start thinking of yourself before other people for a change."

She pulled back to look into his sparkling dark-brown eyes. He stood more than a foot taller than her, and the cocoon of his chest had provided comfort on many lonely nights. She loved him like a brother. A brother who never asked for anything in return.

"I *am* thinking of me." She gripped his shoulders. "This is a good opportunity for me. You know I need the money. I can take a few months away from the city, away from the chaos of the club, and really think about my next move. Maybe after a little time away I'll figure out how to get out from under the shadow of the club world and move into a legitimate business."

"Girl, are you calling me illegitimate?"

"If the wig fits."

"Excuse me?" He placed his hands on his narrow hips. "Do I look like Miss Ambrosia?"

Bee grinned. Since getting into a relationship with Abe, aka Ambrosia, Club Trade's drag queen in residence, she'd never seen Jamie happier. "Now that you mention it . . . I guess couples really do start to look alike after a while."

"See? This is why I never stay in a relationship longer than three months." Jamie turned to the stockpot and lifted the lid, breathing deeply and wafting the sweet tomato aroma toward his face. "I've outdone myself."

"That's what we'll put on your tombstone."

Jamie's face lit up. "Promise?"

Bee grabbed the wine bottle and turned toward the living room. Her relationship with her parents weighed on her, and their last conversation played like a recording in her brain in the errant moments when she least expected it.

"Your brother will never learn to take care of himself if you're always there to bail him out, Bethany." Her mother's voice crackled over the phone. Seemed Aspen had terrible reception. *"We've tried to help him every way we can."*

She gripped her brother's hand, the sharp antiseptic smell of the hospital burning her nose. "You throw money at every problem," she'd said. "And now when money might actually help him, you can't be bothered?"

The silence on the line told her everything she needed to know. They weren't traveling to their son's hospital room. They weren't wiring money. They were returning to their cocktail party, her mother plotting out her next filler appointment in case the minor inconvenience with her kids had caused a new wrinkle line.

Bee had gritted her teeth and turned back to her battered-and-bruised brother. So he'd made mistakes. He needed her. Always had. Always would.

"Bee?" Jamie's voice cut through her thoughts as she loosened her suddenly tight grip on the wineglass.

"Yes?"

"You're gonna go, aren't you?"

She licked her lips. She could almost taste the mountain air, smell the fragrant pine trees. She'd make her money, secure Isaac's finances, and take care of herself for once. She'd give herself a little space and time to sort everything out. And then she'd make her next move.

"Yes," she said. "Yes, I am."

chapter **four**

Denny stood in the middle of his living room, glancing around as if he could summon enough magic to make the barren space presentable in the next fifteen minutes. He cleared his throat, and the sound bounced off the twelve-foot ceiling. He'd never given a second thought to this shell of a home until his mother called.

We want to visit in October. You have space for us?

Anxiety flooded his gut. He'd panicked.

He had space in spades. What he didn't have was furniture, art, rugs, or anything else. In his mind's eye, he saw his mother on the main lanai of the palatial estate his parents moved to after Denny's high school graduation at the top of a hill in Honolulu, overlooking Ewa Plain and Oahu. A smug smile sat on her unlined face as she thought of her less fortunate siblings still living the life she'd moved on from on the mainland and looking forward to visiting her wealthy son in his beautiful home in the mountains.

When he envisioned her entering the barren house and

hearing he had no career plans for the future, nausea rose up in his throat. No job, no wife, no prospects, and no furniture. Just some smart investments he'd made during his playing days and a small chunk from his short-term spokesperson gig last year with Indigo Hotels. What parent *wouldn't* be proud?

Headlights flashed against the far wall, and he hurried out the front door to greet his guests. Sydney's pickup truck barreled over the rocky driveway and stopped a few feet from the sweeping front porch. The previous owners had set up rocking chairs and a giant swing on the porch, and Denny imagined the elderly couple rocking through hundreds of sunsets with lemonade in the summer, hot tea in the winter. He'd probably use it as a space to leave his muddy boots.

When Bee called to tell him she'd take the job, relief washed over him like a cool ocean surf. Sydney had made it abundantly clear Bee needed the cash and to get out of the city for a while, but Denny knew he'd get more out of the deal than she would. The big, empty house had grown lonely, and if he could help out somebody who needed it while adding a little color to his days, why not give it a shot?

"Hey, Denny!" Sydney called out, hopping down from the driver's seat. "We're here."

The passenger-side door swung open, and he had to crane his neck to catch sight of her. One silver Ugg boot dropped to the ground followed by another, and then the door closed and her full form came into view. She wore black leggings with the sparkly boots and a bright fuchsia puffer coat with a fur hood. Early September in the mountains might not bring the heat like summer in the city, but it certainly wasn't cold enough for her ensemble.

He suppressed a laugh. "You look like mountain Barbie."

She dropped her chin, glaring at him with heavily lined eyes, and flicked her silky blond hair over her shoulder. "Syd told me the temperatures can swing pretty drastically around here, and I had to take a train and carry all my own bags—and I didn't know if I'd need a coat or not, so I figured I'd just wear it, but it's kinda hot, right?"

He blinked, momentarily stunned. Was she nervous? This girl who'd seemed so calm, cool, and collected when he'd first met her? She retrieved two huge suitcases from the cab of Sam's pickup, and Sydney winked at him as she climbed back into the truck.

"Call if you need me," she said. She slammed the truck door and pulled away, leaving a cloud of dust in her wake.

"Oh, here." Denny hurried out in his flip-flops as Bee struggled with the massive rolling suitcases on the dirt drive. "Let me get that for you."

"Thanks." She hitched her shoulder as he approached, releasing one of the bags. He caught a slight tremble in her hand as she adjusted, and a flush rose to her cheeks.

"Sorry your rental didn't work out," he said. "But I think you'll like the guesthouse. It's not huge, but it's kinda cozy."

She offered him a tight smile. What could he do to get her to relax? He wanted her to feel safe and comfortable here, welcomed and appreciated. The vibe he got instead was on par with watching someone lay down on a bed of nails.

"I'm sure it'll be fine. Sorry if I'm . . ." She blew out a breath and shoved a hand through her hair. "I had to run a bunch of last-minute errands this morning, and then the train was delayed, and I didn't realize how far from the train station Pine Ridge is, and I feel bad Sydney had to drive all that way to get me."

He nodded slowly. "I get it. You don't have to be sorry. Why don't I show you the guesthouse where you'll be staying, and then we can go on over to mine. I got some food and drinks, but if that's not cool with you, I'll take you into town and impress you with the booming metropolis that is Pine Ridge. It's bingo night at church, and if you're lucky, Edith O'Hare will let you sit next to her and sip off her flask between rounds."

Genuine sparkle reached her gray-blue eyes, and she put her hands on her full hips. The moment he'd asked her to help him out with the house he'd ruled out anything physical between them. He needed her for something bigger than sex, and any type of flirtation would just complicate things. Plus, they were all wrong for each other. He went for googly-eyed, Gucci-wearing jersey chasers, and Machine Gun Kelly was probably more her type.

"I'd actually love to take some time off from any form of nightlife," she said. "Although tomorrow's mission will be to meet Edith O'Hare. She sounds like my kind of lady."

"Your wish is my command."

They dropped her bags in the tiny guesthouse, and she gazed around approvingly without a word. The repurposed shed had a kitchenette, double bed, bathroom, and about as much space as an average two-thousand-dollar-a-month studio apartment in Manhattan. He'd thought it seemed logical that she stay there, but she'd been adamant about finding her own space. After her rental fell through, Sydney had convinced her the guest cabin had everything she needed.

When they entered his house, Bee finally spoke.

"Holy shit." She stood just inside the doorway, her mouth hanging open and her wide eyes scanning the expansive place from ceiling to floor.

The house had been built to take advantage of every inch of the view, with a massive great room serving as the heart of the home and the kitchen and den extending off it. Each of the three main rooms featured floor-to-ceiling windows highlighting the sparkling blue lake and majestic pine trees outside.

When Jared sold him the house, he warned that despite the lake being private, anyone who lived nearby could easily cruise past in a boat and, if the lights were on, vividly see every room in the house. Denny didn't mind. He had nothing to hide. At least when it came to what a neighbor might see through a window.

"So, uh . . . As you can see," he said, "it needs some work."

She kicked off her boots and walked inside, gazing up as if she'd entered St. Patrick's Cathedral. "Denny, this place is insane. I mean, I saw it from the outside last time I was here, but every angle stuns."

"I sort of fell in love with the windows."

In the early evening, the sky's milky shades of violet and indigo reflected in the glassy waters of the lake below, creating a stunning canvas he'd gotten used to in the year and a half he'd been here. Somehow sharing it with Bee made it impressive all over again.

"How could you not," she said on a breath. "This house is going to be *cake* to design. I can't believe you've left it this empty for . . . how long have you lived here?"

He ran a hand across the back of his neck. "A little over a year. I just didn't think I needed much."

She raised her eyebrows, tugged off her coat, and tossed it onto the floor. "All right, crazy. We're gonna change that real quick."

He showed her the dark, moody, wood-paneled den lined with empty built-in bookshelves, save for his handful of game balls, and then led her into the kitchen. Their footsteps echoed off the black granite countertops and shiny wood floors, but she gazed around the blank canvas with the same openmouthed wonderment that she'd given the rest of the house.

"When I agreed to do this," she said, "I realized I could be walking into some millionaire's tacky version of mountain luxury. But this is a freaking gift."

He laughed. "I'm glad you like it. It's overwhelming to me. Just too much empty space, I guess."

"I hate granite countertops." She ran a pointy, emerald-green fingernail over the gleaming surface. "But so far it's the only thing in the whole place I'm not totally in love with."

A warm sense of reassurance skittered across his skin. He wanted her to like it, wanted her to feel inspired here, but ultimately, he had no idea how it would go. As was his usual style, he leaped first and analyzed later.

"Wine?" he asked.

She shrugged, running her hands over the granite like a tarot card reader. "Sure."

He plucked a bottle of red wine from the built-in wine rack in the kitchen island and poured each of them a glass. "Red okay?"

"Perfect."

He handed her a glass and raised his own in a toast. Before he could get a word out, she jumped in.

"Cheers," she said. "To new friends."

"And new adventures."

With her eyes locked on his, she sipped the wine. A barely audible *Mm* escaped her lips.

"I needed this," she said.

"Oh yeah?" He waited for her to continue, but she simply held her placid expression and took a sip.

Sydney had given him just enough of Bee's story to let him know the trip to the mountains might be good for her, but he didn't know details.

"You said something last time you were here about your brother?"

She scratched her shoulder. Again, he waited. Again, silence.

She shook her head and forced a pleasant smile. "It's nothing I can't handle," she said. "This wine is good. Really good. Cab?"

"I have no idea." He lifted the bottle to scan the label but couldn't even find the word "cabernet" among the Italian script. In anticipation of Bee's arrival, he'd asked Yuri of Yuri's Liquor for a couple of his most popular bottles. "I don't know shit about wine. I'm more of a Coors Light guy myself."

She bit her lower lip in an amused smile. "Well, then I

guess I have more to teach you than how to choose paint colors."

"I'd be glad for the education," he said. He swallowed a mouthful of the wine and savored the smoothness on his tongue. "You're right. This is good."

"Take a smaller sip now." Her throaty voice purred. "Let it sit on your tongue for a second before you swallow it."

He complied, but his mind wasn't on the wine. Her chin dropped; her eyelids lowered. Each lusty word sank into his brain. *Tongue. Swallow.* Something stirred below his belt.

"Yeah," he choked out. "Good."

Her eyebrow lifted, and she turned to look out the picture window over the sink. "Thank you for offering me this gig. It came at a really good time for me."

He cleared his throat, thrust back into the present. *Right. The job.* "Uh, yeah. Of course. You need the money; I need the help."

"Right," she said. Her fingers slid around the base of the wineglass as her gaze remained fixed on the lake. "I also needed a little break from . . . life."

"Eh," he said. "Who doesn't?"

"I shouldn't be complaining." A pleasant smile lit her face even in the ever-darkening kitchen. "I'm really fortunate. I guess I'm just ready for a change. To do something for myself."

Something shifted beneath the surface of her smile, but he didn't know her well enough yet to determine what it was. He reminded himself again that she was only here to complete the task at hand. If they got along, great. But they didn't need to bond.

"So," he said. "Where do we start with all this? It's a lot, right?"

"Not at all." A genuine smile replaced her forced one from earlier. "I don't know what your days up here look like, but I'd love to find a home store close by and wander with you. I'll ultimately do most of my shopping out of town and online, but this will be a good start to get a feel for what you like, what you hate. I have no idea what your taste is."

"I don't have any taste." He winked at her, and he could've sworn her cheeks flushed. Damn the low lighting. "I want your taste."

Her wily eyebrow slowly raised, and now it was his turn to blush.

"I want to see what styles and shapes and colors you gravitate toward," she said, righting the conversation like a ship in a strong wind. "Can we do that?"

"Totally. There's a big Adirondack-themed home store a couple towns over, and I've always liked the stuff they put in their windows."

"Perfect. Let's go tomorrow."

"Sounds good." He took another big gulp of his wine, and his stomach whined in response. "Sorry. I'm starving. You hungry? I got a bunch of stuff from the deli—some sandwiches, chips, cookies."

"Oh." She blinked, and then dropped her gaze. "Do you mind if I take something back to my room? I'm exhausted, and I'd love to just take a minute and get my head together."

Disappointment poked at his gut. She didn't want to hang out with him. He cleared his throat. Colleagues, not friends. No big deal.

"Of course. Take what you like."

With a heavy heart and a slightly bruised ego, he watched as she snagged a sandwich from the fridge, grabbed a bag of salt-and-vinegar chips from the counter, and then raised her wineglass at him before disappearing from the kitchen.

chapter **five**

The lake view wasn't nearly as impressive through the smudged little windows of the guesthouse, but Bee took it in the same as she had last night in Denny's kitchen. A suburban kid, born and raised in Garden City, Long Island, she moved to Manhattan the day after she turned eighteen. The idea of nature didn't occupy much of her brain space. Abe and Jamie had suggested camping once, but she'd laughed them off. Why would anyone elect to sleep on the ground when they had a perfectly good bed at home?

As she peered out the cobweb-covered glass at the back of the converted shed, she breathed the pine-scented air, and a peace settled over her. No car horns, no screaming people, no blare of sirens. Just chirping birds and the sweetly scented breeze through the trees.

She slipped into her hooded sweatshirt and headed toward Denny's house, visions of the beefy football player dancing in her head.

Last night, as the sun went down over the lake, and the

mountain air filled her head, and the wine seeped into her veins, he began to look just a little too dreamy. *I want your taste.* He hadn't meant it that way, but her body certainly heard it that way.

She'd wanted to stay in that moonlit kitchen, gazing into his deep brown eyes and wondering what his animated face might do if she kept talking, kept poking fun at him. But if she'd stayed, she'd start to fall. And she didn't have time for that.

She rapped on the imposing front door, and it swung open immediately. He grinned down at her. The morning light caught amber flecks in his damp black hair, and a wave of clean, cool soap scent wafted out at her. He must've just taken a shower.

A shower . . . Rivulets of water cascading down those chiseled abs . . .

He cleared his throat. "Hey. Good morning."

Shit. She hadn't had time to suitably scratch her itch back in New York, and she'd pay for it now. She didn't imagine the findings on Tinder in Pine Ridge were particularly rich.

"Good morning," she said. "Ready?"

"Yep. Let me put some shoes on."

In his brief absence, she pulled her hormones together. He wasn't even her type. Robbie, her last significant relationship, was a heavily tattooed hipster always dragging Bee into his personal and financial issues. A performance artist, Bee had initially been attracted to him because of his creative ambitions and insatiable thirst for life. After Bee stuck by him during rehab for opioid addiction, newly clean Robbie decided it wasn't the right time for a relationship and disappeared from Bee's life.

Someday, Robbie had said in a voice mail he left while Bee was at work. Someday my future partner will thank God I had a woman like you in my life.

It hadn't made the breakup any easier to swallow.

"You look cute," Denny said, yanking the front door closed behind him.

Bee ran a hand over the word FUN on the front of her gray hooded sweatshirt. She'd had no idea what to pack for early fall in the mountains but figured sweatshirts and jeans would get her through the next couple months. Had she gone out of her way to make sure her hair was freshly highlighted and each outfit had some element of her personality in it in case he noticed?

Maybe.

"Thanks," she said, trying to force the blush from her cheeks. "How far away is this place?"

"About a fifteen-minute drive." He walked over to his big black SUV and clicked a tiny remote to unlock the doors. "I figured we'd grab breakfast first. That cool?"

She breathed deep, the crisp morning air filling her head. She'd declined his dinner offer last night because she didn't need any excuses to spend nonwork-related time with him. If she could keep her distance and restrict their interactions to decor-focused only, she had a shot at avoiding his glittering eyes and lopsided smile. If they started sharing their life stories over wine, she'd be toast.

But a girl had to eat.

"Sure," she said. "But we should make it quick. I want to really dive in today."

His brow furrowed. They climbed into the car, and as he started the engine, he shook his head. "Am I a gross eater or something?" he asked.

"What? No. I mean, I don't think so."

"This is the second meal you've tried to get out of with me." A grin tugged at his lips.

"That's not true." She cleared her throat and gazed out the window as they ambled over the rocky driveway. "I just want to get cracking, you know? I'm really excited about this project."

The smile on his face remained as if he didn't believe

her. *Whatever.* It was her story, and she'd stick to it if it killed her.

They arrived a few minutes later at the Black Bear Diner. The heavy bacon scent floating in the parking lot air made her stomach groan with hunger. She'd inhaled her sandwich last night, but it wasn't enough to tide her over to the morning.

Mila Bailey, Sydney's soon-to-be sister-in-law, raised a hand in greeting and told them to sit wherever they liked. As Bee followed Denny through the bustling little diner, curious eyes trailed her. She stuck close to Denny as if his towering figure could protect her from judgment.

She slid opposite him into the booth he selected and picked up a menu to shield most of her from the room. "Syd told me everyone here is super friendly and inclusive," she said. "I don't really have any reason to think otherwise, but it almost seems too good to be true. You don't typically associate 'inclusive' with 'small town.'"

"This place is the best," Denny said. A tiny smile curled onto his lips. "There are a handful of prickly assholes, but you know. Every town's got 'em."

Bee's eyes darted around the restaurant. People seemed to have returned to their coffee and conversation, but her heart still hammered in her chest. Her preconceived notions about small-town life were hard to ignore.

"Everything okay?" he asked. His gaze narrowed in concern.

"Fine." She shrugged. "I'm just . . . cautious. Around new people. I don't exactly fit in around here."

The tiny smile returned to his face. She wanted to touch that face, trail her fingers over his smooth brown cheek. He had the closest shave she'd ever seen.

"What's different about you?" he said. "Your tats? I can barely see them. Except for these."

He ran a gentle finger along the base of her thumb where the word "go" was written in curvy black script. With the same cool, deft finger he traced the index finger of her other hand where the word "be" was written in the same script.

Goose bumps rose up on her neck as his gaze deepened. She swallowed down her discomfort, but the feeling of exposure remained. She may as well have been naked, the way his dark eyes narrowed in on hers and stripped away her armor.

"What do they mean?" he asked. His finger still connected with hers, and the contact left her brain as thick as tomato soup.

She drew in a ragged breath, digging for an answer.

"Hey, guys!" Mila barreled into their little bubble, and Bee looked up, startled.

"What's up?" Denny said. "Mila, did you meet Bee when she was in town a little while back?"

"Yeah," Mila said brightly. "I was grateful to meet someone who also has zero interest in football."

"Great." Denny laughed. "Kindred spirits."

"Coffee?" Mila said.

"Please." Bee held up her chipped white mug like a disciple waiting for the blood of Christ.

"It's so cool you're helping Denny decorate his house," Mila said as she poured hot dark coffee into Bee's waiting mug. "Only took him a year to give in and admit he needs more than a mattress."

"I'm still not convinced," Denny said. He stretched to his full, impressively wide arm span and leaned back on the booth. "But Bee's got great taste, so I'm letting her try."

"Can't wait to see it." Mila placed her free hand on her hip. "Bee, if you need a break from this guy, let me know. I'm not sure if I told you, but I work part-time as an assistant pastry chef at Indigo Hotels Adirondack Park, and we have a killer bar. I'd be happy to entertain you sometime."

Bee bit back a smile. Maybe people around here really were kinder than she'd given them credit for. She'd always thought small town equaled small-minded, but the warm, welcoming vibe at the Black Bear Diner and from Mila felt anything but.

"That's really sweet of you," Bee said. "I'm totally taking you up on that."

After Mila took their food order, she scribbled her phone number on Bee's napkin and then disappeared. Denny's eyes returned to Bee's, all warm and probing.

"So," he said. "What do they mean? The tattoos."

Damn it. She thought maybe he'd forgotten. "They're reminders."

"Be?" he asked. "You need a reminder to . . . be?"

"In a way." She grinned. "As in, don't hold back. Whoever you are, do that. Go forward. Be."

He nodded slowly. "I like that."

"Also, I got it when I was eighteen as a little bit of a 'screw you' to my parents." Her mother had physically gagged as if, instead of a tattoo, Bee had shown her a dead mouse. Bee went out the next day and got another one.

Denny nodded again. "I like that, too."

"What does yours mean?"

He ran a big, strong hand over his shoulder, a nostalgic grin settling on his mouth. "*Honu*. The turtle. It symbolizes a long and prosperous life in Hawaiian culture."

"Ah, you're Hawaiian."

"Mostly Filipino Hawaiian, but my mom can trace her lineage on one side all the way back to native Hawaiian royalty. You can thank those native roots for my height. Everybody else in my family is about five foot."

She nodded, waiting for more. He scratched his nose, breathed deep, gazed out the window. When he looked back at her, something in his eyes shifted. Whatever vulnerability he'd approached disappeared in one flick of his gaze.

"So these are reminders," he said, touching her fingers again and melting her insides in one go. "What are the rest?"

"The rest?"

"The rest of your tattoos. I saw the roses during your first trip here."

She suppressed a laugh. Most men who asked about her ink loved it because it turned her soft, feminine form into something bangable. It made her more dangerous, more complicated. In all the years she'd had them, not one sexual partner had ever bothered to study them. Or her.

"They've all got different meanings," she said. "Different stages in my life, different things that are important to me. And then there are the reminders."

Mila returned with steaming plates of eggs, pancakes, and bacon, and Bee's mouth watered. The restaurant patrons might have been different, but a diner was the same in Manhattan, in Pine Ridge, and everywhere in between. Bacon smelled the same wherever it sizzled.

The conversation stalled as they tucked into their breakfast, and after a few bites, Bee looked up to find Denny's plate nearly empty. He shoveled huge forkfuls of eggs and potatoes into his mouth, and only after a few moments of her staring did he look up.

"What?" he asked, mouth full of breakfast food.

"Sorry." She bit her lip to tamp down the shock. "You just . . . Wow, you eat fast."

His cheeks filled with color, and he wiped his mouth and set down his fork. "Yeah. I always have. I come from a huge family, and if you wanted a full plate, you had to eat before somebody else came along to take it from you."

She nodded slowly. Her own family meals growing up were mostly silent. Her grouchy, overworked father—when he could be bothered to attend dinner at all—was usually too exhausted from a day on Wall Street to put effort into family conversation. Her mother picked at her sparse plate in an endless effort at achieving her goal weight, and Isaac texted his way through meals. Sometimes Bee brought a book.

"You know you're an adult now, right?" Bee teased.

"You can order ten more plates if you're still hungry. And aside from me snagging a potato, no one's taking your food from you."

He crossed his arms over his chest, his sparkly eyes lighting on her once again. "No way in hell am I giving you a potato."

"Who said anything about giving?" In one quick movement, she speared a crispy potato with her fork and popped it into her mouth.

His grin curled further, revealing the edges of his straight, white teeth. "Well, that's it. You forfeit these."

He grabbed the nearly full plate of pancakes in front of her and set it down on his side of the table. "That's the rule. You take from me, I take from you."

"Unless you want a fork in your arm, I suggest you give that back."

They stared goofily at each other, their smiles belying their threats. He locked eyes with her as he dug into her stack of pancakes, cutting off a huge triangle and shoving it into his mouth.

If you kissed him now, he'd taste like butter and syrup. She exhaled, admonishing herself. She couldn't keep the lusty thoughts at bay.

This boy might ruin you.

After breakfast, they drove a few miles north to Donnerville, where Adirondack Home Furnishings promised a wealth of mountain-themed decor. The sprawling store looked more like Bass Pro Shop than the quaint little place she'd anticipated, but when they entered, Denny's face lit up like a kid on Christmas morning.

"Holy shit." He bounded over to an eight-foot, taxidermied black bear positioned next to the entrance in a frozen but ominous pose and ran his long fingers through the fur. "We gotta get this."

"Hi there!" A tiny salesman approached, a perma-grin pressed into his round face. The top of his head gleamed like a cue ball, and he ran a hand over it before extending his reach to Denny. "Welcome to Adirondack Home Furnishings. I see you've got great taste."

"We definitely want this," Denny said.

"No." Bee bit back a smile. "I mean, possibly. For now, we're going to keep looking."

Denny shot her a confused glare. "We can look for other stuff, but I know I want this."

She rolled her eyes. The last thing she needed was for the salesman to think they were impulse buyers with a lot of money. Worst-case scenario, he recognized the wealthy football player standing in front of him.

"We just walked in," she said. "Let's see what else is available, all right?"

"Whoa-ho-ho." The salesman laughed. "I see who wears the pants in this marriage."

"You see who wears the *what now*?" she snapped.

"All right, all right." Denny put his big paws on her shoulders and steered her away from the entrance. "Nobody's making assumptions about anybody's pants. We'll let you know if we need anything."

Bee's face flushed with anger as Denny led her into a secluded aisle featuring racks of scented candles.

"Take it easy, yeah?" he said. "I've got money. And that was cool as hell."

"We're here for inspiration," she reminded him. "I can get all this stuff at swap meets, garage sales, wholesalers. This place is tourist central and everything is marked up like crazy. Plus, anybody who tosses out a misogynistic line like, 'Who wears the pants' does not deserve a dollar of our business."

"Was it that?" he said, grinning. "Or did it piss you off he thought we were married?"

Her stomach fluttered as she looked up at his amused face. The guy must've been a terrible poker player.

"I don't know what you think you know about me, but I'm not some badass, anti-commitment city chick. Marriage doesn't scare me. And some random dude in Hicksville, USA, assuming I'm your wife scares me even less."

Or maybe it made me super turned on.

"Hicksville?" His grin morphed from amused to disappointed. "Don't discount the people here. They might not know the difference between types of caviar, but they'll help you out when you need it. You of all people should know how valuable that can be."

He moved down the aisle, and she stood in her embarrassment. Of course, she knew how valuable generosity could be. She'd essentially dedicated her whole life to taking care of other people no matter if they thanked her or not.

The truth was, she was a fish out of water in North Country. Visiting for the weekend was one thing, but living here for a couple of months was another. Her defenses rose sky-high the minute Sydney's pickup truck pulled off the highway onto the single-lane road leading into Pine Ridge. What if instead of being embraced by the town, she was shunned? Mocked or held at arm's length because she came from someplace else? She'd felt like an outcast in her family throughout her entire adolescence by everyone but her brother, and she'd sooner cut off her own arm than be made to feel that way again.

She'd settled in a comfortable existence in Manhattan, surrounded and supported by a community she'd never experienced or expected. Now that she found herself submerged in so-called normalcy, she'd never felt so exposed.

With her heart in her stomach, she wandered the store and found Denny in the bedroom furniture department. He stood stone-faced next to a four-poster bed made out of logs and covered with a buffalo plaid duvet.

"This is . . . something." She touched the smoothed, lac-
quered wood and tried to find a redeeming quality. "Fits the
theme."

"I like it," he said. "Is it cheesy?"

She studied his face before proceeding. He seemed
strangely affected by the bed, and she didn't want to insult
him. "Maybe? But that's fine. Today I just want you to tell
me what you're drawn to, and then I'll come up with some
renderings and swatches and mood boards to show you. We
don't have to make any decisions today."

He ran a hand up one of the four posters, and she ad-
mired the tendons popping out of his thumb and wrist and
trailing up into his forearm. Her brain made the short leap
to imagining him on the football field. She'd never lusted
after athletes, but the strength in one of this man's append-
ages distracted her in an alarming way.

"Maybe something like this in the guest room," he said.
His eyes remained trained on the bed, the blank stare frozen on his face.

"You could also tell me if you're looking for something
specific with your parents in mind."

Finally, his eyes flickered away from the bed and over to
her. "Yeah? Is that weird? They'll probably be the ones to
stay in the guest room most often."

"Not weird at all. It's your house. I want to turn it into
something you love. Every room of it."

He stared at her for another moment before licking his
lips and letting his hand fall from the bed frame. "My parents have really high standards."

Over the years, Bee had honed her ability to pick up on
the tiny threads people tossed out in conversation. Threads
they wanted you to tug on.

"Oh yeah?"

"Yeah." He looked back at the bed. "I mean, disgust-
ingly high. My younger siblings are all really successful.
I've got a brother who's a doctor, a sister who owns a tech

start-up that she's in talks to sell to Google, and another brother who's premed. I'm the delinquent child."

Her heart seized up. "You are not."

He tossed her another glance, his lip quirked in a half sneer. "You're being nice, but one Torres family event and you'd see it a different way. I am definitely the black sheep of my family. Mediocre grades, never read anything beyond comic books until I got to college. My dad used to ask us trivia questions at dinner, and I got one right. One. In my entire adolescence."

She waited patiently for him to continue, giving him the space to open up on his own time.

"I became a freaking professional athlete," he said. "But they didn't respect that the way a lot of other guys' families did. And maybe . . ."

Again, she waited. His stare fixed on the bed.

"I dunno," he said. "Maybe it's why it was easy for me to quit when it got really tough."

She nodded slowly. "Was it really that easy?"

His gaze cut to hers. "Well, no. But nobody really understood it. Nobody I played with. Guys thought I was crazy to give up my career."

"But you did."

"Yeah." He dragged a hand across his mouth. "There were parts of it that were hard to give up. The team aspect of it. Some of those guys were closer to me than my brothers. And I will always love the game, no matter how messed up that sounds. I still love to watch it, still love reading about innovative plays and the skill it takes for a team to have a winning season. But ultimately, I couldn't figure out why I was putting my life on the line for rich dudes sitting up in a box who'd never played a single down."

"Did your parents understand *that*?"

"I never exactly put it to them like that." His sharp cheekbones shifted, the tiniest hint of a dimple appearing in his cheek. "They don't really understand anything about the game. They always thought that any guy with a little height and a little speed could be good at it if he wanted to be."

He ran a hand through his silky dark hair and then pasted on an easy smile. "Sorry. You didn't realize I hired you to be my therapist, too, huh?"

"I've been told I'm easy to talk to," she said. "So I don't mind."

His face softened, his eyes zeroing in on hers. "You are. Easy to talk to, I mean."

A fluttering between her legs made her clear her throat and take a step backward. A dangerous thought wiggled its way into her brain. What if they slept together—no strings attached? People did it all the time. They'd never end up together in a serious way, but what harm could come from helping each other out every once in a while?

The vibe between them flowed like ocean waves; powerful and undeniable. He must have felt it, too. She pressed her lips together, watching him, studying his angular face, and wondering if he'd considered the same scenario.

He flashed his teeth at her, breaking the reverie. "Wanna take a look at the couches and stuff?"

She nodded, not trusting her voice. They wandered slowly through lanes of plaid couches, patchwork leather armchairs, and deerskin lamps. Everything screamed "mountain kitsch" while Bee wanted "mountain chic." His place would look so much better filled with minimal pieces with rustic appeal.

She pulled out her phone to tap a note to herself while he sidled up next to her.

"Let's go out for dinner tonight," he said. "You haven't seen the town yet, and on Wednesday nights Taylor's has trivia. It sounds lame, but it's really fun. Everybody goes. Mila, Jared, Sam, Sydney. A bunch of their other friends."

Dinner. She breathed deep, imagining that handsome, chiseled face lit by candlelight. Then she imagined a room full of people who all knew one another, friends who had already achieved a natural ebb and flow in their relationships. Without Jamie and Abe to lean on, she'd be on the outside. Again.

She scratched her shoulder. "Well . . ."

Disappointment lined his eyes. She'd already caused that sad-puppy face three times in the twenty-four hours she'd been in Pine Ridge. Maybe the evening wouldn't be so bad with Denny accompanying her.

"Okay," she said. *But no candles.* "But someplace casual."

"Really?" His whole face lit up, and something small and quiet eased down deep in her soul.

"Really." She sucked on her cheeks to contain her smile. "I mean, you don't even have Wi-Fi in the guesthouse. What else am I gonna do, read a book?"

"Oh shit." He smacked a palm to his head and tugged at his wild hair. "There's no Wi-Fi in the guesthouse. I didn't even think of that. Whenever you need it, come to the house. There's a key on that set I gave you, and I'll write the alarm code down for you. You're totally welcome. Any time."

"Thank you."

"All right." He crossed his arms over his chest, settling into a satisfied stance. "Dinner tonight. And then trivia after. It's not club-hopping in Manhattan, but it's gonna be fun. I promise."

She grinned. With Denny by her side, it might be even better.

chapter **six**

Denny watched as Bee tilted her face to the left, then the right, her long, wavy, golden blond hair dancing in the late summer breeze, and jogged across the street. Her absurdly tall high-heeled boots clicked on the pavement, and she held her fluorescent yellow bag tight under her arm, all but announcing, I'm not from here!

When she'd climbed into truck to head out to dinner, he laughed. Out loud. For a while.

She'd glared daggers at him, demanding to know what was so funny. He finally spit out that most of the trivia-night attendees would be in casual clothes. Jeans, boots, hoodies. She said these *were* her casual clothes. He dropped it.

At dinner, she'd peeled off her leather jacket, and he nearly had to pick his jaw up off the floor. She wore a tight white T-shirt with black jeans that looked like they'd been applied with paint. Her curves stretched the fabric in ways that turned his vision spotty.

Now, as she jogged across the road, her hair flowing behind her, he wondered again—as he had earlier when she'd listened to him blather on about his family and his career—if he'd really asked her here because he needed the house decorated, or if he'd asked her here because he wanted to be around her.

He followed her inside, breathing in a lungful of the spicy perfume that surrounded her like a cloud. At dinner, conversation flowed between them as if they were old friends. He opened up about his rigid parents, and she spoke about Club Trade, Jamie, and Abe with a warm glow on her face.

Denny liked her. A lot. Maybe too much.

He'd never been able to say he really liked a girl. There were hot girls and fun girls, party girls and girls down for anything in the bedroom. He'd wanted to spend time with some over others, but he'd never been able to look at a girl and honestly say, "I like you."

Commitment meant expectations, and Denny Torres was not built for commitment. Even though he explained himself to every woman he'd ever been with, some of them forgot. Especially after the games.

His life in Pine Ridge was a sharp left turn from his NFL normal. Most people in the area under forty were married with at least two kids. He'd found a good group in Syd, Sam, Jared, and Mila . . . but no single women. Anywhere. Even if he wasn't looking for a relationship, a man had needs.

Bee snaked around the tightly packed tables in Taylor's, making her way toward where Syd and Sam sat at a table in the back making googly eyes at each other. They'd just recently tied the knot, but they looked at each other like two teenagers alone in a room together for the first time.

"You made it!" Sydney said. She leaped out of her chair to squeeze Bee in a hug. "Of course you're dressed for a Thursday night at One OAK."

Bee rolled her eyes. "I absolutely refuse to wear hiking boots and Wranglers."

"You do you," Sydney said. "But ultimately, practicality wins out here. I give you until the first snowfall before you're popping into the hardware store for thermal long underwear."

Bee barked out a sarcastic laugh and removed her jacket. Every pair of male eyes in the place turned to survey the goods. She might not have fit in here in Mountain Town, but nobody seemed to mind.

"I'm gonna grab a drink." She placed a gentle hand on Denny's forearm. Shocks sparked as their skin touched. "You want something?"

"Two Coors Light, please." He flashed a grin, and she rolled her beautiful eyes again. Something sparkled on her skin. Shimmery powder, maybe. Or maybe her skin had a natural glimmer to it. He wanted to look closer.

Denny settled down at the table as Bee made her way to the bar, and Jared joined the group.

"Dude," Jared said. "What's the deal? Now women are up and moving cities for you?"

Denny ran his hand across his mouth and cracked his knuckles. "She's helping me with the house."

"Yeah," Sydney said. "But you like her, right? I mean . . . come on."

Denny studied Sydney's face, her deep brown eyes glittering. What was it with women always wanting to set a guy up with their friends? He'd had more jersey chasers shove their friends in front of him than he could count. Sometimes they both wanted to play.

"*Come on* what?" Denny asked. Bee wasn't one of those women.

"She's freaking gorgeous!" Sydney squeaked. "And you're single. She's single. You're two of the sweetest people I know. I've always known you'd totally hit it off. Now she's here. What's the problem?"

Denny trailed his hands over his face, trying to summon the words. What was the problem? Where should he begin?

"It's not like that," he said. "She's helping me. I'm paying her. She'll leave at the end of October, and I'll stay here."

"Yeah, that's what I thought, too." Sydney grinned at her husband, and Denny wondered if the woman would leap over the table to get after it right there and then. He'd met Sydney only after she'd already become a tried-and-true Pine Ridge resident, but he'd heard plenty of stories about how she blew into town from New York City with a chip on her shoulder and a plan to stay just a few days. Sam Kirkland had swiftly and effectively changed all that.

"Never underestimate the panty-dropping powers of Pine Ridge, my friend." Jared swallowed the last of his beer as Sydney let out a disgusted scoff.

"Where's Mila?" Sydney asked. "I like you a million times better when she's around."

"Yeah, me too. She's working. Again." Jared's tone turned somber. "Denny, dude, don't ever marry someone who's supercool and talented and has a lot going for her. She'll be way too in demand to spend time with your sorry ass."

"Eh, I dunno," Sam said. He yanked his baseball cap down over his eyes and draped an arm across the back of Sydney's chair. "I totally outkicked my coverage, and I get to see my wife all the time."

Denny laughed. He definitely hadn't had that problem. He'd scarcely met a woman he could stand to be around for more than three days at a time, let alone someone he wanted to commit to for the rest of his life. As far as he was concerned, the type of woman Jared described was the only one worth settling down for.

He just hadn't found it yet.

"Here you go."

He smelled Bee before he saw her, and as she set his two beers down in front of him, he breathed in for maximum exposure. The idea of friends with benefits appeared in his mind again like a vision.

She took the chair next to him, her knee brushing against his. Something twitched below his belt.

He gritted his teeth and shifted away from her, angry with himself that a simple brush of her knee turned him into an animal. He'd had less of an anatomical reaction from women flashing their breasts at him.

A few more of Jared's friends joined the group, and shortly after the host announced that trivia would start in ten minutes, one more person approached.

"Allison!" Sydney said. "You made it!"

Syd stood up from the table to squeeze Allison in a hug.

Shit. Denny had been dodging Allison for weeks. Her teenage son played for the local high school football team, and the message she'd left on his voice mail alluded to the fact that she wanted Denny to mentor the kid. He'd be the last person any parent should want teaching their kid about the benefits of playing pro sports.

"Bee," Sydney said, "this is Allison. She teaches at Pine Ridge High, and she's been throwing some YA book recommendations my way."

"Denny," Allison said, her eyes widening. "I'm so glad you're here. I wanted to talk to you if you have a second. Not sure you got my messages."

"Oh yeah, I never check 'em," he lied. "But we can talk, for sure."

He shifted uncomfortably in his chair and noticed Bee fidgeting, too. He knew Allison was married but she didn't wear a ring. Was Bee jealous of another woman paying him attention? A man could dream.

"Ladies and gentlemen!" The host's voice boomed through the low rumble of Taylor's as people scrambled to take their seats for trivia. The music lowered, papers shuffled on each table, and Bee turned toward the front of the

room, brushing his thigh again and forcing goose bumps to
pop up on his arms.

Jesus, dude. Get your shit together.

"Welcome to Taylor's trivia!"

A roar rose up from the bar.

God bless small-town living.

"As a reminder, please put your phones in the baskets on
your tables and no touching them while you're playing. If
you do pull your phone out, we ask that you go sit at the bar
so we can be absolutely sure you're not cheating."

"Why don't you just cut the Wi-Fi?" Jared called out.
"Seems like a surefire way to make sure nobody can contact the outside world."

Every Pine Ridge resident in the place laughed. Without
Wi-Fi, cell phones were useless.

"Thanks anyway, Kirkland." The host continued, "I'll
read each question once, give you fifteen seconds, read it a
second time, and then you've got two minutes to decide on
an answer. Tonight's theme is sports."

A shot of adrenaline pulsed through Denny's veins. Is
this what it came down to now? He got his competitive
juices flowing at bar trivia instead of on the gridiron? He'd
fit in an extra workout or a swim tomorrow. His brain and
body needed it.

"Okay, here we go," the host called out. "Round one,
question one."

Allison clutched a pencil, poised over the paper as if
speed counted. The entire group leaned in, smacking their
lips at the thought of the hundred-dollar bar-tab prize.

"Name two teams in the NFC East division of the NFL."

Denny forced himself to sit back, giving the others a
shot to chime in. At one point or another in his NFL career,
he'd played against all the teams in the NFC East. A warm
nostalgia filled his chest as he remembered the tightness of
his jersey, the click of cleats on the tunnel's cement floor,

the greasy scent of concessions floating down from where the crowd gathered and flowing into the stadium.

He gnawed at his lip. His life was different now. He'd never dispelled the rumors about his potential return to the NFL, but his heart just wasn't in it anymore. The workouts kept him in shape, and in conversation with his family, his return was imminent. But deep down, he couldn't picture ever returning to the league.

"Um, Buffalo?" Allison offered, blinking around the group.

"Good grief," Sydney grumbled. "Give me that."

Sam's wife knew her stuff and quickly scribbled the names of two NFC East teams. She could probably complete the entire round on her own.

"You want another one?" Denny asked Bee. He gestured toward her empty cocktail glass before standing from the table. Talking about football made his stomach swirl in a way he didn't like.

"Sure," she said. "Vodka soda. Thanks."

He held her gaze for a moment longer, letting the kindness in her eyes soothe his anxiety. She'd been strangely silent since they walked in, but he never forgot she sat next to him, their knees brushing and sending goose bumps skittering across his skin. Before any other part of him could react to her, he turned away and headed for the bar.

While he waited for the bartender to acknowledge him, someone slid onto the stool to his left. "I'm such an idiot when it comes to football."

Denny gritted his teeth and turned his attention to Allison. "It's not everybody's jam."

"My son loves it, though," she said. "He's a huge Jets fan."

He wished she'd just get to it already: whatever she wanted from him, whatever token she felt she was owed by simply living in the same town as a guy who used to play. No matter how much he loved Pine Ridge and the relative anonymity it afforded him, he couldn't escape his identity as a football player.

"Funny," he said, "I notice more Giants fans around here than Jets."

Her lips lifted in an expectant smile. "So I sort of wanted to ask you something. I hope it doesn't come out desperate."

Here it comes.

"Eh, I'm sure it won't." His fingertips tingled as if watching the quarterback prepare for the snap.

"My son plays football." She twisted her fingers together. "The team is good. I mean, it's a collection of kids from a bunch of local high schools, and they're not winning the state championship anytime soon, but they're the best team the schools have had in years. I think they really have a shot at a winning season."

He rapped his knuckles on the bar, desperate for the bartender to approach so he could grab his drinks and sit down next to Bee again. She hadn't pressed him on his former career during dinner, and for that, she'd quickly become his favorite person in Pine Ridge.

He stole a glance behind him in time to catch her piercing stare. She blinked rapidly and tilted her head away from the bar.

She's totally jealous. A warm, fizzy sensation rose up in Denny's chest.

"Anyway," Allison continued.

The fizzing in his chest disappeared as quickly as it had surfaced.

"They're really good kids. Hardworking and talented. They just . . . I think they need some inspiration. They don't have a lot of former students to look up to since no one they know ever made it very far. I think if they had a former pro to spend some time with them or even just an afternoon . . ."

Denny pasted on a phony grin, determined to let Allison down easy. But maybe she could see it in his eyes. His heart just wasn't in it.

"Hey, look," he said, using every ounce of energy to keep his tone light. "It's awesome that your kid's on a good team. Sounds like they'll do just fine with or without me. I just . . ."

What could he say? *I'm busy?* Everyone in town knew just how not busy he was. Plus it was a lie. People could accuse him of being a lot of things, but he refused to allow "liar" on that list.

"I get it." She tossed a hand in the air as if literally chasing away the notion. Her cheeks spotted pink. "Sorry, it was a bold ask anyway. I see a lot of kids around here whose dreams feel impossible, and I thought that if they could see someone with their own eyes who'd actually done it, those dreams might seem a little bit more attainable."

His body tensed, from his calves through his gut and up to his jaw. Everything in him said, *Show up.* He knew better than anybody how important it was to have someone to look up to. For him, it wasn't pro athletes. It was a coach who treated him like a valuable human, no matter if he pulled a C in chemistry or made the play of the game. Coach M. took the time to know him. All of him.

He touched his pocket, sure he'd felt a buzz. When he checked the screen, it remained blank. Phantom texts. His guilty conscience reminding him he owed Coach a call back.

"I'll think about it," he grunted.

Allison's face lit up. "Amazing! I mean, great. Here's my number. Please, please call if you want to drop by a practice. Honestly, no commitment. Whatever you feel like."

She snagged a pen from the bar and scribbled her phone number on a napkin before sliding it toward him. She raised both hands and stepped backward.

"Thanks, Denny. Seriously."

"Eh, don't thank me yet," he said.

Allison returned to the group wearing a triumphant smile, and Denny caught Bee's eyes once more. Her full eyebrows pinched in the middle. Maybe trivia was a bad idea. Was it the small, townie bar that bored her, or did she simply not enjoy being around him and his friends?

You okay? he mouthed.

A forced, close-lipped smile pressed into her face, and she nodded tersely. Unconvinced, Denny turned back to the bar. He ordered their drinks and glanced down, Allison's phone number staring up at him.

Huh. Had Bee watched the entire exchange? She was only in town to decorate his house. And he had to keep it that way. Anything more than that would be a mess he didn't have time to clean up.

He paid for the drinks and returned to the group where Bee sat silently as the group argued over who coached the '85 Bears. Her demeanor had shifted so drastically from when they were alone, he worried something was wrong.

"Thank you," she said as he handed her the cocktail.

"Yeah. No problem."

He waited for her to say something—anything—about her muffled energy, but she simply turned toward the group and sipped her drink. Had his interaction with Allison bothered her? Could she be that jealous already? And what were he and Bee anyway? Contractor and contracted. Nothing less, nothing more.

On the drive home from Taylor's, Bee remained stony and silent. He couldn't figure her out.

"Did you have an okay time?" he asked as they turned into his driveway.

"Yeah, it was fun." She pawed through her purse, avoiding his eyes.

"Did I do something to piss you off?"

With a long sigh, she rested her hands on her purse. "No. Not at all. I'm sorry if it came off that way."

He waited. He pulled the truck up to the house and cut the engine, suspending them in quiet darkness.

"Well, thanks for tonight," she said. "I think tomorrow

I'm going to do some work on my own and let you know where I land."

His skin prickled. What did that mean? He wouldn't see her tomorrow?

"Okay. You, uh . . . you want to go for a hike tomorrow afternoon? I'm trying to spend as much time outside as I can before it gets too cold."

Her pretty face twisted into something akin to horror. "Hiking? I don't really hike."

"Oh, come on. Give it a shot. We're not scaling mountains."

"I have a meeting with Sydney tomorrow morning," she said. "Flesh out some ideas about textiles for your house."

His jaw tensed. "After?"

She turned to look out the windshield, her eyebrows lowered and her lips worked overtime. "Okay."

Frustration roiled in his chest. "Look, you don't have to hang out with me. I'm starting to wonder if maybe I'm pushing you into being friends, and I know that wasn't part of the deal. If you're just being nice and you'd rather I back off, say the word."

Her gaze snapped back to him, her expression open and surprised. "No. God, no. I'm so sorry."

His frustration amped up. Then what? What was up with her?

"I'm super out of my element," she said. Her shoulders lifted. "When you first offered me this job, I thought it would be a fun, easy way to make some extra money. It never occurred to me that I wouldn't fit in."

"Sydney told me she felt the same way when she first got here," he said.

"Syd's different."

Once again, he waited for her to continue. Since she'd arrived in Pine Ridge, he sensed her holding back. Like a dam always on the verge of flooding.

He leaned back in the driver's seat, resting his weight on

the door. "You've barely scratched the surface of the town. I know it seems small and boring, but I promise, there are a lot of amazing things you haven't seen yet."

"It's not that."

"Okay?" he said. "Then what is it?"

"I have never really felt like I fit in."

He waited, but she stared at him as if he should already understand. "Fit in where?"

She shrugged. "Anywhere."

He ran a hand across his chin, taking a moment to figure out where to go next. There was plenty he didn't understand about women, and he sensed even his minimal knowledge wouldn't touch on whatever bothered Bee.

"Was there something about tonight that made you feel that way specifically?" he asked.

She paused. "I just feel like some people . . . some women especially . . . have it easy."

"Allison?"

Bee's eyes flashed as she glanced at him. "Yeah, I guess. She has this confidence. This unabashed confidence."

"You do not strike me as somebody who lacks confidence."

Her spine straightened. "What does that mean?"

He'd said plenty of wrong things to women over the years. He needed to get this right. "You're . . . stylish."

One side of her mouth lifted into a grin.

"You didn't notice all the dudes staring at you tonight?" he said. "You're . . ."

Incredibly gorgeous.

Finally, the words found him. "You dress like you don't care what people think of you. And you run a club, which doesn't seem to me like the type of gig you get if you're a wallflower. If you're not superconfident, it doesn't come off that way."

"Thanks, I guess?" Her grin stretched.

He hoped his stumbling compliment landed as intended.

"That actually makes me feel pretty good."

Earlier, at the home store, she'd given him space and time to continue talking at his own pace. Tonight, he returned the favor. He sat quietly, waiting for her story to unfold.

"I grew up with very strict, conservative parents," she said. "Not politically conservative. But there was a plan I was supposed to follow, a guidebook on how to be a success in the eyes of society. Everything that felt natural to me was somehow unnatural to them. Sometimes, when I'm around new people, I get that feeling all over again. Like I'm a kid doing the wrong thing. Like I don't fit."

She sucked on her lower lip and stared out the windshield.

"I can understand that," he said. "Funny how sometimes what's supposed to be conventional feels all wrong."

She wrapped the strap of her purse around her finger, unwound it, and wound it again. "I've never really felt normal."

"What's normal?"

"I dunno." She shrugged. "What you said. Conventional. Married at twenty-five to a tall, confident guy who works in finance. Two kids by thirty. A house in the suburbs."

"Sounds like a 1950s TV version of normal."

Her stormy blue eyes found him in the dark cab. "Yeah, and the Jones family's."

"Your parents were tough on you?" he asked.

"They just never understood me." She laughed. "Oh God, how cliché did that sound?"

He grinned as her stony veneer began to crack.

"Maybe," she said, "it's more accurate to say they never tried to know me at all. It was like they had kids because they were supposed to, but they had no idea what to do with us. They weren't really *kid* people. I remember they had friends who took their kids to Disney World, and they laughed about what a waste of money it was because who took a vacation for the sole purpose of a child's entertainment?"

He winced. "Damn."

She raised an eyebrow, as if to say, *I know, right?* His family hadn't traveled much, even when they had the money, but no matter how much his parents disliked each other, they always paid attention to their kids. If fifteen-year-old Denny had been consulted, he'd have said too much attention.

"My parents made it very clear they didn't want their own lives disrupted in any way," she said. "And so as I got older, they put out this expectation that the next step would be college, a responsible job, and a family and kids in a house in the suburbs. Like it was the only natural path. And that just never felt right to me."

She'd begun to open up, but he didn't want to pry. The air in the truck crackled with newness, as if their relationship were a brand-new pair of sneakers right out of the box and he had to break them in. For every superficial topic they'd covered at dinner, nothing compared to the burgeoning connection they forged in the dark cab of his truck.

"But you're happy, right?" he said. "Who cares if you don't have kids and a house? That picture-perfect bullshit doesn't necessarily work out for everybody who gets it."

"I don't know." She tugged on her earlobe and looked at him with an exhale. "My life in New York is the opposite of my parents' life on Long Island, and something about that doesn't feel right, either. I thought if I could do everything differently, something would start to make sense. And bits of my life make sense. I've grown to love some of it. My friends. Parts of my job. My community. But I get a little nervous that maybe I *do* want some of the life I grew up with, too."

The tumult showed clear on her face, worry lines creasing her forehead.

"It doesn't have to be one way or the other," he said.

She laughed bitterly, running her hands through her hair. "I have basically spent my entire life fighting against what my parents believe in. I don't know how to find a happy medium now."

A smile creeped onto his face. "I might know something about that."

She matched his gaze. "Why were your parents so against you playing football?"

"For all the reasons you mentioned when we met, and then some." He swallowed down the bad taste in his mouth. "Career instability, injuries, and on top of everything else, it's a career based on physical acumen. Or . . . at least that's what they thought. They never saw the strategy or the studying or the mental acuity it took to be successful in the sport. They only saw a bunch of grunting dudes on a field kicking the piss out of each other."

He inhaled, and on the release, let go of the anger. He knew firsthand how much more football required than simply showing up and pummeling people. And despite wanting to get out, his love for the game still ran deep. He couldn't explain it. He was tired of having to try.

"But I wasn't good at anything else," he said. "So to my parents, my siblings, everybody who knew me, football became who I was. Who I am. *What* I am."

She tilted her head, studying him closely. She'd nailed it earlier. She really was easy to talk to. It had been years since he'd spoken aloud about his parents and his past, and she pulled it out of him without his even noticing.

"So, what are you gonna do now that it's over?" she asked.

A tension headache tugged at his temples. He couldn't breathe, as if the airplane window had cracked at thirty thousand feet. He didn't want to go down this road tonight. He didn't want to have to answer the question his parents would inevitably require an answer to the moment they crossed the threshold of his new home. *What now?*

"I don't know," he said.

"What made you land in Pine Ridge?"

He couldn't answer that one, either. "I liked it here?"

A short laugh huffed past her lips. "Is that a question?"

He tugged the keys free of the ignition and opened the driver's side door. "Hey, I'm beat. I'll see you tomorrow, yeah? Just come over when you're done with your meeting."

He ignored her confused brows, climbed out of the truck, and slammed the door.

chapter **seven**

The Loving Page bookstore wrapped around Bee like a cashmere blanket. She stepped inside as a cloud cleared the sun, and the entire store lit up like high noon on a tropical beach. White pillar candles burned inside vintage glass lanterns in a cluster near the cash register, their sea salt and peach scent filtering through the air and sending shoppers to coastal beaches as they perused the artfully curated displays of summer reads. Seashells filled blue glass bowls on the bookshelves, and canvas totes stamped with Summer Reading and Pine Ridge Is for Lovers adorned a rack in the window.

Sydney had kept the giant sailboat in the window but added beachy, ocean vibes to the decor.

"This place is freaking stunning," Bee said.

Sydney gripped Bee's shoulders and pressed a kiss to her cheek, as genuine flattery glowed on her sun-kissed face. "Thank you. Just a couple of changes since you were here. I like to keep it fresh in case of repeat customers. Even if it is a lot of work."

Bee set her purse down onto the little red velvet sofa and plucked a chunky copy of *Summer Island* from the side table. "Is it mostly you here by yourself? Or do you and your mom split shifts?"

"Are you kidding?" Sydney said. She settled onto the couch and propped her feet up on the glass-topped coffee table. "I wish she'd stay away. Ever since GMA profiled us, she hangs out every day, chatting with customers and doing absolutely no work."

"Aw, she's like your spokesperson. I love that."

Sydney raised an eyebrow. "I just wish she'd unload a box every once in a while. But I have to admit, it's been nice spending so much time with her. She'll be thrilled to meet you."

A knot formed in Bee's chest. She hadn't spoken to her own mother in over a month. Not since Isaac's accident. Not since her millionaire parents refused to chip in even a hundred bucks for his medical bills. Not since they'd shown their hand.

"I can't talk to you when you're like this, Bethany."

Bee filled in the blanks for her mother. Hysterical, over-reacting, dramatic.

"I'm telling you he needs help," Bee said.

"Your brother always needs help. Do you have any idea how many exorbitant bar tabs I've covered over the years? The insurance claims on the car? The scams he's fallen into that any half-bright human would've seen coming a mile away?"

Bee winced. For all the years she'd had the grenades tossed at her, she still couldn't fully protect herself when they hit. Half-bright, dim-witted, slow. Never enough. And always too much.

"We're not covering him this time," her mother said.

"And if you do, then you're just as deserving of failure as he is."

Syd squeezed Bee's hand. "You okay?"

Bee cleared her throat, forcing her face into a neutral smile. "Totally. Just mentally envisioning Denny's house. It's gonna be so much fun to decorate."

The front door of the store swung open, the tiny bell overhead jingling to announce Allison's arrival. She looked different today, her makeup toned down from the previous night's lips-and-lashes look. Bee loved makeup, but if Allison let her, she'd teach her about individual lashes and matching her lipstick shade to her skin tone instead of the color of Barbie's dream car.

"Hey, girl!" Sydney rose from the couch to squeeze Allison in a hug. Allison's white-blond ponytail swung as Sydney rocked her back and forth before releasing her.

"Good to see you," Allison said. She raised an awkward hand at Bee. Was it because of last night? Bee hoped she hadn't slipped into cliché girl mode and been cold to Allison simply because this beautiful woman had chatted with Denny for a few minutes.

Admittedly, Bee had assumed Allison was flirting. But so what if she had been? Denny didn't belong to Bee in any way. And the last thing she ever wanted to do was treat a woman with disrespect based on how they each felt about a man. Part of developing her own sense of confidence in an unfamiliar place was pushing past the petty bullshit. *Starting now.*

Bee stood up from the armchair where she'd been sitting and wrapped Allison in a warm hug. "I can't thank you enough for coming." She pulled back to find Allison's face open and surprised. "Syd told me you've got tons of hookups and some gorgeous original designs you've done yourself?"

Allison's pale cheeks flushed with color as she lowered

her overstuffed purse to the ground. "Sydney is way too kind."

"No, I'm not," Sydney said. "Your original stuff is stunning. We carry a few of her pillows, and I've been bugging her to do some throws and lampshades, too. You'd be shocked at how many people want funky lampshades."

"I teach at the high school," Allison explained to Bee. "Between that and my husband and two kids, I just don't have a ton of time to work on this. I wish I did. I love doing it."

Allison spread samples across the coffee table as Sydney poured them each a mug of hot cinnamon tea. Bee gazed over swatches of nubby white cotton, plush faux-deerskin, and smooth, matted grass, as Allison explained her process. Growing up among the trees and lakes of Pine Ridge, her inspiration came from nature, the textures, colors, and motifs all originating in the land, sea, or sky.

Bee laid out her vision for Denny's home, displaying a mood board on her laptop but also infusing Denny's amiable personality into the explanation.

"Well, you know him," Bee said. "I'm not sure how much time you've spent together, but he's a big kid. As intimidating as he looks, he's sort of sweet and easygoing. He wants things to be soft and comfortable and homey, you know?"

Sydney's lips curled into a smile, and she lifted her mug to her mouth, blocking the insinuating smile.

"What?" Bee said, her cheeks hot.

"Sounds like you have a little crush," Sydney said.

Allison grinned, adopting Sydney's suggestive voice. "Oh yeah?"

"What is this, middle school?" Bee said. She willed any suggestion of happiness from her features, narrowing her gaze and daring Sydney to continue.

"Oh, come on," Sydney said. "You have to admit he's cute."

"Of course he's cute," Bee said, tossing her hands in the air. "He's smokin' hot. That's not debatable. But I do *not* have a crush."

Bee swallowed down every lusty thought she'd had about Denny in the past couple of days. The trace feelings were simply the product of not having been laid in months. Denny was stubborn and goofy and used to women falling at his feet. Men like Denny complicated things, and she had enough complicated people in her life.

Bee's phone lit up with Jamie's happy grin, made up in purple glitter in a photo from last year's Pride Pier Party. Her throat clogged. Having Sydney here lessened the loneliness, but no one could fill Jamie's shoes.

She clicked the down button to silence the buzzing call and returned to Allison's samples. A delicately woven, natural wool fiber caught her eye, and she plucked it from the selection.

"I'm thinking draperies for the library," Bee said. "Obviously, we're on a really tight timeline, so our options might be limited. But I'll send you measurements when we're done here, and you can tell me what we can source by early October."

Allison jotted something in her notebook and nodded as Bee's phone lit up again with another call from Jamie. It wasn't like him to call, let alone twice in a row.

"Will you give me a second?" she said. With her heart in her throat, she hit the green Accept button and pressed the phone to her ear as she walked swiftly to the front of the store. "Jamie? What's going on?"

"Hey." The single word barely carried over the line. "Sorry to act like a stalker and call you relentlessly."

"It's fine, what's up? I can't really hear you."

"Sorry," he said again. His voice remained low and muffled. "Is that better?"

"Not really."

He huffed out a frustrated breath. "Isaac's here."

The hair on the back of her neck stood at attention as if an icy winter wind blew against her bare skin. Pine Ridge was exceptionally warm that day, and she'd happily donned a sleeveless crop top for her meeting. Suddenly she wished she'd worn a sweater.

"What do you mean?" she said. "*Here* as in my apartment? With you? He's supposed to be at home. Recovering."

"Oh, he's . . . recovering."

"Jamie," she snapped. "Can you find a private place to explain all of this to me?"

He huffed again, and a few seconds passed before she heard the faint closing of a door. "Okay. I'm in the bathroom."

"Spill it, please."

"He showed up about an hour ago," Jamie said. "With luggage. He said your parents won't let him stay at their house, and he's got no place else to go."

Anger burned in her chest, hot and fiery, and she clenched her stomach as if muscles alone could contain the emotion. Isaac had plenty of places to go, plenty of trust-fund buddies with spacious apartments in Tribeca their mommies and daddies paid for. He'd come looking for his sister.

"He didn't even know you were gone," Jamie said. "You didn't tell him?"

The anger continued to churn. She typically texted him if she went out of town, but he never remembered she was gone or for what reason. Didn't it figure, the one time she hadn't planned ahead.

"No. I . . . thought he was going to my parents'. I thought maybe he wouldn't have any dire emergencies until I got back."

A warm hand landed on her shoulder, and she turned to face Sydney's pinched brow. "Everything okay?"

"Yeah," Bee said hurriedly. "Sorry, it's just Jamie."

Her lips tightened. "Something wrong?"

"I'm sure it's fine." Bee shoved down all the reasons Isaac had demanded her attention in the past. He'd lost his friend's cat; he'd locked himself out of the house; his car ran out of gas on the Long Island Expressway. If he'd shown up unannounced at her apartment, she couldn't even fathom why.

Sydney placed a gentle hand on Bee's elbow and squeezed. "Take your time."

As Sydney sat down with Allison, Bee turned her back toward them to shield her face. Whatever news she was about to get would surely show all over her features the moment Isaac dropped it like a bomb at her feet.

"Jamie?" she said.

"Yeah, babe."

"So Isaac's there."

"Isaac's here."

"Can you put him on?" She didn't want to talk to him, didn't want to get sucked into his gravitational pull. But she needed to know what was going on and fix it before it got out of hand.

"Are you joking me right now?" Isaac's nasally voice pierced through the muffled silence. "How *dare* you take a mountain vacation without me?"

She breathed deep. "Listen, I'm right in the middle of something, so I don't have a lot of time. Mom and Dad won't let you stay with them?"

"Like you're surprised. They changed the freaking locks."

Maybe her parents really were putting their foot down this time. Isaac had tested them so many times, and his motorcycle accident must have been the final straw.

"All right, well . . ." She ran a tense hand across the back of her neck.

"Just text me the address where you're staying and I'll drive up."

The tips of her fingers tingled, and she glanced back at

Sydney and Allison. Both reclined in their respective chairs, typing on their phones, attentions occupied.

"Ike." She gritted her teeth. Ike was a pet name. She couldn't soften. If she allowed even the slimmest of openings, he'd wriggle in and win her over, and he'd be sharing her guest cabin within the day. "You can't come here. This isn't a vacation, I'm working."

"Don't make me torture Jamie to get the address."

"You are *not* coming here. I'll text you when I'm done with my meeting. Don't bother Jamie; he's doing me a huge favor." Without her best friend, she'd have had to find a replacement tenant for the apartment above Club Trade. She'd bailed on the rent early and promised Gerald she wouldn't leave him high and dry. Jamie to the rescue.

"Bother?" Isaac's melodic laugh skipped across the line. The laugh that seduced everyone from lovers to his friends' parents. "Jamie loves having me here. I mixed him a perfect mojito within five minutes of walking through the door. He's gonna beg me to stay."

Jamie needed alone time like flowers needed sun. He'd never allowed a partner to move in with him and often cited "self-care" as a reason he couldn't hang out with Bee. She imagined him locked in the bedroom, begging Isaac to take off.

"Please, just stay out of his way," she said. "I'll text you later."

She ended the call, and, with her pulse hammering, returned to the couch.

"I'm so sorry," she said, lowering herself to the red love seat. "Family shit."

Allison pressed her lips together politely. "The worst kind."

Bee and Allison selected a few more fabrics before moving on to vintage clocks and kitchen decor for Denny's home while Sydney drifted in and out, handling customers as they entered the store looking for romance reads.

By the time Allison packed up her bag and hugged Bee goodbye, Bee had a lump the size of Long Island stuck in her throat. Isaac had sidelined her plans more times than she could count. When she'd applied and been accepted to the interior design program in London, something finally felt right. Like her life belonged to her for once. And then Isaac swooped in and derailed that, too.

And now he was coming to Pine Ridge.

Well, shit.

Bee tucked her laptop into her shoulder bag and hovered near the romantic suspense shelves while Sydney finished ringing up a smiling customer. She scanned the spines, the variety of fonts and colors blurring together until she found the LGBTQ+ shelf.

"You really have such an impressive display," Bee said as Sydney sidled up next to her. "You've got the rainbow completely covered."

"We get more interest in the Amish romance section," Sydney said, "but I'm trying to tell myself it's a small, up-state town. They're open, and they're beginning to get interested. Baby steps are okay as long as they're being made."

"I agree. Little by little is sometimes the only way."

"I'm thinking of doing a loaner program." Sydney removed *Tula Times Two* from its spot and reshelved it six books to the right. "Allison was telling me a couple of kids at her school are having a tough time fitting in. She's thinking at least one might be struggling with their sexuality. I didn't start reading romance in earnest until I moved here, but I've had a bunch of customers tell me that romance novels exposed them to sexuality in a way that felt safe. And these days the genre is all over the place, including all types of main characters with sexuality across the spectrum."

Bee's antennae went up. She licked her lips. "You want to lend diverse romance novels to the high school?"

"Sort of." Sydney tugged a slim copy of *She's All I Need* from a tightly packed shelf to reveal a cartoon cover featuring two Black women embracing. "I want to create a teen book club. With Allison. We'll cover all types of age-appropriate books, but focus on non-white, non-cisgender authors and characters. I'd love to lend copies to the kids so they don't feel pressured to buy, and open it up to anyone interested—"

"Let me help you!" The words shot out of Bee's mouth with enough force to rattle the windows.

Sydney grinned. "Oh, is that something you'd want to participate in?"

"Oh, you saucy minx, you." Bee's mouth curled into an all-knowing smile that matched Sydney's. "You knew exactly what you were doing, didn't you?"

"The idea came up when you told me you were gonna be in town for a while. I know you used to volunteer at that youth center in Chelsea, so you've got the experience with kids. And I mean, you can't *just* decorate Denny's house. You'll be bored out of your mind."

For a moment, Bee had forgotten all about Denny. Their brief but intense conversation the night before had left her shaken, affected by him in ways she hadn't expected. He really listened.

Bee had moved away from her hometown, had created authentic, close relationships with great friends in New York who loved her unapologetically, and yet exposing herself to new people still turned her insides to Pop Rocks. No matter the family she'd created for herself in adulthood, she still remembered the two who birthed her, sitting across from her at the dinner table when she was fifteen years old, chirping politely whenever she attempted to open up about something tough, "Oh, Bethany. You'll get over it." As if her identity, her hopes, her fears were all phases she'd eventually outgrow like low-rise jeans and acne.

Bee swallowed down the painful memory and ran her thumb across the *be* tattoo on her knuckle. *Be. Easy as that.*

"Or," Sydney said, the smile fading from her face,

"maybe you have too much on your plate already? Is everything okay with Jamie and Isaac? If you're overwhelmed
with stuff back home . . ."

"No," Bee said. "Jamie's call was . . . nothing. I've got
time. And you have absolutely exploited my pressing need
to make kids across the spectrum feel loved and supported,
so bravo you."

Sydney tossed her head back as she laughed before
wrapping her arms around Bee's shoulders. "You're right.
That's exactly what I meant to do. Thanks for seeing
through me and stepping up anyway."

Bee promised Sydney she'd brainstorm a few book ideas
based on her own expansive shelf of YA romance before
hopping on the bike Denny had lent her and heading out of
downtown.

Warm late-summer breeze whipped through her hair, a
chorus of insects rising up around her like orchestra musi-
cians tuning their instruments. Sunshine flickered through
branches and clouds and kissed her cheeks in mottled bursts
as she sped around the corner of Denny's desolate street.
She breathed deep. Okay, so she'd never been an outdoor
kind of girl. Pine Ridge felt like so much more than that.

Carefully dodging fluttering monarch butterflies sun-
bathing in the drive, she pulled her bike around to the
guesthouse and used the toe of her formerly white sneaker
to tug at the kickstand. She stood outside the cabin, adjusting her bag on her shoulder and gazing out past Denny's
massive house, down the sweeping emerald lawn to the
sparkling blue lake below.

"You're back." Denny's booming baritone gave her heart
a kick start. He loped across the front porch and down the
strip of grass separating the main house from the guest
cabin, a worn white T-shirt and seafoam-green shorts hanging on his powerful frame.

"I'm back." She bit her lower lip, but the smile remained.

He grinned back, his face open and warm in the glowing midday light.

"How'd it go?" he asked.

"Sort of awesome."

He stood too close, hands on hips, smiling down at her as if she were the only thing in the world worth looking at.

"Oh yeah?"

She realized she'd been silent too long for any normal person's comfort level.

She cleared her throat. How could a girl think with those sable-brown eyes exposing her like that? "Um, yeah. Sydney's starting a book club for kids from the high school. She's gonna focus on diverse authors, diverse content. You know, anybody who's not a straight white person."

He grinned. "Very cool."

"Isn't it?" Ideas rushed feverishly around her brain. Study guides and conversation starters. Themed snacks. Authors she loved. "I'm going to help her with it. I love young adult books, and there are so many options. You just have to dig a little, but I love the idea of sharing those great books with kids who might not know they're out there."

"Wow," he said. "So it was a successful design meeting then."

"Oh, shit." *Duh.* She twisted her purse strap with both hands. "Of course. The design meeting. That went super well, too. Allison and I came up with some really beautiful options for your draperies. . . ."

"I'm pulling your leg." His grin widened, his shiny white teeth and glittering eyes mocking her. "I mean, I'm stoked that you locked down draperies. But you seem pretty excited about the book club."

She scratched her shoulder. He made her feel giddy. Foolish. Out of control.

"I guess each has its exciting aspects."

He nodded before scanning her body, his eyes flickering

down and back up as her flesh reacted in kind. Goose bumps prickled across her skin.

"You ready to hike?" he said.

Hope slowly leaked out of her chest. *Dummy.* He hadn't been checking her out. He'd been silently judging her outdoor-inappropriate outfit.

"Sure," she said. "Do I need to change or something? I've never really hiked before."

"Nah, you're good. As long as you don't mind those clothes getting wet."

Prickling dread creeped from her scalp to her spine. "Why am I getting wet?"

His smile widened again. "There's a swimming hole along the route we're gonna take. You don't have to swim, but it might be nice to have the option."

"Oh." She begged the clanging alarm bells in her brain to shut the hell up. "Sure. It's shallow?"

He blinked before crossing his arms over his chest. "I'm not sure. You don't have to go in."

She loved water from a safe distance. Give her an enclosed room forty stories up with a view of the Hudson River, and she'd enjoy the hell out of it. Drop her into a watering hole with unknown depths and the breath froze in her lungs.

"Okay," she said, "well, I guess I should change either way."

"Cool. Meet you down by the lake. Trailhead's on the other side."

With long, graceful strides, he strode on bare feet down the slope of lawn toward the lake. Before she could hurry into her cabin and change, her phone buzzed inside her purse. A moment of longing poked her chest as she remembered her bike ride just minutes prior, blissfully free of cell service or Wi-Fi. Another plus-one for the mountains.

She yanked her phone out of her bag, and her heart sank immediately into her stomach. Isaac.

Please call me? I think I pissed off Jamie.

She sent Isaac a FaceTime request, and he answered after the first digital ring. His flawless, heart-shaped face
practically glowed from the screen, his skin creamy and
bright with the newest, priciest treatments. Apparently,
Mom and Dad had locked him out of their house but not
their line of credit.

She breathed deep, dragging herself back to the present.

"Hello, gorgeous." He smiled, the toothy grin a near exact replica of her own. People said they couldn't see the
resemblance in the Jones siblings until they smiled.

"Hi, Ike," she said. "What did you do to Jamie?"

"Eh, it's not even worth mentioning."

"Right." She bit the inside of her cheek. Jamie would tell
her eventually. "What's up?"

"You never texted me." His sandy-blond eyebrows
pinched, revealing a glimpse of the little boy she'd grown
up with. "I need help, Bee. Can I please come crash with
you for a while? I promise I'll stay out of the way."

"You can't come here." Was the fight even worth it?
When Isaac said he was doing something, he found a way
to make it happen. St. Moritz for New Year's at fifteen
years old? He'd called her at midnight New York time to
tell her 2009 was already a drag. Gaga tickets to a sold-out
show in Vegas during a nationwide airline strike? He texted
her photos backstage with his arm around Gaga's shoulders, both of them bedazzled and stunning in head-to-toe
black.

"I know you're worried I'll be super needy," he said.
"But I promise, I won't be. Cross my heart. I just can't get
around the city like this. I'm still on these crutches, and my
neck's all messed up. Have you ever tried taking the sub-
way stairs with crutches?"

She swallowed the sour taste on her tongue. She couldn't
articulate what scared her about his visit. Part of her wanted

to sink into Pine Ridge, pretend nothing existed outside the idyllic mountain town. Part of her didn't want Isaac to spoil it.

"There's nowhere for you to stay," she said. Her voice came out meek and mild.

"I'm easy, you know that. I'll bring a yoga mat and sleep on your floor. I mean, this guy who hired you is giving you a room, right? Or . . ." His face lit up. "You're not staying *with* him, are you?"

If only. She cleared her throat. "No, I'm not staying with him. I'm in his guest cabin."

"Perfect!" Genuine relief glowed on his face. She'd never known him to be unsure of himself or worried about how he'd get by. Maybe this time he really did need her help.

"There are conditions to you coming here," she said. "You can't just pop up and crash and laze around all day and drink all night."

"Okay, *Mom*," he said, rolling his big brown eyes.

Bee raised an eyebrow. "I'm serious. Find something you can do online."

"Like . . . work?"

A bitter laugh escaped her throat. "Sure. Work. Or you can volunteer. The Trevor Project will let you volunteer from home with just a phone line or a computer connection."

He nibbled his lip. "Okay, I guess I can do that."

"Great." She grinned, satisfied that even if he did only want her to take care of him, she'd get something out of the deal either way. "I'll call my contact there and get you set up, okay?"

"Amazing!" He squealed with glee, using the heel of his hand to shove aside a rogue strand of honey-blond hair. "I can't wait."

"Before you get too excited, let me run it by Denny first. It's his place, he's being super generous in letting me stay here, and I don't want to abuse it. Okay?"

"Of course," he said. "This is gonna be so much fun. We haven't been on vacation together in years. Since all of us went to the Berkshires, right?"

"Ike." His name snapped off her tongue. "*Not* a vacation. Do you hear me?"

"Right, right, right." He held up a hand as if to physically stop her from continuing. "Are you allowed to have any fun at all? Or are you literally punching a clock?"

As if on cue, Denny rounded the corner of his house, eyes narrowed and lips parted.

"I have to go," she said into the phone hurriedly. "I'll text you later."

"Mm-'kay. Love you."

"Love you."

As the two words slipped from her tongue, Denny stopped. He blinked a few times, the surprise clear on his face.

"Hey," he said. "I, uh . . . Sorry. Didn't realize you were on the phone. I didn't mean to interrupt anything."

"Oh, no, it was just my brother." She nearly laughed. He hadn't asked who it was. Simply apologized. But she needed that point to be very, *very* clear.

"Ah." His face melted into an easy grin. "Let me just grab my shoes and we can go."

chapter **eight**

A mosquito whizzed past Denny's ear. Moisture hung in the forest air, coating his skin and turning it sticky with sweat and condensation. The swimming hole called his name like an old friend, visions of crashing waves at T Street back home distracting him momentarily from the clouds of insects. He missed the water. Missed the surf. Missed entire days spent outside, the bridge of his nose tender as the sun set over the ocean and turned the sweeping horizon fiery orange.

He'd thought about settling on the West Coast. After growing up in Orange County, he spent years playing for LA before Carolina picked him up. His younger days had centered around Southern California. But when he thought about regular dinner invites from his obnoxiously successful siblings, each of them trying to outdo the others with stories of grants and projects, lifesaving medical triumphs and earth-shattering technological developments, he bolted to upstate New York. The role of "fun uncle who visits once a year" suited him just fine.

Bee trudged along the root-laden path ahead of him, sporadically slapping at the backs of her bare arms. Curly tendrils of hair clung to her neck, the heat and humidity tugging random strands from her haphazard hairdo. He couldn't see her face, but judging by the slaps, the labored steps, and the pervasive silence, he could only guess she hated every minute of the hike.

"Don't forget to look up every once in a while," he called out.

She tossed a glance over her shoulder. A terse smile sat on her lips. The girl clammed up too much, turning into one of those little-kid diaries bound by lock and key whenever the wind shifted. Sure, she was hot. The tats really did it for him, especially the delicate line of script down her spine, revealed when she lifted her hair into a loose knot on top of her head.

But tats or not, she'd been in Pine Ridge for a few days, and he still felt like he was auditioning for her. He'd never put in that much effort for a woman. Especially one flitting in and out of his world like a butterfly.

They rounded a bend in the trail and sidestepped a patch of mud, the product of water runoff from a tiny waterfall just up the hill. His mouth lifted at the corners. They were close.

"I think the swimming hole is up here," he said. "Jared told me the tiny waterfall turns into a bigger stream and it's just past that."

"Cool."

He breathed deep, trying to let her icy demeanor slide off his shoulders. Maybe he should've come alone. But he was tired of doing things alone, and he could only ask Jared on so many outings. The guy had a fiancée and a job to worry about. In the past couple of months, the constant invites had begun to feel desperate.

The trail rose ahead, and the faint rush of water greeted them. As they continued along the path, the gushing grew louder until they crested the hill and found the oasis.

Sun filtered through the trees, lighting on the swimming hole and turning everything in its path to gold. The surface of the pool shimmered and rippled, the modest waterfall providing a constant flow. Denny practically salivated at the thought of stripping off his damp T-shirt and plunging in.

"You game?" he said, dropping his water bottle and kicking off his sneakers.

She turned to face him, her pallor ghostly white under flaming red cheeks. "I dunno."

He paused his frantic striptease and narrowed his gaze. "Can you swim?"

"Of course I can swim." Her eyes flicked to the swimming hole and back to him. "Is this safe, though? I mean, what's at the bottom?"

He wanted to laugh, but something told him she wouldn't appreciate it. He'd only ever been concerned with what was below the water in Hawaii when they got too close to the reefs.

"I guess it's mud and rocks," he said. "But it's probably too deep to touch the bottom. If you can swim, you'll be fine."

She sucked her lips and twisted her water bottle with white-knuckled fingers.

"Bee, seriously, you don't have to go in," he said. "Hang here. Or just put your feet in. I'm dying, though, so I'm gonna hop in, if that's cool?"

She nodded, a rigid gesture that made him think she'd rather be dead than get in the swimming hole. Jesus. He definitely should've come alone.

With his nerves practically vibrating in anticipation of cool relief, he tore off his shirt and picked carefully across the slippery rocks. Spray off the waterfall coated the rocks with just enough moisture to make them dangerous, and he couldn't imagine her dragging his concussed body out of these woods.

Using the stream bank to steady himself, he lowered his body into the cold water. Liquid embraced him, rushed across his skin and elicited an audible sigh from his throat. He ducked under the surface, letting the cool, prickly sensation wash over him.

He flipped his head back and pinched his eyes, water streaming down his face. "Holy shit," he said. "This feels really good."

She chewed on her lip, anxiously gripped her water bottle, and watched him unblinking. Maybe she needed a little encouragement.

"Sure you don't want to come in?" he asked. "Seriously, at least dip your feet in. After that hike, you won't be sorry."

Her chest rose and fell, her gaze never faltering from his. After a few more moments of listening to the gentle rush of water over rocks, she crept toward the edge. She lowered her body slowly, with all the poise and control of a ballerina onstage, and touched her bare toes to the water.

Finally. Her audible exhale floated toward him, and he paddled closer, suddenly wanting to be next to her. Whatever kept her from diving in, she'd gotten over it and given into the pull of the liquid relief.

He swam closer, and just before he reached the edge, his hand brushed the bottom of her foot.

A shrill scream ripped from her throat, the placid expression replaced by an openmouthed stare of pure terror. She clambered backward on the rocks, unable to gain footing because of the slick surface. The more she struggled, the more she panicked. Her chest turned a blotchy shade of crimson.

"Hey!" he called out. He launched himself onto the slippery rocks, unconcerned with his own safety at the moment, and crouched down next to her.

She covered her mouth with trembling hands, her knees

inches from the edge of the rocks and covered in dirt. Yelps escaped her mouth as she struggled for breath.

"Bee." He slipped an arm around her shoulders, her skin warm from the sun, and pulled her toward his chest. "Hey. That was me, I accidentally brushed your foot. You're all right."

She sank against him, her body folding into his chest as if she wanted to curl up there and disappear. Her fragile state didn't stop him from noticing the warm, flowery scent of her hair as it tickled his nose.

"I'm sorry," she said.

She looked up, her wide sky-blue eyes rimmed with red. With shaky hands, she wiped at her splotchy cheeks.

"What just happened?" he said.

Her chest rose and fell dramatically as she continued to stare at him, her face more open and vulnerable than he'd ever seen it. She pulled away enough to create space between them, but he felt her as if she were still tucked into his chest.

"I have a weird thing about water," she said.

"Okay." A strand of hair caught in the corner of her mouth, and he tugged it free. She didn't move.

"Can we go?"

She couldn't be serious. A reaction on par with Jamie Lee Curtis in *Halloween*, and all she could say was *Can we go*?

"That's all I get? You have a weird thing about water?"

"Everything's a joke to you." Her cheeks burned red; her full lips set defiantly.

"I'm sorry," he said, the sentiment losing steam with the groaning in his voice. "I'm trying to understand, but that was extreme, right? You have a *thing* with water? Help me out here, Bee."

Her chin rose as if he'd challenged her to a duel. "I don't want to talk about this. I just want to go."

He gritted his teeth, waiting for something. An explanation. A crack in her defenses. Instead, she stood tall, crossed her arms over her chest, and stared him down.

"All right," he said. "Let's go."

Denny wiped the sweat dripping from his nose. His muscles ached, his weak foot protesting against repeated use. And still his heart barked at his head like a dog left out in the rain.

The first day they met, she'd had Sydney by her side. So cool and confident. But alone with him in the mountains, all her comforts stripped away, she'd retreated. Pulled back. If she'd never exposed the creative, New York–bravado side of herself, he'd have a much easier time stomaching the walled-fortress version. The version of her who'd avoided him for a solid twenty-four hours.

He wanted Cool Bee back. Bad.

He tossed the sweat towel in his hamper and gazed out the basement window, the view nearly eye level with the sloping lawn. The lake beckoned, his itch to swim not sufficiently scratched by yesterday's botched swimming-hole trip.

Without changing from his mesh gym shorts, he exited through the sliding-glass basement doors and hurried outside. The crunchy, late-summer grass cushioned his bare feet as he made his way down the lawn. With one push off the rickety dock, he dove into the glassy lake, the cool water shocking the breath from his lungs.

He propelled himself toward the middle of the lake, slippery little fish skittering out of his way as he tore through the water. Solo workouts weren't doing it for him anymore. He needed something more, something that burned his lungs and challenged the very core of his work ethic. Something that seemed unattainable and out of reach.

As much as football had always been somewhat about pleasing other people, it also satisfied the part of him that craved competition. Few things in normal life compared. Coach M. told him most guys felt that way after they left the league. If he could ever summon the guts to write the man more than a *Hope all's well* text, he'd ask for a reminder on how anybody got through the quiet boredom of post-NFL life.

He owed Coach M. a call. But he had to get everything in Pine Ridge settled first. He needed to see how his parents would react. If his new life wasn't good enough for Ernie and Rosa Torres, he couldn't imagine sharing it with the rest of the people in his world. Especially those who expected the best.

Denny somersaulted through the water, speeding back toward the boat launch and scaring the fish again. When he sensed the shore approaching, he popped up, gulping at the cool, clean air. Just as soon as he inhaled, the breath left his lungs again.

Bee sat on the dock, her bare legs dangling off the edge, crimson red toenails skimming the surface of the water. Her skin glowed in the early-evening sun, the light catching the flaxen highlights in her loose, wavy hair.

"Hey," she said.

He swam cautiously to the edge of the dock, careful to leave a few feet between them.

"Thought you had a thing with water." He wiped the droplets trickling into his eyes, shoved his hair back before resting his arms on the wooden planks.

Her gaze trailed along his arms and skimmed down his torso to the surface of the lake. She could not actually be checking him out right now.

Could she?

"I almost drowned once," she said. The words slipped past her glossy lips as if she'd told him she'd just taken a nap.

"Oh shit."

"When I was a kid," she said. "It's not some glamorous

story about getting sucked into an undertow in Bali or something."

He raised an eyebrow, a snarky retort on his tongue. *No jokes.* "No?"

Her gaze narrowed, her toes continuing to skim the lake's surface, creating ripples that reached his ribs. Curving black lines peeked out from the leg of her cutoff denim shorts. The edges of a lion's mane.

Despite the nagging below his shorts, he turned his attention back to her face. Not the time for wondering what the whole tattoo looked like or where it ended.

"What happened?" he asked. "I mean, if you want to tell me."

A tiny, wry smile found her lips. "My brother and I were on the beach in Nantucket. I was twelve, and he was eight. My parents were always letting us do our own thing, go where we wanted as long as we showed up for meals. They didn't realize, or maybe they didn't care, that it was late in the season and there were no lifeguards on the beach. There were No Swimming signs everywhere, but Isaac's always been a defiant little brat, and he went in anyway."

She rubbed a hand over her eyes and looked back to the surface of the lake. "He yelled out to me that the water was so nice and that I was totally missing out. I went in after him, and I swear, two minutes passed before we were way too far out from shore."

"Jesus, Bee."

The delicate muscles in her neck flexed. She sat up straighter. "We could both swim, but not well. I started to panic. Shortness of breath, numb limbs, the whole deal. I felt like I was sinking, like I had weights on my feet, and I swallowed some water. If Isaac was scared, he didn't show it. Or at least that's what I remember. I fainted at some point, and he pulled me out. Someone farther down the beach saw us and gave me mouth-to-mouth."

Denny blinked at her, trying to see through the facade.

Her voice remained even and unwavering, as if she read from a newspaper article.

"What happened?" he said.

"The guy on the beach called our parents, and they came and picked us up. I was just kind of dazed when they showed up, so they didn't take me to the hospital or anything. I think they were more annoyed that they had to leave their friends' luncheon than anything else. After that they started hiring vacation chaperones."

Disbelief blurred Denny's vision. Some people should've been legally forbidden from having children.

"That sounds pretty freaking scary."

She shrugged. "According to my parents, we were just being dramatic."

He lowered his voice. "You could've died."

"Well, I didn't." She cleared her throat. "It's just that ever since then I've had a little bit of a . . ."

"Thing with water."

She turned her gaze on him, her eyes reflecting the gray tones of the lake. The breeze picked up, rippling the water's surface and lifting her hair off her shoulders.

"I should've said something when you first mentioned the swimming hole," she said. "It seemed silly. Obviously, I'm not so scared of water that I can't be around it. It's peaceful, actually. Sitting here with you."

A trickle of water danced down his temple, cooling the burning skin at his neck. He felt all lit up when she looked at him like that.

"There she is."

Her eyebrows touched in the middle. "What?"

"You've seemed, uh . . ." Would she throw her defenses back up if he said it?

She crossed her arms, her forehead remaining wrinkled.

"It seems like," he continued, "you've been sort of uncomfortable since you got here. When we first met, you were like the coolest, most confident person. I've seen moments of that since you came to help me. But for the most part, you've been nervous."

A dark cloud passed over her face, and she turned her gaze back to the lake. "I've done scary shit, you know? I got a call once at four a.m. from someone who found a friend of mine passed out on the street in this really dangerous neighborhood in Brooklyn. I went out there by myself to pick him up. In hindsight, I realize that was risky."

He nodded. "Very."

"It's easy for me to do that kind of stuff." She trailed her fingers across the rose tattoo on her shoulder. "It's easy to focus on other people. To take myself out of the equation."

He waited for her to go on. To explain herself. But she sat still, one hand hooked on her shoulder, eyes trained on the lake. Wheels turned in her head, but nothing passed her lips.

"I have the opposite problem," he said.

She finally looked up. "Oh yeah?"

Goose bumps and fish skittered across his legs, the chill of the lake finally getting to him. He pushed himself onto the dock, water splashing up around him as he looked out at the darkening sky. The air had already cooled significantly. Soon they'd need sweatshirts.

Or body heat.

He cleared his throat. "I'm more of a *me, myself, and I* guy."

A short laugh escaped her. "Of course. You're a hot guy in his thirties. Why should it be any other way?"

A blush started at his toes and spread like wildfire through his legs, groin, and chest until it reached his face. "Really?"

Her jaw tightened as she grinned. "Yes, really. Don't pretend like that's news to you. Even married Allison seemed smitten the other night."

"Eh, she's got a kid who plays football for the high school. She's been hounding me to volunteer with the team."

"No way," she said. "Mr. Me, Myself, and I?"

Her tiny grin spread to a full-on smile, and he matched it. "Funny."

"She wants you to work with the team?"

He rested his hands behind him, leaning back and allowing the last remnants of sun to dry him off. "She mentioned coming to a practice or something and talking to the kids. It's not really my thing."

"Spending an hour with some teenage boys who love football isn't your thing?"

Tightness spread across his chest. "I don't have any life lessons to share. I don't have any words of wisdom. Everybody thinks that just by virtue of playing in the NFL you suddenly become a motivational speaker with a really inspiring life. I . . . am not that guy."

"I think you're underestimating yourself."

A duck lifted off the lake, flapping its wings and disappearing over the tree line. He envied the bird.

"Yeah, I dunno," he said.

Bee dipped her hand in the lake and flicked water at him, the cool drops peppering his face. "You scared?"

His lips parted in disbelief. "Scared? Of some kids? No."

"I bet some of them could beat you in a race."

A flare of competitive juices shot up into his chest. "I run the forty in four point four."

She laughed, tucking her chin and scrunching her face up in genuine joy. He warmed all over.

"Wow, okay, so now I know what gets you riled up," she said. "I'm teasing. I'm sure you're a very fast runner."

He wanted to scoop up a palm full of water and splash it at her, but she didn't trust him yet. And she certainly didn't trust him around water. It took everything in him not to push her boundaries.

"So," she said. "What are you scared of?"

The last sliver of sun disappeared behind the clouds and a chill settled over him, his skin tightening under the remaining drips of lake water. He loved North Country, but he didn't know if he'd ever get used to the cold. California blood ran through his veins, islander DNA in his cells.

"*You* said I was scared," he said. "I'm not."

"Then why don't you do it?"

He weighed his response. The people of Pine Ridge had pestered him since he'd arrived. They wanted to hear all his stories, and they wanted to tell him theirs. He knew every Pine Ridge record holder in town, had heard every victory tale three times over. He didn't want his life here to be about football.

"It's a lot of pressure," he said finally. "What do I have to teach a kid? I quit. I got so much shit from so many of my teammates. It's gonna take a long time for the stink to wear off, you know?"

"Can I ask you something?"

He met her gaze, her eyes glowing in the hazy, pale blue sky.

"Who do you look up to?" she said. "Did you have an idol or a mentor growing up?"

He didn't even have to think. "My high school coach. Coach Maiava. Samoan guy."

She tilted her head, waited for him to continue. Finally, a subject he'd talk about freely and without reservation.

"He valued hard work," Denny said. "But he also cared about us being well-rounded people. My parents taught my brothers and sister and me to chase the thing we were best at, to put it at the center of our lives. To make it our identity. And Coach M. pushed community service, good grades, social stuff. He told us to spend time with our teammates, form bonds off the field, too. It was the time in my life when I actually loved playing football."

He paused and ran a hand over his mouth. Coach M.'s text a few weeks back had just been a friendly greeting. A quick note to say hello. A few days later he'd emailed to share some photos of his newest grandson, and Denny had replied only with platitudes. He owed the guy a real response. And soon.

"College was a totally different scene," Denny said. "College athletes get all kinds of passes for the rest of it as long as they're excelling at the game. The NFL is even worse. So I got to put 'being a good person' on the back burner. Everything but football became far less important."

As the words poured out of him, he actually heard them. He looked over at where she sat grinning. Like she'd just cracked the code.

"Okay," he said. "I get it. Damn, you're good."

She laughed again, the coarse, throaty sound that let him know he'd done something right. "And I barely even tried."

"You think I should go, huh?"

She shrugged. "I think if you really explored the reasons why you *don't* want to go, you'd realize they're not good enough. One decision doesn't define you. Maybe what those kids *really* need is someone who's been through it and has a real experience to share. As opposed to the glamorous life they see on TV."

He snorted a bitter laugh. "You think a guy who quit the league early is more interesting than a guy who played till he was forty, made hundreds of millions, and made it into the Hall of Fame?"

"Honestly, yeah. I do." She scrunched her nose and kicked her feet to a silent rhythm. "All they'll care about is that you're there."

"Look at us," he said. "Saving the youth of Pine Ridge one football practice and book club at a time."

Her smile faded, and she tugged at the strap of her gray tank top. Her feet went still. "Hey, I wanted to ask you something. You can totally say no. It's your house."

"What's up?"

"My brother," she said. "He got into a motorcycle accident a couple of weeks ago. A couple of days before I met you, actually."

"Oh yeah," he said. "I remember."

"He needs some help." She paused and tugged at her shirt again. "He called and, um, asked if he could come up here. Just for a few days. A week max. Until he can get on his feet. He's sort of a helpless idiot, and he doesn't have anywhere else to go . . ."

"Yeah," Denny said. "Of course."

Helpless idiot with nowhere else to go. Denny was pretty sure he'd been described exactly that way by a few of his girlfriends.

She stared at him for a moment, lips parted as if waiting for the catch. "You sure?"

"Of course. No bed in the guest room yet, but you can blame my decorator for that." He winked, but she didn't flinch. Back to serious mode apparently.

"Oh, no," she said. "He'll stay in the guesthouse with me. I wouldn't want to put you out."

"Bee." Had she grown up rich? Flashes of a proper, well-bred girl revealed themselves in the moments that challenged her. "It's cool. I've got so much space I don't even know what to do with it."

She shook her head, sending her hair fluttering around her shoulders. "Thank you, but no. He'll stay with me. I don't want him to get in your way. It's just . . . easier."

In one swift movement, she tucked her feet under her body and stood up.

"You going in?" he said. "You want to have dinner?"

Shit. What was he doing? After she'd thrown up her defenses at the swimming hole, he'd promised himself the friend thing was over. No more invitations, no more desperate attempts at some semblance of a platonic relationship. But she'd shown him her softer side. He couldn't deny it had stirred him up.

She dipped her chin, her gaze deepening as if she'd already given in. He'd sit at the edge of the lake with her until the snow blew in if he could.

"I can't," she said, the apology clear in her tone.

"Should I stop asking for whole meals?" he teased. "Is a happy hour, wine-and-cheese type of deal more your thing?"

A sweet laugh passed her lips, and she lowered her chin further, a silky lock of hair falling over her cheek. She pushed it back and set her warm gaze on him again.

"I'm sorry. I just have a lot of work to do tonight. I've got less than two months to turn your house into a home your mom and dad will love. It's gonna go fast."

She pushed herself to standing, raised a hand at him, and walked away.

Another chill prickled across his skin. "Sure is."

chapter **nine**

Bee clicked Send on an email to a furniture dealer near Albany who had the perfect couch in stock. Sourcing furniture, contractors, and decor within the tight time frame Denny had laid out for her proved challenging but not impossible. Whenever she scored a particularly gorgeous piece, her adrenaline soared.

"Refill?" Mila Bailey appeared with a full carafe and a scowl.

"You read my mind," Bee said. "Thanks."

Mila refilled Bee's coffee and glared out the diner window toward North Country Realty, a hand on her hip. Her sparkling engagement ring caught the midafternoon sun streaming past the booth Bee had commandeered as her makeshift office the last couple of weeks.

"Everything okay?" Bee asked.

"Sure." Mila's lips worked overtime. "Jared's just being zero help on the wedding. I'm not even asking him for all that much, you know? Just his opinion."

Bee suppressed a smile. "Tell him he's being cliché. Reinforcing gender stereotypes."

Mila laughed. "I'm sure that'll *really* get him to weigh in on flowers. He's an incredible partner in so many ways, and yet the wedding stuff . . . total fail."

Bee's phone buzzed on the tabletop, and she glanced down, a flutter in her stomach telling her it was Denny before her brain could even process the name. She opened the text.

Happy hour today?

"Damn," Mila said. "I can only imagine who *that* might be."

Bee forced the smile off her face but guessed her scarlet cheeks gave her away. After their heart-to-heart on the dock, Denny and Bee had started regularly meeting outside to share a beer and conversation. Sometimes she brought a good bottle of red wine, sometimes she let him pour her an icy Coors Light. They always brought cheese. She always looked forward to it.

"How's that going?" Mila asked.

"Fine," Bee said. "I've found some really great pieces for the house, and I'm right on schedule."

"Yeah, 'cause I was talking about the furniture." Mila rolled her golden-brown eyes. "How's it going between you two?"

Their afternoons together were heaven, the highlight of her day. But her brother put a damper on everything. Isaac arrived with a flourish, having used some cash he earned from selling a few things at a designer resale store for a black SUV to deliver him to Pine Ridge.

He'd spent his first full day in town complaining about the lack of Wi-Fi and the early closing time of most of the town's nightlife. In the days following, he'd turned his gripes on Bee's busy schedule and inability to entertain

him 24-7. When she reminded him of his promise to virtu-
ally volunteer, he'd gritted his teeth and blamed the tech-
insufficient town as the reason he hadn't called her friend
at the Trevor Project yet.

Denny had been kind and patient, but when she'd mentioned Isaac might stay for a few more weeks, she couldn't
help but notice the weakened smile, the glitter disappearing
from his eyes.

"It's great," Bee said. "We get along well. He's an easy
client."

Mila snorted. "Mm-hmm. Client."

"Stop." Bee laughed and closed her laptop. "Seriously.
Clients and friends. That's it."

"Yeah," Mila said. "Just friends. I sang that tune for a
long time, too, girl."

Mila flashed her engagement ring at Bee with another
smile and turned to the table behind her, refilling their
mugs with coffee and leaving Bee to mull.

Her phone buzzed again.

I'm taking your silence as a yes. You're bringing the
cheese. I'm bringing the drinks. Spoiler alert: no
blue mountains on the bottles.

Bee tucked her computer into the canvas tote Sydney
gave her, emblazoned with the Loving Page logo, and
tossed some money down on the table. After shouting a
goodbye to Mila, she hopped on her bike and headed back
to Denny's.

Summer weather had vacated quickly after Labor Day,
and Bee suspected she wouldn't need her shorts or tank
tops anymore that calendar year. She tugged her oversize
wool cardigan around her ribs and parked her bike against
the side of the guest cabin before hurrying inside.

"There you are!" Discarded clothes covered every surface of the tiny cabin, an especially impressive mountain

on the bed, and sitting on the pile like a disgraced king atop his throne was her brother.

"Here I am," she said. She dropped her bag near the door and scanned the room. "Unless you're tidying up your life, I'm gonna need an explanation."

Isaac clicked a few times on his laptop and then shut it, turning his glittering smile on her. "First of all, hello. Hi. Love your hair like that. How was your day?"

She breathed deep, every nerve in her body buzzing like electricity. "Not bad. How was yours? What did you do today?"

"Well." He shoved his willowy body off the bed and hobbled on one good foot and one medical boot toward her, his placid smile never wavering. He wrapped his long arms around her and squeezed. "Funny you should ask. I've had a very productive day."

She gripped his arms and pulled back to look into his face. He had a secret. One quirked eyebrow told her so.

"Oh yeah?"

"I started an Etsy page so I can sell some of my clothes," he said. "I can't wear most of it since I lost weight, and I need the cash if I'm going to stay here with you until October."

Dread washed over her. "October?"

His mouth tightened into a grimace, and he tilted his head, a lock of sandy-blond hair falling over his eyes. "Babe. It's only another month. I'm still recovering, so obviously I can't work."

Her stomach tightened. Was Denny already sitting down on the dock? He was probably wondering where she was. "I don't know, Ike. That's a really long time . . ."

"I thought we were getting along," he said. His bottom lip jutted out like when they were kids, and he'd finished his ice cream and wanted "just one bite" from her cone.

"We'd get along a lot better if you cleaned this place up."

He leaned in to hug her again, tucking his chin behind her shoulder. "I will, I promise."

Would he? He'd never been on his own before. If she could just get through the next month and set him up with enough savings to cover living expenses for a couple months, maybe then he'd really grow up and move on. Every other twenty-five-year-old without a trust fund seemed able to make it happen. Why not Isaac? And by the time he'd gotten his feet under him, she'd be on her way to a new, settled life in London. Two thousand miles away from the younger brother she'd cared for since birth.

"Hey, how are you getting internet in here?" she asked.

He flopped back onto the bed and retrieved his phone.

"Using my phone as a hotspot," he said.

Her gut tightened again. "And who pays for your phone?"

He flashed her a smile. "The one thing Mom and Dad haven't cut me off from."

"Yet."

He grinned again. "The good news is, strong Wi-Fi means I can finally make good on my promise to you about volunteering. I connected with Marcello at the Trevor Project, and we have a call scheduled for later today. Aren't you so proud of me?"

She swallowed everything she really wanted to say. The kid wanted a cookie every time he completed a task he'd already committed to. Maybe she'd given him those handouts for too long. Maybe now was the time to stop.

"I'm proud you're investing in your community," she said. "It's long overdue."

He rolled his eyes. "I attend the Elton John AIDS Foundation gala every year. Those tickets don't come cheap."

"Oh God," she groaned. "You're insufferable."

"You want to watch a movie?" he said, tapping at his phone. "There's some new impossibly bad Tori Spelling thing on Lifetime. *Mama's Little Murderess* or something equally ridiculous."

"I can't," she said.

"Ooh," Isaac cooed. "Another platonic afternoon with Mr. Baseball?"

She grinned despite trying to give him the stink eye. "Football. And yes. A platonic afternoon."

"What a waste," Isaac groaned. "Can't believe you've been here almost a month and nothing's happened. How come? Not your type, huh?"

Every reason Bee didn't want to go down the Denny road rattled in her brain. It had become the mantra she fell asleep to. *Too unstable. Too goofy. Too used to getting what he wants.*

And when that didn't work, she let herself reminisce about the day at the swimming hole when she'd tucked herself into his chest. The panic attack had almost prevented her from fully enjoying his smooth skin against her cheek, the way he'd jumped to her aid without hesitation.

Almost.

"Totally not my type," she said. "I'll see you later."

"Hey, what are we doing for dinner?"

Her chest burned. She tried to remind herself he could barely walk, let alone make himself meals. "There's a sandwich in the fridge."

His lip curled. "Ugh, again? Can we go out?"

"I don't have a car," she reminded him. "And I don't think you'll fit in the basket of my bike."

"Let's ask Mr. Baseball to go to dinner." He raised his sandy-blond eyebrows at her. "Someplace romantic. I wouldn't mind staring into that gorgeous face by candlelight."

"Goodbye, Isaac. Enjoy your sandwich."

Without waiting for a reply, she pushed through the cabin door and hurried down the lawn toward where Denny sat waiting. After their second happy hour, he'd dragged two big wooden Adirondack chairs to the dock, and it had since become her favorite place on the property.

"Shit. I forgot the cheese."

He looked up, his kind face with the sharp cheekbones open and warm and not the least bit bothered.

"I brought string cheese just in case." He reached into the pocket of his hooded sweatshirt and held up four mozzarella cheese sticks.

"Wow, you were banking on me forgetting?" She hugged her sweater tighter around her and nestled into the big wooden chair. He leaned back, too, as if he'd been waiting for her to really settle in.

"Nah, it's just that this variety of cheese pairs really nicely with the craft beer I brought." He winked, and her lower abs contracted in response.

He handed her a pint glass filled with foamy golden liquid, and she sniffed before she brought it to her lips. One sip told her it wasn't Coors Light. "Ooh, that's good."

"It's called Big Wave from Kona Brewing Company." He drank from his own pint glass and licked the residual froth from his upper lip. Her throat dried up at the sight of his tongue.

She'd all but given up on finding someone to scratch her itch in Pine Ridge, and with Isaac sharing her one private space, she couldn't even get off on her own. But being around Denny made her feel something different. Something deeper.

Of course, she'd fallen into the trap that surely every other woman who'd ever been around him had fallen into, but she'd also grown comfortable in his presence. She simply liked being around him. His blatant sexual energy enhanced the experience.

"I like how you're branching out," she said.

He laughed, his eyes crinkling up in his face. "Yeah, I might even try an IPA. It's about to get crazy."

She gazed out at the lake, a pair of mallards paddling

slowly from one side to the other. Peace settled over her shoulders. She could see why people settled in North Country. Even the wildlife seemed at ease.

"How's the Golden Boy doing?" he said.

With half a smile, she turned her eyes on him. "You don't like him, do you?"

He lifted his wide shoulders and adjusted his large frame, stretching his legs toward the edge of the dock. He often went barefoot, and that afternoon she noticed a long, white scar on the top of his right foot.

"Nah," Denny said. "He's cool."

"He can be a spoiled brat."

Denny took a long drink of his beer. "You know him better than I do."

All the peace she'd acquired since sitting down evaporated with his response. "Look, if it's a problem, him being here, just say the word. You've been super generous in putting me up at your house, and I don't want to spit in the face of that."

Denny dropped his head against the back of the chair as a slow, lazy laugh escaped his throat. "How come you get so formal when you talk about him?"

Her throat went dry. "I don't."

"You *totally* do." He turned his lopsided smile on her. "You even sit up straighter. It's really cute."

Her legs turned to Jell-O. She'd been called cute a handful of times, and she could only roll her eyes at the half compliment. When Denny said it, she liquefied.

"He can stay as long as you want him here," he said, as if he hadn't just decimated her. "It's fine with me."

"But?"

"Nah," he said, "I just want you to be okay having him around."

Damn. He saw right through her.

"Are you?" he said. "Okay having him around?"

"Of course." She said it before she could really think. "He's my brother."

Denny pressed his lips together and raised his eyebrows in a *Oh, really?* look. "Okay."

"He's going through a transition," she said. "Mom and Dad cut him off, and he's not used to taking care of himself."

His gaze narrowed.

Whoops. She hadn't told him about her family. Not really.

"Your parents were bankrolling him?"

She sucked her teeth. "Yeah."

She knew what came next. He'd ask about her. He'd ask if she had a trust fund, if Mommy and Daddy still paid her rent and sent her ten-thousand-dollar checks on her birthday. People loved to make assumptions about kids who grew up with money.

"Huh," Denny said. He looked back over the lake and drank the last of his beer. "I can see that."

Could he see her? Did her behavior say, *I refused a dime after I turned eighteen because of the strings it came with?* Did he see in the way she treated other people that she ripped up those checks and had spent years reshaping her relationship with her money-solves-everything parents only to have Isaac mess everything up?

She tucked down everything she wanted to say, every personal achievement she wanted him to know about. If he really cared, he'd ask. And she'd tell.

"I decided to help out the football team," he said.

She blinked. The moment had passed. Relief trickled into her racing heart. "That's amazing."

"I told Allison I'm not making any promises." He ran a hand over his face and set his pint glass down on the arm of the chair, rotating it slightly as he spoke. "I'm not trying to be a coach or anything."

"I think you'll be surprised by how much you like it," she said. "Volunteering can get super addictive."

"How's the book club going?" he asked. "Your first meeting is coming up, yeah?"

The ache in her chest lessened, and she grinned. "Two weeks. I'm super excited. Sydney said six kids signed up already, which seems like a good number to me, and she and I are working on a study guide to fuel the conversation. It's gonna be good. Really good."

Dusk settled over the lake, the sun obstructed by clouds and a fine mist hovering around the tree line. Denny's lips curved upward, his face shadowed but warm in the dim late-afternoon light. Did he make every woman who spent time around him feel this seen? This honed-in on? She'd met charismatic people before, had fallen for more than a few, but Denny's charm exuded from his skin like pheromones. Against it, she couldn't win.

He scrubbed a hand across his mouth, and for the first time she noticed his pinkie finger. It extended out from his hand normally, but at the first knuckle, it jutted abruptly outward at an unnatural angle. Simply imagining how it happened made her skin crawl.

He paused; his hand poised over his mouth. "Does that gross you out?"

She cleared her throat. "What?"

He raised his hand in the air and bent the wonky finger. "My messed-up pinkie."

She couldn't hide her smile. "Sorry, I didn't mean to stare."

"You can stare. I've broken or dislocated a bunch of my fingers, and this one just didn't set right." He shrugged. "Hazard of the trade."

"Tell the high school kids the story of how it happened," she said. "They'll eat it up."

His gaze drifted back to his empty pint glass, his fingers working lazily along the rim. Did he feel the same sparkling chemistry between them? Or did he simply dole out the charm to everyone he spent time with? He'd mentioned more than once that while he loved Pine Ridge, it did lack a certain level of excitement he'd become used to. Maybe flirting with the new girl satisfied a little bit of his craving.

"I should go in," she said. "I've got some orders to place. The painters are coming tomorrow. I told you that, right? And then the floor's being stained on Friday, so you'll have to avoid the front room for a day or two."

"I can do that," he said. "Maybe I'll go camping for the night or something. That could be cool."

A laugh escaped her throat as she retrieved her empty pint glass and stood up. "Sleeping in the woods when you've got a perfectly good bed at home."

"You ever done it?"

She raised an eyebrow. "Honey, no. Do I look like I camp?"

He leaned back in his chair, letting his eyes roam her body. She nearly melted from the heat of his stare. "You could get there. Say the word, and we'll try it out."

She tucked down all the things she'd like to try with him and breathed deep. *Inhale. Exhale. Focus breathing. Squash the lust.*

She grinned. "I'll definitely let you know."

A sharp crack of wood. Rattling glass in the window-panes. The clicking of the door handle as someone tried it from the outside.

Bee sat straight up in bed, her heart slamming against her ribs. Blood rushed in her ears, and she clutched her phone tight to her chest. Calling 911 was her only option.

Unless she didn't have service . . .

She swallowed the lump in her throat and forced her bare feet to the ground, the icy floorboards sending shocks into her shins. On tingling legs, she crept toward the cabin door, her eyes slowly adjusting to the inky darkness. Nighttime in the mountains swallowed up light like a demon from beyond.

"Stupid lock." In two liquor-laden words, her heart slowed. She drew in a shaky inhale and unlocked the door.

Isaac stood just outside, stumbling backward on his medical boot, as his head lolled to the side. "Thank God!" He lurched at her, knocking her backward with his full weight and a wave of whiskey-laced breath.

"What is wrong with you?" she snapped. She shoved him away from her.

"Nothing." He rose to his full height and made a feeble attempt at focusing his stare. "I had a few drinks with some guys in town. Matt somebody? Or Mike? One of 'em dropped me off. Nice people around here."

Fury tickled her throat as it rose up through her stomach and past her lungs. Her entire body filled with simmering anger.

"You have a key," she said. Her voice trembled with rage he probably didn't even notice. "Did you break the door? I thought I heard something break."

She inspected the frame of the flimsy wooden door but couldn't find anything broken. After pushing it shut, she turned back and found him snuggled in her bed.

"Oh, hell no." She crossed the room in two paces and yanked the covers back. "Get out, you asshole."

"Jusss . . ." He cleared his throat and felt around for the covers, his eyes glued shut. "Jus' one night. You can have my yoga mat. Surprisingly comfortable."

Her head pounded, her vision blurred. If she could, she'd lift him out of the bed and toss his ass out into the cold. Let him sleep it off out there.

Instead, she snatched her cardigan from a hook by the door, shoved her feet into boots, and slammed the door behind her as she tore outside. One more minute in the tiny cabin with her drunk brother, and she'd have burned the place to the ground.

With her phone's flashlight guiding the way, she trudged down the lawn, dew sprinkling her ankles and dampening the bottoms of her cotton pajama pants. Rustling in the bushes beside her forced her heart into her throat for the second time that night, but she pressed on. She'd dealt with drunk, aggressive men at four in the morning in the West Village. She could certainly handle a rogue possum or racoon.

She blinked against the pitch-dark night, stumbling over a tree root, until a cloud passed the moon and the outline of the dock materialized before her. The lake beyond reflected just enough light to guide her down the rickety wooden structure and into an Adirondack chair.

She swallowed down a mouthful of the cool, moisture-laden air and hugged herself, hunching her shoulders against the chill. September nights in New York meant jeans instead of a skirt. September in the mountains meant wool sweaters. Most of the time she'd embrace the cooler temperatures. Tonight, she gritted her teeth against them.

The anger prickling her skin began to dissipate as she soaked in the pure stillness of the lake. Every few minutes, motion broke the glassy surface and a gentle ripple moved toward the shore. The sweet scent of pine trees hung in the air, so pungent and pure she could taste it on her lips.

The quiet creak of a door sounded behind her, and she sat up, peering over her shoulder. No way Isaac would be up and moving. Nothing short of a tornado would wake him during that type of drunk.

Nylon rustled as the figure approached, the swinging, graceful gait bringing a smile to her face.

"Hey," Denny said. His voice remained low as if he didn't want to disturb the quiet.

"I'm so sorry," she said. "Did Isaac wake you up?"

He made his way onto the dock and stood before her. He wore a track jacket over sweatpants and sneakers, his silky hair shoved into a cowlick on one side. Despite his rumpled appearance, his face shone brightly down at her.

"No," he said. "I was up. I'm kind of a night owl. Saw you down here and thought maybe something was wrong."

She licked her lips, debating on how much to divulge. Her New York friends knew all about her complicated relationship with her parents, Isaac's willingness to accept all their handouts, and the caretaker role she'd adopted since she and Isaac were kids. The Jones family was as much a part of her as her love of Ariana Grande and her affinity for neon. She didn't have to explain herself to her closest friends, and she'd taken it for granted.

"Isaac came home sort of toasty," she said. "He crashed in my bed, and I got pissed off and needed a little air."

Denny nodded slowly, crossing his arms over his chest and making her feel six inches tall. "You're gonna sleep out here, then?"

She hadn't thought that far ahead. "I dunno. Maybe."

"Hey, uh, the guest room mattress showed up, right?"

With a disapproving purse of her lips, she lowered her chin. "Yes."

"Someone should probably test it out to make sure it's comfortable before my parents come. Don't you think?"

"Nice try."

"There's a lock on the bedroom door," he said. "You'd be perfectly safe."

She lowered her chin further. "Because you're a threat? I know you too well at this point to be afraid of you, big man."

"I'm honored that you trust me." He grinned. "I come from a lot of very proud people. And I see where you're coming from. You're stubborn. I get it. It's cute as hell."

The remnants of her Isaac-directed anger flared up before morphing into something like flattery.

"But you don't have to prove anything," he continued. "You're not gonna fall asleep out here. Trust me. It's cold and damp, and I've seen a black bear hanging out down here late at night."

Her teeth clenched. Black bear? Slightly scarier than a drunk idiot on West Fourth Street.

"Fine." She breathed deep as his grin stretched wider. "But stop calling me cute. I'm sure that gets you really far with girls who want nothing more than to bag a professional athlete, but it doesn't do it for me. Okay?"

At least, it shouldn't do it for me.

She stood up as he stepped back. His forehead wrinkled. "Sorry, I didn't mean to offend you."

"You didn't offend me." She prepared for the tirade about how annoying and PC every woman was these days, how nobody could even give a compliment anymore. She'd heard it a thousand times from a thousand straight men.

She edged past the Adirondack chair, careful not to brush up against him, and climbed the sloping lawn toward his house. After weeks of studying the home, measuring angles, walls, and windows, and planning every inch of decor, she knew the space as if she lived there herself. Still, it wasn't her house. She waited on the deck just outside the sliding-glass kitchen door, hugging her cardigan close. A single, dim bulb cast a weak glow around her.

He stepped onto the deck, walking slowly until he stood mere inches away. For a moment, he paused, his forehead wrinkled in what she now recognized as concern. He brushed his knuckles against the palm of his hand.

"You know," he said, "I probably have called women cute before. Women who may have been interested in me."

She huffed out a bitter laugh. "You don't say."

Her retort didn't seem to faze him. "But I didn't mean it that way with you."

The glowing yellow porch light cast his angular face in shadows, his lowered brow hiding his sparkling brown eyes. She couldn't read his face, but the heavy, languid feeling in her limbs told her the mood had shifted.

"You didn't?" she said.

He licked his lips before reaching out to tug a strand of hair caught in the corner of her mouth. Just like he'd done at the swimming hole. Her entire body lit on fire as his rough skin brushed her cheek.

"I'm sort of . . ." His hand fell at his side. She missed his touch already. "Learning from you."

Ouch.

"Learning?" she said.

The left side of his mouth tugged into a grin. "There aren't any sheets on the bed yet, but I'll grab 'em for you. I want you to stay in the guest room as long as you need to, okay? Let Isaac have the cabin. I have a feeling you'll be way more comfortable here."

With one last panty-melting stare, he reached for the door handle and pulled. He raised a hand, ushering her inside, and on legs as shaky as a newborn deer, she went.

chapter **ten**

Denny had planned to go camping while the floors were being refinished. He'd intended to spend a night solo in the mountains, communing with nature and taking some much needed contemplative alone time to figure out what the hell he was doing with his life.

Then Bee moved in.

She'd stubbornly fought back when he suggested she take the guest room over the lakeside deck chair, so he thought she'd put up more of a fight when, the following day, he said she should simply stay put while Isaac was in town.

She barely blinked before saying, "Okay."

The guest bathroom didn't have so much as a shower curtain, and while he suspected that was tops on her to-buy list, she borrowed his master bath in the meantime. The first morning in his house, she'd showered and left the bathroom filled with honey-scented steam. He'd decided then and there to postpone the camping trip.

"Today's the last day I'll have to mooch off your insanely amazing shower," she said, pouring herself a cup of hot coffee. She'd made a pot every one of the four mornings she'd been sleeping in the guest room, waking him with the heavenly scent. He'd never lived with a woman before, but he'd begun to enjoy it.

"Oh yeah?" He gratefully accepted the mug she passed him.

"I seriously considered a guest bath reno after using it, but your stupid tiny budget wouldn't allow for it." She sipped her coffee, her sky-blue eyes sparkling with mischief from behind the rim.

"Whoever built this house either loved their long showers or they had a thing for group sex."

She turned her back to him but not before he caught the flush in her cheeks. For a brief moment, he let himself indulge in a fantasy of her in that shower, soaping her silky curves as steam filled the cavernous space. Side-by-side rain showerheads meant he could join.

He cleared his throat, willing away the beginnings of an erection. Probably for the best that she stuck to her own bathroom from now on. Down the hall. Three doors away.

"Sorry," he said. "Didn't think you'd be bothered by the sheer mention of an orgy."

She turned back toward him, one eyebrow raised and a smirk on her lips. "I'm not bothered."

Turned on? He begged his subconscious to shut up already.

"Should I be?" she said.

He shrugged. "I dunno."

The smirk remained as she watched him. "Ever done it?"

He swallowed. "Done . . ."

"Group sex," she said.

His heart stutter-stepped. "I—"

Sure, he'd done it. He'd indulged in all manner of cliché athlete behavior, especially in college. But he'd never seen himself as a man defined by his sexual résumé the way some of his teammates did, and he especially didn't want to share that part of himself with Bee.

"I have." The words darted out of her mouth with clarity and purpose.

He blinked rapidly, unable to hide his surprise. "Seriously?"

She laughed and leaned back against the sink, crossing her arms over her chest. "Yeah. It was fun. You've really never had multiple partners at the same time?"

"No, I have." His skin crawled. Would her face shift into judgment? Would he blink and she'd suddenly be wearing a mask of disdain?

"You're shy?" she teased.

"I am not shy."

"You don't have to be. Not about this. Not with me."

He licked his lips. He didn't come from a family that openly discussed sex, and despite spending most of his life in locker rooms listening to men swap filthy stories about their sexual conquests, he'd never talked to a woman about it. Not even women he'd slept with.

And definitely not women he was actively trying *not* to want to sleep with.

"You also don't have to tell me," she said. "I'm not prying. I guess sometimes I forget not everyone is as open about sex as my friends from New York."

"I've done some stuff," he said. "Maybe I've been around athletes too much of my life, but anything more feels like I'm bragging. And all that shit doesn't really seem worth bragging about."

She bit her bottom lip, studying him as he squirmed. "Admirable."

He huffed out a short laugh. "Eh. Maybe my parents' ideas about keeping the bedroom door closed stuck with me into adulthood, you know?"

"I think it's generational," she said. "If my mother heard me openly discussing group sex, she'd die of embarrassment and then haunt me for the rest of my living days. Hiding in the closet, whispering any time a guy came into the room, *Close your legs, Bee. No one will ever buy the cow if they can get the milk for free.*"

A half snort, half laugh escaped him, and her laughter rose with his to the high ceilings of the kitchen. "Your mom sounds really great. Really open-minded."

Bee retrieved her coffee cup from the counter, lifting the white stoneware mug to her lips. She swallowed and dropped her gaze to the island. "It took me a long time to realize their closed-off way of living wasn't necessarily the right way."

Maybe she was onto something. He'd spent a lot of days toiling away under the mentality his parents had instilled in him. And where had it gotten him? Thirty-two years old and he still allowed their judgment to control his life.

"It's amazing the ways our parents can mess us up," he said. "I guess we're all still figuring it out."

She breathed deep, her eyes settling on his. He sensed her mind working overtime. She turned back to the coffeepot, refilling her mug and giving him a moment to clear his thoughts. Having her in his home consumed him. In more ways than one.

"I'm going to the high school today," he said. "Three o'clock. You need a ride anywhere?"

"I'm good, thanks. Big furniture delivery today, remember? You're about to have a living room you can use."

"That's right." He'd never been so excited about a couch. When she'd handed him the fabric sample, a nubby wool in soft slate gray, he envisioned sinking into its depths every Sunday to watch the games. In those fantasies, he wasn't alone.

"Can't wait to hear how your first day with the team goes." Her eyes lit up like sparklers. "Kinda wish I could stop by and watch it all play out."

"Don't you dare." He smiled, but inside his stomach flipped.

When he'd reached out to the head coach at Pine Ridge High, he'd told him he might be interested in stopping by. He should've known Coach Parker would leap at the chance to have a former NFL player spend time with his kids. Before the call ended, he found himself agreeing to attend an entire practice the following day.

"Well, good luck," she said. "And maybe tonight when you get home, we can celebrate by watching your newly mounted TV on your newly acquired couch with some pizza?"

The nerves eased the tiniest bit. He smiled. "I'd like nothing better."

D enny tugged a sweatshirt over his head as he pulled the front door shut behind him. Sun beat down but couldn't shake the chill coming in off the lake. Lust and longing and nostalgia competed for space inside his chest. Sunny and cool. Football weather.

"Denny!" The voice came from Bee's cabin.

"Hey, Isaac."

Bee's brother, dressed in varying shades of black, hobbled across the driveway wearing a huge grin. The guy hadn't done anything particularly terrible, and yet his presence got under Denny's skin like fire ants.

"You mind if I catch a ride into town?" Isaac's grin remained as he stared up at Denny, his eyes shimmering in the sunlight. The look was practiced, perfected, probably effective on everyone from teachers to cops to potential hookups.

Denny saw right through it. "Yeah, sure thing, dude. You got an appointment or something?"

"Yeah," Isaac said. "An appointment with some microwave dinners. You stole my personal chef from me."

Denny glared as he climbed into his SUV, but Isaac softened the moment with a wink. He sensed truth in the joke. As much as Bee wouldn't let herself cater to her brother, Denny knew she'd move mountains to help him. If that took the form of providing regular meals while Isaac was on the mend, he wouldn't have been surprised.

With Isaac in the passenger seat, Denny pulled out of the driveway and onto the main road, careening easily around the mountainous curves.

"You doing physical therapy or anything?" Denny asked.

Isaac turned his dreamy gaze from the window to look at Denny. "Nah. Not yet. My ankle split in one clean break, so the doctors wanted to wait for it to heal a bit before I had surgery, and now we're waiting for that to heal before I start PT."

"Damn." Based on what Denny had seen in the NFL, it sounded logical. But Isaac's blasé description irked him. "Bikes are pretty scary shit."

Isaac laughed, casually draping his arm against the car door. "Not any scarier than facing three-hundred-pound men who want to literally drill you into the ground."

Denny scraped a hand along his chin, massaging his face in an effort at easing the tension there. He couldn't run from who he was. That much had become painfully clear.

"At least I had insurance."

Isaac's grin drooped. "Lucky you. I didn't know I didn't have insurance. My parents tossed out a lot of idle threats during my lifetime, and the lapsed insurance is the one they actually made good on. Go figure."

Denny brought the car to an abrupt halt at a stop sign and turned to look at Isaac. He tried his best to quell the annoyance in his voice. "Good thing you had your sister to bail you out."

"You're right." Isaac's placid gaze remained steady on

the scene outside his window. "They don't call her Mama Bee for nothing. She's giving to a fault."

"It's not a fault," Denny said, his voice simmering. Nothing about Bee's goodwill could be misconstrued as negative.

Isaac raised an eyebrow. "She could've made a lot of money hustling for part-time gigs in New York. Instead, she opted to move up here because you called and said you needed her. She barely knew you. I mean, granted you're hella cute, and I'm sure that helped your cause. But maybe this move wasn't necessarily in her best interest."

Denny's face heated as he pulled the car forward onto the main road leading into Pine Ridge. "I offered to pay her way more than what she ultimately accepted."

"Oh, I'm sure you did. That's what I'm saying. She's making adequate money, but what really got her up here was her bleeding heart."

Denny's head spun. Had he inadvertently coerced her into a job that didn't serve her? Sydney said Bee needed the money, but he hadn't fully realized she may accept the position because she felt sorry for him.

"She told me she wants to move to London," Denny said. The words sounded feeble coming out of his mouth. Isaac seemed to know a lot more than he did. "I guess I figured she was leaving New York anyway. Might as well make a stopover in Pine Ridge."

Isaac pursed his lips, his eyes growing three sizes. "I know she quit her job and all, and it *seems* like she's serious about making a change, but I just don't see her moving to London. She's got friends in New York; she's got me. People who need her. The amount of people who would be absolutely lost without her would blow your mind. She'll go back. It's only a matter of time."

They rode in silence the rest of the way, Denny's mind full of questions. The picture Isaac painted of his sister didn't mesh with the woman he'd come to know in the past couple of weeks. Sure, it took her a minute to settle into small-town life, but she fit here. She made friends easily.

Didn't she? Or did she gravitate toward people like Sydney who needed help with a book club? Or Denny who needed his entire home decorated on short notice?

Guilt scratched at his throat as he dropped Isaac in front of the grocery store. He thanked Denny for the ride and limped inside. Denny remained at the curb, wondering if he'd helped Bee or taken advantage of her completely.

By the time he got to the high school, his nerves fired on every level. He'd googled himself that morning just to double-check what image came up first. He wasn't disappointed.

He climbed out of his truck and ran a hand through his hair as he approached the field. Despite the nerves bouncing around like Ping-Pong balls in his gut, the scent of fresh-cut grass and the sight of the bleachers stirred his excitement. He hadn't been on any type of football field in at least a couple of years. It terrified him in the best way.

With the sun shining in his eyes, he squinted at the crowd of young men in practice pads gathered in the middle of the field. Coach Parker blew his whistle every three seconds, and the boys, in turn, touched their toes with alternating arms.

As Denny passed through the opening in the chain-link fence, Coach Parker raised a hand and jogged toward him. Denny inhaled, steadying his stance.

"Coach Parker." He extended a hand, and the coach shook it tightly.

"Oh man," Coach Parker said. He grinned, hitching his shorts up under a modest gut. "Can't tell you how excited these kids are to have you, Denny. Do you prefer Denny? Mr. Torres?"

"What's your protocol?"

"We like the team to call adults 'mister,' if you don't mind."

Denny grinned. "Or missus, right?"

Coach Parker laughed. "Of course. I got an earful from my teenage daughter the other day about pronouns. I'm no expert, but I'm learning."

Denny wished Bee were around to hear it.

"Happy to be called Mr. Torres."

Coach Parker faced the field, shoving his aviators up on the bridge of his crimson nose, and placed his hands on his hips. A bright red lanyard hung from his neck over a white polo shirt emblazoned with Pine Ridge Titans logo.

White and red. Denny's high school colors. Coach Maiava would lose his mind with happiness when he found out what Denny was doing. He swallowed down a pang of nostalgia.

Coach Parker waited until the boys finished warming up before he called them over. As they jogged from the center of the field, a buzz began to grow within the group.

"Holy shit," somebody called out. "It really is him."

"Language, Mr. LaMotta," Coach Parker called out. He pointed at a tall kid in the back of the group.

"Sorry, sir."

Denny forced back a smile. God, he'd missed this part of it.

"Take a knee, please," Coach Parker said. "Take a knee."

The boys all dropped to one knee, a sea of faces staring up at Denny with wide eyes and openmouthed grins. He tried to remember back to his teenage years and how he might've felt in front of a real live professional football player. It seemed like a lifetime ago.

"As I mentioned yesterday," Coach Parker said, "Denny Torres has generously agreed to spend some time with us. I thought today we'd chat a little and get some of your questions out of the way before Mr. Torres weighs in while we practice. That sounds good to everybody?"

A rowdy chorus of "heck yes" rose up from the group. Denny planted his feet and readied for questions.

"I should start," Denny said, "by thanking you all for letting me hang out. I've missed being on the field, so it's really my privilege to be here. Anybody have a question?"

Every hand shot up. Denny pointed to the sailor-mouthed kid in the back.

"Is it true you turned down a ten-million-dollar contract because you got scared of getting hit?"

Adrenaline slowly leaked out of Denny like air from a punctured tire. For a few blissful minutes he'd forgotten what he'd ultimately be known for. Not his stats. Not his records. Not his game-changing interception in the NFC Championship game in 2016.

He'd be known for giving up.

"Mr. LaMotta," Coach Parker snapped. "What did we talk about yesterday?"

Denny's cheeks burned. What *had* they talked about yesterday? *Hey, pretend like this guy's not a total embarrassment to the sport, all right? We really need him to hang around.*

"It's cool," Denny said. "I realize there are a lot of rumors floating around about me. But I'd rather talk about game play. That off-the-field shit isn't half as interesting."

He caught the swear word as it skipped off his tongue.

"Sorry, didn't mean to curse."

The hopeful smiles on the kids in front of him slowly transformed into blank stares. He'd been on the field five minutes and had already managed to disappoint them.

"Can we stay game-focused, please?" Coach Parker said. He shifted awkwardly, crossing his arms and nodding at Denny as if to keep things moving.

Another hand shot up, and Denny pointed at a wiry little kid in the front. Probably a third-string kicker who doubled as a running back. Sizes in the group ran the gamut from refrigerator to smaller than his tiny mother.

"Go ahead," he said to the kid.

"Hey, that press conference where you cried," the kid said, flashing a buck-toothed grin. "Did you get a lot of crap about that from your teammates?"

"Guys, come on." Coach Parker clapped his hands twice. "I said *game*-focused. Anybody want to ask Mr. Torres what a safety's greatest asset is? Anybody want to ask him what it feels like to pick off some of the greatest quarterbacks in the league? Anybody want to know what it's like to play in Green Bay in ten-below temperatures?"

Denny's limbs trembled, his heart skipping in an irregular rhythm. His collar choked him, the chilly September air suddenly stifling. Why had he ever come here?

The questions finally veered away from his disgraceful exit from the league to his career highlights before Coach Parker split the team up into groups and directed them to opposite ends of the field.

Once the kids were out of earshot, Coach Parker clapped a hand on Denny's shoulder. Despite all his time in professional sports, his traveling, his sexual conquests, the millions he'd made over the years, he still felt like a little kid on the field being consoled by his coach. It knocked the wind out of him.

"Don't let 'em shake you," Coach Parker said. "They're kids, you know? They think pro sports is all glamour and no effort."

"It's totally fine," Denny said. "I was the same way when I was a kid. I know they don't mean anything by it."

Coach Parker offered him a tight-lipped smile. "Maybe today you stick by me and get a feel for the team as a whole? And then when you come back, you can work a little more closely with the secondary."

The rest of practice passed by in a blur. Denny had never been so quiet, so reserved. He imagined what they'd say about him in the locker room. How they'd always thought he'd be such a cool, dynamic guy but meeting him in person had dashed all their expectations.

He climbed into his SUV after a handshake from Coach Parker and a promise to let him know when he'd attend another practice.

With his heart in his throat, he drove aimlessly. He crossed through downtown, passed the small chain of lakes signaling the town limits, and kept on driving.

He'd always anticipated a long and illustrious football career, his days filled with models and parties and cash. The reality of the league had shocked him, and it didn't take long for the shine to come off the apple. Everything he loved about the game quickly became tainted as friends got cut before they played their first regular season game and injuries ended careers too soon. Football was a business and the players merely a commodity.

When finally forced to examine football's place in his life, he found it was all he had. Everything his parents had ever suspected about him became startlingly clear. If football was all he used to be, what was he now?

Milky twilight settled over Pine Ridge as Denny made his way slowly back home. His chest felt hollow, emptied of all the emotions that had raged there hours before. He pulled into his driveway, cut the engine, and pinched the bridge of his nose.

He looked up at his house, the lights glowing brightly from every room. Through the wide front windows, he saw Bee.

She rushed from the kitchen to the living room, striking a match and lighting the cream-colored candles atop the fireplace. With graceful motions, she fluffed the pillows on his brand-new couch and adjusted a gray-and-white-patterned blanket on the ottoman.

She bent over, the bottom of her shorts riding up to reveal more of the lion tattoo on her thigh. He turned away. He wanted to see more of that tattoo, wanted to see more of her. But not like this. Not like a creep peeking through the window.

And definitely not now.

He took one more moment to himself in the car. As soon as he went inside, she'd ask about today. She'd want to hear that his life had been changed by helping people, that he suddenly had a new lease on life because he'd connected with the Pine Ridge youth.

He couldn't lie to her. He ran his shaky hands across his face, drew in a steadying breath, and climbed out of the car.

chapter **eleven**

The front door opened with a long, quiet squeak, and Bee jumped a little as the silence broke. She thought Denny would be home from the football practice hours ago but relished the extra time she'd been given to spruce up the living room.

Every delivery arrived within its window—a feat she did not take for granted—and the room began to take shape. She'd need to hand-shop a few more items of decor but even in its unfinished state, the room stunned.

The oversize slate-gray couch sat perpendicular to the soaring bay windows, facing the brick fireplace to center the room. The sofa, with its wide cushions and generous depth, begged a man of Denny's size to sink right in, dared him to stretch out his legs and nap or read or watch hours of television. Below the couch she'd layered rugs in varying shades of cream, gray, and light brown to brighten the room and add to the overall texture. Buttery yellow and dove-gray pillows accented the space, and an architectural, worn leather armchair pulled it all together.

"Wow." His voice carried over her shoulder, and she spun around to face him, her hands clasped at her heart.

"You like it?"

He stepped cautiously into the room, sending her a timid smile. He paused over the couch, gazing down at the massive piece of furniture before turning to the trio of lamps made of bamboo. They'd been sanded down to their pale, natural-wood base. She'd selected them because they reminded her of Hawaii.

"This is bamboo?" he said. He lifted his soft gaze to look at her.

"Yeah." Her voice caught in her throat. She couldn't have anticipated such an emotional reaction. It chilled her from her toes to her neck.

His teeth trailed over his bottom lip as the subtle grin grew. "This is cooler than I could've hoped for, Bee. Seriously."

She beamed. "Really? It's not done yet. Once I add in the rest of the little things, I think you'll see it makes a big difference. I have some plants coming later this week, coffee-table books Sydney ordered for me. But for now . . . it's getting there."

"It's incredible." He gazed around at the room. "I love it."

"I'm so glad." She kept her hands clasped at her chest, afraid if she moved she'd burst of happiness.

He turned back to her and dropped his chin, the scent of cold mountain air and spicy, cedar cologne breezing toward her. "Thank you."

Kiss me. The thought nearly knocked her backward. She'd never spent so much time with someone she wasn't sleeping with, and yet she felt closer to him than men she'd dated for years. Being around him was easy. Safe.

"Pizza's in the oven," she said. "You want to eat in the kitchen or in here?"

"I feel like my grandmother saying this, but let's eat in the kitchen. I'd be devastated if that couch got dirty on day one."

He followed her into the kitchen, and she set out plates from the pewter set she'd purchased. She feared he'd be against so much white in the house, but he seemed to trust her. If the living room served as an indication for the rest of the house, he'd love every inch.

She waited until he'd devoured his first slice to ask about the football practice. "How'd it go today?"

He swiped a hand across his mouth and tossed the pizza crust back in the box. "It was all right."

She picked a greasy piece of pepperoni off the top of her slice and popped it in her mouth, eager to hear more but giving him space to continue. The pinched look on his face told her it wasn't good news.

"I dunno if I'm gonna go back," he said.

"What? Why?"

He shrugged, avoiding her eyes. "They've got their rhythm down. Great coaching staff. I don't want to disrupt anything, you know?"

"No, I really don't. I thought they just wanted you to be sort of a mentor, not a coach."

"Yeah, what a great mentor I'd be." He huffed out a sarcastic laugh. "NFL has-been Denny Torres told me to study hard and it turned me into an A-plus student. World-class coward Denny Torres told me to listen to my coaches, and now I'm the goddamned president of the United States."

"Hey."

He looked up, a storm brewing in his darkened eyes.

"None of that is true," she said. "How can you talk about yourself that way?"

"I'm not looking for pity." His tone remained light despite the chaos swirling on his face. "It's facts. It's who I am. And it's fine, I can't go back in time and change it. But I'm not exactly the perfect guy to be giving advice to kids. All they wanted to talk about today was how I quit. What an inspiration. The guy who had everything and gave it up."

She leaned on the kitchen island in her best imposing stance. "So the reality is that you just don't want to have to face your past."

He rolled and cracked his neck before sauntering to the fridge and grabbing a can of Coors Light. With a defiant crack, he popped the top and chugged.

"I don't have to be a role model," he said. "Kids have plenty of great people to look up to. They don't need me hanging around, confusing their goals. Nobody should look up to the guy who just happened to be talented at something but had no other vested interest in the thing he dedicated his life to. Kids should be looking up to botanists and lawyers and that woman who started the Me Too movement."

She'd heard the argument from addicts more than once. *This is who I am.* The problem was that was just an excuse to avoid trying to be better.

"You're scared," she said. "It's that simple."

"You already tried that one," he said. "Remember? Last time you tried to convince me I should do this?"

"It was true then; it's true now."

He raised the can to his lips and drank again, smirking as if he couldn't have cared less.

"Allison told me the team's pretty good," she said. "That they have a shot at a winning season for the first time in years. But they're unsure of themselves. Their reputation precedes them. Funny, right? See the similarities there?"

"Maybe I just don't feel like facing my failures every day for the next three months," he said.

She grinned. There it was. The truth. She knew it would come out eventually.

"Who said this has to be all about your failures?" she said. "This is actually a shot at letting people see you for *more* than your failures. You just have to get over your fear."

"You talk a big game for somebody who's afraid of water."

A single, disbelieving laugh passed her lips. She couldn't even be mad. It was such a low blow. "Nice try."

"Oh, come on, Bee. Face your fears."

Her chest filled with defiance. "Is that what it's gonna take?"

He paused, a frown forming. "What do you mean?"

"I face my fears, you face yours?"

What the hell are you suggesting? Visions of fish and bottomless bodies of water and slippery eels flashed through her mind. What was at the bottom of that lake anyway? What might nibble on her toes if she dove in after dark?

But she needed to shock him into a realization. If diving into her fear headfirst gave him the push, so be it.

"I'm lost," he said.

Before common sense had a chance to creep in, she tore off her sweatshirt. His lips parted as his stare fell to her chest and the skimpy white sports bra that covered it.

"Let's go." She crossed the kitchen, yanked open the sliding-glass doors, and tore out into the violet-soaked night. Her heart raced, nearly choking her, as she galloped down the sloping lawn toward the deck where gently rocking water lapped at the shore.

Would this be easier in the dark? Fear clogged her throat and clouded her vision, but she couldn't stop now. She charged down the dock, pushed off the rugged edge with one bare foot, and plunged into the frigid water.

For a moment, she was weightless. The rush of bubbles filled her ears as the shock of the cold water froze her limbs. With one great kick, she pushed past the surface and broke free of the water, gasping at the space above her for air.

"Are you insane?" Denny shouted.

She shoved her hair back from her face and looked up. He stood at the dock edge, staring down at her with a gaping mouth. The sky behind him was streaked with indigo and purple clouds, a delicate crescent moon hanging behind them among a blanket of stars. Denny's muscular form stood out in hazy contrast, his dark hair and clothes almost causing him to disappear into the night sky.

"I did it," she choked out. She forced her mind away from whatever might lurk beneath her bare feet. There were surely fish, but was there seaweed? Could her feet get caught? Was there anything bigger down there?

"All right, you proved your point," he said. "Now get out."

She kicked her legs, swimming farther away from the dock. "No. Not until you agree to go back to practice."

Her teeth chattered, the water slow to warm around her skin. If not for the creatures potentially swimming just below her feet, waiting to drag her to her watery death, she might have actually enjoyed it.

He paused for one more moment before slowly removing his sweatshirt. She watched with rapt attention as he peeled off his T-shirt, kicked off his sneakers, and dived into the water.

Bee gasped, struggling against the suddenly choppy current, until he popped up six inches to her right. He inhaled sharply, shaking his head until his hair flipped to one side, an easy grin on his face.

"Now what?" he said.

The current slowed, the water between them settling. She couldn't tear her eyes from his mouth, his curvy lips glistening in the moonlight.

He drifted slowly toward her, his breath warming her face as it released in quick, regular exhales. Her arms and legs kept her body afloat, but her brain threatened to sink, overwhelmed and overloaded.

"Now what?" she whispered.

Her chin teased the surface of the lake as he closed the few inches between them and gently pressed his lips to hers.

She shivered, the chilly lake and the warmth of his mouth filling her body with sparks. With one hand curled around his neck, her fingers brushing against the silky strands of his dripping hair, she drew him closer, devouring the taste of him as his tongue met hers.

He pulled away slowly. She opened her eyes, desperate to hang on to the sparkling sensation he'd cast over her. The weak moonlight cast an eerie glow across his face, and she soaked in every angle, every softly curving inch.

She trailed her tongue over her bottom lip, the faint taste of hoppy beer and his delicious skin still lingering there.

"Come on," he said. "Let's go in."

The lake water slapped against her as he kicked back and propelled himself toward the dock. He watched her, his lopsided grin visible even in the darkness. What did he mean *Let's go in*? The way her blood rushed around her body, like the first shoppers at a closeout sale, she hoped it meant *Let's go inside, where there are beds and condoms*.

Her heart pounded. Whatever threatened to pull her under below the water couldn't compare to what threatened above.

He pushed himself onto the dock before extending a hand and helping her out. Their impromptu swim rendered them towel-less, and his eyes flickered briefly to her chest. He hadn't been subtle about his appreciation for her body, not since the first night she'd met him. She tried to summon a snarky response, but nothing came. She liked the attention. She liked that he wanted to look.

They climbed the lawn, silence hovering between them, and by the time they reached the house, she was as torn up as ever. She slept in his house, worked for his money, existed in a brief timeline alongside him before she'd leave his orbit forever. Kissing could get tricky. Anything more would be plain dumb.

Through the cloud of uncertainty, a tiny voice called out inside of her. Her head may have been a mess, but a very different part of her knew exactly what it wanted.

Denny slid the kitchen door closed behind her and flipped the lock. When he turned back to face her, she moved in. Shoving all warning bells to the back of her mind, she placed her hands on the damp, taut skin at his abs and looked up.

His jaw dropped; his eyes wide. But the shock lasted only a second.

He cupped his hands around her jaw and closed his mouth around hers, breathing in and slipping his tongue past her lips, exploring her carefully as if she were made of glass.

She was on fire, alive and electric from limb to limb, and she snaked her arms around his neck as her toes briefly left the floor. He clutched her waist, drawing their bodies together. A half erection pressed at the base of her stomach through his soaked gym shorts, and a shudder ran through her, the cold and lust mingling to send her body into shock.

With one hand tight around his neck, she let her other hand slide down his chest. Her feet returned to the floor as she enjoyed the firm planes of his torso careening into the tautness of his back.

"Can we go upstairs?" she said.

"You sure?"

She held back a laugh. *Sure*? How much more of an invitation did he need?

"Why wouldn't I be?"

A damp strand of his hair tickled her forehead. She wanted to feel him everywhere.

"I dunno," he said.

All at once, he stepped back. Her soaking clothes hung on her like faulty armor, and a chill spread across her skin.

She crossed her arms over her chest. Maybe *he* was the one who wasn't sure.

"No," he said gently, stepping closer. He brushed a knuckle across her cheek. "Don't give me that look. Please. I'm not—"

She tilted her head. She needed an answer. Quickly.

"I'm not saying I don't want this." He scraped his teeth over his bottom lip again and again. Those perfect lips. She wanted more of them.

"If we both want it, then . . . what?"

He paused, his cool knuckle lighting on the curve of her cheek. His soft breath whispered over her skin.

"We're just having fun, right?" she said. "It feels natural."

His hand dropped from her face, the dreamy gaze in his eyes replaced by stony resistance. "Is that what it feels like to you?"

No, it's deeper and scarier than that, but how do I say that out loud when I have no idea what I'm doing with my life?

"I—" The words died on her tongue. "I don't know."

She bit the inside of her cheek. Where did they go from here? Saying anything further felt like a trap, but all she wanted was to slip back into his arms and sink into his taste.

"I'm gonna go to bed," he said. "It's been a really long day."

"Wait," she said feebly. "I didn't mean it that way."

"Nah," he said, ruffling his hair. "You're right. I'm gonna crash. Probably for the best."

He watched for a single beat. Was he waiting for her to fight him on it? She wouldn't hang around, begging someone to kiss her.

"Okay," she said. "Well, I guess . . . good night?"

Denny sighed and sauntered out of the room, his shoulders lowered and resigned. Bee glanced around. Pizza crust, half-empty beer cans, her discarded sweatshirt on the ground; remnants of their abandoned good time.

She couldn't bear to climb that same staircase, following him upstairs but retreating to her own room. Instead, she retrieved her sweatshirt from the floor, slipped her feet into flip-flops, and headed to her cabin.

With a twist of the cold, rusted door handle, she let herself into the dark cabin, Isaac's heavy breathing the only sound. She kicked off her flip-flops as he cleared his throat and lifted his head.

"No way," he said. "You forfeited this bed. After three consecutive nights, it becomes my property."

She dropped her chin and raised an eyebrow. "Is that something you learned from your finance buddies?"

"No, Bee, that's like, the law of beds."

She found a pair of pajamas in her suitcase and closed herself in the bathroom to change out of her wet clothes. Her head swam, all thoughts overtaken by the memory of Denny's mouth on hers, the cool intensity of his kiss. And then, the words she didn't even mean falling off her tongue like acid rain and burning everything in their path. Night: ruined.

She emerged from the bathroom and shuffled over to the bed, peeling back the covers and sliding in next to her brother. The double bed forced him toward the wall, and he groaned as he went.

"Do I even want to know why you're back here?" Isaac grumbled, tugging at the covers until properly cocooned.

"No." She lay flat on her back, staring up at the wooden ceiling slats. Her eyes adjusted to the dark, and the dusty, generic light fixture occupied her gaze.

"We haven't shared a bed since we were teenagers." His voice lowered with a tinge of nostalgia, barely carrying over the blankets.

"And that was only because you were too drunk to even realize I was there."

His melodic laugh filled the space. "That was a really fun trip. I met those guys from Mexico City . . ."

A slow exhale left Bee's lungs. After the incident in Nantucket, their parents began hiring chaperones to watch their kids on vacation. Bee typically found a quiet place to read, while Isaac became an expert at losing the chaperones and making his own fun.

"That wasn't the trip Mom got food poisoning, was it?" Bee asked.

"No, that was Buenos Aires." He laughed again. "She was more upset that she ruined her white suit than anything else."

He rolled over and patted Bee's cheek with a baby-soft hand. "You sure you're okay, boo?"

She nodded slowly, her eyes affixed on the darkened light fixture. "Remember when Mom and Dad told us we were too old to be sharing a bed on vacation?"

"And then I came out, and the semantics of it all confused them to the point they stopped caring?"

Bee grinned. Isaac had never officially come out to his sister. He'd never had to. As different as they were, they'd always had an unspoken connection. To Bee, Isaac's sexuality had always just been a part of who he was. No need to pay extra attention to it. In her adulthood, she'd gravitated toward others who owned their identities in a similar fashion.

Isaac's voice shrank. "Have you talked to Mom and Dad?"

"Nope." Her parents hadn't made a single attempt at calling. She hadn't, either. She knew what they'd have to say, and she didn't want to hear it.

"They were really pissed at me."

She shifted her gaze in time to see his face drop. Maybe he cared what they thought of him after all.

"They had every right to be pissed at you," she said.

"They don't get to turn a blind eye to every stupid thing I've ever done and then pretend one day to give a shit." He rolled back toward the window, shielding his face. "This is just their way of getting what they want. They've tried everything else, now they're trying to freeze me out."

"What do they want?"

"They want me to get a job," he said. "Dad set me up with this friend of his who needed a marketing guy, and I blew off the interview. I mean, I didn't even blow it off. I told him I wasn't going. It wasn't the right fit for me."

Bee squeezed her eyes shut, anger pricking her skin. "Then what *is* the right job for you?"

"I don't know." He tugged the blankets closer around him. "I really need to be fulfilled. To do something I'm passionate about. Otherwise, what's the point? You're so lucky. You've had lots of things you've been passionate about, and you've made loads of money from them. I envy you."

Words floated around in her brain, but she couldn't manage to vocalize a single one. She'd heard it before. He acted as if she fell into money, that she hadn't put blood, sweat, and tears into the projects that sustained her. He conveniently forgot about all the years she'd waited tables, worked retail, and filled in last-minute at her friends' events and shows. There was no passion involved in wrangling nearly naked dancers at DragCon.

"I'm gonna go to sleep," she said.

"You're not sleeping here tomorrow night, are you? This bed is too small for both of us."

Her stomach churned, and she clasped her clammy hands on top of the quilt. After the events of the evening, she couldn't imagine where she'd sleep tomorrow.

"You're free to leave whenever you like, you know," she said. "I hear there are lots of beds for rent in New York City."

Isaac didn't make a peep.

chapter **twelve**

Bee woke up with Isaac's hand tossed over her face. Darkness told her the sun hadn't yet come up, but her bedside clock told her otherwise. She slipped into jeans and a sweatshirt, brushed her teeth, twisted her hair into a messy bun, and ventured outside.

"Ugh." Misty rain filled the air, brightening the pine scent surrounding Denny's home and almost lifting her spirits as she crossed the lawn to his front door. If the weather had to be gross, at least it smelled like heaven.

She knocked on the front door and had to wait only a moment before it opened. The warm, toasted scent of rice wafted out at her. Denny licked his lips, his face revealing no hint of emotion, and stepped aside to let her in.

"Good morning," she said.

"Morning." He closed the door and stared down at her, leaving a discernible space between them. "You sleep okay?"

"In the double bed next to my little brother, the blanket hog?" She shrugged.

"You didn't have to leave, you know."

"Felt like a little space might not be the worst thing for us."

His eyelids lowered, heavy and curious as he studied her.

"You hungry?" he said.

"Sure."

She shoved a loose strand of hair into her bun and paused as he walked into the kitchen. Would they pretend last night never happened? Go back to being friends with tension the way they had been since she'd arrived in Pine Ridge?

She made her way into the kitchen and found him standing over the stove, lighting the gas burner and adding butter to a frying pan.

"You cook?" she asked. "I've been here almost a month, and I had no idea."

He tossed a coy smile over his shoulder before turning back to the stove. "You seemed really opposed to eating with me, so I didn't want to press my luck beyond beer and cheese on the dock."

"I'm not opposed to eating with you." She bit her lip and slid onto a barstool at the kitchen island. "I . . ."

Didn't want to fall for you.

"I get it," he said. "You're here to do a job. I keep confusing the situation."

"That's not it," she said. "You shut me out last night before I could explain myself. Can I try now?"

He tapped his spatula against the frying pan and set it down on the counter before turning to face her. He crossed his arms over his broad chest, stretching the fabric of his light gray T-shirt and settling his deep gaze on her.

"I'm open," she said. "To seeing what happens."

He sucked on his cheeks and lowered his eyebrows. "I don't know what that means."

"Yes, the plan is to leave here when the job is done," she said. "But . . ."

Heavy silence filled the room while he watched her struggle to find words that explained her thoughts but didn't expose her heart completely.

"There's something different about you." Her voice came out breathy and quiet. Vulnerable. Stripped down, the way he made her feel all the time. "There's something different about who I am when I'm with you. I can't say I've felt that way in a long time. So maybe it's worth taking the time to find out what that's all about."

He massaged his chin, his gaze deepening as he looked at her. Despite her grungy outfit, she'd never felt more desired.

"If you want," she added.

His throat contracted as he swallowed, slowly walking around the kitchen island to where she sat. He slid his big hands along her thighs, lighting at the crease at her hips and stealing every ounce of her breath.

"Guess I should've let you finish last night." His soft voice whispered across her face.

Her pulse beat against her skin as if it wanted release. "That doesn't scare you?"

He lowered his chin and brushed his nose against hers. "Do I look scared?"

The acrid scent of burnt butter drifted between them, and his nose wrinkled. She looked to the stove where a curl of black smoke rose up from the frying pan.

"Oh shit." He hurried over to the stove and flipped off the burner, tossing the frying pan into the sink and filling it with sputtering water.

She sat, disconcerted and dizzy, the promise of his kiss still floating above her head. Before she could wonder about her next move, he sauntered back to the kitchen island. His tongue flickered across his lips before he tucked a hand behind her neck and kissed her.

She dropped her head back, deepening the connection as he sunk against her, cradling her jaw delicately in his huge hands. He tasted vaguely sweet, his tongue sweeping gently against hers. She wanted the kiss to last forever, the slow, languid movements lulling her into a bliss she hadn't felt in years.

As she ran her hands down the front of his T-shirt, he pulled back with hesitation, as if he wasn't quite ready for it to end, either. When they parted, a wide grin stretched across his face. He looked down to where her fingers tucked into the waistband of his black joggers.

"Sorry." She snatched her hands to her chest, the heat in her cheeks spreading down her neck.

"You don't have to be sorry." He trailed a thumb across her lips. "Maybe it's too late to ask this, but was that all right? Me kissing you?"

She stopped herself from shouting, *DUH!* She'd nearly ripped his pants off without even realizing it. With a timid grin, she said, "Um, yes. That was more than all right."

He leaned in again, brushing his warm lips across hers before standing up straight. "I'm gonna try breakfast again. Don't distract me this time."

Her brain fizzed, a dopey smile on her face, as he went back to the stove, rinsed the frying pan, and tried again. She felt like she'd had one too many vodka shots, her thoughts heavy and floaty and just out of reach.

"You like Spam?"

She turned toward him, blinking to focus. "Spam?"

"Yeah." His shoulders flexed under the gray T-shirt as he moved between the frying pan and the sink, stirring butter and retrieving a carton of eggs from the counter. "Ever had it?"

He could've been speaking Greek the way the questions crashed against her eardrums. "Um, no. Spam? No, I've never had it."

"You're gonna love this."

He darted around the kitchen, snatching bottles of hot sauce from the refrigerator and plucking eggs from the carton. With deft fingers, he cracked the eggs and flipped paper-thin slices of Spam in the same frying pan while she tried to force away visions of him doing other types of skilled things with his hands.

By the time he set a plate down in front of her, she'd regained enough cognitive function to inhale the spicy scent wafting up at her.

"What is it?" she asked. Two fried eggs stared up at her from atop the thin slices of fried Spam and a bed of white rice.

He set a bowl of dark brown gravy between them and took the stool next to her. His eyes glowed. "Loco moco."

"Right. Sure. Of course."

He grinned, teasing her with his gorgeous lips. Now that she knew what they tasted like, how they felt against hers, it didn't seem right that they should be used for anything but kissing.

"It's Hawaiian comfort food," he said. "My mom is an incredible cook, and she'd make all kinds of amazing stuff for us kids growing up. This is the easiest dish in her arsenal, but I asked for it all the time."

"We didn't eat a lot of Spam and rice out on Long Island," she said. "But it smells delicious."

"After last night . . ." His voice dropped. "That practice made me feel kinda shitty about myself. And then I totally dropped the ball with you. I thought this would make me feel better."

She crossed the few inches between them and squeezed his forearm. "Thank you for sharing with me."

He held her gaze for a beat before blinking, as if to shake himself out of the moment. "You should eat it with gravy. It's better that way. But I didn't want to overwhelm you with too many flavors if that's already enough for you."

"Nah," she said, reaching for the ladle. "I want the full experience, please."

"Oh! Coffee." He leaped out of his seat and hurried to the coffeepot, filling two mugs and setting one down in front of her.

She couldn't remember the last time someone other than Jamie or her local takeout place had made her a meal. Denny made sure she had a napkin, filled a water glass for her, even handed her a fork. It was perfect. Every bit of it.

"All right," he said, reclaiming his seat. "Dig in."

Bee cut a triangle of fried egg with her fork, the runny yolk seeping into the rice, and scooped up a big mouthful of Spam, rice, egg, and brown gravy. She lifted the fork to her lips as he watched, his eyes twinkling as the saltiness flooded her senses.

"Holy mother of . . . ," she mumbled through the food. "Why is that so good?"

His smile grew three sizes as he tucked into his own plate. "Right? I don't know. I mean, I'll eat Spam any way you make it, but this is my favorite."

They ate quietly, occasionally punctuating the silence with a groan of pleasure or a mumbled, "So good." He finished well before she did, but he waited for her, watching as she enjoyed every bite.

"Even though you didn't know I'd be here," Bee said. "And technically you didn't make this *for* me, you should know, no man has ever cooked for me. So this is kinda making me feel like a queen."

He dropped his chin. "You're joking."

She shook her head. "Never. Frozen pizza, takeout, microwave mac and cheese. But never a fully cooked meal."

He raised his eyebrows as he carried their plates to the sink. "That's downright shameful, Bee."

As he started on the dishes, she sipped her coffee and studied him from behind. A thin, curious thread of discontent wove its way from her stomach into her chest, tightening as it reached her throat. It whispered like a bad omen.

This could never work.

Denny's strong arms dipped into hot, soapy water, scrubbing the frying pan as his silky dark hair flopped over his forehead. The better he looked, the surer she became. She could fall for him, really fall for him, and then what? He'd rely on her. Need her. The way everybody else did. Until he didn't need her anymore. She'd poured her heart out, told him she'd be willing to explore what bloomed between them, but her gut begged otherwise.

"Hey."

He looked up, his face dewy and fresh from the steamy water. "Yeah?"

"The kiss . . ."

His eyes darkened as he smiled. God, he was sexy. "Yes?"

Take it back. Take it all back now. Before the whole thing gets too heavy.

She sucked in a breath as he leaned on the counter, his flexed forearms and amused smirk making quick work of her logical brain.

"I wouldn't mind doing it again." The right thing to say—the adult conversation she should've broached—shrank back inside of her like a scared turtle. She always tried to control things, always tried to see the consequences before they sidelined her.

Denny wouldn't let her go there. He chased away the potential downfall with a half smile or a plate of Hawaiian breakfast. She struggled against the defenses she'd built since childhood, constantly wondering why those walls were up in the first place.

His smile widened. "Wouldn't mind, huh? That's not really the reaction I was going for. Guess I'll have to work a little harder."

Winged creatures, something that dwarfed butterflies, flapped in her stomach. God help her if it got any better.

He slid the last of the dishes into the dishwasher and wiped his hands on a dishrag before leaning on the kitchen island. Since the previous night, his eyes held a softness when they landed on her. The look was nearly as intimate as the kiss.

"Can we do something today?" he said. "Kayaking or hiking or something? I promise we can stay far away from swimming holes."

"I can't," she said. "I'm going to Vermont with Sydney today to pick up a light fixture for your office."

He dropped his head dramatically, lifting it with a groan and a pout on his lips. "Just forget the rest of the house. The living room is good enough."

She grinned, rising from her seat. Every fiber of her being told her to circumvent the island, slip into his arms, and pretend nothing existed outside the walls of his house. But a voice from beyond, a reminder of old hurts, wiggled past the desire and reminded her that Denny couldn't exist in her real world.

"Something tells me your parents would find it weird that the guest room has a mattress but no bed frame, and the office has a chandelier but no desk."

"I'll cancel their trip." He worked his way around the island, the grin pressed into his face. She inhaled deeply to steady herself.

"Need I remind you what I'm here for?" she said. Her voice came out breathy, unstable.

Without laying his hands on her, he stepped close, overwhelming her with the scent of cedar and lavender dishwashing soap. His proximity dared her to maintain space.

"Do we need to talk about anything?" He spoke low and even, his gaze narrowing and a rogue lock of hair falling over his forehead as if Nora Ephron directed the scene from afar.

"No." If he stepped any closer he'd see her ribs struggling to hold on to her heart.

"I'm letting you take the lead here, all right?" he said. "I'll back off as much as you want."

She craved him, like breath in her lungs, like water in her parched throat. She didn't want him to back off. She wanted him to push every boundary. She wanted him to step over every line.

"I'm just aware of how messy this could get." She nibbled her lip, afraid to say the words out loud. "I want to have fun and . . . see. What happens. But I also don't want to ruin something that didn't need to be ruined. We should go slow. You know what I mean?"

Whether he realized or not, he shifted backward and increased the space between their bodies. "Totally."

She hated the space, fought it like magnets turned backward. She pressed onto her toes and laid a gentle hand on his rock-hard abs, closing her eyes as she kissed him.

With a slow inhale, she sucked his bottom lip. He responded eagerly, closing his mouth on hers and claiming her without restraint.

"Bee," he breathed, barely breaking contact. "You have an interesting take on going slow."

He nudged her bottom lip with his, and she struggled to think straight.

"Sorry." Her hand remained firmly planted on his torso. "You're a really good kisser."

In another life she'd drag him upstairs and get down to what her body screamed at her to do. But she was tired of getting hurt. Tired of being used. Tired of mistaking chemistry for something more.

His grin reappeared. "Let's just take a minute. All right?"

"Yeah." She lifted her face, sinking against his mouth and delighting in the delicately salty taste.

"Bee." He pulled away, a laugh tripping off his tongue. "I meant, take a minute apart."

"Oh." A lazy grin found its way to her face. "Sorry."

"You're dangerous."

"Thought you weren't scared."

His eyes glittered. "Maybe I lied a little. You're pretty intimidating."

She breathed deep, rubbing her clammy palms on the legs of her jeans. "I'm gonna go now. Before I make even more of a fool out of myself."

As she slipped past him, he grabbed her hand, tugging her back into his orbit. He pressed a soft kiss onto her lips. "Just so there's no confusion, I'm not on the fence about this. I know what I want."

A jolt of electricity hit her in the chest, her voice struggling to escape. "Got it."

With a squeeze of his hand, she paused once more to soak him in—the soft T-shirt, the fitted black joggers, the tousled hair and half smile, all making a mockery of her self-control—before turning and walking out.

Sydney squealed, her hands tightening on the wheel of Sam's truck. "I knew it! Should I add matchmaking services to the menu at the Loving Page?"

Bee's shoulders quaked with laughter, and she gazed out the window. Hunter-green trees sped by as they headed back to Pine Ridge, the almost-over-the-top deer antler chandelier nestled safely in the bed of the pickup truck. She'd waited all day to fill Sydney in, the secret threatening to spill out every second they were together.

"Let's wait and see how it all pans out before you go using our photo in your fliers," Bee said.

"Why?" Sydney shot her an accusatory look. "What's the problem?"

"No offense to you or this sweet little town," Bee said, "but I can't live here. There's no future for us."

As much as I might like there to be.

"You say that . . ."

"Seriously," Bee said. Scenes from her childhood filled her mind, the repressed, nuclear family structure choking the creativity and independence right out of her. Who would she become if she lived in Pine Ridge? How much of herself would she lose?

"Okay." Sydney tugged at a strand of her long chestnut hair. "Have you talked to him about this? Does he definitely want to stay in Pine Ridge permanently?"

Bee couldn't contain her laughter. "He just bought that house. He's paying me to decorate it. Why in the world would he up and move to London or New York City or São Paulo with somebody he just met after all that?"

"It's São Paulo now, huh?" Sydney said, the chiding clear in her smirk.

"You know what I mean."

"Maybe you're more than somebody he just met." Sydney shrugged, making a futile attempt at looking innocent.

"Has anyone ever accused you of reading too many romance novels?"

"Yes." She sipped her iced coffee and replaced it in the cup holder. "My husband. Every day."

Bee leaned back in the passenger seat, tucking her feet up under her the way her mother used to scream at her for. The truck passed the **WELCOME TO PINE RIDGE** sign, and she grinned. She'd developed a deep affection for the place, despite her best efforts at remaining unaffected.

"If I was talking to anyone but Bethany Jones," Sydney said, "I'd suggest you just get it in while you're here."

Bee laughed. "Yeah, but you *are* talking to Bethany Jones, so you know that's a physical impossibility for me."

"Ms. A Night or a Lifetime."

Bee couldn't be mad. Her heart decided for her. She'd

had plenty of one-night stands, a few casual encounters, but the minute someone took her to dinner or sent her flowers, it was all over.

"This is a weird scenario for me, though," Bee said. "I mean, I'm here for another month, at least. And we already kissed. I can't just close the door on that."

Sydney eyed her cautiously. "Is it the strangest thing to suggest you try something new?"

Bee gazed out the window as they passed the Black Bear Diner, North Country Realty, and the Pine Ridge Library. She'd considered it. More than once. Could someone train themselves not to catch feelings? To enjoy someone else fully without emotional attachment?

"I don't know," Bee muttered. "I'm not sure he's somebody I want to practice that on."

Sydney pulled into Denny's driveway a few minutes later and cut the engine. She turned to Bee and tilted her head. "Listen. I'm obviously shipping you two. Hard. But trust your gut, you know? I'd hate to see either of you get hurt."

Bee tugged at the silver hoop in her ear. What would it take to save her heart at this point? Disappearing in the middle of the night with nothing more than an "I'm sorry" note?

"Thanks," Bee said. "Now help me with this monstrosity so you can run home to your husband and make dinner and touch his butt or whatever married people do."

They both laughed as they lowered the door on the truck bed and eased the chandelier out. Dusk settled over Denny's little neck of the woods, but the house remained dark.

"I've never been here at night," Sydney said as they waddled across the lawn, the huge fixture dangling from their arms. "You can see into every room from the driveway. There's absolutely no privacy, is there?"

"Not really." Bee balanced a polished deer antler on her thigh as she fished in her pocket for her house key. "There's something sort of sexy about it, though."

Sydney's eyes sparkled. "Maybe it's the smoke show who lives here."

"Girl." Bee grinned. "Does your husband have any idea how you feel?"

"Of course. Pretending like Denny isn't hot would be a flat-out lie. And we don't do that."

They shoved past the front door and deposited the chandelier in the office, where, in a few days' time, an electrician would hook it up. Sydney hugged Bee goodbye and hopped back into Sam's truck. A flash of headlights illuminated the house as she pulled out, leaving Bee alone.

Hours passed. Bee ate Golden Grahams by the handful, clicked around cable, and poured herself a glass of wine. She peered out the windows every half hour or so, waiting for an arrival that never came.

Maybe Denny was avoiding her. She had stupidly asked for space, after all. When his new wall clock ticked to eleven, she picked up her phone and texted him.

I'm back from Vermont—movie?

She hit Send, and a moment later, a bell sounded on the second floor. A yelp of disbelief escaped her lips. He'd been home the entire time and hadn't announced himself?

She climbed the stairs, flipping on the hall light as she went, and approached the master bedroom. Despite the open door, she knocked.

"Hello? Denny?"

A faint blue light glowed from his bedside table, illuminating the otherwise dark room. She approached slowly, as if he might be sleeping. But the bed was made, pillows artfully arranged the way she'd showed him at the home store.

With tense fingers, she picked up his phone. The screen lit up as she lifted it.

7 New Messages.

Her face pinched. What began as curiosity led to anxiety and shifted into dread. The man wasn't glued to his phone, but she hadn't seen him leave the house without it, either.

Had his car been in the driveway when she'd pulled up with Sydney? She held on to his phone and jogged downstairs, looking out into the driveway, where his big black SUV sat, dark and undisturbed.

She licked her lips, her throat turning sour as she gazed out the window. Lights glowed from the guest cabin windows, and she hurried out on shaky legs to talk to her brother.

"Isaac." She called his name as she opened the door. Isaac reclined in bed, clicking around on his laptop.

"Thanks for knocking," he said. "I could've been jerking off in here."

"Have you seen Denny?" She didn't have the brain space to stop and scold him.

"Mm . . . this morning, maybe?" He tapped away at the computer and smiled.

"Can you focus for one second?"

With one raised eyebrow, he looked up. "What's going on?"

"He's not home. It's weird. It's eleven o'clock. Where could he be?"

Isaac shook his head and turned back to his computer. "Are you serious right now? He's a grown man. Maybe he's with a woman or something. You don't know his life."

Her stomach turned. She hadn't thought that far. Would he do that? He'd kissed her this morning, told her she didn't need to wonder about where he stood. Could he be that bold of a liar?

"His phone was on his nightstand," she offered.

"Maybe he forgot it." Isaac's face remained unaffected. "It's not like having a phone does you a lot of good in this town anyway. Chill out. You always do this. Not everybody is bleeding in a gutter the moment they do something out of the ordinary."

Bee glanced down at the phone again, shame creeping across her shoulders. Denny didn't belong to her. His phone wasn't within her jurisdiction, and neither were his whereabouts. She'd be mortified if he came home and found her snooping around his bedroom, clutching his phone.

"Okay," she said. "I guess I'm being sort of dramatic, huh?"

"Uh, *yeah*."

She breathed deep, crossing an arm over her waist. "All right. Forget I was ever here."

He grinned. "I already have. Bye, boo."

She pulled the cabin door closed behind her and shivered against the chilly night air. With one last glance at the still driveway, she turned and walked back into the house. Isaac was right. Denny was an adult, free to do whatever he liked, whenever he liked.

But something in her gut told her it wasn't that simple.

chapter **thirteen**

A sharp ray of sunshine beamed in through the guest bedroom window. Bee blinked against it, grasping blindly for her phone. She found it tucked under the pillow and hurriedly checked the screen.

No messages.

She'd barely slept, waking every half hour or so to check her phone or listen for any signs of life from within the house. With a pit in her stomach, she climbed out of bed and padded down the hall to the master bedroom. Even before she walked in, she knew nothing had changed. Silence singed the air. Denny still wasn't home.

Her cheeks burned, her stomach yawned with a mixture of hunger and fear. She hadn't eaten anything beyond cereal and a glass of wine last night after Sydney dropped her off. The thought of food made her nauseous.

While trying to shove down her threatening panic, she changed into jeans and sneakers and grabbed her bike. It couldn't hurt to ask around town if anyone had seen him. Even if it did make her sound insane.

She rode to the Black Bear Diner and dropped the bike against the side of the building, neglecting the lock. She scanned the parking lot and surrounding storefronts for any sign of Denny, but she only saw unfamiliar faces among the otherwise placid, early-morning scene.

She pushed through the diner door and found Mila behind the counter, slicing up one of her famous apple pies. When she saw Bee, she grinned and shoved her springy curls out of her face.

"Hey, Bee." The cheer on her face dropped as soon as Bee approached. "What's going on? You look wiped."

Bee bit down on the inside of her lip, trying her best to settle her nervous face. "I'm probably overreacting, but have you seen Denny lately?"

Mila puffed out her cheeks as she looked skyward. "Mm . . . I don't think so. A few days ago, maybe?"

"Okay." Bee's stomach continued to churn.

"Why?"

"He didn't come home last night." Hearing the words aloud sent a chill down her spine. She couldn't ignore the dread. "His car and phone are at the house, and I don't know him *that* well, but it just doesn't seem like him to up and disappear. He's not really a loner. You know?"

Mila nodded slowly, her cat eyes narrowing. "Let me call Jared."

She snagged the cordless phone next to the register, entered a number, and placed a hand on her hip while she waited. Her brow pinched, the worry matching every dark thought Bee had had that day.

"Hey," Mila said. "Have you heard from Denny today? Or seen him?"

As Mila's forehead creased, lines deepening into chasms, Bee's throat dried up.

"Huh," Mila said. Her eyes flickered up to Bee, and she

pulled the mouthpiece of the phone toward her chest. "Jared saw him yesterday afternoon, and Denny said he was going for a hike."

"Ask him where." The directive flew out of her mouth before she could think twice.

Mila relayed the question and turned back to Bee. "Behind his house. There's a trail back there."

The swimming hole. Adrenaline surged through her limbs, and Bee reached for the phone. Mila handed it to her without a word.

"Jared?"

"You think something's wrong?" Jared said, his voice crisp and low.

"He didn't come home last night," Bee said. "I thought maybe . . . I dunno, I thought maybe he crashed somewhere else. At someone else's house or something. But he didn't take his phone or his car, and it just didn't seem like him, and I got worried."

"Yeah, you're right," he said. "That's not like him."

"I know that trail behind the house." Bee's feet tingled as if they couldn't believe she hadn't set off yet. "I'm gonna go check it out. Maybe he fell or . . ."

"No," Jared said sharply. "Don't go back there alone. Mila's friend Nicole is a volunteer with Adirondack Mountain Rescue. We've heard too many stories of people going out on their own to look for somebody and getting in trouble themselves. Let me handle it, okay? I'm gonna make some phone calls, and I'll meet you at the diner. Just stay put."

Bee ended the call without saying goodbye, wanting Jared to get on the phone with search and rescue as fast as physically possible. She handed the phone back to Mila and attempted to swallow the lump in her throat.

"What did he say?" Mila asked. Tension creased the corners of her eyes.

"He said he's gonna make some calls," Bee said. "Your friend? Nicole?"

"Yes," Mila said. "Nicole's super levelheaded, and she's helped with dozens of search and rescue missions with AMR. I think you have to call the cops first before AMR will jump in? But I'm sure Jared's calling her first for advice. Here, babe, have a seat."

Mila filled a water glass and slid it to her, but Bee couldn't sit. She could barely stand. Her skin prickled and itched, her chest full to bursting. What was taking Jared so long?

Time stretched on, seconds crawling into minutes, and finally the diner door burst open and Jared entered. He hurried over to the counter, his face flushed and focused.

"I called the cops," he said. His eyes darted between Mila and Bee. "They're dispatching EMS and a couple of team members from Adirondack Mountain Rescue. I told them where I thought Denny went hiking and that nobody had seen him in almost twenty-four hours, and they're heading out now."

"I'm going, too." Bee turned on a heel, but before she could make it any farther than the register, Jared grabbed her elbow.

"No." His voice stamped the moment like punctuation. "I told you, Bee. They don't want inexperienced people out there with them. It's not helpful if they're trying to save someone's life and then you slip and break an ankle."

Her lips fell open as a strangled sob caught in her throat. *Save someone's life.* Her stomach turned into a ball of ice.

"Well, I can't sit here."

"Bee." Sydney rushed into the diner, the same cold, stoic look on her face that Jared had walked in with. "I just heard about Denny."

"Jesus." Bee dragged a hand over her shoulder. "Word travels fast in this town."

"My mom listens to the police scanner," Sydney said with a shrug. "What's the plan, J?"

"Search and rescue is heading out on the trail we think he took," Jared said. "We just have to wait."

"Nicole's with them?" Sydney asked.

"Yeah."

Sydney turned to Bee and wrapped her in a hug. "Come on. I'll drive you back to Denny's, and we can wait there. Nicole will let us know as soon as they find him."

"I've been on that trail." Bee's voice screeched, as tight as a violin string. "I'd stay out of the way. I know where I'm going."

"Come on," Syd said, guiding her toward the door with a firm arm around her shoulders. "They're going to find him, and he's gonna go back to his house, and we'll be waiting for him when he gets there."

Sydney sped to Denny's house, her face set and determined, while Bee focused on her breathing in the passenger seat. They still knew nothing. Her vivid imagination tempted her into believing the worst, but Sydney's steady stream of positive reassurance pulled her back from the edge. Her teeth chattered, and her foot bounced, all the energy coursing through her desperate for a release.

People typically called Bee in moments of panic because she always maintained a level of cool. She'd talked NYPD out of arresting her intoxicated brother, paid off cabdrivers with cash and charm after helping vomiting friends home from parties.

But when it came to Denny, her cool evaporated. She morphed into the one who needed consolation instead of the one in charge. She fought against the riptide and still, it pulled her under.

They arrived at Denny's house to find an ambulance, a cop car, and two dark green forest ranger trucks parked in his driveway. Bee gnawed her lip as she climbed out of Sam's truck, watching a small cluster of people hustle around the edge of the lake toward the trailhead.

"Want to go in?" Sydney's hushed voice startled Bee out of her trance.

"No," Bee said. She watched the search and rescue team, most clad in hiking boots, trudge into the woods. "I won't be able to relax. I'm going down to the dock, and I'll just . . . wait."

Sydney nodded as Bee remained firmly planted in place.

"I was worried before," Bee said. "I sort of felt something was off. But this . . ." She gestured toward the opposite side of the lake, where the team had disappeared into the forest. "This is scary."

"He's going to be fine," Sydney said. "You'd be surprised how many people that team has helped. People get lost, they sprain ankles, they underestimate the cold and get disoriented."

A shiver crept up Bee's neck. "He's an athlete, Syd. If he sprained an ankle, he'd find his way out."

Sydney placed a hand on Bee's elbow. "Go down to the dock. I know it's still morning, but I'm grabbing us a couple of beers. It'll take the edge off."

Bee lowered herself into one of the big Adirondack chairs Denny had dragged down the lawn for them. She perched on the edge and hugged herself, her knees bouncing as she gazed over the glassy water.

All she could do now was wait.

Minutes dragged by. Sydney returned with beer, and Bee drank her bottle slowly. Sip by sip. Instead of calming her, each drink of alcohol seemed to heighten the twisting in her stomach. But she had to do something. And so she drank.

The sun rose high over the lake, forcing Bee to squint as she watched the opposite bank. She set her second empty beer bottle onto the deck beside her, and as she returned her gaze to the water, something among the trees shifted.

"There they are." Bee barely recognized her own voice through the *whoosh* of blood pounding in her ears.

With her breath in her throat and her hands clasped at her chest, she watched helplessly as the first few people from the search and rescue team emerged from the woods. The tallest of the group, a man in a dark green polo and khaki pants, moved as if caught in slow motion.

One step. Then another. The big man's arm hooked around something behind him.

Bee squinted her eyes further to catch a glimpse.

"Oh God," she breathed. "There he is."

The group surrounded Denny from behind, guiding him along the trail to the edge of the lake. He limped, his head bowed, his pace threatening the last tender threads of control Bee had left.

"He looks okay," Sydney said. "I mean, he's walking."

Bee stared as if she could telepathically hurry him along. The group ambled along the edge of the lake, their forms growing ever larger as they approached the dock.

The first few people traversed the last curve of the lake toward Denny's dock and waved at Sydney. One of them casually called out a greeting as they headed for the driveway. Bee wanted to shake them, throttle their necks, and demand information.

With her nerves in tatters, she broke free from the dock and ran the last twenty feet separating her and Denny.

She stopped short, sucking in a breath as she reached the slow-moving group, and placed a hand gingerly on Denny's arm. His skin felt cool and clammy beneath her fingertips.

"What the fuck?" She hadn't meant to curse at him.

His mouth quirked. Half smile, half wince.

"Sorry. You were worried about me, huh?" His voice scraped out, ragged and labored.

She scanned his body for visible injuries, but all she saw were flat white packs strapped to his legs and arms and an emergency mylar blanket wrapped around his shoulders.

"You absolute asshole." She hadn't expected the tears, but they flowed freely without warning. He didn't belong to her, and yet simply being next to him replaced something she hadn't realized she'd been missing.

"He's fine," one of the women behind him said. "Low body temperature, but we're pretty sure it's not hypothermia. Dislocated shoulder, but Rodney here popped it back in, so with a few days' rest, he should feel fine. Mostly just a big ol' bruised ego."

Denny gritted his teeth. "Have you met Nicole? She's great."

The woman bared her teeth as if she couldn't stand to be in the presence of this idiot. "Read a Hiking 101 manual the next time you go out, okay, Torres? Headlamp, flashlight, compass, water, extra layers. This isn't East LA. It's mountain country."

Bee walked alongside the group like a spectator to the world's saddest parade. Denny winced every few steps and refused to look her in the eye. By the time they got him to the driveway, his cheeks flushed with exertion.

"Thanks, everybody," he said.

"We're not done yet," Nicole said. "We have to take you to the hospital. Get you checked out. You're dehydrated, you need an IV—"

"I don't need to go to the hospital." He shrugged off the helping hands and stepped slowly toward the house, as if he'd aged fifty years in twenty-four hours.

"It's protocol," Rodney said. "Don't be a hero."

Denny laughed, shallow and unaffected. "I'm not going to the hospital. I've had every injury under the sun. I've dislocated a shoulder before. Been dehydrated more times than I can count. Hypothermia's a new one, but Nicole said herself she doesn't think my body temperature got low enough to even qualify. I'm gonna go upstairs, take a shower, eat every bite of food in the house, and go to bed."

"But if it *is* hypothermia," Nicole argued, "you shouldn't immediately get into hot water. . . ."

"It's not hypothermia," Denny said. "Do you need me to sign a release or something?"

A casual smile hung on his lips. His indifference only fueled Bee's anger. How dare he act like he'd caused a minor hiccup in everyone's day instead of wreaking havoc on her nerves and demanding the time and attention and efforts of a whole town.

"You're refusing medical attention?" Rodney said, the disbelief clear across his ruddy face.

"I just don't need anything more than a shower and a sandwich." Denny placed one hand on his hip—Bee guessed the hand that wasn't controlled by the bum shoulder—and waited for someone to respond.

"I'm here," Bee offered. "If he needs anything."

Nicole shook her head, tossed her hands up in front of her. "Fine. Rodney? You have the release form?"

Rodney retrieved a form from one of the green pickups and handed Denny a pen. He and Nicole looked on with disappointment as Denny signed his name.

"Don't let him go to sleep," Nicole warned. "Make sure he drinks tons of fluids, and maybe try to talk him into seeing a doctor today."

"A doctor would laugh me out of the room," Denny said. "Seriously, I'm fine. Nothing a good night's sleep won't cure. Thanks for the help, Nicole. I appreciate it."

Nicole stared, her expression stony and unimpressed. "You're welcome."

The team vacated the property as Bee looked on, her insides whipping around like a flag in the wind. Sydney sidled up next to her.

"You need anything?" she asked.

"No," Bee said. "Thank you, Syd. Seriously. You and Jared and Mila . . . I'm usually the one taking care of everything. I'm really grateful for your help today."

Sydney grinned, zipping up her denim jacket against the

chilly autumn temperatures. "I told you this place sucks you in."

She squeezed Bee in a hug, made her promise to call later, and drove away.

Bee glanced back at Denny's house. He'd gone inside, as quickly as his grandpa body allowed, and she watched through the towering windows as he opened the refrigerator. When he pulled out a can of Coors Light, her jaw dropped.

"Unbelievable."

She jogged into the house, passing a discarded pile of heat packs and the emergency blanket in the foyer, and only stopped when she reached the kitchen. He took a long, slow pull from the can before setting his sights on her and wiping a hand across his mouth.

"You're drinking a beer?" she stammered. "Seriously?"

He exhaled, sucking in cheeks that seemed to have sharpened in the day since she'd seen him. "I don't need Mama Bee right now, okay?"

"Denny, you could have *died*."

With a frustrated groan, he shuffled past her and climbed the stairs. She caught up in no time, cornering him in his bedroom. In the shadows cast by the bedside lamp, his gaunt face forced a pain in her heart. Could he have lost weight in that short amount of time? Purple half-moons hung below his eyes. How could someone that big and capable succumb to the elements so quickly?

"Tell me what happened," she said. If he wouldn't respond to tough love, maybe a different approach was necessary.

"I got turned around, I fell, and I thought it would be easier to hunker down for the night than get myself even more lost. No big deal." He picked his phone up off the nightstand and tapped a few times, the careless grin fading a bit from his face as he read. She wondered how her texts read. Desperate? Scared? Neurotic? She'd been all that and more.

"No big deal?" she countered.

"I just want to take a shower, eat something, and forget it ever happened. All right?"

"You selfish prick."

His gaze snapped up. She finally had his full attention. "What?"

Her mouth opened in pure, unadulterated shock. "You think you can disappear for a whole day and nobody will care? That you can just gloss over the whole thing and go on with your life pretending I wasn't sick over what might've happened to you? You needed a rescue team to save your ass from the woods. You're not an island, Denny. People care about you."

He swiped a hand across his chin. "Seriously, Bee, don't sweat it. I was in my head, and before I knew it I was off the trail. Then I tweaked my damn ankle. I'm fine. I don't want you to have to worry about me, yeah? I'm not one of your friend's friends who needs a couch to crash on or a drugged-up club kid."

With trembling fingers, her nerves on overdrive from a full day of worry, she crossed the room to stand before him. She breathed in, the earthy scent of his skin grounding her and giving her strength to continue.

"If you don't want me to care about you, say the word." She tightened her jaw, willing the tremors from her limbs. "I will pack up my stuff and I'll go back to New York, and I'll forget I ever knew you. But I can't stay here and pretend like I don't give a shit. And I refuse to believe if the situation was reversed, you wouldn't give a shit about me."

He ran a hand through his hair and blew out a controlled breath. "I would. I do. Care about you."

"If you cared about me, you'd really let me in."

His jaw ticked. "Thought you were tired of being needed all the time?"

"Only when it doesn't count."

She heard the words fall from her mouth, realized how

she must've sounded to this man she'd known for only a few weeks. If he was surprised, he didn't show it.

"All right," he said softly. "I get it."

A moment of fear flashed across his face, quickly replaced by an impish grin. What had they become to each other since she arrived in Pine Ridge? She wasn't ready to voice it, as much as it occasionally tripped off her tongue in the most hurried, haphazard fashion.

"I was really worried." Her words squeaked out, tears threatening again. Emotion flooded her body, begging for a release.

He licked his lips. "I'm sorry."

She swallowed, shoving the sadness down, and massaged her face. Exhaustion washed over her. She needed sleep, food, a full day of deep breaths and quiet. She knew she should go, let him get cleaned up, but she couldn't bring herself to leave his side.

His strong hand closed around her wrist, coaxing it away from her face before sliding up her arm. He palmed the back of her head and gently massaged his fingers into her hair.

"Bee." His voice soothed. "I am really sorry."

She looked up at him through bleary eyes. "Don't ever do that to me again."

"Promise."

Her breathing began to slow, her heart returning to a more normal pace.

"I really need a shower," he said. He trailed his full bottom lip with his teeth, the invitation clear on his face.

She had a thousand questions, needed a thousand answers. She needed to know why he'd gone into the woods alone, how he'd gotten hurt, why he hadn't made his way out. But standing in front of him with his capable hand supporting her heavy head, the promise of what came next proved too enticing to ignore.

With her fingers linked in his, she turned toward the

bathroom. Midday sunlight filtered in through the skylight and bounced off the wide bathroom mirror, illuminating his face enough to see a smudge of dirt on his jaw.

He trailed one hand casually across her hip as he reached into the massive shower and turned two handles, igniting both rain showerheads one after the other. As the bathroom filled with delicate steam, he reached down to cup her jaw and press a warm kiss to her lips.

In the past twenty-four hours, her adrenaline had soared and plummeted, making a mess of her nerves. With his soft lips caressing hers, she came completely undone. She couldn't control herself any longer. The grip she'd used to maintain her sanity since he vanished had weakened and loosened until nothing of substance remained.

She melted, breathing him in as their tongues tangled. She tasted beer and the familiar, smooth flavor of his skin and mouth.

Steam floated between them, and she ran her fingers under his T-shirt, reading every ridge and muscle with concentrated effort. He reached one arm behind his neck and yanked the garment off, tossing it on the floor as his silky dark hair settled back over his face.

She used her fingers to comb his hair back, stretching to her full height to kiss him again. She had no idea how weak he felt or how tired his limbs, but he explored her mouth with all the fervor of a man refreshed.

She pulled off her own sweatshirt, kicked off her jeans, and before she could remove anything else, he placed his hands on her arms and paused. His eyes trailed from her shoulders downward, pausing decadently when he reached the middle.

He slid against her, burying his face in the crook of her neck, and breathed in. "I've fantasized about what you might look like naked since the day we met," he said. His breath warmed her skin against the steamy chill of the bathroom. "It's better than I thought it would be."

His hands glided across her hips, and he stared down at the scene etched into the skin covering her thigh: a male and female lion head staring boldly into the distance. *Pride*. The word was hidden in the leaves surrounding the lion heads, and only those privileged enough to get a close-up view ever noticed.

She didn't trust her words, instead tugging his shorts and boxer briefs down past his hips until he stood before her, all taut, ropy muscles and impressive length. If he could stare at her, she'd take her time staring at him.

But looking wasn't enough. She wriggled out of her panties and bra, desperate for her skin on his. She slid her hands over his shoulders and pressed against him, his erection tightening between them.

With one arm wrapped around her waist, he lifted her off the floor and stepped around the glass partition into the shower. Water rained down on them from above, hot enough to draw a gasp from her throat.

"Too hot?" he asked, his wet lips ghosting across hers.

"No." Her skin sizzled, from the shower and his touch all at once. "It feels incredible."

She reached for his loofah and bodywash, squeezing soap onto the white puff and working it until suds cascaded over her fingers. His gaze lowered as she dragged the sponge over his arms, soaking in every inch of light brown skin and rinsing away the dirt.

She trailed her fingers over his pecs, fingernails tracing and teasing his taut nipples. The water washed away the soap before she lowered her mouth to his chest and sucked at the wet flesh. His hips responded, softly digging into her belly.

A moan escaped her throat. She wanted him, her core aching to feel him buried deep. But she also wanted to savor every moment of his glorious body, of having him for the first time.

She made small circles with the loofah over his stunning

abs, past the full curve of his ass, and down his legs, pausing as his erection came level with her face.

With one lingering gaze up at his pinched expression, water sprinkling down around her, she tossed the loofah onto the shower floor and wrapped her hands around his thighs.

The small tiles dug into her knees as she straightened, his cock begging to be tasted. She wrapped her lips around the velvety head and swallowed, taking him all in at once.

"Shuh . . ." A single sound floated down from his throat as she palmed the base of him and worked her lips gently across the rest. The faint taste of bright, citrusy soap danced along her tongue, and she moaned with pleasure, developing a slow, steady rhythm that made him twitch.

"I'm . . ." The word choked out over her head, and she looked up. He gripped the shower wall with one arm while the other hung limply at his side. "I'm too weak for this. I can't stand up in here."

She pulled back, a lazy smile on her lips. "Maybe we need to get you reclined."

His mahogany eyes deepened as he shook his head. "Not yet."

With both hands on her shoulders, he guided her to the shallow ledge at one end of the shower. Thick clouds of steam filled the space, trickles of water running down her body as she sat.

His searing gaze traveled from her neck to her breasts, finally lighting on her hips, and he slid his shoulders between her thighs with his eye on the prize. She stretched wide, allowing him full access, and he dived in greedily.

He lapped at her, no teasing bites or wasted kisses. He knew what he wanted, and her body responded just as quickly.

His tongue traveled across all her most sensitive spots, sucking and playing and drawing her closer to an imminent release. He moaned, the deep, guttural sound shivering through her hips like electric current.

She squeezed her eyes shut tight, bright lights exploding behind her lids, as he coaxed her toward climax. She climbed higher and higher, her thighs spread wider, and he pulsed his tongue over her clit until she exploded.

Waves of pleasure washed over her, her hips rolling across his face and one hand clutching his wrist as he propped her thigh up. She cried out. Her voice bounced around the black-tiled bathroom, and just as she began to come down, he lifted his eyes to meet hers.

With one last touch of his tongue, he pulled away and grinned. "God, you taste good."

As her vision cleared, she noticed the grayish tone of his skin, the drooping eyelids. He'd just taken care of her in the most intimate way possible. It was her turn to care for him.

She stood up from the shower ledge and linked her fingers with his. "Sit under the showerhead."

He lowered his face to trail his mouth across hers. "I want you so bad, but I feel a little woozy."

"Just sit." She braced his good arm until he lowered himself shakily to the shower floor, and once he was settled, she grabbed his shampoo.

She leaned over him, lathering the soap in his soft, silky hair and inhaling the sharp, peppery scent that reminded her of luxury-car interiors and expensive suits. She trailed her fingernails delicately through his scalp and used the pads of her fingers to massage his temples and neck.

While she rinsed the shampoo out of his hair, he dropped his head forward and groaned. She paused. For a moment, she worried he'd passed out.

"Denny?"

"This is better than a blow job."

She choked back a laugh and rinsed the last suds from his ears, iridescent bubbles gliding down the glistening curve of his spine. "Once you're feeling better, I'll see if I can't change your mind about that."

She stepped out of the shower and snagged a towel before helping him to his feet. She swung the towel over his shoulders as best she could, and he tugged at the corners until it covered both of them.

He grinned his half smile down at her, his eyes still hazy and unfocused. "They say body heat is the best thing for hypothermia."

"Coors Light and body heat, huh?" She clutched her hands to her chest, letting him caress her back with the soft towel. "Did you set out to get hypothermia on purpose?"

"You left me with a raging hard-on yesterday morning. Had to get you to give in somehow."

Manic laughter burbled out of her chest as fresh tears sprung in her eyes.

"It was just a joke," he said. "Bee, I wouldn't—"

"I know," she said. "I'm not . . . I don't know why I'm crying. I think I'm exhausted. And maybe a little drunk."

He held her tighter as a short laugh breezed against her cheek. "Drunk, huh? I knew I tasted beer on you."

Tasted you. A shock of desire coursed through her again, and she looked up at him. Their naked bodies huddled together under the towel, but until his joke, it hadn't seemed sexual. She liked being close to him. She couldn't get close enough.

"Come on," she said. "Let's get you something to eat."

chapter **fourteen**

Bee shifted, a barely audible moan escaping her throat. Denny's arm had fallen asleep half an hour ago, but he'd have rather lost the limb than woken her up. She promised she'd stay awake for a movie, but Lloyd and Harry had barely left for Aspen before her eyelashes fluttered and deep, heavy breaths passed her full lips.

Sleep eluded him. He'd dozed off a few times last night in the woods when he couldn't fight it off any longer, but every snapped twig, every owl call, drove his heart back into his throat. When he did drift off, he dreamed about the headlines. FORMER NFL PLAYER DENNY TORRES EATEN BY A BEAR.

He'd seen the documentaries. He knew you didn't mess around with nature.

He leaned cautiously toward the coffee table, snagging one of Bee's discarded pizza crusts. She'd scampered around the kitchen, delivering him a bowl of cereal on the couch while she prepared the rest of the meal. Frozen pizza, tater tots, bagels with cream cheese, leftover rice with sriracha. She plied him with water, refused to bring him any beer, and as soon as she'd eaten half a slice of pizza herself, had promptly conked out.

He breathed deep, savoring the scent of his Molton Brown bodywash on her skin. He'd nearly fainted in the shower—from the hunger, the dehydration, the radiating pain in his shoulder—but afterward, seeing her in his big T-shirt and gym shorts, hair wet from their bathroom romp, he'd almost suggested abandoning the food for another go-around.

When he'd headed out for his hike the day before, he hadn't considered telling anyone. He wanted Bee to join him, but it never occurred to him that anyone should know where he was. He'd been on his own his entire adult life, never having to check in with anyone outside of the coaching staff of whatever team he played for at the time. He heard his dad's voice saying, *You're a big strong guy, you don't need help.* And he hadn't.

Until he slipped on that trail.

The night before had been chilly, but he'd never expected frozen conditions. He wanted to see the view from the ledge, but instead, his foot caught the ice at a weird angle, and he slipped, landed on the hard ground shoulder-first, before rolling off the edge of the trail into a bed of pine needles below.

He thought he remembered which direction he'd come from, but he'd strayed from the marked path to get to the ledge, and two hours later, the sun had disappeared. He knew he couldn't progress in the dark. He hunkered down using pine boughs to cover himself and settled in until daylight.

"I fell asleep." Bee's low, throaty voice drifted up from where her head rested in the crook of his shoulder.

"You sure did."

She pushed against his arm, sending a shock of pins and needles through his limb. He winced, and her brow knit. "Oh God. Was I lying on your bad arm?"

"No," he said. He flexed and stretched his hand. "It just fell asleep."

"So you were basically immobile for the last hour." She pressed her lips together. "That was super nice of me."

"I don't mind."

A feathery lock of honey-blond hair hung over her forehead, and he reached up to tuck it gently behind her ear. The way she'd responded to him in the shower, her untethered reaction, made her skin like steel and his fingers like magnets. He wanted her under him, against him, connected.

He'd never had anyone give him hell for going out on his own. He'd always been the Torres kid who could fend for himself, the one bullies didn't mess with. Independent. Self-sufficient. No matter how scary the scenario, he'd brush it off and so, too, would everyone else in his life.

When Bee turned her fire on him, he felt it. To his core. She wouldn't let him joke his way out of anything.

"How do you feel?" she asked. She glanced down at his shoulder like she could see the answer there.

"So much better," he said. "Now if I can just get some sleep, I'll be good."

"You want me to help you upstairs?"

He trailed his finger across her cheek where sleep creases marred her otherwise flawless face. "Nah, I'm good. You don't have to help me move around anymore. My shoulder's a little sore, but I can walk."

She raised one eyebrow as if she didn't believe him.

"Seriously," he said. "Mama Bee can chill for a while. I don't want to see her again. Yeah?"

Her full lips dipped at the corners, two dimples appear-

ing where he'd never seen them before. "Your voice got all
bro-y."

"Oh yeah? Like this?" He slipped into the California-
tinged accent he heard on the beaches growing up and sub-
sequently lost after moving away. "Got a nug of bud, bruh.
Totally amped, it's gonna go off today, dude."

"Wow." Her eyes creased up as she laughed, flashing her
wide smile at him. She tucked her feet up under her, co-
cooning under his arm. "A little bit Hawaiian, a little bit
SoCal. You need a flat-brimmed hat and some Vans."

"Oh, trust me. I've got 'em." He settled his gaze on her
perfect mouth.

She tipped her chin up and parted her lips, the memory
of her promised blow job making his groin tingle.

He dipped his tongue into her mouth before closing his
lips over hers, inhaling the lush scent of her skin. She re-
ceived him eagerly as one hand dragged through his hair.
When she kissed, her whole body softened into him. The
only time he ever really saw her soften. Aside from the
shower . . .

He wanted her upstairs, in his bed.

Or right here.

He leaned back into the couch, and she took the hint,
straddling his lap while her eyes blazed. She pressed her
hips into his growing erection and huffed out a heady
breath.

"Seems like you're feeling *much* better," she said.

He tugged off the T-shirt she'd borrowed and gripped
her around the waist, savoring the masterpiece perched on
top of him. The rose tattoo covered one shoulder, but something else had been hidden underneath even her tiniest of
tank tops.

Three thin lines of black script decorated the smooth
stretch of skin below her left breast, and he leaned in to read
them. She shuddered as he approached her naked chest.

So subtly is the fume of life designed,
To clarify the pulse and cloud the mind,
And leave me once again undone, possessed.

He paused, reread, and lifted his gaze. "What does it mean?"

She clasped her hands behind his neck, keeping him close. "It's a poem. Edna St. Vincent Millay. It's about, um . . ."

Curious how the things she had the most difficulty discussing were the things she'd chosen to have permanently injected into her skin. The public and the private. The mystery of it all.

"It's about," she continued, "knowing that a lover could completely crush you but giving in anyway. Love is designed to ruin us. And we let it."

He trailed his thumb over the quote, her skin silky and warm beneath his touch. "Kind of a scary thought."

"No scarier than spending a night alone in the woods." She traced the curve of his ear, sending chills down his neck. "Have you ever been in love?"

He exhaled sharply, wanting to laugh but not wanting to burst the bubble of the moment. "No."

Her brow pinched. "No? Not even when you were really young and didn't know any better?"

Hard no. His longest relationship lasted five months, and they broke up because she couldn't handle the schedule of a professional athlete. His rookie teammates had women clinging to them like lemurs, waiting for the big pro-sports payoff, and Denny's last girlfriend ran scared from it. A sweet girl from a solid middle-class family, she hadn't wanted the life of an athlete's partner or any of the fame that came with it.

Denny had been disappointed when she broke it off, but it was nothing a few nights out on the town couldn't remedy. It wasn't love. Just two people with a mutual attraction who happened to be around each other at the right time.

He swallowed the story and looked Bee in her pale blue eyes. "Nope. Always seemed like a lot of work to me, and nobody I've ever been with was worth the effort."

She pursed her lips as if he'd just said he didn't like puppies. "I never really felt like I had a choice in the matter."

"What do you mean?"

Her chin lowered. He loved that she sat exposed in front of him and made no moves to cover herself up. They could have a conversation about the deep stuff with nothing between them but air.

"I guess I've just fallen into relationships," she said. "Fallen into love. I meet someone, get super attached, and suddenly it's six months later and we're practically living together."

He froze. He hadn't set out to fall for her, but imagining she played out the scenario often and with different actors turned his stomach to a solid block of ice.

It took her a moment, but when the words fully hit her, her grin faded. "I mean . . . I don't mean this. I'm not *living* with you. This is a completely unique scenario."

His heart pummeled his ribs. She'd lulled him into a safe space, coaxed him into comfort with her stunning body and steely attitude and soft heart. He'd been floating peacefully near the shore, and in one swift move, she'd yanked him out to sea.

"We're not in love," she said. Her full lips parted as if she didn't believe what she'd said.

In love. They couldn't be. It was too soon.

Wasn't it?

He nodded slowly. His head felt like it was filled with whipped cream. Her shoulders curved toward him, her posture itself turning into a question mark.

The thought of her leaving for parts unknown opened a

tiny fissure in his heart. He imagined her reading the newspaper at a posh British coffee shop, sipping wine at sidewalk cafés in Paris, riding on the back of some Italian guy's Vespa in Florence. Pine Ridge and that football player she helped out once would be distant memories, a brief detour she'd taken on her way to bigger and better things.

He sealed up the chasm in his chest, pretended he was just emotional and tired after the day he'd had. He'd rather have another broken finger than explore why he cared about Bee leaving him behind.

She leaned forward, sinking into his chest and crushing her full breasts against his ribs. He drew her hair over one shoulder to get a better view of her bare back, and as he lifted his gaze, his heart nearly leaped out of his chest.

"Holy shit."

Headlights flashed against the far wall of the living room, illuminating the entire space.

"Who the hell is that?" She snatched up his T-shirt and held it against her chest.

He squinted against the lights as they swept back around, revealing Isaac standing in the driveway with a hand raised. When he looked at the house, his jaw dropped and he clapped a hand over his eyes before scurrying toward the guest cabin.

"Jared did tell you there's no privacy here," she said.

"There would be without someone crashing in the guest-house."

She slipped the T-shirt over her head, and he released an exaggerated moan.

"Hey, come on," he said. "I thought we were just getting started."

The lightness had evaporated from her face. "You want Isaac to leave, huh?"

HELL. YES. Isaac drifted in and out of the property, demanding Bee's attention and taking advantage of her generosity. As far as Denny could tell, Isaac offered nothing but nostalgia and the pull of family. The thought of Bee giving her brother her hard-earned money made him want to punch something.

"I told you," he said. "I don't care if he's here or not. Would I like to have sex with you on this big, beautiful couch without worrying he might see us? Yeah."

She licked her bottom lip and shifted her hips, awakening his fading erection.

"But," he said. "I also just want you to be cool with him being here. I know he's injured and all, but it seems like he's more than happy to take whatever you give him."

Her face clouded over as she lifted her leg over his lap and climbed off. With her chin tucked and her eyes averted, she crossed her arms over her chest. The tight buds of her nipples pressed against the fabric of his thin gray T-shirt, and despite her demeanor, he held out hope for couch sex.

"He's my brother," she said. "I'm trying to help him out."

"I know," he said. "You're one of the most generous, giving people I've ever met. But it just seems like maybe Isaac's never had to stand on his own before. Your parents didn't give him what he wanted, so now he's coming to you for it."

"Listen." Her gaze locked on his, her eyes the color of a stormy morning sky. "I'm doing this my way, okay? You don't know everything about my family. I'd appreciate it if you didn't weigh in."

He lifted his hands skyward. "It's my house. You brought him here. And forgive me, but you keep asking for my opinion on it."

She rubbed at her eyes before looking away again. He couldn't tell if she believed what she said, or if she just tried to hold tight to an argument she'd long seen as truth.

"I'm gonna go to bed," she said. "I can't even think straight, let alone talk to you about this."

A defeated exhale sailed past his lips. "You sure?"

"Yeah."

He leaned forward, resting his elbows on his knees. Sharp pain shot up his bicep into his shoulder and he jerked backward.

"You're still in pain?" she asked, her mouth tightening.

"It's no big deal." He stood up, looming over her, and she let him. "I was sort of hoping you'd sleep in my bed tonight."

A coy smile tugged at her lips as she looked up at him. "Oh yeah?"

His hands itched to touch her, practically cried out to brush against her full breasts, the dangerous curves of her hips and waist. They'd kissed, cuddled, and tasted each other. But she didn't belong to him yet. Her armor remained.

"It's gonna be tough sleeping in that big empty bed knowing you're just down the hall," he said.

She stepped toward him, inching her fingers around his waist until they snaked up his back. "I think maybe tonight you should get some sleep. And then tomorrow . . . we can talk."

He gritted his teeth behind a smile. He didn't like that idea one bit. "Okay. I'll wait."

With her hands still holding him tightly, she pressed up onto her toes and placed a sweet, tender kiss on his lips. He summoned all of his self-control to kiss her back gently.

She pulled back and grinned. "Good night."

Denny awoke on his bad shoulder, pain stabbing through his arm. He'd tried to sleep flat on his back, but habit won out, and even his fingers tingled in discomfort. He'd have to track down a doctor today for access to something stronger than Aleve.

He breathed deep, inhaling the pungent scent of freshly brewed coffee. A smile crept over his face. He indulged in a vision of Bee scurrying around his kitchen, preparing the coffee in her little shorts, tattoos peeking out, hair flipped to one side.

She'd scared him last night. He hadn't meant to put on such an obvious display of cliché male commitment-phobia, but when she'd firmly stated they weren't in love, he felt compelled to defy her. Who was she to tell him what he didn't feel? Maybe he couldn't name the deep, clawing sensation in his chest when she looked at him, but he knew it wasn't some fleeting feeling he'd be over the day she left town.

He thought they'd shared something different. At the very least, they'd become friends on a deeper level than most he considered close. He knew more about her than most women he'd dated, and a hell of a lot more than anyone he'd ever slept with.

But her side of the story sounded different. Like he was just another charity case she was willing to bleed for. It should've sat with him just fine, soothed the part of him that feared losing himself to love. All it had done was keep him up long after he'd laid his head down on the pillow.

As he tugged on a T-shirt and ran a hand through his increasingly wild hair, something irked him. He'd ignore her flighty relationship past, but he couldn't stop the incessant nagging in his gut. He didn't want to be counted among those she'd loved and left.

He jogged down the stairs and sauntered into the kitchen, a smile already on his lips for her. But when he entered the kitchen, the only thing waiting for him was the coffee and a note, written on North Country Realty notepaper Jared had left after Denny bought the place.

Went into town early—see you later! Bee

He stared at the note, at the way her name turned into a capital "B" with two little curlicues following. Even her handwriting had style.

With hot coffee in hand, he went out to the deck and

settled into a patio chair, leaning back and surveying his property. A breath slowly released from his lungs, and with it, the tension from his shoulders.

A steady rain had pummeled Pine Ridge the night before, and a fine mist clung to the treetops, warm earth and cool air combining to create a mystical atmosphere. The glassy lake reflected the clouds, shrouding the entire view in a wash of gray. He breathed in the fresh, cool scent of pine and damp soil before bringing the mug to his lips and sipping, the bitter black liquid scorching across his tongue.

God, he loved it here. Jared had initially told him about the property in passing, probably assuming Denny couldn't have cared less about a big house on a quiet, private lake in the mountains of North Country, New York.

But then Denny had visited the property on his own. He soaked in the view, the soaring windows and exposed beams, the crackling sounds of nature providing a soundtrack straight out of a Disney cartoon. Something felt right. Something clicked.

Sometimes his gambles didn't pay off.

Sometimes they did.

He stared down into the coffee, the liquid so thick and dark it barely registered against the black mug. Black and white dishware in a log cabin in the woods. He'd never have chosen it himself. But then, Bee did a lot of things that never would've occurred to him.

His house phone rang shrilly, yanking him out of his quiet space. He ducked inside and snatched it from the wall after the third ring.

"Good morning, my boy."

He checked the wall clock—10:15 a.m.; 4:15 a.m. in Honolulu. Rosa Torres never slept.

"Hi, Ma. Why are you up so early? Or are you just getting home? What time do nightclubs close out there again?"

His mother huffed out her version of a laugh. "Always the clown. How are you doing?"

"I'm good." The events of the last forty-eight hours flashed through his mind. She didn't need to hear about any of that. "How are you? How's Dad?"

"Good, good. We're both doing fine."

He paused, waiting for the rest.

She cleared her throat. "Talked to your sister yesterday."

There it is.

"Oh yeah?" Denny said. "What's she doing?"

"Well, you know, they're thinking of moving." Her words were clipped, the hint of an accent she'd worked hard to erase still nipping at the ends of her sentences. "That house is just too small for all those kids."

In one line she said a mouthful. His sister lived in a four-thousand-square-foot, million-dollar home in Orange County with her two kids and husband. The house was neither too small nor did she have too many kids. The subtle dig reminded Denny of where he should be in life.

"They'll figure it out," he said.

"Speaking of houses," she said.

Subtle. So freaking subtle.

"How's yours coming along? Last time I talked to you, I heard an echo. You have any furniture yet? Should we bring our own mattress?"

"Now who's the clown?" he teased. "I have furniture. More than ever. I think you're gonna love it, actually."

He envisioned his parents entering his home, Rosa's face lighting up when she saw the sleek but welcoming couch, the bamboo lamps, the thoughtful touches Bee had added to every corner. They'd love it. Who wouldn't?

"*Ooh,*" she cooed. "I like the sound of that. Am I going to be able to cook for you? You have pots and pans? Dishrags? All that?"

"All of it," he said. "I've uh . . . got somebody helping me."

The line went quiet. For a moment, he wondered if she'd hung up.

"Hello?" he asked.

"Who?"

Motherly intuition could travel thousands of miles, it seemed.

"A friend of a friend," he said. "She's an interior decorator. She's thought of stuff I never would have."

His gaze caught the floating shelves made of natural wood she'd had installed next to the fridge to showcase the black and white dishware. The simple touch elevated the entire room.

"Hm." The quiet sound said more than any words his mother could've spoken aloud. She'd never been particularly warm to any women Denny had introduced her to, instead encouraging him to expand his career beyond football. Look ahead. Establish himself. Women came second.

"Hey, listen, Ma," he said, his skin suddenly itching to be outside and away from her reach. "I have to run. I've got a full day ahead of me."

The lie slipped out easily, as if his brain told him exactly what would appease his mother enough to end the call on a good note.

"Well, that's nice to hear," she said. "I can't wait to visit and see what you've been up to."

He gripped the edge of the counter until his knuckles turned white. What *had* he been up to? Disappearing into the woods and making out with his hot decorator. The stuff parents' dreams were made of.

"Same here," he said.

"Your father sends his love," she said. "Talk to you later, my boy."

He gritted his teeth, gazing around the kitchen. Maybe none of it would make a difference to his parents without all the rest. A career, a direction, a sense of purpose. He remembered the crestfallen stares of the kids at football practice and imagined the same sad expression on his parents' faces. What did he have to show them? What could they be proud of?

He needed to get out. He needed to see Bee.

Denny climbed into his SUV and headed into town. He hoped he'd find Bee's bike parked outside the diner, and when the black mountain bike came into view, he grinned, the tension of his phone call evaporating into the cool mountain air.

As he pulled into a parking space directly in front of the restaurant, he saw her through the front window, huddled over her laptop with a furrowed brow. She looked up, locking his eyes and pressing her lips into a half smile.

Relief trickled into his chest. He'd worried, briefly, that he'd show up and she'd wonder why he'd followed her. *Act first, think later.* The mantra had gotten him into hot water in his past. With Bee, maybe it worked.

He walked into the diner, the little bell jingling over the door as he entered and joined her in the front booth. He snatched a home fry from her near-empty plate and popped it into his mouth, the cold, soggy potato telling him she'd been there awhile.

"Hi," she said. "You want something? I can grab Mila."

She'd swept her hair into a ponytail, the graceful curve of her neck exposed, and when she turned to wave Mila over, he caught sight of a little black safety pin tattoo behind her ear.

When she turned back, her cheeks flushed. "What?"

"Huh?"

"You have a weird look on your face."

He blinked away whatever showed on his face. Her body was a treasure map, and he wanted to find every last gem. "How many are there?" he said.

Her brow pinched. "How many *what* are there?"

"Tattoos."

The confusion on her face eased, and a smile replaced it. "I lost count."

"That can't be true."

As the blush in her cheeks deepened, her tongue slicked over her lower lip. His heart kick-started like a race car about to spin out from the starting line. The vision of her naked torso popped into his mind, and he couldn't shake the lust coursing through him.

"Mr. Torres!" A teenage voice broke through his reverie, and he looked up as two lanky kids he recognized from the football team approached. The taller one hitched his backpack up on his shoulders as the shorter one hung back, skepticism clear on his face.

Who could blame him? Never meet your idols, they said.

"Hey, guys," Denny said. "How's it going?"

"Hey," the smaller one said, looking at Bee. "You're that lady from the bookstore, right?"

She grinned. "That's me."

"My friend Emma's really excited about your book-club thing," he said.

"Ah, okay, you must be Andrew," she said. "Aren't you supposed to come, too? Your name's on my sign-up sheet."

In all of Denny's own drama, he'd never even asked her how the book-club planning was going. Shame prickled his skin. She was right. He really was a selfish prick.

The kid shrugged, his eyes darting between Denny and the taller kid, who Denny now remembered as the snarky Mr. LaMotta.

"He wants to go to the book club instead of hanging out at Mariah's," LaMotta said, his face twisting up. "Mariah's mom's got this unbelievable bar in her basement . . ."

"All right," Denny said, holding his hands up. "I don't want to hear anything I'm gonna have to tell Coach Parker about."

"Like you care," LaMotta said on a laugh. "My dad's one of the guys on the rescue crew who saved your ass yesterday. I'm sure you've done tons of stuff worse than having a couple of drinks before you turned twenty-one."

Denny's chest singed with the fire of a thousand tiny burns. LaMotta and his friend stared at Denny in amusement, but Bee's gaze said something very different. She raised one eyebrow, her mouth set in determination. He could almost hear her say it. *Go on, asshole! Set them straight!*

"LaMotta, right?" Denny said.

"Yeah."

"What do you want to be when you grow up?"

The kid smirked. "I'm gonna play in the NFL."

Wrong. Denny wouldn't crush anybody's dreams straight up, but he'd seen enough of the kid's performance at practice to know he'd be lucky to walk on to a Division III college team.

"All right," Denny said. "Say that happens. You work your ass off in high school, and college teams are clamoring after you. You get drafted. You're a pro football player, wearing the uniform, girls are hanging all over you . . ."

"Keep talking." The kid laughed, nudging his friend.

"It's the dream, right?"

"No shit!"

Denny folded his hands on the tabletop. "All right, cool. The average NFL career is about three years. And that's the *average*, which means plenty of guys play for only one or two years. Some guys never play a single regular season down."

LaMotta's cocky smile wavered. "Yeah, but Ben McKenna's been playing for, like, twenty years."

Denny choked back a laugh. "You trying to compare yourself to Ben McKenna, five-time Super Bowl champion quarterback?"

His friend chuckled, and LaMotta shot him a look. "Well, no . . ."

"Let's say you *are* the next McKenna," Denny continued. "Do you know what his favorite cocktail is?"

LaMotta's smile faded further. "I, uh . . . I don't think he drinks?"

"That's right. He doesn't drink. Do you know what time he goes to bed at night?"

"I think pretty early."

"Right again," Denny said. "Pretty early. You ever heard anything about his reputation as a teammate?"

The kid's face settled into a grimace. "I heard he's cool."

"Very cool. A leader. Reliable, hardworking, dependable, and smart." Denny paused for effect. "A one-in-a-million type player. You starting to get it?"

LaMotta's lips worked, and he tossed another glance over his shoulder at his smirking friend. "I guess."

"You want to be good at something—hell, you want to be good at *anything*—it's not just gonna be handed to you," Denny said. "Maybe you try to bring a little bit of that attitude to practice, yeah?"

LaMotta adjusted his backpack again, checked the faces of everyone in the group, and looked back at Denny. "Yeah, maybe."

Denny barked out a laugh. "*Yeah, maybe?*"

"I mean, yes, sir." LaMotta squeezed the straps of his backpack together and stood a little taller.

Mila stalked over to the table and waved a receipt in front of the boys' faces. "I know you're not trying to walk out on a tab, Ethan. Just because you work here part-time doesn't mean you get all your meals for free."

LaMotta's cheeks burned as his hands plunged into the pockets of his skinny jeans. "Oh shit, sorry, Mila. My bad."

"Get out of here," Denny said. "I got it."

Both boys' faces stretched into grins.

"Thanks so much, Mr. Torres," Andrew said. "We really were gonna pay."

"*You* were gonna pay," Mila said, sending LaMotta the stink eye.

"No, I was, too," LaMotta said. He turned back to Denny. "Thanks, Torres. Seriously. Are you gonna be at our next practice?"

Bee grinned widely before her teeth scraped across her bottom lip. Did this turn her on? He thought he'd been spouting pure crap to these kids, but maybe he was onto something.

"Yeah," Denny said. "I'll be there. Can't wait to see you prove yourself."

LaMotta reached his skinny arm out, and Denny clapped his hand.

The boys turned to leave, and Denny called out. "And hey. Next time your friend wants to go to a book club meeting, don't give him crap for it, all right? Remind me to tell you about how much Ben McKenna reads."

Mila dropped the boys' tab on Denny's table as the two kids headed outside, leaving Bee and Denny alone. For a moment, she said nothing. Just stared. A sexy smirk sat on her lips.

"Was that so hard?" she said.

He scrubbed his hands over his face and leaned back in the booth. "Yeah, in fact. I can't stand Ben McKenna. That squeaky-clean son of a . . ."

A melodic laugh danced past her lips, and she leaned forward over the table, her soft, drapey black sweater hanging low enough to expose a peek of cleavage. She sat up straight, all her glowy attention focused on him.

"I'm really proud of you," she said.

For the first time in his adult life, he had no words. His throat dried up. The way she looked at him . . . like she really saw him. *Proud of you*. He'd never trusted those words, and suddenly they meant everything.

She cleared her throat, scratched her shoulder, and dropped her gaze. He didn't know why or how he'd push her too far, but it seemed to happen often. He didn't care. It was too late now. She'd wormed her way into his life, filtered into his bloodstream. If she wanted out, she'd have to say so.

"Can I take you out?" he said.

Her eyes snapped back to his. Good. He wanted her attention however he could get it.

"On a date?" she said.

"Yeah. A proper date. We can go a couple of towns over, get a drink, go out for dinner."

She licked her bottom lip, but it didn't dampen the smile. "Yeah. Okay."

"Really?"

"You're surprised I said yes?"

He grinned. "A little? But I won't question it. Six o'clock?"

"Tonight?"

He shrugged. "Unless you're busy."

She shook her head, her dangly silver earrings dancing against her jaw. "I'm free. You're not tired or anything? Your shoulder—"

"Nope." He stood up from the table. "I feel great. I'm actually gonna run and get a workout in. See you tonight."

Confusion crossed her face, but he didn't want to discuss it any further. He didn't want to give her any space to change her mind. The night stretched ahead of him, possibilities endless. He owed her. Dinner wouldn't make a dent in his debt, but he'd sure as hell try.

chapter **fifteen**

Bee gazed at herself in the rectangular mirror over the bathroom sink in Denny's guest cabin, her reflection slightly obscured by the mottled glass. Her skin prickled with anticipation. She hadn't felt nervous about a date in years, but her stomach churned, and her fingers tingled as if she readied for a cliff-diving expedition.

"Where's he taking you?" Isaac called out from the bedroom.

"I don't know." She flipped her hair to one side, revealing the glittering ear cuff she'd added to her look. "Ugh."

She tugged off the ear cuff. Denny had seen her stripped down to nothing but lip gloss and gym shorts. How did she impress a guy who seemed to like her completely bare?

"This is sort of new for you, huh?" Isaac said. "He's like, an all-American hunk. Your type usually veers more toward strung-out-rocker-chic."

"I guess." She replaced the ear cuff. If he liked her, he liked all of her. Makeup, glitter, and everything in between.

She emerged from the bathroom, and Isaac gasped. He clapped a hand over his mouth. "Sorry."

"What?" she snapped.

"Nothing." He pressed his lips together as his eyes glittered. "You look like a stone-cold fox."

She'd chosen to get dressed in the guest cabin because she'd left all her fancier clothes in the closet there. Denny had gone out of his way to ask her on a proper date. She owed it to him to dress like she was going on one.

"You're sure?" she said. "I feel overdressed."

She smoothed her hands over the black, long-sleeved crop top she'd donned with her black, high-waisted, pleated silk skirt. Spiky stilettos, nude lips, and smoky black eyeliner completed the look. On any other night in New York City, she'd blend right in.

Tonight she didn't want to blend in. Not with Denny.

"You're totally overdressed," Isaac said. "That's why I love it."

"What are you doing tonight?"

"I'll probably end up at Taylor's," he said. "A couple of Sam's friends offered to pick me up. Maybe go bowling? Did I really just say that out loud? Something tells me the bowling alley here doesn't have bottle service."

She clenched her jaw, begging the words "Then get the hell out" not to fall off her tongue. If he complained one more time about Pine Ridge, she'd let loose. After Denny's disappearance, Sydney and Jared and Mila and the rest of the town had rallied around her, no questions asked. They forged into the woods to help Denny without hesitation. They were good people, and she was beginning to love it here.

"Just remember to be nice, all right?" she said. "Don't be such a pompous asshole all the time."

"Damn," Isaac said, raising his eyebrows. "Don't hold back."

She paused, giving him a once-over as she breathed

deep. Maybe something about the accident had humbled him. Maybe he was finally ready to stand on his own two feet.

"Have fun," she said. "You need money?"

"Thank you," he said with a quiet smile. "But, no. I'm good. I love you. And be safe."

She retrieved her leather jacket, grabbed her purse, and headed outside. As she closed the door behind her, she looked up to find the shadowy silhouette of a tall, beautiful man in front of her. He waited beside the car, leaning on the passenger-side door. A sweater the color of woodsmoke stretched across his defined chest and shoulders, and paired with expertly fitted navy-blue trousers, he looked downright edible. His half smile beckoned her forward as his teeth flashed in the dusky, early-evening light.

"Hi," she said. A smile teased her lips. She couldn't help it around him.

"Hi." His eyes roamed her body. "You look insanely beautiful."

"Thank you. It's not too much?"

She approached, legs wobbly from skinny heels on the uneven gravel driveway but also from the nerves pulsing in her veins. He reached an arm out and clasped her hand in his.

"Nah," he said. "You're never too much."

Every inch of her radiated with warmth, and she lifted her chin until he got the hint and met her halfway. Even in her tallest heels, she didn't reach his face.

His hands gripped her waist as he closed his lips around hers, drawing her into his solid body and breathing her in all at once. His skin tasted faintly of shaving cream, and she trailed a hand over his smooth cheek. If they stayed in the driveway making out all night, she wouldn't even miss dinner.

He pulled away slowly, and she opened her eyes with great hesitation, not wanting to release her hold on their perfect moment.

"Come on," he said. "Let's take this outfit out on the town, yeah?"

Most of the time his accent stayed hidden, but in the rare moments she heard the islander in his voice, she turned to putty. He opened the passenger door for her and held her hand as she climbed into the SUV.

He climbed in beside her, and as soon as the vehicle roared to life, the plucky sounds of a ukulele filled the cab. A sweet, rich Hawaiian-tinged alto flowed from the speakers, and Denny reached hurriedly for the volume.

"Sorry," he said. "I was jamming earlier."

"Don't be sorry." She reached for the same volume knob and turned it back up. "It's so pretty."

As he pulled the SUV out of the driveway, he slid a gaze in her direction. A grin tugged at his mouth. "You like this?"

Bee had heard stereotypical Hawaiian music before, heavy on the ukulele and sunshine lyrics, but the music that filled Denny's car had soul. A deeper, sweeter sound poured from the speakers, the simple melodies burrowing under her skin and holding on to her attention.

"Yeah," she said. "I guess I don't know much about Hawaiian music outside of Don Ho."

His smile deepened, his teeth flashing in the dashboard light. He draped one hand over the steering wheel as they careened around the mountain road's tight curves.

"I'll play you some of my favorites," he said. "This is my cousin's band. They do a couple songs you'd know. Some covers. But mostly they stick to traditional Hawaiian music. My dad played a lot of these records when I was growing up, so it's got my heart, you know?"

It's got my heart. Yeah, she knew. It probably felt a lot like she did now, her chest swelling with warmth as she gazed at his glowing face.

"I didn't grow up with a culture like that," she said. "I

mean, there are definitely things that make me miss my parents and home sometimes, but nothing like that."

"What are the things that make you miss home?" he said.

Home. It didn't conjure images of family Christmases or a shiny, happy breakfast table complete with pipe-smoking father and doting mother serving hot pancakes. She thought first of Jamie and Abe, their weekend brunches and vacations to Sonoma. Her friends had replaced her family. It was them she missed most.

"Well," she said, digging deep, "I guess I miss the people who knew me when I was young. Sometimes I feel like my life has been split up into two parts, you know? And my parents, my childhood friends . . . they don't fit into the adult life I created for myself."

"Except for Isaac," he said.

She checked his face. No sign of sarcasm.

"Yeah. You're right. He bridges the gap whether you want him to or not." She chewed the inside of her lip. "I just want him to be okay on his own, you know? I know it comes off like I'm coddling him, and maybe I am. He's just not as independent as I am. He never has been."

Denny ran a hand across his chin and stopped at a red light. He turned his serious eyes on her. "Can I ask you something kinda . . . personal?"

"Sure."

"You told me your parents were covering him," he said. "Financially."

"You want to ask if they cover me, too?"

He shifted but didn't say anything.

"No," she said. "They don't."

The red shadow on his face flashed to green, and he turned his attention back to the road.

Another minute passed before she continued. She'd seen money define so many people. It colored her parents' whole world. Who had what, when they got it, how they used it.

She couldn't deny the importance of financial stability, but she didn't want anything to do with the power dynamics that came along with being wealthy.

"For the record," Denny said. "I never thought that about you. The way you low-balled yourself when I first asked you to decorate for me didn't exactly give me spoiled-princess vibes."

She smoothed her hands over her silky skirt. Her mother had sent it to her for her last birthday, probably envisioning it paired with a modest white blouse and stockings. But maybe she'd be happy knowing her daughter liked it anyway.

"I grew up pretty spoiled," Bee said. "But it never really stuck. I had everything I could ever want. We traveled a lot, always flew first-class, got tons of presents for Christmas. But all I ever really wanted to do was read books and draw. Isaac didn't mind if my parents disapproved of his behavior, but I tried to keep under the radar. Just seemed easier."

She checked Denny's expression again. His lips curved upward as he glanced from the road to her face and back again.

"My parents aren't bad people," she said. "They're just . . . cold. If I cried or complained or even if I was too happy, they'd tell me to button it up. Chill out. That I was being embarrassing. I mean, embarrassing to *who*? Strangers in a restaurant? Their stuffy friends? I'd be alone with my mother in our own house and she'd tell me to tone it down."

She grimaced. "I tried. I was a total rule follower. I got really good grades, I never got in trouble. The only times they ever punished me were when I let my emotions get the best of me, but I learned eventually to hold it all in. And then it came time for me to go to college, and I thought, *This is it. This is my opportunity to be myself.* I told my parents I didn't want to go to college, and they said if I didn't go, they were done. No more financial support."

"Wow," Denny said. "That was it?"

She shrugged. "That was it."

"But Isaac gets a free pass to do whatever he wants, and the money keeps coming for him?"

"As long as he checked their boxes, they gave him his allowance." She huffed out a short, bitter laugh. "He has a master's in communication because they told him they'd buy an apartment and let him live there while he got it. Can you believe that?"

Denny's eyebrows rose into his forehead as if he could not, in fact, believe it.

"But I knew how much a private college would cost, and I just couldn't imagine wasting all that money for something I didn't even really want to do."

"Sounds pretty responsible for an eighteen-year-old kid."

"My parents thought it was the most *irresponsible* thing they'd ever heard of," she said. "We didn't talk for almost a year. I called a lot, and they never called me back. I only heard through Isaac that they were doing okay. They were just so mad at me. They thought freezing me out would change my mind, I guess."

She could still feel the pangs of rejection when she remembered the sound of her mother's cold, clipped voice on the voice mail message. *You've reached the Jones residence.* All the unanswered messages. All the effort Bee made.

"Guess they didn't realize how stubborn you are, huh?" Denny said. His eyes twinkled in the oncoming headlights. Could he know her that well already?

"I think they overestimated the power their money could have," she said. "But I did all right. I took any job anybody would offer me and finally worked my way up at Club Trade. I found a whole community of people who embraced me, even at my worst. Even at my loudest, my most obnoxious."

Denny pulled his SUV into a driveway, turning into a

shadowy parking space next to a restaurant called Antonio's. He cut the engine, clicked off his seat belt, and turned to look at her. He propped his arm onto the door, letting her know in one motion that he wasn't done listening.

"And now you actually want to go back to school," he said. "On your terms."

She couldn't fight the grin tugging at her lips. "Yes. Exactly. And I've looked into tons of programs, but London feels . . . appropriately far away."

His brow pinched. "What does that mean?"

How could she say, *I need an ocean between me and the people who need me if I'm ever going to truly do what I want* without sounding like a total pushover?

"I guess I just want some space," she said. "And crossing the Atlantic seemed like a good way to do it. Maybe I'm being dramatic."

He smirked. "Maybe."

"If you knew my brother better, you might agree."

"So do you talk to your parents now?" he asked.

"Yeah." A jolt of memory pinged in her brain. "I mean, I did. Isaac sort of brokered a conversation, and they actually listened to me. My dad cried, which up to that point I had never seen him do. They're very emotionally stunted people, and money was the only way they knew how to support me. Once I took that away I think they felt sort of lost."

"Makes sense," he said quietly.

"I just had to take them at face value." She stole a glance at him, his face creased and focused. "And since that conversation, we've had a pretty good relationship. Until . . ."

Her voice faded, and her attention fixed on her lap.

"Until?"

"Until Isaac's accident." She massaged her temple. "I guess between the accident and not having insurance and refusing to take a job they wanted him to take, they'd finally had enough. They wanted to keep him under their thumb, even though he's an adult, you know? And when they heard I'd helped him out financially, they stopped talking to me again, too."

"Damn," Denny said. "That's a lot of manipulation right there."

She shook her head, pressed her hands against the dashboard until her elbows strained. "It's just really disappointing. I thought we'd made progress, and then they go and show me who they are all over again. They haven't changed at all."

He shifted his large frame and pursed his lips. "Sounds like your brother doesn't have the cleanest track record, either. I'm saying this as somebody who's tested people's patience, you know?"

She touched her teeth together, attempting to swallow a grin. Was he referring to his disappearance in the woods? He'd done a lot more than test her patience.

"That's fair," she said. "I did wonder about that. If maybe they'd gotten tired of being worried about him all the time."

"Or feeling like they were enabling bad behavior."

She nodded, a slow rise and fall of her chin. "Yeah. Maybe."

She stared past him into the parking lot, a stretch of desolate, dark gravel stretching between their car and the restaurant.

"The thing is, though," he said. "I don't think you can turn it off and on. When you sign up to care about somebody, you don't get to decide when to be there and when to disappear."

She smirked. "This coming from someone who's never been in love before."

"Why do you think that is?" His eyes darkened. "I mean, I've had good people in my life. Girls who probably deserved more from me than I gave them. But I think I've always known when I decided to love somebody, that would be it. No taking it back. No conditions."

She tilted her head, studying him. It wasn't a line. It was something he'd thought about. She'd never *decided* to be in love—it caught her like a shark caught fish. But it often left her ruined, wrung out, spent. She'd never had the kind of love that turned her into something better.

"So," she said. Her voice caught on the word. "Why haven't you ever done it?"

He pushed himself upright, closing the space between them. Cold night air slipped into the car as they sat in the parking lot, but her skin heated the closer he came.

"I can't control all of it," he said. "When I meet somebody worth loving that hard, I'll do it."

Her muscles tightened, anticipation pricking her skin. He leaned across the console, dipping his chin until his mouth caught hers. His hand buried in her hair as his tongue probed at the seal of her lips. She welcomed him in, opening as he slid against her.

Flames licked at her insides as he breathed in, stealing her air and heightening her senses. Desire made her dizzy, and she clutched fistfuls of his soft wool sweater to ground herself.

We shouldn't. The line screamed through her brain, but all other sensation drowned it out. She popped off her heels, and in one deft maneuver, crawled over the console into his lap.

With knees tucked up around his hips, she arched her back and pressed against him, desperate for as much of him as she could have. He reached down next to the seat, and with a low, whirring noise, they reclined until he laid almost completely flat on his back.

His strong hands traveled up her waist, pausing as his fingertips brushed the undersides of her breasts. Their mouths worked together, the rhythmic motion extending to their ribs down to their hips. He grinded against her, the pressure of his erection teasing the crux of her legs.

She wanted more. The layers of clothes between them

tortured her. He gripped her ass, bunching the skirt in his hands and finding her bare skin below. The tips of his fingers brushed the edges of her black lace boy shorts, and she choked against the lust scratching at her throat.

She snaked one hand between them, finding and fumbling with the button on his pants. The button popped, the zipper lowered, and soon she had him clutched in her feverish grip.

"I don't have a condom," he whispered. His warm breath cascaded across her cheek before he turned his attention on her neck and sucked her skin between his teeth. Her vision clouded.

"I do," she said. She reached out blindly, feeling around the passenger seat for her purse, finally having to turn her full focus on the task. As she leaned over, digging through the endless array of lipstick, keys, and mints, he lifted the bottom of her shirt. Through the thin, delicate fabric of her bra, he closed his teeth around her nipple.

"Oh God," she breathed. Fireworks popped off behind her eyelids as her fingers closed around a small, square packet.

He tugged the lace down, finding a sliver of space between her shirt and bra to work his magic. He flicked his tongue across her sensitive flesh, gripping her ass tighter as he sucked.

"Your mouth," she said, barely able to form words, much less sentences. "Holy hell."

He groaned against her chest, the heat and vibrations combining to scramble her brain even further. She returned her attention to his open zipper and pulled back just enough to roll the condom onto his waiting cock.

His lips parted, his gaze hazy, as if confused that she'd stopped him from putting in good work. He slid a hand between her legs and tugged the middle of her boy shorts to one side. It was all the direction she needed. She raised her hips, and with one hand, guided him inside of her.

She wanted to look at him, wanted to stare into his beautiful face while he filled her up, but she couldn't. The slow, sinking sensation as she lowered her hips further and further over him siphoned away all other brain function.

He wrapped his arms around her body, holding her closer as his hips slowly rolled. A thumb swept across her nipple, and he gently massaged the nub as it tightened. She dragged her tongue across his earlobe, unable to decide where or how she wanted to taste him. Any bit she could get would have to do.

He buried his face in her neck. The heat from his mouth and the pressure from his hips driving against her again and again lit every nerve on fire. She gripped her thighs tighter around his waist, begging the orgasm to hold off. He felt too good, tasted too sweet. She'd never have him again for the first time, and she wanted to remember every moment.

Her nerves braced, her teeth clenched, the moment upon her like an oncoming freight train. And then suddenly, he slowed. His grip loosened, he relaxed backward, and one hand nestled behind her neck.

She opened her eyes slowly, his sharp cheekbones and full lips appearing before her. The words "What's wrong?" sat heavy on her tongue until carefully, purposefully, gently, his hips rocked against her. Labored breaths gripped her lungs.

Slow. He wanted it slow. He slid in and out of her, the friction amping up the drumbeat pulse between her legs. If he meant to hold off bringing her to climax, he'd done exactly the opposite. Her breaths came quicker, her face went numb.

She grabbed his wrist and slipped two of his fingers into her mouth, rolling her tongue against the powerful digits and mimicking the rhythm of his hips. His lips bunched, his brow furrowed, and his single-handed grip on her ass tightened.

If he wanted all the control, he wasn't going to get it. She lowered herself until she pressed against him, ribs to ribs, and slid his fingers from her mouth. While he continued to rock against her, she kissed him. Slow and purposeful, controlled and deep.

As he slid his tongue past her lips, she melted into him. She'd never been so absorbed, so utterly focused and powerless at the same time. He held her in every way possible; in every way she'd never let anyone else touch.

With one hand buried in her hair and the other gripping her hip, the climax seized her. In one colossal crash, she tensed up, pulsing against him as he held her, and bursts of light exploded behind her eyelids. She stifled her cry against his shoulder, the taste of soft wool filling her mouth.

She dragged her mouth against his neck and sucked his flesh between her lips until he tightened against her. He shuddered as she clung to him, a life raft in the shifting waters of her world.

He panted, his warm breath ruffling her hair and summoning goose bumps along her neck. She pulled back to look at him. She ran a trembling finger across his dark eyebrow, committing every inch of his face to memory. His cheeks flushed, his breath came quick. How could she sit across from him at dinner after that?

"Holy shit," she said. "We're in a restaurant parking lot."

He grinned, his lopsided smile making her legs shiver all over again. "Whoops."

She placed one shaky hand on the car door and pushed herself to sitting, yanking her top down but not yet ready to move from his lap. He wrapped his hands around her hips and twitched again inside of her.

"Bee . . ." He swallowed, the column of his neck contracting as his jaw worked. He reached one hand up and smoothed a strand of her hair back.

The mood shifted. What had once been hot and passionate and mind-melting turned somber and sweet and terrifying. She didn't want to hear what came next.

"No," she said. "Just . . . whatever you're gonna say. Don't say it yet."

The corners of his eyes creased.

"I don't want things to turn heavy right now," she said. "Okay?"

With one hand still holding firmly to her hips, he reached down and the seat whirred to life, lifting him upright until they sat nose to nose. Before she could question the instinct, she leaned forward and kissed the curve of his full lower lip.

"You afraid to hear what I have to say?" he asked.

Her throat closed up. Fifteen minutes earlier he'd hinted that he could love her. *Afraid* didn't scratch the surface.

"No," she said. "What just happened was kind of perfect. I want to leave it that way."

He breathed deeply; his eyes focused on her mouth. The second they separated, real life would rush in around them, and they'd be moving forward toward the inevitable ending. Why couldn't they stay here, in his SUV, touching each other and kissing and talking for the rest of their lives?

His lips parted, but before he could speak, his phone buzzed where he'd left it in the center console. With a heavy heart, she climbed off his lap and slid into the passenger seat. It seemed that real life wormed its way in no matter how hard she tried to keep it out.

After discreetly tucking the used condom into a takeout napkin and zipping himself up, he retrieved his phone. His eyes narrowed at the screen.

"Everything okay?" she asked.

He tapped the screen and held the phone to his ear. "It's the alarm at the house."

The hair at the back of her neck stood on end. She'd felt safe in Pine Ridge from the moment she and Sydney drove past the **WELCOME** sign on their way into town. She couldn't imagine someone breaking into Denny's house.

Denny greeted the person on the other end of the phone,

and in the silence that followed, his sharp features tightened further. He propped an elbow up on the door and massaged his lips.

His gaze flickered over to her.

"Nah," he said quietly. "I don't want to press charges. He's staying with me. He must've forgotten the security code."

Bee's throat dried up. Her heart dropped into her stomach as Denny pinched the bridge of his nose, promised the person on the phone they could vacate the property, and hung up. He replaced the phone in the console before starting the engine and pulling out of the parking lot.

She tucked her trembling hands between her legs, every nerve in her body on the verge of overload. Denny remained silent, but the waves of energy coming off of him spoke volumes.

"Isaac was in your house," she said.

"Yep."

Bile threatened the back of her throat, and she turned her eyes to the road ahead. She wanted to shrivel up and disappear. Denny had been nothing but kind and generous to Isaac, overlooking any shred of inconvenience her brother inflicted on him. And he repaid him with disrespect.

"Denny . . ."

He tilted his head, pursing his lips and waiting for her to continue. But she couldn't summon the words to properly express her anger, her frustration, her overwhelming disappointment.

"Don't freak out just yet, all right? Let's talk to him once we get home."

They drove back to Denny's house in silence, Bee's fingers massaging the flat planes of her phone as if she could communicate with Isaac through osmosis. Her empathy for his plight, the deep well of compassion she'd long maintained for him, had all but dried up. He could take advantage of his sister. She'd allowed it her whole life. But she couldn't stand back and watch him manipulate Denny.

By the time they pulled into the driveway, Bee shivered from head to toe. The car had barely come to a stop before she snatched her shoes from the floor of the SUV and climbed out, stalking across the cold, sharp gravel in her bare feet.

She bit the inside of her lip, tasting blood and realizing she must've been chewing the entire ride home. As she neared the cabin, her heart rate soared. She twisted the knob and flung the door open.

The cabin sat empty, Isaac's stuff piled everywhere but no sight of the man himself. She dropped her shoes on the floor and spun toward the house, where Denny stood waiting.

"I think he's in the kitchen," Denny said. His voice remained low and cautious. She wanted him to let Isaac have it, too, but the words bubbling up inside of her had to come first.

She stormed through the front door, pounding on heavy heels into the kitchen, where her brother stood washing dishes. He turned over his shoulder, his eyes downcast, and forced a quiet smile.

"Hey," he said. "So sorry I tripped the alarm. I thought I'd clean up a little for you guys. You know, do something nice for Denny since he's been letting me stay in the guesthouse all this time."

Her teeth chattered. "Spare me the lies. Put the dishes down and look at me."

Isaac cleared his throat. He set one of her newly acquired white stoneware mugs down in the drying rack, shut off the tap, and turned around, his hands dripping water onto the floor.

"Dry your hands off," she snapped. "Can't you see you're getting the floor all wet?"

With wide eyes, he grabbed a dish towel and wiped his

hands. "Jesus, calm down. Nothing even happened. Greg and his friends came by to pick me up, and since Denny's fridge is always stocked with beer, we just stopped in to grab a roadie. I didn't know I'd set off the alarm until the cops showed up. Denny doesn't mind, right?"

Bee started, looking sharply behind her. She hadn't even realized Denny was standing in the kitchen.

"I dunno, dude," Denny said. "If you'd asked, I'd have been totally fine with it. But busting in while I'm out . . ."

"You're right," Isaac said. "I get it. I'm sorry."

Sorry. He'd apologized to Bee so many times the word had lost its meaning.

"You're such a spoiled brat," she said. "Just taking whatever you want no matter who you hurt."

Isaac's pale cheeks flamed red. "I didn't hurt anybody. And I already ordered stain remover for the wine spill."

A new wave of anger rose up inside of her, and she gripped the island in front of her. "Wine spill?"

He crossed his arms over his chest, his jaw tightening in defiance. "I opened a bottle of red I saw in the wine rack, and Greg's stupid friend Fiona tripped on the coffee table and fell right into me."

Bee's vision turned spotty. "Where?"

Isaac tossed a hand toward the living room. The living room she'd managed to turn into something special, despite a tight timeline and the challenge of interpreting someone's style she'd only just met. She'd worked so hard. And he'd spit in the face of all of it.

"In there. It's this tiny spot on one of the couch cushions. It'll come out, though. I've used this stain remover before and—"

"Get out."

"Bee . . ." His eyes brimmed with tears.

"Get out now," she growled. "Get out of Pine Ridge. I'm so tired of you acting like you're owed something, Isaac. Everybody else works hard for what they have, and you just walk in like it all belongs to you. You don't do *shit*. You have Mom and Dad's money, or my money, and now you're taking advantage of Denny's generosity, too."

Isaac's entire face bloomed crimson. "I made a mistake, Bee. I didn't burn the house down. Cut me a freaking break."

"That's just it!" she said. "You don't care what any of this means to anybody else. You don't care that I've covered for you a thousand times, that I've bailed you out of more jams than I can count. You don't care that I've worked hard to design this house or that somebody paid good money for the couch you ruined. You don't care. Maybe it's time I should start not caring, too."

"Good luck with that," he said. "You and your holier-than-thou attitude, like putting in some hours at a charity makes you better than everybody else."

Her skin stung as if he'd tossed actual barbs. "Just get out."

He stood as tall as his booted leg allowed, his mouth hanging open in surprise. "Where am I supposed to go?"

She shrugged. "I don't care."

Tears pricked her eyes as she turned and walked out of the kitchen, past Denny hovering awkwardly in the kitchen doorway, and away from her selfish brother. She climbed the stairs and made it as far as the landing before the first sob erupted from her throat.

She draped herself across the guest bed, her face buried in a pillow as the sadness rolled out of her in waves. All she'd done for him, all she'd put herself through on his behalf. None of it amounted to anything. He just took, and took, and took some more.

Denny's low voice carried upstairs.

"Come on," he said. "I'll give you a ride to the train station."

"You don't have to do that," Isaac said. "I'll just get a cab."

"Dude," Denny said. "You'll never get a cab here. There's one guy with one car and it usually takes him at least an hour to show up. And the train station is about an hour and a half away from here. Just pack up your stuff and be ready in twenty minutes. I'll meet you outside."

Bee sat up on the bed, dragging a wrist across her cheek. Isaac didn't even deserve loaned cab fare from Denny, let alone a ride to Utica Station.

Denny's heavy footfall grew louder as he climbed the stairs, one slow step after another. She wiped at her cheeks as his figure appeared in the darkened doorway to the guest room. He leaned against the doorjamb, gazing at her with serious eyes.

"You okay?" he said.

She shook her head. Something long tested had finally snapped inside. She'd lost her brother. Or maybe she'd never really had him in the way she thought.

"I am so sorry," she said. "I can't even begin to tell you how sorry I am. That I invited him here, that I let him stay so long, that I gave him the impression he could trespass on your property."

"Thank you for saying that." He traipsed into the room and ran a hand over her head, smoothing back her hair. "But this is not your fault."

"I know him." She licked her lips, her gaze trained on the woven chocolate-colored rug beneath Denny's feet. "I know how he operates, what he's capable of. It was stupid of me to think he wouldn't pull that shit here. It *is* my fault."

The sound of Denny's slow exhale filled the space between them. He combed her hair back again with strong fingers, the repetitive motion soothing her weary mind.

"He's your family," he said. "He needed your help. It's not the craziest thing in the world, you know."

She looked up, his fingers tucked behind her ear. When they first met, she'd been attracted to him, but in the past couple of weeks, she'd been blindsided by the ferocity of her feelings. He was soft and kind, powerful and assertive. She'd never met anyone like him.

"You really don't need to drive him to the train station," she said. "Let him wait for the cab. He's probably never waited for a cab in his entire life."

"I want to know he's on his way out," he said. "For both our sanities."

He leaned down, melding his lips to hers in a quiet kiss. She placed timid fingertips on his cheek, wanting as much of him as she'd had half an hour ago in his car.

"Can I ask a favor?" he said. His breath warmed her earlobe as he spoke.

"Anything."

"If you go to sleep early, can it be in my bed?"

She inhaled sharply, a smile finding her despite the night's tumult. "Yeah, I think I can do that. As a favor to you."

He stood upright and grinned. "Too generous for your own good, Bethany."

As he turned toward the hallway, her heart slammed against her ribs. *Bethany.* Had she even told him her full name? How long had he known it, how long had it rolled around in his brain unspoken?

She sat on the bed, listening for him long after he'd gone.

chapter **sixteen**

A cool breeze snaked beneath the collar of Denny's sweatshirt, and he shivered against the autumn air. He'd been in Pine Ridge for a year and a half and still hadn't adjusted to the abbreviated summer. In Southern California, they'd still be enjoying the heat. As he gazed out over the Pine Ridge High School football field, he remembered being soaked in sweat moments after suiting up.

Coach Parker's kids enjoyed cooler temperatures, which meant they could work twice as hard. Denny had reminded them of that fact during warm up. The kids who'd rolled their eyes got to run extra laps.

The shrill bleat of a whistle sounded as purple evening light tickled the edges of the sky, and Coach Parker commended the boys on a great practice. He clapped a meaty hand on Denny's shoulder and grinned up at him as the boys trudged off the field.

"Can't thank you enough for coming by today," Coach

Parker said. "I know last time was a little bit rough, but I think they really respect you."

Denny's chest swelled. He'd stopped envisioning practice as a time to impart wisdom and started treating it like work. The drills were shorter, the language tamer. But the push and pull was the same. When he gave a kid a note and watched him implement it, resulting in better-quality play, accomplishment rose up inside of him like he'd just finished four quarters alongside pros.

"You have a really good team here," Denny said. "And, uh . . . sorry about what happened last time. I got all up in my own head."

Coach Parker smiled, his cheeks reddening. Denny'd heard a couple of kids on the team talking about how Coach Parker was their favorite teacher. How he made their government class tolerable. Some of those kids would surely cling to lessons their coach imparted long after their high school careers ended.

"No apology necessary," Coach said. "You've been through a lot these past few years. It's part of the reason why I wanted to have you come in."

Denny scoffed. "You wanted to teach these kids to be goof-offs and squander huge opportunities?"

"I wanted them to learn from somebody who's learned himself." Coach Parker hitched up his pants. "Somebody who's figuring out a life beyond football. They don't need examples of guys who seem to have it easy. I mean, those guys are all right, too. The Ben McKennas and Derek Tahoes of the world. But let's face it, these kids aren't gonna go pro. A few of them might play in college. I'd rather they see somebody who's finding his way outside of the NFL. That's real life. That'll help them out when they take jobs in offices or schools, you know?"

Denny gazed out over the field, the grass matted with dirt and the effort of a group of hardworking kids. No one except Coach Maiava had ever encouraged him to work hard no matter the job. His parents, grandparents, uncles, and aunts had drilled into him that there were prestigious careers and there was everything else.

"I guess you're right," Denny said. "Excellence no matter what you're shooting for."

"Somethin' like that." Coach checked the phone clipped to his belt and hitched his pants again. "Listen, I know this is probably small-time for you."

"It's not." He didn't care what Coach Parker planned to say next. He needed him to understand how much it mattered, how much Denny needed it, too.

Coach Parker grinned. "I appreciate that. But I also want you to know that if you want to come again, I need a commitment from you. If we ask these kids for consistency and effort, we have to give it back to them. I don't blame you if you don't want to join us for the season. But I need to know up front."

Denny's throat dried up. *I need a commitment.* Four words that had never agreed with him. "Now to December, right?"

Coach laughed. "God willing, through November. If we make it that far. For now, we focus on the playoffs."

Denny nodded slowly. "I'm in."

With another barking laugh, Coach's eyebrows shot up under his white baseball cap. "Just like that? You can think it over if you like."

"Nah." Denny extended his hand, and Coach shook it. "I don't need to think it over. You have a really great program here, and I'd be honored to be a part of it."

Coach clapped his other hand over Denny's, and for a minute Denny thought the man might cry. His face pinched, the cheeks turning cherry red.

"Fantastic." He dropped Denny's hand and hitched his pants again. "I should also tell you, in addition to the practices, we throw a couple of fundraisers and events throughout the season. First one's a week from Friday, if you can make it. A big bonfire at my place on Tupper Lake."

Denny grinned, his face warming despite the cool temperature. "That sounds awesome. I'll be there."

With one more clap on his hand, Coach Parker told Denny to have a great evening and left him alone on the football field feeling like he'd just won the Super Bowl.

He drove into town, coasting on the day's good vibes. After Friday night's debacle, he needed some positivity. He'd been ready to pummel Isaac. Not because he'd been an idiot and made Denny's house his own, but because he'd trampled all over his sister's big heart. As Denny watched the overwhelming shame and anger douse Bee's personality, he could only stand back and let her handle it.

When he'd arrived home after the silent three-hour round-trip drive to Utica, he found her in the living room scrubbing at the couch. Her face tight, her formerly styled hair twisted on top of her head in a haphazard knot. He allowed himself a moment to watch, her torn-up T-shirt slipping off one shoulder as she scrubbed vigorously.

He knew a relationship between them couldn't work, told himself over and over again she wouldn't stay in Pine Ridge. There was nothing for her there. And yet, he let himself fall. He couldn't help it. He meant every word of what he'd told her in the car. The moment he met someone worth loving, he'd do it with every ounce of himself. No matter what.

His SUV careened around the turn to Main Street, and he saw Bee's bike parked outside the Loving Page. He'd offered to rent her a car for the duration of her stay, but she refused. When the first snowfall came in mid-October, she'd change her tune.

As he parked his car along the curb in front of the Loving Page, his phone buzzed in steady intervals. He checked the screen and grinned.

"Hi, Ma."

"Hello, my boy. Do you have towels?"

"On me?" His eyes flickered to the back seat of his truck.

"At your house."

He closed his eyes, massaging his brow and summoning patience. "Yes, Ma. I have towels at my house."

"Okay, okay. Good. If you don't have any, I can order some and have them shipped to you."

"I have some." He waited. That surely wasn't the end of it.

"You have enough for guests?" she said.

There it is.

"Yes."

The guest room. He hadn't considered where Bee would go when his parents arrived. She'd stayed put in his guest room—okay, in his bed—since Isaac left, but would she return to the guesthouse eventually? Exposing his parents to his new life in Pine Ridge was enough for one visit. Maybe explaining his relationship with the tattooed club promoter who encouraged him to volunteer his time could wait a while.

"Okay," Rosa said. "I wasn't sure if that girl stocked the whole house."

His face heated. He knew he shouldn't have told his mother he had someone helping him decorate. The mere mention of a woman in his life set Rosa on edge, like a shark smelling blood in the water.

"Her name is Bee," he said. "And she'd be a pretty terrible designer if she only outfitted one bathroom, yeah?"

"I don't know what you're paying her for," Rosa said. Her words trembled with defensiveness.

"Don't worry about it." He tried to keep his tone calm. "Everything is gonna be ready for you when you get here."

She sniffed, her suspicion carrying clear across the thousands of miles between them. "Okay, okay."

He knew she'd bring towels with her, just in case. "Everything else okay?"

"Oh, yeah," she said. "Everything is fine. I'll let you go. Love you, my boy."

"Love you, Ma."

He ended the call and dragged a hand down his face, reminding himself that in two weeks, his parents would have come and gone. One visit couldn't dictate his future, and whether he played professional sports or helped coach a high school team, he was still their son.

A wry smile settled over his lips. He could have the mantra injected into his skin, tattoo it on his forehead to read every day, and it still wouldn't stick. One sideways glance from his mother, and he'd be reduced to that ten-year-old kid again, knowing he didn't quite fit into her mold of the perfect kid.

He climbed out of his car and walked into the bookshop, his spirit lifting as the bell over the door signaled his arrival. Bee stood next to Sydney at the register wearing a bright blue-and-white tie-dyed hoodie, big gold hoops dangling from her ears. She looked up, her smile stretching as they caught eyes.

"There he is," Sydney trilled. "Were your ears burning?"

Bee shot her friend a narrow-eyed look.

"Kidding," Sydney said. Her Cheshire cat smile told him otherwise. "We were talking about this new sports romance series that just came in about a football player and his edgy decorator—"

"And their nosy friend who married the town mechanic?" Denny cut in. "Yeah, I think I read that one."

Sydney's cheeks flushed, and she tossed a tiny pine needle–filled pillow at Denny as laughter spilled out of Bee. He approached the register and tucked his hand in Bee's, kissing the *Be* tattoo on her knuckle. When her hand stiffened, he paused. Did she care what Sydney saw? From Sydney's teasing, he could only assume she knew every detail of what happened in his car at Antonio's.

"You guys ready for your first book club meeting?" he said.

"So ready," Sydney gushed. "We had ten kids sign up,

which is insane considering the entire school only has a hundred and twenty students."

"We should expand to surrounding schools," Bee said. "I mean, the football team is made up of kids from three schools. Why shouldn't the book club be?"

"Totally," Sydney agreed. "We'll see how the first one goes and adjust from there."

"What's the book?" Denny asked.

Bee held up a green-and-pink-patterned paperback with the title *Chrissy Went Home* splashed across the cover. "It's a really good opening book, I think," she said. "It's like a Gen Z take on *Are You There God? It's Me, Margaret.*"

"Did you get any of that?" Sydney said with a smile. "*Are You There God? It's Me, Margaret* is this book that practically every young woman has read at some point in her life—"

"I know," Denny said. He plucked the book from Bee's fingers and scanned the back cover. "I have an older sister."

"You've read it?" Bee asked.

He lifted his eyes to look at her. The dreamy grin on her lips caused a rush of endorphins through his body. Had Sydney not been standing two feet to his right, he'd have snatched her into his arms and kissed her. Hard.

He raised an eyebrow. "Yeah. And I'm glad I did. Nobody ever taught me about periods. So thanks, Judy Blume."

"Wow," Sydney muttered. "Bee, do you want me to give you guys five minutes so you can just get down to it right here, right now?"

Bee's eyes crinkled up, but the way she looked at him made him think she was considering it. "I wish it was acceptable to tell the kids of this town that you can have *that* kind of effect on somebody just from the books you've read."

"When we're alone," he said, "I'll tell you in *explicit* detail how many issues of *Sports Illustrated* I've got under my belt."

Bee's face pinched with laughter again, and she placed

a cool hand on his arm to steady herself. He wanted to keep going, summon every quippy line in his arsenal, if it meant she'd keep laughing.

"Denny," Sydney said, "when are you gonna have a big housewarming party so we can all see your place?"

"That's an amazing idea," he said. His eyes widened as he looked at Bee as if for permission. It was as much her space as it was his.

"No way," she said. "Not until *after* your parents visit. I'm scarred after the shit Isaac pulled last week."

His smile faded. "Ah. Right."

A chill settled over the conversation, and Sydney cleared her throat, busying herself with a stack of books beside the register. He hated that Isaac had tainted Bee's Pine Ridge experience.

"The weekend after my parents leave," Denny said. "Friday night."

Sydney tapped her phone. "The twentieth?"

"Sure," he said. "Everybody's invited."

"Everybody?" Bee said. She grimaced. "RIP beautiful glassware."

Worry tinged every conversation lately, as if Isaac's misstep proved that no one could be trusted. He nudged her hand with his.

"Let's take a walk," he said. "It's beautiful out right now."

Bee licked her lips, studied him for a moment. "Okay."

She slipped into her coat, promising to call Sydney the next day about book-club details and hugging her goodbye before she and Denny left the shop.

A brisk wind breezed across his cheeks, and he hunched his shoulders against the chill. Bee zipped her jacket, and before he could wonder whether she'd freeze up or not, he took her hand and linked his fingers with hers.

Instead of stiffening like she had in the shop, she leaned into his body, falling into step as they strolled down the sidewalk out of town. He breathed in, the woodsmoke-scented air blending with her clean, spicy perfume and lulling him into a state of near euphoria. He felt happy. At peace. Soothed in ways he hadn't been in years.

Maybe ever.

"Have you heard from Isaac?" he asked.

"Nope."

They hadn't spoken about the incident all weekend. When he got home Friday night, she asked if Isaac got on a train okay, Denny told her he didn't wait to find out, and that was it. He followed her up the stairs into his bed and held her as she drifted off into a fitful sleep.

"I'm sure he's all right," Denny said. "He's got a lot of friends in the city, right?"

"Tons." Her voice remained low, nearly carried away on the wind. "I'm not sure why he didn't stay with one of them in the first place. Maybe he burned all those bridges, too. I really thought I'd get a call from Jamie telling me he showed back up at my apartment."

My apartment. The words dug into his skin. A subtle reminder that his home wasn't her home, that even if she didn't go to London at the end of October, even if she didn't return to her old life, she wouldn't be staying here.

"Maybe he really did need some tough love," Denny offered.

He gazed down to catch her expression clouding over with doubt. "I dunno. Maybe. Maybe this wasn't the fireable offense, you know? He's just done this so many times."

"I think you handled it well," he said. "Even if it doesn't feel like it right now."

"I don't want to talk about it." She mumbled, staring straight forward as they reached the end of the sidewalk. The road curved ahead, leading them farther away from town and into the forest. The air grew richer with the pungent scent of pine.

"Does it smell this good here in every season?" she asked. She breathed deep, her chest rising under her honey-brown utility jacket. He grinned, remembering the day she arrived and how she promised he'd never see her in mountain clothes. With the hood of her tie-dyed sweatshirt jutting out and her gold hoops dangling like Christmas ornaments, she'd found a way to make even the functional jacket look stylish.

"Yeah, it does," he said. "It's a weird place, right? If you'd told me three years ago I'd be living in a little mountain town in northern New York, I'd have told you to get the hell out. Now I'm sort of in love with it."

Her cheeks rose in a grin. "It's a very weird place. I expected . . . something different. I don't know what."

Shivers skittered across his skin. Did he dare take it one step further? "Do you like it here?"

"I love it here." She shrugged, keeping her eyes fixed on the road ahead. "It's a really nice escape."

Huh. An escape. Like an all-inclusive resort in the Caribbean. Not somewhere to settle.

He traced the smooth skin of her hand with his thumb, lines running through his head like a script. He didn't often question himself or plan the next comment. But he didn't want to scare her away. He had to be thoughtful.

They followed a tight curve in the road until they came upon a scenic pull-off, approaching the guardrail to gaze out over Fourth Lake. The sky glowed with early-evening light, broad brushstrokes of tangerine and violet coloring the landscape and reflecting back on the glassy surface of the water. A heron took off from the shoreline and cruised by in front of them.

"Seems like Sydney's bookstore is doing really well," he said. He clenched his teeth. Did it sound obvious?

She leaned into him, keeping her eyes focused on the lake in front of them. "Amazingly well," she said. "I'm so proud of her. She spent a lot of really unhappy years in New York. To see her with Sam and her mom and making the store a success . . . It's pretty magical."

His confidence soared. "I bet a lot of people don't realize what they're missing if they've only ever lived in big
cities."

Finally, she turned, an all-knowing grin curling on her
lips as she looked at him. "Maybe not everybody's cut out
for life in a small town."

His head told him to shut up, but his gut didn't listen.
"Maybe you don't really know until you give it an honest shot."

Her grin melted away, and she looked back over the water. "Don't do that."

"Do what?" *Smooth, dude. Pretend like you're dumb
enough not to know what she means, and she'll definitely
want to be with you.*

"You know what you're doing," she said.

She refused to look back at him. He cupped a hand
around her elbow, urging her to face him, but she resisted.

"I just want to talk," he said. "I'm not trying to pressure
you or anything."

"You absolutely are." Her voice sharpened. "I'm not a
casual dater. I already told you that. And if you push me too
hard, I'll fall for you, and then I *will* move here, and we'll
be in a relationship until you decide you don't actually want
to spend your life in Pine Ridge. Then you'll move away,
and I'll have changed my whole world for somebody . . .
again . . . who needed me but only for a season. I refuse to
be the person who helps you through a transition and then
gets discarded when you're on the other side of it."

His hand fell from her elbow. "Whoa."

"You wanted to talk." She tucked her arms over her
chest, her sharp jaw working back and forth.

A whisper of icy wind snaked under his sweatshirt as
the sky melted into indigo.

"I don't always have a plan," he said. "I like following
my gut when something in my life tells me to. I didn't plan
on moving here, I didn't plan on connecting with somebody
in town for the weekend, and I definitely didn't plan on hir-

ing her to decorate my house. But all those things happened. I'm glad they happened. Now I want to see what comes next."

She exhaled, her striking blue eyes shifting toward him. "I can't live here."

He heard his mother's voice. *Leave it alone!* Every time he hugged the family dog too hard; every time he picked a scab; every time he teased his fragile sister. Moderation wasn't in his vocabulary.

"Can I ask why not?" he said.

She twisted her neck, giving him her full attention along with a stunned, openmouthed stare. "What would I do here? Open Club Pine Ridge? Start a support group for the one kid in town who might be at risk? Decorate the homes of the three new people who move here each year?"

"Sure," he said. "All of it. None of it. You could take your time and see what worked."

"And my income would come from . . . ?"

"I'd cover you until you figured it out."

The crease between her brows softened, and she stared at him unblinking. For a minute he thought she was considering it. Like he'd turned the key and unlocked the magic words.

"No, thank you."

Three words stripped the last shreds of warmth from the moment.

"I didn't mean it that way," he said.

"I don't care how you meant it."

Her voice remained cool and calm. He'd rather she yelled at him.

"If you think I'm ever going to take a handout from you, then you don't know me at all."

Every story she'd told him about her parents, her brother, their complicated relationship with money, and everything she'd rejected since childhood came screaming back to him all at once.

bold love

223

"Bee," he said softly. He tried to step nearer to her, tried to close the space between them, but she moved backward, her face warning him against any further motion. "I didn't mean it that way. I like you. A lot. If you wanted to move to Pine Ridge but you couldn't because you didn't have a job, I would want to fix that for you. Not cut you a ten-thousand-dollar check. Make sure you had a roof over your head and food in the fridge until you could cover it yourself."

She licked her lips. Did her face soften? He couldn't tell. Night filtered in around them like slow-rising tide.

"I grew up broke," he said. "My parents didn't start making money until I was in grade school. And even after they started making money, they made damn sure their kids didn't know it. My mom clipped coupons; we rode the bus; we wore hand-me-downs. And we were happy. I think I have a pretty good handle on how to use my money. What's worth spending on and what isn't. If I can make things easier for somebody I care about, I want to do that. But there will never, ever be any strings attached."

She lifted her shoulders, her lips twisting into a scowl. "You say that."

He huffed out a laugh, taking one timid step toward her. He needed to be closer, needed to feel her in his orbit. "It's the truth. I never give expecting something in return."

"It's human nature to expect something back," she said.

"Well," he said, "I don't. Respect, maybe. Appreciation is nice. But other than that, I give what I want, to who I want. And that's it."

One eyebrow slowly lifted as she looked at him. She took one step forward. And another. Her hands lighted on the waistband of his joggers, sending a flood of adrenaline through his limbs.

Darkness shrouded her face but couldn't dim the intensity in her eyes. "Why do I believe you?"

Something tightened in his stomach, twisting until he couldn't breathe. He had jumped from the plane without a parachute, but a strong wind carried him safely through the air.

"I don't always make the right decision," he said. "But I'll never lie to you. It's not my style."

She pressed up onto her toes and stretched until her mouth landed on his. He squeezed his eyes shut, inhaling until he tasted her on his tongue, in his head, and down into his lungs. He tucked a hand behind her neck and drew her closer, licking against her mouth until she softened and melted, her body turning pliable.

Headlights flashed around the curve of the road, and Denny pulled Bee into his chest, drawing her closer to the guardrail. As the lights swept over them, the car came to a stop and the passenger-side window lowered.

"Get a room!" Jared shouted before laughing and peeling away.

She collapsed into Denny's chest as they returned to darkness. Her body shook as she laughed. "Tell me again," she said, "About the joys of small-town living?"

He trailed a hand along her jaw and lifted her chin to kiss her again. "That's one thing New York and Pine Ridge have in common. No privacy whatsoever."

"The difference is, no one in New York cares what you do. I can't say the same for this place."

"That's fair," he said. "But I have to tell you. It's been nice having people care."

She narrowed her gaze and folded her hands behind his neck. "Let's go home."

He grinned, trying and failing to keep his hopes in check.

She'd said it. Just like that.

Home.

chapter **seventeen**

The Loving Page buzzed. Bee had seen the shop busy, quiet, and everything in between, but the energy a group of teenagers brought to the place was unrivaled. Sydney had lowered the overhead fluorescents, and the soft, purple glow of twilight filtered in from outside as kids shrugged off coats and dropped their overstuffed backpacks by the door.

"I have to commend you on the turnout." Allison folded her arms over her chest and grinned as she surveyed the room. "I've tried dozens of tactics to get kids involved in extracurriculars, and the most I get is five or six kids."

Bee breathed a deep, satisfied inhale. "I may not have kids of my own, but I know teenagers. They don't show up for much."

"Well, they showed up for this."

Kids gazed around in wonder as they entered the shop and surveyed the space. The cozy bookstore had been transformed into a youth-friendly wonderland. Bee had set out tons of snacks on the coffee table—Twizzlers, popcorn, Sour Patch Kids, McDonagh's chocolate chip cookies, Pop-chips, and four flavors of seltzers—and the selfie station behind the couch promised features on the Loving Page's thriving social media.

"Bee," Sydney called out from the back office. "Did you pick up that cutout we had printed for the selfie station?"

"Sure did." Bee scuttled behind the red velvet sofa and retrieved the cutout, holding it in front of her face and striking a supermodel pose for Allison. "Am I cute?"

"The cutest!" A booming male voice cut through the room, and Bee's heart nearly dropped into her stomach. Barreling toward her, all but shoving teenagers out of his way, was Jamie.

He wrapped his long arms around her, squeezing tightly and drowning her in the heady scent of Tom Ford Tobacco Vanille. A rush of emotion flooded her sinuses, and before she could pull back enough to see his face, tears pricked her eyes.

"What are you doing here?" she said. He held tight to her shoulders but stepped back to grin down at her.

"Where there is a gay book club," he said, "so, too, am I."

Sunglasses shielded his eyes, but his skin glowed as if he'd just had a facial. He wore a drapey black sweater decorated with a silver star and paired with black leather pants, a stunning red Prada bag tucked in the crook of his arm. She couldn't have loved him more.

"It's not a *gay* book club," she said, still clutching his arms. "We're talking about a book with a nonbinary main character who happens to be best friends with a cisgender gay boy."

"Girl, I don't care about the book. I'm here to see you." He kissed her cheek and pulled her in for another hug. "You've been here a month and a half, I'm more than due for a vacation, and it seemed time for a visit. Plus I heard through the grapevine about Isaac's little stunt and thought maybe you could use some moral support."

Her chest caved, the warmth of seeing an old friend swelling inside of her.

"Have I mentioned lately that you're my favorite person in the whole world?"

He removed his sunglasses and winked. "No. You haven't. But do go on."

"I'll properly gush later when we're alone. You're staying with me, right? Denny has a cute little guest cabin you can stay in." She wouldn't have to explain to Jamie why she wasn't using it herself.

"You're very sweet," he said. "But I booked myself at that gorgeous new hotel just outside of town. If I'm staying for a week, I'm staying in style."

Her sinuses prickled as she squeezed him in another hug. She couldn't wait to give him a tour of the bookstore, show him around Pine Ridge, and introduce him to all of her new friends.

"Jamie?" Sydney burst out of the office, her eyes wide with excitement. Jamie released Bee and crushed his old friend in a hug.

"It's been too long," Jamie said. He stood back, beaming at his girlfriends. "I'm proud of you two. Can't wait to sit back, relax, and see what this shindig is all about."

Jamie snagged the stool behind the register while the rest of the kids filtered into the store, and Sydney gave them her welcome speech.

Happy chatter settled into conversation, which melted into a seated discussion of the book. Bee didn't know what to expect from small-town kids, but from the way they dialogued, joked, and teased one another, Pine Ridge kids were the same as New York City kids, Long Island kids, and everyone in between. Some loved the book, some called out obvious disconnects with the way kids actually relate to one another, and some had suggestions for next time.

As the group broke up, a few stragglers shoved candy and seltzer into their backpacks, and Jamie watched with a restrained smile from behind the counter. He hadn't jumped into the book discussion, but Bee had caught him smiling when the more vocal of the group expounded on societal expectations based on gender.

The last book-club participant waved at Sydney, Bee, Allison, and Jamie, leaving the adults alone in the store, each of them gazing at one another with satisfied smirks.

"Damn," Allison said. "Well done, ladies. Not only did you get ten kids, but you actually kept them here for the entire event. I can only do that when I promise extra credit."

"The selfie station was a huge hit," Jamie said, wrapping his arm around Bee's shoulders. "That was you, right?"

"All Bee," Sydney said. She hadn't stopped smiling all night.

"We have one permanently installed at Club Trade, thanks to Mama Bee," Jamie said. "Never underestimate the power of vanity."

"Now that the kids are gone," Allison said, "Can we go get a drink? This calls for a celebration, right? And throughout the course of the discussion I had ideas for about ten more books these kids would love."

Sydney locked up, and the group made their way down the street to Utz's bar, riding high on the day's accomplishments. They settled into a corner booth, and Bee had to cut off the rapid-fire conversation to ask who wanted what to drink.

"Whiskey sour," Allison said.

Sydney grinned. "Ooh, same, please."

"You know what I like." Jamie winked. "And a round of tequila shots, please. The good stuff. This round's on me."

He handed her his credit card, and she turned to make her way to the bar. Utz's teemed with bodies, a chorus of loud conversations filling the space. Bee hadn't been out much since she arrived in Pine Ridge, only meeting Sydney and her friends for drinks a handful of times. With Jamie in town, and the joy of a successful book club under her belt, she itched to party.

She placed her hands on the sticky bar top as Hank the bartender sent her a short wave to let her know he'd be right over. Just as her mind drifted to Denny, a big, lean body slid against her, two strong arms caging her into the bar.

Warm breath heated her neck, and a deep voice purred into her ear. "Come here often?"

She bit her lip, lust shooting through her veins. With all the control she could muster, she turned her chin and said, "Mm, not really. I've got a man at home, and he gets *real* jealous."

Denny's large hand slid across her back and down to the curve of her butt as he stepped to the side, leaning on the bar with a grin. He shoved his hair back, a lock falling over his forehead and grazing the curve of his dark eyebrow. She reached up to brush it away.

"You look very good from behind," he said. "I noticed your jeans before I realized it was you."

She ran a hand over her high-waisted denim. "I wanted to look as stylish as possible so the teenagers wouldn't think I was an out-of-touch asshole."

His grin stretched. "I want to hear everything."

Her cheeks ached from smiling. "I'm here with Allison and Sydney. And Jamie! My best friend from New York? He showed up to surprise me."

"Seriously?" He looked over her head to glance around the bar, finding and waving at the corner booth where her friends sat. "That's awesome. You must be so pumped."

"It was a really good night," she gushed. "Having him here made it even better."

"Well," he said, "I just stopped in to grab a beer with Jared and Sam. I'll let you hang with your friends."

His gaze remained happy and placid, no traces of jealousy or hurt on his features. He said what he meant. She kept looking for hidden meaning. And she kept coming up short.

"No way," she said, slipping her hand into his. "Come hang out with us. Bring the boys. I'm ordering shots on Jamie, so I'll order some for all of us."

"Shots will definitely entice Jared, and Syd's over there, so Sam will be easy to convince. I'm a harder sell, though."

The apples of his cheeks tinted pink.

"Oh really?" She stepped closer, her breasts brushing against his ribs.

"Eh, maybe not." He lowered his face to hers, kissing her slowly on the lips. For a moment, she considered pulling away. Everyone in the bar would see them, everyone would know they were sleeping together. They'd expect her not to hurt him. They'd expect her to stay.

The moment of blinding insecurity passed quickly as his warm, soft lips caressed hers. The subtle slip of his tongue teased her mouth. She wanted to disappear with him, yank him into the bathroom, and touch and taste him until she'd had her fill.

He pulled away before she did, his grin reappearing. "I'll grab Jared and Sam and meet you over there."

Hank took her order and loaded up a tray with the drinks. She balanced the tray on one hand, memories of her restaurant days flooding over her, and when she approached the booth, her friends looked up with identical smiles.

"I'm not sure any of you has ever been so happy to see me," she joked.

"Excuse me?" A shrill voice sounded behind her, and she set the tray down before turning toward it.

A woman close to her own age wearing a tight ponytail and an oversize black sweatshirt stood a few feet away, her hands on her hips and an accusatory look on her thin, puckered face.

"Hi," Bee said.

"Hi." The word snapped like a rubber band. "You're Bee Jones, right? You ran that book-club meeting for the kids tonight at the Loving Page?"

"Yeah."

"I'm Jen Cody, Andrew's mom," she said. "I thought he was going to a school-sponsored book club tonight."

"It was school-sponsored," Allison offered. "I'm Andrew's English teacher. We met last week at parents' night?"

The woman glared at Allison and turned back to Bee. "I'll be contacting the school about this, then. I saw the book you had those kids read. It's perverse."

Bee's hackles rose. *Perverse.* She'd heard the word hurled at her friends more times than she could count. She'd heard it used to demean, cut down, and embarrass. *Not tonight, Jen Cody.*

"It's not perverse," Bee said calmly. "There's absolutely nothing in it that you wouldn't find in a PG-thirteen movie or on any youth-oriented TV show. Allison read it before we assigned it, and she ran it by the principal just to double-check."

"I don't care *what* the principal said," Jen snapped. "You needed to run it by the parents. I know what it's about, and I know what kind of message you're trying to push on our kids."

Bee tamped down a smile. She'd heard it all. The "gay agenda" had become a joke in her group of friends. "What kind of message is that?"

Jen tightened her grimace, her eyes darting from Bee to the table behind her. Bee couldn't see Jamie, but she imagined the glittering, defiant stare on his face, daring the woman to say anything derogatory about the gay community.

"You know what I mean," Jen said finally. "I know it's *cool* to be gay these days, but some boys really do just like girls. You don't have to push your beliefs on these impressionable teenagers. That's all I'm gonna say about it. You won't see Andrew at another meeting."

She leaned around Bee to point a skinny finger at Allison. "And I'll be calling the school about *you*."

"Everything okay?" Denny sauntered over, a pint glass in his big hand and a confused stare on his face. When Jen turned to face him, she stumbled back a step as if she'd confronted a bear.

"Oh."

Denny stood at least a foot and a half taller than Jen, and in the soft white button-down shirt that highlighted his broad shoulders and chiseled chest, he had the same effect on her that he did on most women.

"I . . ." Jen cleared her throat and reclaimed her rigid stance. "I was just saying to these people that I don't care for the reading material at tonight's book club meeting."

"Andrew's mom, right?" he said.

She stood taller, her cheeks flushing red. "Right."

"Andrew's a really nice kid," Denny said. "I'm helping out with the football team, and I've seen him do great things on special teams."

"Well." She cleared her throat again. "Thank you."

"But what's really great about Andrew," he continued, "is how well-rounded he is. I hope more of the football players take his lead. If he stays interested in sports *and* books, he'll have a shot at getting into a good college."

She blinked rapid-fire, her lips working as she shifted her weight from foot to foot. "That's nice to hear."

"So maybe you should be thanking *these people*, instead of yelling at them."

She gazed back at the booth. "It's not that I don't want Andrew to read. It's that I don't want him reading books that are too mature for him."

"Did you read the book?" Jamie chimed in.

Jen paused. "I read some reviews online."

"Read it," Bee said. "It's fantastic. And then maybe you and Andrew can talk about it. He had some really insightful things to say at the meeting tonight."

Jen tucked her arms across her chest and looked back at Denny. A pleasant smile graced his lips. Had he ever been more attractive?

Jen scratched her cheek. "Maybe."

"And I hope you'll let Andrew come back to the book club," Bee said. "We're still deciding on the next book, but I'd be more than happy to call and chat with you about it before we tell the kids."

"I'd appreciate that."

Bee waited, but something told her that was the end of it. Jen threw one more glance at Denny, tweaked her mouth into a smile, and marched out of the bar.

"Whew," Jamie quipped, sipping his cocktail. "Have y'all been dealing with that since you came up with this idea? Am I in a modern day *Footloose* where the kids aren't allowed to read books that aren't about straight white people?"

"No, this is new," Allison said. She tugged a strand of her long blond hair and stared wide-eyed at Bee. "Most of the parents I deal with are pretty accepting of the reading material I select. Even the principal didn't have anything to say about the book."

Bee's veins pulsed with adrenaline, her body recovering from fight-or-flight mode. She'd been confronted with a lot of Jen Codys in her life, and she used to cower down. Even when she'd first arrived in Pine Ridge, she expected more people like the concerned mother.

Something had changed. She felt stronger now. More equipped. More supported. More sure.

As Sam and Jared joined the group and Jamie, Allison, and Sydney erupted in an animated recap of the confrontation, Denny sidled up to Bee and brushed her hip with gentle fingers. Tension seeped out of her.

He lowered his mouth and said quietly, "That was pretty impressive."

She looked up, unprepared for the heat in his gaze. "We're quite the team."

"Busting up small-town homophobia one mom at a time."

"Hey," Jamie called out. Bee tore her eyes away from Denny in time to catch the group's all-knowing stares.

"Yes, darling?" She slid into the booth and leaned into Jamie, nuzzling his chin as Denny sat down beside her. Maybe she could convince Jamie and Abe to move to Pine Ridge with her. Maybe they could all open a nightclub/interior design business that offered youth counseling on the side. Maybe she could have everything that made her happy all in one perfect little package.

And maybe Mom and Dad will take a vow of poverty and donate all their money to struggling families.

"I have so much tea about Gerald," Jamie said. "I don't want to bore everyone else with it, but maybe tomorrow we can go for coffee and I'll fill you in?"

"Oh God," she swooned. "A proper gossip session? Man, I've missed you."

"Pine Ridge gossip is kinda different, huh?" Sydney said.

"Maybe not quite as juicy." Jamie winked. "Don't you miss it, Syd?"

Sydney shook her head, grinning across the table at her husband. When Syd and Sam locked eyes, anyone in the room could see neither regretted their choice for a second.

"Nah," Sydney said. "Living in New York felt like being high all the time. When you sober up, you realize there are a lot of little things in life that can make you feel the same way. And they're real."

"Good grief," Jared groaned. "I think I'm gonna throw up."

"You're full of shit," Sam quipped. "I saw the wedding

vows you wrote for Mila. Even Hallmark would call them sappy. And we all know the second she texts you she's done at work, you're gonna disappear."

Jared's face twisted in a forced display of indifference, but Bee had seen enough of him and Mila together to know how he really felt. He'd have moved heaven and earth for his future wife.

"Damn," Jamie said, raising his arched brows. "This place really sucked you all in, huh?"

Beside Bee, Denny shifted, energy radiating off him like a live wire.

"Good thing you don't have a drag scene here," Jamie said. He wrapped an arm around Bee and pulled her tight. "Or a nightclub. Or a salon. Or a yoga studio. Or a Gucci . . ."

"Oh, please," Sydney said. "Bee doesn't need all that."

Bee's old life flashed before her eyes, a barrage of glitter and high heels and beautiful people and complicated relationships. A tiny part of her ached for it, and just as soon as the nostalgia set in, Denny's big, strong hand crept across her thigh and squeezed.

Her heart crumbled. Jamie gripped her on one side, Denny held her on the other.

As the night progressed, and the group enjoyed the drinks and the company, Bee sank further into her feelings. She couldn't stop her hands from reaching for Denny. She needed to feel him, needed to know that she hadn't created him in her mind.

As the bartender announced last call, they paid their tab and left the bar, friends splitting off and waving goodbye. Jamie kissed Bee's cheek before promising to scoop her the following morning on his way into town from Indigo Hotels Adirondack Park.

Denny drove Bee home in silence, every few minutes one of them stealing a glance at the other. The three drinks she'd had at the bar warmed her skin and turned her body to liquid. If she'd had to decide in that moment whether or not to leave Pine Ridge—in a darkened cab cruising over mountain roads with Denny's intoxicating cologne lulling her to pure bliss—she'd have changed her address in a moment. It all seemed so simple.

They pulled into his driveway, and he opened the door for her, helping her down and inside the house. She trudged immediately up the stairs, desperate to strip off her clothes and get into bed with him.

By the time he joined her in the master bedroom, she'd peeled off her jeans and blouse, standing half-naked next to his bed. He stood for a moment just inside the doorframe, one side of his mouth pulling into a grin.

"Hi," she said.

"Hi." He stood still. Waiting.

"Are you okay?"

"I'm great." The smile remained. He blinked. Crossed his arms over his chest.

"Well, then, what are you standing there for?" she said.

His face broke into a wide smile, deep laughter coming from his throat. He finally moved into the bedroom, the low lamplight bathing his face in golden tones. She ran her hands across his firm pecs and over his shoulders, draping herself against him as he placed light fingers on her waist.

"You're drunk, baby."

Baby. Just set me on fire, why don't you.

"I'm not drunk," she said.

"Liar." The amused grin still played on his lips. "I don't mind. But I don't want to have sex like this."

"Oh, come *on*," she groaned. "I'm not blackout. I just feel kinda loose."

"Yeah, trust me," he said. "It's not easy to say no to you."

"Then don't." She pressed up onto her toes, brushing her mouth against his. He returned the kiss with a chaste press of his lips. She exhaled, realizing she wasn't going to get much further.

"Let me get you some water," he said. "I'll be right back."

She slipped into bed, breathing in the faint scent of his cologne on the sheets. The room faded to black as he re-appeared next to the bed with a full glass of water.

"It's here if you want it," he said. He brushed her hair back from her brow and gazed into her eyes.

"You're the best person I've ever met," she said.

The amusement faded from his face. "Oh yeah?"

"Yeah." The liquor boosted her confidence. The moment hung heavy with truth, and she had to let it out. "Sometimes I get nervous that I'll never meet anyone better than you. And how could I live with myself if I left here knowing deep down that you're as good as it gets? And that I chose not to stay?"

His brow turned rigid, his hand falling from her temple.

"Shit," she said. "That came out wrong."

"This isn't something you have to decide right now."

"Yeah, but when? I want to stay here, Denny. But like, how could that work?" Tears welled up in her eyes. "Shit. Sorry. I'm not crying. Maybe I did have too much to drink."

"Tequila shots will do that to you."

Her chin quivered as she stared back at him, attempting to will away the seriousness on his face. "Your parents come next week," she said. "And then what?"

He took a long, deep breath. "I don't know."

"What if I stayed?"

"I don't know."

She turned her face into the pillow, letting the cool, smooth fabric soothe her burning cheeks. When she looked back at him, his face remained stony.

"Well, what *do* you know?" she said.

"I know we should table this conversation until tomorrow." He stood up straight. "Just go to sleep, all right? I'll be back in a minute."

"Wait." Her strangled voice stopped him short, and he

turned to gaze at her with loving eyes. "Where are you going?"

"I'm gonna lock the front door and turn out the lights. That okay with you?" He winked, and her entire being lit on fire, incinerated from the toes up.

"Oh," she said. "Okay."

She watched his form move toward the door, his shoulder flexing as he reached for the light switch and flipped it off. He glanced at her once more, paused, and walked out.

How long have you known him?" Jamie asked, sipping his coffee. A tiny blond waitress Bee had never seen before stopped at their table to refill their mugs.

"Where's Mila?" Bee asked the waitress. The young woman shrugged and snapped her gum.

"I dunno. She's been working at the hotel more these days, so Benny cut her hours way down."

Nothing felt right this morning. From Bee's throbbing head to the overcast, drizzly weather to the lack of friendly faces at the Black Bear Diner. She wanted to show Jamie the beauty of Pine Ridge, but it seemed the picturesque town had taken a sick day.

The waitress vacated their table, and Jamie repeated his question.

"Almost two months?" Bee said. "That weekend I came up here to visit?"

"Gosh, that's right." He stole a strip of bacon from Bee's untouched plate. "Feels like a hundred years ago. The city sucks without you."

"I spoke to Abe last week," she said. "He said you two have never been better."

"That has nothing to do with you being gone." He paused with the bacon halfway to his mouth. "You think you love him?"

"Jesus, I don't know. It's barely been two months. How could I love him?"

The question had plagued her for days. It wasn't a question of *if*. It was a matter of figuring out what to do about it. Denny had upended all of her plans, thrown everything she thought she knew into chaos. She'd pulled up an airline website the week before but couldn't pull the trigger on a flight to London, finding every excuse under the sun why she shouldn't go quite yet.

"You know you fall fast and hard," Jamie said. "Who was it you were using the l-word with after three dates?"

She grimaced. "Simon. He was *so* perfect in the beginning."

"Such a classic story," he said. He sipped his coffee with a loud, purposeful slurp. "He's exactly who you want him to be until he starts actually being himself."

Simon was the first serious relationship Bee had in the city. She hadn't seen any of the red flags until it was too late.

"I think Denny is exactly who he claims to be," she said. "He's himself whether you like it or not. I just . . . I do this all the time. You know that. I'm overlooking something. I *have* to be."

"Did I ever tell you about how Abe and I met?" Jamie said, tearing a bite of bacon from the strip and tossing the rest back on Bee's plate. "Ugh, I can't eat that. Don't let me."

She tossed a paper napkin over her plate, the sight of the food turning her stomach. Her hangover required greasy Chinese food and a cold, light beer.

And an orgasm. Denny had left the bed before her that morning, disappearing into his gym. The thought of a solo orgasm depressed her.

"I know how you met," she said. "I was there, remember? Ambrosia's first appearance at Club Trade."

"Oh, no." Jamie leaned back in the booth, and his lips

curled into a devious smile. "That was the second time we met. The time we pretended like we hadn't *already* met."

"Okay, enough with the teasers." She sipped her ice water. "Give me the story."

"We met at the Jock." He raised one eyebrow. No embellishment necessary.

"You did not."

"We did. I was there with a couple of friends, he was there with a couple of friends, neither of us really wanted to be there, and *bing bang*—literally—*boom*, we're having sex in the corner."

"Wow," Bee said. She couldn't wipe the smile from her face. "Good for you. I didn't think you were really into that whole scene."

"I'm not!" His heavily lashed eyes flew open. "You've known me since I was eighteen. Even when I was a kid, I didn't really do that. Casual sex is one thing. The Jock at four in the morning is another."

"So, what happened?"

"He asked for my phone number, I gave him a fake, and then two weeks later, who shows up to Club Trade in full drag talking about *When's my spot*?"

"Oh my God," she said laughing. "I remember you two didn't hit it off right away, but I didn't know that was why."

He lowered his chin and folded his hands on the table. "I was at a place in my life where I couldn't imagine dating someone I'd hooked up with at a club. It wasn't gonna be my story. I thought it would define us. I thought it would define *me*."

"Who among our group of friends would've blinked if you'd told them where you really met?" She raised one accusatory eyebrow and shoved a loose strand of hair into her mess of a bun.

"No one," he said. "It wasn't about other people. It was what I told myself I needed."

She clenched her teeth and tried, unsuccessfully, to avoid his pointed stare.

"Babe." He closed his hand around hers. "You've got the biggest heart. Which means you've been walked on a *bunch*. I see you trying to put your guard up and put yourself first. But just because you decided what that should look like doesn't mean anyone's gonna hold you to it."

She breathed deep and glanced out the window. Denny's big SUV was parked outside the hardware store. He'd been talking about refinishing the dock himself. He really loved that house. Without realizing, she'd fallen in love with it, too.

"It's not about appearances," she said. "I'm scared. What if he's just like everyone else I've ever been with? What if I'm just repeating patterns? I took a break from the club scene. I made one step in the direction of changing things for myself. I'm on the road to a completely different life. I can't backtrack now."

Jamie held his hands up in front of him. "I want you to do whatever makes you happy. I, personally, could never move to a tiny town in the mountains. That said, if a giant hunk of man meat like Denny Torres was waiting for me in that tiny mountain town, the odds would look a little better."

Bee cracked a smile, pressing her fingers against her forehead as the hangover headache thumped loudly against her temples. "God, Jamie, he's so freaking sexy."

"He seems like a really good guy, too."

"He's the best guy," she said. She glanced out the window again as the man himself exited the hardware store, four cans of paint dangling from his deft, capable hands. He loaded the paint into his back seat and turned toward the diner, grinning when he saw her.

She raised a hand and waggled her fingers. An ache in her chest radiated through her limbs as he waved back and climbed into his SUV before driving away.

"And no red flags?" Jamie said.

A single laugh escaped her. "Of course there are red flags. He's a guy, isn't he? He's impulsive and bold. And he's never been in love before."

"Ah," Jamie said with a grin. "Now I know why you like him."

"Exactly." She laughed, tearing tiny pieces from her napkin.

"But he's been reliable, right?"

She ignored Denny's sojourn into the mountains alone. And even then, he'd simply apologized to her and admitted he could've done things differently. Denny was different. He did everything she'd always wanted a man to do.

It terrified her.

"Yeah," she said. "Very reliable. Honest. He's unabashedly himself."

"Maybe you're looking to retire Mama Bee." She should've known Jamie would flesh it all out. He always zeroed in on the real issue, digging into it like a cavity. "Maybe you finally met someone who fills that space in your life and it's scaring the shit out of you."

Her fingers froze mid-tear and she looked up at him. Her best friend. The caring, considerate brother she'd always wanted. The person who knew her better than anyone and yet let her be herself—whatever form that took.

"Maybe," she said.

"I think being Isaac Jones's sister messed you up more than you care to admit," he said. The mention of her brother's name squeezed her chest. "He took a lot from you, and I think you've been trying to correct that piece of your past with the men in your life. But you're learning, Bee. You're getting to a better place. I see you."

She slid her hand along his, gripping his fingers tightly. "You're in the wrong business. You should've been a psychologist."

"Baby, I'm a bartender." He winked. "Same thing."

chapter **eighteen**

Seven oh two. Flight 330 on Delta by way of Hawaiian Airlines had landed exactly one hour earlier, meaning Rosa and Ernie Torres were en route to Pine Ridge as the sun peeked over the tree line and turned Denny's typically calm demeanor to ash. He'd been awake for hours.

"Baby." He whispered against the warmth of Bee's neck, allowing his lips to brush the soft skin under her ear. "It's seven o'clock."

She grunted into the pillow, burrowing further under the covers. The day before, she'd moved all her belongings from the main house to the guesthouse, agreeing that it wasn't the best moment to explain to his parents what was happening between them.

Denny had suggested it, but Bee had nodded along. If they couldn't even explain it to each other, how would they explain it to his parents?

Every day, Denny had to force his brain into relaxed mode. He couldn't make her mind up for her, couldn't coax her into staying just a few more weeks. Or maybe months. A year, at best. But she hadn't booked her flight out of town yet. She hadn't returned to New York. That was something.

"Five more minutes," she said. Her eyes remained tightly closed. He couldn't blame her for wanting sleep. They'd stayed up until two in the morning, taking turns making each other come. Despite all his time in the gym, that morning he woke up sore.

He patted her butt and jogged down into the kitchen. He checked the refrigerator for the fifth time that morning, surveying the eggs, milk, fruit, and other grocery items that said *A responsible adult lives here.* He'd left four cans of Coors Light in the door and moved the rest to the basement. A bottle of Rosa's favorite sweet white wine had replaced them.

"You want me to make coffee?" Bee shuffled into the kitchen, her eyes still half-closed. Her shorts rode high on her butt cheeks, exposing the lion heads on her thigh. She ran a casual hand over her tangle of loose blond hair and yawned as she reached over the counter for the coffee grounds.

All at once, his entire body flooded with emotion, the mere sight of her puttering around his kitchen like she belonged there—because she *did*—summoned the words he'd been tending for two weeks and forced them from his lips.

"I love you."

She spun around, her eyes wide as saucers as the glass canister slipped from her hands and shattered against the polished hardwood floor.

"Shit," she muttered, staring down at her bare feet. Shards of clear glass and chocolate-brown coffee grounds spread out in every direction.

"Just stay there." He hurried to the pantry and retrieved the broom and dustpan, dropping to the floor to start sweeping. Neither of them spoke a word as he carefully brushed glass and coffee away from her and deposited the remnants into the trash.

When he'd cleaned most of it up, he returned to where she stood, wide-eyed and silent with lips parted, and hooked an arm around her thighs.

She released a tiny yelp of surprise as he lifted her over his shoulder, away from the mess, and into the living room. He lowered her down, avoided her gaze, and returned to the kitchen. He'd rather have picked up the last glass shards with his teeth than discuss her reaction.

He wet a paper towel and wiped up the tiniest bits as she crept back into the kitchen. His stomach twisted, his already-frayed nerves charged up into overdrive.

"Denny." Her throaty voice hummed through the kitchen. The kitchen she'd decorated. The home she'd created for him.

"I'm not taking it back," he said. He tossed the paper towel into the trash, tied off the garbage bag, and carried the whole thing into the garage where a larger bin waited. By the time he returned, her face pinched, and she balanced on one foot, the other tucked up in an awkward yoga pose.

"I don't want you to take it back," she said. "I just wanted to . . . apologize for my reaction. You caught me off guard."

He wet his lips, taking her all in. She didn't want him to take it back. But she hadn't returned the sentiment, either.

"Today is about your parents coming," she said. "Let's just focus on one thing at a time. Okay?"

He stepped toward her, gingerly, cautiously. Her shoulders dropped as he approached. "Sure. If that's what you want to do."

She pursed her lips, the tiny dimples on either side of her mouth appearing. "I don't want to complicate things. You know?"

"No, I don't." With steady hands, he cupped her jaw. "I love you. It's not complicated. I don't care if my parents are coming or if you decide to go to London tomorrow. It's just how I feel. I wanted to say it out loud. In case you were wondering."

A wrinkle of worry creased her brow, and he placed a kiss there.

"I'm not ready to say it back," she whispered.

"That's okay." The stabbing sensation in his chest begged otherwise, but he kept that bit to himself. "I didn't mean to scare you."

She held tightly to his wrists and stretched toward him, pressing her pillowy lips to his. "I'm gonna get out of here, okay? Whenever you want me to meet your parents, just let me know."

"Sure. And you're still coming with us to the bonfire tonight, right? At Coach Parker's?" Bringing his parents along was a gamble, but confidence about his place in life surged inside. He hoped it spilled out and convinced them he was on the right path.

"Yeah," she said. "Definitely."

Bee slipped into shoes and headed out, leaving him alone in the fully transformed house. He gazed around at all the special touches she'd added; the architectural light fixtures, the layered frames on the mantel, the family photos from his younger days perched atop a carved wood tripod side table.

Every piece spoke to him. And every piece said *Bee*.

At eight fifteen, as he stared out the front window, a shiny blue rental sedan cruised up his uneven driveway. The nerves popping in his stomach turned to flapping birds as he hurried outside to greet them.

"Hey, boy!" His father climbed out of the driver's seat, rising to his full five-foot-eight height and sending a wide smile at his son. Denny crossed the ten feet separating them with a few long strides and crushed his father in a hug.

"Man, it's good to see you," he said.

His father pulled back, beaming up at Denny.

"So good to see you." Ernie's eyes brimmed with tears. "It's been too long." It was all the emotion Denny would get out of him, but it was enough.

"Ma." Denny hurried to the passenger side to help his mother out. She grabbed his hand with her tiny one, and he all but yanked her clear out of the car. When Bee found his old family photos, she busted up laughing at Denny towering over the rest of his family. One member of each generation grew to Denny's height, the native Hawaiian genes strong in a handful of Torreses.

"Oh, Denny," Rosa cooed, reaching for his neck. She hugged him to her chest, always treating him like a little boy. He drowned in a cloud of her floral perfume and sank into the familiarity of her arms. Despite his complicated relationship with his parents, having them in his home felt like the last puzzle piece snapping into place.

"You need a haircut," Ernie quipped. "No barbers around here?"

"I like it like this," Denny said. He stood up straight and ran a hand through his hair. He couldn't have cared less about his hair, had actually meant to get a trim just before Bee arrived, but the way her fingers trailed through it, tugging and caressing the strands, he definitely wouldn't part with it now.

Denny helped his parents with their bags, struggling with the massive, unwieldy suitcases. "Jesus," Denny grumbled, "What did you pack? You're only traveling for ten days."

Ernie and Rosa planned to spend three days with Denny before driving to the coast of Maine to spend the rest of their East Coast trip with Rosa's cousins in Portland. Denny loved his parents, but he'd be glad to send them off before they started rearranging his kitchen cabinets and complaining about the cold.

"You know your mother." Ernie rolled his sable-colored eyes. All the Torres kids had Ernie's animated eyes, and more than one ex-girlfriend had told Denny looking at his father was like looking into the future.

"If you brought towels," Denny said. "You'll be sleeping outside on the deck."

Rosa laughed, pressed a hand to the cluster of gold chains at her throat. "Wait until you see what I brought you. You'll want me staying in the presidential suite. No, no, don't take those up yet. Some of it has to go into the refrigerator."

Denny lowered the suitcases to the ground and watched in wonder as his mother unpacked. First came the double Saran-wrapped Tupperware packed in dry ice.

"Lomi lomi salmon," she explained. "Put that in the fridge."

Denny accepted the Tupperware with wide eyes. "You brought lomi lomi salmon all the way from Hawaii?"

"Of course she did," Ernie said. He folded his arms across his gray polo shirt and adjusted his baseball cap. Always ready for golf, no matter the place, no matter the time. Maybe before his parents left town Denny could take him to a local course. It had been years since they'd played together.

"And lumpia," Rosa said. She lifted a foil-covered, Saran-wrapped package from another box of dry ice and held it up to Denny with a glowing smile on her red-painted lips. "I didn't know if I'd be able to find the good wrappers here, so it was easier to make them and bring them along. Put those in the freezer."

"Ma," Denny said, "You didn't have to do this."

She tossed a hand at him and tucked away the layers of plastic she'd used to wrap everything. "I'm sure you don't eat well here."

The joy leaked out of Denny like air from a punctured tire. In a moment, he was a kid again being scolded by his mommy. She'd brought food because she assumed he survived on ramen noodles and beer. A helpless little boy, forever more.

After the last of the perishables made its way to the kitchen, Denny carried his parents' bags upstairs to the guest room. As he stepped past the doorframe, the hair on his arms stood on end. Bee's scent still hung heavy in the air, the spicy perfume infusing the room.

"Ooh, it smells nice in here," his mother said.

Denny shook the lust from his veins and set the suitcases down in one corner of the room. "This is it. You like it?"

Bee had taken his tacky log cabin bed idea and transformed it. The room soothed in shades of charcoal and barn red, plaid throws and overstuffed, sky-gray pillows welcoming guests and begging them to sink into the plush richness of the fabrics. On the walls, she hung folk-style paintings from local artists, and a reclaimed wood bed frame tied it all together.

Ernie and Rosa glanced around the room, his mother's chin tightened in an unreadable expression. "It's nice. Dark, no?"

The *whoosh* of disappointment flooded Denny's chest. Thank God Bee wasn't around to hear the room called "dark." She'd made every effort to lighten the place up while keeping the cozy atmosphere alive.

"It's overcast today," Denny said. "Maybe that's why it feels dark. Let me show you the rest of the house."

He led them downstairs, starting with the basement gym to get the boring stuff out of the way, and ending in the living room. He felt like a used-car salesman, gushing over windows and high ceilings, lamps and rugs and color schemes. The tighter his parents' expressions, the more desperate he became.

By the time they toured the office, a thin sheen of sweat covered his upper lip.

"Isn't that chandelier cool?" He gestured over his head where the massive deer antler light fixture hung. "Bee found it at an antiques store in Vermont."

Rosa placed her hands on her hips as her narrow gaze settled on Denny. "You like this girl?"

Denny's heart slammed against his ribs. "Huh?"

"That's about the hundredth time you've said her name

since we got here," Rosa said. "Seems like maybe you like her. As more than a decorator, I mean."

"Yeah, no. I mean, she's cool."

Ernie shot a half grin at Rosa.

"I'm not sixteen, you know," Denny said. "I'm not asking her to the prom."

Rosa rolled her eyes and tugged at the gold cross around her neck. "Always so defensive."

Denny gritted his teeth. How to explain that he became defensive when he was attacked? His parents were the king and queen of subtle digs. So subtle, in fact, it was nearly impossible to call them on it.

"She doesn't live in Pine Ridge," he said. "She's from New York City, and she's just here to help me decorate. You'll meet her tonight. She's cool."

"With all this build up," Ernie said, "She better be *cool*."

His father's grin stretched into a wide smile, his full set of teeth shining in the light of the chandelier.

"Both of you," Rosa said, tossing a hand at her husband and son. "Such clowns."

Denny made coffee from a bag of reserves in the freezer before his parents retired to the guest room to nap. With a few minutes to himself, he crossed the lawn to the guest cabin. Only after he knocked did he consider Bee might want some space from him.

The front door creaked open a moment later. Bee tightened a towel around her chest, her face wide and open and smiling.

"How'd it go?" she said.

His gut twisted. He promised himself it was the only lie he'd ever tell her. "They loved it."

Her shoulders rose, the smile stretching wider. "Come in."

He stepped inside, shutting the door behind him, and breathed in the dewy air rich with the scent of her honey bodywash. The smell stirred up desire in his veins.

Before he could think twice, he slipped a finger underneath the towel at her chest and tugged until it fell at her feet. Her soft, shimmery body, still damp from the shower, stood before him like a heavenly vision. One of those golden-hued paintings of an angel sent from God.

"I can't stay," he said. He knew his parents too well. They'd nap for half an hour and then start roaming the house in search of things to tidy, inquire about, or fix.

"Just came for a quick creep?" She closed the space between them, pressing herself against his chest and wrapping her arms around his waist. His dick stood at attention.

Did he have time? Not for all the things he wanted to do with her.

"I actually came to tell you we'll leave at six tonight," he said. "Seeing you naked is an added bonus."

He closed his arms around her shoulders, gazing down at the dangerous curves of her hips and ass. If he wasn't going to see the moment through, he had to get out now.

"All right." He cleared his throat and peeled her arms off of him. "I gotta go. It's been a while since I had to hide a hard-on from my parents, and I'm not really trying to relive those days."

A sly smile crossed her lips. "I'm so glad they like the house."

Ah yes. His lie. That was one way to kill an erection. "You really nailed it."

"I'll be ready by six," she said. "Can't wait to meet them."

Denny turned and exited the guest cabin with his heart in his throat.

chapter **nineteen**

Denny's SUV bumped over the uneven roads leading to Coach Parker's cabin on Tupper Lake, and Bee had to physically will her muscles to relax. Rosa Torres sat next to Bee in the back seat, her floral dress pressed within an inch of its life and her curls set to match. She'd nodded hello at Bee when Denny introduced them, and beyond that, had ignored her completely.

Five more minutes, and she'd be able to disappear into the crowd at Coach Parker's. Allison promised she'd be there. Jamie headed out of town that morning, despite Bee's pleas to get him to stay longer. He made her circle in Pine Ridge complete, rounding out her group of new friends with just a dash of New York.

Denny's car careened around a bend in the road, and a cabin appeared in front of them flanked by folding tables covered in food and a roaring bonfire at the edge of a small, pristine lake. Crowds of people already congregated around the fire, drinks in hand, and a few kids tossed a football in the expanse of green lawn just beyond the smoking grill.

"We didn't bring anything!" Rosa gasped, clutching a fist to her chest.

"Yes, we did," Denny said calmly. "There's a case of beer in the trunk, and Bee got cookies."

Rosa exhaled loudly. Bee hadn't known what to expect from Denny when it came to his parents. He acted like a big kid most of the time, but around his parents he became subdued, passive in a way she hadn't seen from him yet.

Denny let his parents out of the car as close as he could get to the party, and Bee accompanied them while he parked down the street.

"Doesn't it smell amazing here?" Bee said, breathing deep as the scent of pine filled her lungs. "I still can't get over it."

Rosa sniffed, her nose wrinkling as if she'd stepped inside a fish market. "As long as you don't have allergies, I guess."

Ernie offered Bee a tight-lipped smile but remained mute. Bee remembered her first week in Pine Ridge, when she and Denny browsed at the Adirondack home store. The salesman at the store would be dead-on assuming who wore the pants in the Torreses' marriage.

Denny approached, balancing the case of beer on one shoulder and holding the boxes of McDonagh's chocolate chip cookies under his arm. Bee hurried to relieve him of one burden.

"Give me that," she said. She grabbed the bakery boxes and held his gaze for a moment, the intimacy of one quick look setting her body ablaze. She didn't know how she'd stay away from him at the party, but she knew she had to try.

They joined the other guests, Denny introducing his parents around to the coaching staff and some of the kids.

Bee gave them space, finding Allison near a huge cooler filled with ice and drinks. She wanted Denny to introduce her around with the same beaming look of pride he held for his parents.

Her heart sank as she watched them. What would he introduce her as? His decorator?

Maybe.

"You're not driving, right?" Allison said, handing her an icy can of Adirondack Brewery's IPA.

"I don't even know if I'm going home with them," she said bitterly. She cracked the can and took a drink.

"What does that mean?" Allison tucked an arm across her chest as they both watched Rosa and Ernie shake Coach Parker's hand. "They don't know you're together?"

Bee huffed a laugh. "*I* don't even know we're together."

Allison's chin dropped, a wry smile on her lips. "Sorry to tell you, but the whole town knows how he feels about you. If *you* don't, then I don't know what to tell you."

"It's complicated." Bee tipped the can up, swallowing another drink. "Hey, I read that book you recommended. *Prom Queen*? I inhaled it in one night. It's so freaking good."

Allison lit up as she launched into a list of all the things she loved about the YA sci-fi romance novel, and as she gushed, Bee kept one eye on Denny and his parents.

He set them up at a picnic table with drinks and plates of food, and a few of the football parents joined them in conversation. Denny clapped a hand on his father's shoulder, his mouth forming the words, "You need anything?" before Ernie raised a hand shooing him away.

Even from across the lawn, with dozens of people between them, Denny looked up and found her in an instant. He raked a hand through his hair, letting his smoldering gaze linger on her.

She couldn't fight it anymore. The words bloomed in her chest like roses in the sun, and before she could shut them down, they soundlessly passed her lips. Allison turned away, reaching for another drink, as Bee mouthed, *I love you.*

His sharp cheekbones lifted as his mouth formed a half grin of disbelief.

"Wow," Allison said. Her voice crashed through the moment, and she patted Bee's hand with a smirk. "Good luck hiding all that from his parents."

As Allison walked away, Denny crossed the lawn. In the time it took Bee to take another drink from her beer, he approached. He stood too close to keep their relationship a secret, but the dopey smile on his face told her he didn't care.

"Can I talk to you for a second?" He brushed her hip, his fingers hooking into a belt loop.

"Denny, hi!" Two enthusiastic football parents decked head to toe in Pine Ridge High colors hurried toward Denny wearing wide smiles and dragging their teenaged son behind them.

"Shit," Denny muttered. He turned his fiery gaze on Bee, stopping her breath in her throat. "I'm not done with you."

She bit back a smile. "You better not be."

Early evening blurred into night, and soon the bonfire replaced the sun, lighting up the faces of the dozens of people in attendance. Coach Parker welcomed the players, staff, and families, and told everyone to please eat their fill and enjoy his home.

Bee fell into easy conversation with the parents of a few of the kids she'd met at the book club, even chatting amiably with Jen Cody after her son had practically forced them to say hello to each other. When Bee noticed Ernie and Rosa alone at their picnic table, she made her way over.

"I was just about to grab myself a beer," she said. "Can I get you two anything?"

"I'll take another Coors Light, if they have it," Ernie said.

Bee grinned, happy for a task. She retrieved the drinks and sat down opposite them at the picnic table.

"Are you comfortable in the guest room?" Bee asked. The fire warmed her back and lit Rosa's and Ernie's faces with dancing orange light. She saw bits of Denny in both of them. Ernie's eyes and Rosa's nose. Even with Denny clear across the party, she felt like he was there with her.

"Sure," Rosa said. "We don't need much."

Bee brushed off the subtle dig. "Denny was really adamant about making sure you both felt at home there. He had you in mind when we designed it."

Rosa's penciled eyebrows lifted into her forehead, her lips pursing. "I don't know why he'd spend so much time and money on a house up here. Or why he'd get involved with some kids knowing he can't really commit."

In Rosa's words Bee heard her own mother's digs. *You'll never get back what you think you're giving to these kids, Bethany. There's giving back, and then there's wasting your time.*

Bee steeled herself. "I don't want to speak for him, but I think he likes it up here."

Rosa grimaced again. "Sure, but what will he *do* up here? Work at the local diner? Become a teacher?"

Bee bit back all the retorts hot on her tongue. Pine Ridge subsisted on the hard work of all the diner workers, teachers, and others with careers deemed less admirable by people like Rosa Torres. Bee had never met such kind, noble people.

"I don't think he's made a plan yet," Bee said. "But the kids on the team love him so much. If he did decide to coach or become a teacher, I think he'd be really good at it."

"Hey." Denny slid next to her at the picnic table, sipping at a beer.

"We were just talking about how great it is that you're working with the football team," Bee said. "And I was telling your parents that if you did decide to work with kids as a career, that it would be a really great fit for you."

Denny licked his lips, his wide eyes darting from his parents to Bee and back. A deer in oncoming traffic. "I haven't made any decisions yet."

Bee's gaze narrowed. "What?"

"I mean, who knows what I'll end up doing?" Denny said. "I could get into broadcasting or work for the coaching staff of an NFL team."

"Any front office would be lucky to have you," Ernie said. His father nodded as if that settled everything.

Bee stared unflinchingly at Denny, waiting for an explanation. Broadcasting? Coaching for a pro team? She'd never heard either of those plans pass his lips. And neither of them kept him in Pine Ridge. Just when her own visions of life in Pine Ridge were beginning to take shape.

"Will you excuse me?" Bee's voice squeaked past her lips.

"Hey, wait . . ." Denny grabbed her hand but she shook him off. When she looked down, the pleading on his face almost made her stay.

Almost.

"I'll just let you talk to your parents," she said. Her throat dried up. He was leaving after all. He'd go where the offers took him, impulsive and hasty in all the ways she'd been afraid of.

Another hour passed, and as the crowd at Coach Parker's thinned out, Denny found Bee chatting with Allison and told her they were heading out. He tried to squeeze her hand, but she pulled away.

She didn't really know him at all. She only knew Pine Ridge Denny, the Denny who hid away in a big house in the mountains to escape his problems. And he only knew that tiny piece of her. They'd brushed up against each other as each of them took a different path, meandering around on their way to somewhere else.

Denny, Bee, and his parents drove silently back to his house, the low, tinny sounds of adult contemporary radio filling the car. Bee stared out the window, her eyes glazing over as the dark forest blurred in front of her.

They pulled into Denny's driveway. He cut the engine, and Rosa and Ernie wished Bee a good night without looking at her before disappearing inside.

"I'm coming over in fifteen minutes," Denny said. He lowered his chin, but the intimacy of his posture felt off somehow. Inauthentic. Like she'd seen the truth of his plans and his future, and they didn't match up with what he'd told her all along.

"I'm gonna go to bed." She cast her eyes at the driveway, hugging her jacket tighter around her body. Stupid mountain coat. She never should've purchased something she wouldn't wear in London. She'd book her ticket tonight and figure out the rest of the logistics later.

"Well, I want to talk," he said.

She gritted her teeth. Whatever she decided to do with her life, it couldn't be about him.

Without responding, she left him in the driveway, closing the guest cabin door behind her. She glanced around at the tiny space she'd barely inhabited, wishing against her better judgment that she could climb the main house stairs to his bedroom and burrow beneath the expensive sheets as his big, warm body cocooned around her.

She retrieved her laptop from where she'd left it on the nightstand and pulled up a discount travel website. Her fingers trembled as she typed.

JFK to Heathrow.

She rubbed her lips together. Which date should she choose? Denny's house was finished. The book club didn't meet for another month, and she couldn't stay that long. If she stayed another month, she'd lose her nerve and stay forever. And then what? Hunker down in Pine Ridge until Denny decided he couldn't be caged in any longer and disappeared to Vegas or LA or someplace else where bars stayed open past nine?

One week. She'd give herself seven days to tie up loose ends, plan out the book club with Sydney and Allison, and put her heart on hold.

A quiet knock interrupted her planning. She opened the front door, and light from the driveway spilled across the floor.

"Can I come in?" His dark hair fell over his forehead, and she fought the urge to brush it back. In the past four hours, he'd changed. She finally, truly saw him amid the backdrop of his whole world; beyond the bubble of the sleepy little town she'd found him in.

"Of course," she said. "It's your house."

He glared until she stepped aside, letting him into her space. She closed the door, shutting out the light, and waited for her eyes to adjust to the gently moonlit space.

He stood for too long facing away from her, his posture rigid and tense. Was he waiting for her to touch him? To force him to look at her?

And then she saw it. The computer. Open to the confirmation of her plane ticket purchase.

A steady, whistling exhale filled the space and froze her heart.

"You're really going," he said.

"Yeah."

He turned slowly, his eyebrows pinched. "Because of tonight? I don't really have plans to go into broadcasting, Bee. I mean, if the opportunity came up I guess I wouldn't immediately turn it down, but it's not what I really want. I just said that to get them off my back."

Did he hear himself? When she needed absolutes, he gave her noncommittals. When she needed assurances, he gave her questions. Why should she change the course of her own life for someone who kept changing his mind?

"It's not because of tonight."

A frustrated sigh passed his lips. "Then I don't get it."

"We both knew this was temporary," she said. The words had as much impact as cheap bodega coffee. "The project is over. The house is decorated."

As he dropped his chin, his eyes darkened. "You said you *loved* me."

You loved me. She'd never chosen it before, and she wasn't choosing it now. It had simply found her, sought her out like a heat-seeking missile. But she wouldn't let him know that. He'd refuse to let her leave under those circumstances.

"And you said your feelings were the same if I got on a plane or not," she said. "Remember?"

"Well, I lied."

The moment stretched between them, as fragile as a spiderweb and just as intricate. "You lied?"

His jaw ticked, and he crossed his arms over his chest. "I don't want you to leave. My feelings don't evaporate the moment you get on that plane, but I thought . . ."

He didn't need to voice the words. She knew. Denny willed things to happen, said them out loud to send the ideas off into the universe so that they might materialize. If he told her he loved her, she'd stay. Simple as that.

But there were two people in the relationship. And she got a say, too.

"Why are you doing this?" he said.

Her sinuses prickled as if she'd choked on ginger ale. "We've been through this."

"No." Slowly, he stepped closer. A soft breeze carried his warm cologne and nearly wrecked her. "I'm not asking why you feel like you need to get on a plane and go to London. That much I get. You want to go to London, let's go to London. I'm asking why you're leaving. Now."

She straightened her shoulders defiantly as scenes from Coach Parker's cookout came rushing back. One word from his parents and he turned back into the kid who didn't measure up. The kid who'd do anything for their approval.

"Why haven't you been honest with your parents?" she said. "If you really do want to settle down here and work with the kids and start a different kind of life, why haven't you said it? Out loud?"

He shoved his hands through his hair, nervous energy infiltrating the tiny space. "I just don't want to hear it from them."

"Hear what?"

"That this isn't real life." His eyes blazed. "That volunteering is a waste of time, and I can't spend the best years of my life holed up in some mountain town avoiding the hard shit. That only people who are avoiding something could ever be truly happy in a place like this."

A bitter smile settled on her lips. "Gosh, I didn't think I was gonna agree with your parents on anything."

"Yeah, well, you have that in common. You're both wrong."

"Or maybe we all see something you don't."

"I'm *here*, Bee." He pressed a hand to his chest. "It's been more than two years since I left the league. I bought a house in Pine Ridge. I'm not going anywhere. Maybe I've made some stupid decisions in my past, but this isn't one of them. I want to be here. So maybe I haven't voiced it yet because something in me still needs them to say I did good. So what?"

"Who else knows you've chosen this?" she said. "Your old teammates? Your high school coach you keep in touch with? I've never even heard you mention friends who don't live in Pine Ridge. How about your sister or your brothers? Have you told them you're settled up here?"

He breathed deep; his jaw ticked. "I want to establish a life here before I let anybody else in."

She barked out a laugh. His defiance only reinforced her

hypothesis. If he didn't openly commit to his life in Pine Ridge, it would be that much easier to abandon it.

"Two years," she said. "And you haven't even told anybody but your parents that you live here."

"I don't get it." He took a step closer. "Why don't you *want* to believe this?"

She paused, her T-shirt sliding slowly down her arm. A flicker of desire crossed his face as he caught her exposed shoulder. She yanked the shirt back up.

"I'm not choosing to believe anything," she said. "I've been through some shit. I've seen people's patterns. Even if you really think you're doing the right thing by living here, it's only a matter of time before you realize it's not sustainable. That it's not you."

He paused, his shadowy face darkening. "Because you know me so well."

"I do." Her eyes widened. "I know tons of people just like you. The Isaacs of the world, the reasons I need Jamie and Abe to stay at my apartment some nights. The impulsive, change-their-mind-every-ten-minutes, there's-something-better-around-every-corner type of guys. When this gets boring, where to next?"

His face pinched, and he dragged a hand across his eyes. When he looked back at her, resignation colored his stare. "You've had me pegged from the moment we met. Nothing I could've done would've changed your mind. Right?"

Her chin quivered, fear turning to adrenaline. She'd wanted him to be different.

Silence stretched between them.

"Nothing else to say, huh?" he said. Disappointment hung on every word. He dragged his teeth across his lower lip, teasing her with memories of what that mouth could do. "All right."

With one hand buried in his hair, he walked past her toward the door. Words clawed at her chest, begged her throat for release. *Please don't go, please don't go, please don't go.* But her teeth clamped shut.

He reached for the doorknob, and the words she knew she shouldn't say exploded from her throat.

"I don't want to lose you," she said. "Can't we . . . can we at least be friends?"

He turned, his expression tight, the corners of his eyes creased. "Friends?"

"Yeah." Her throat clogged with panic. "I'm not leaving for another week, and I don't want this to be the last time I see you. You know?"

His mouth hung open in an incredulous grin. "A week. You're not gonna be here for the housewarming?"

Shit. The housewarming party he'd been so excited for.

"I will be, but I fly out the next day. I'm not sure if I'll be able to make it. Packing and all that."

"That's a weird start to a friendship," he said.

She'd never heard him sound so bitter.

"I'm trying," she said. *Trying not to lose you completely.*

"I'll make sure you have a check before you leave."

As he opened the door, nausea spread through her stomach. She'd nearly forgotten about the job, the payment, the money she didn't want. The reason for all of it.

"Your parents didn't like the house, did they?" she said.

His lips worked, his gaze settling into neutral. "You know, it took me a while. But I finally realized it wasn't for them anyway."

chapter **twenty**

Denny yanked the golf clubs out of the trunk of his SUV. He'd liked to have spent another hour in his gym, but he knew no matter how much physical exertion he expended, nothing would relieve the anxiety flaring in his gut.

"That was a nice course," Ernie said.

Denny slammed the trunk closed and lugged the clubs into his garage. "Yeah. I'll go back for sure."

Denny thought that after playing eighteen holes, Ernie might want to have a beer. Talk with his son. Instead, he remained close-lipped for the duration and declined the drink, parroting platitudes that surely came from Rosa whenever Denny tried to broach the sensitive topics. Football. The future. Bee.

"Hope your mother didn't get too bored while we were gone," Ernie said, following Denny into the house.

"Oh, I'm sure she kept herself busy cleaning every inch of the house." He couldn't keep the sour tone from his voice. Since the night before, when he saw the ticket confirmation on Bee's computer, his whole world had turned gray.

"She's just trying to be helpful."

Denny shook his head, hoping his father didn't see. He shuffled into the kitchen, where Rosa stood at the sink, scrubbing the black marble countertop with a stiff bristled brush.

"Ma," he barked. "Leave it, will you?"

"Black countertops," she moaned, not slowing down for a second. "Who picked these? That decorator? I'd have done white in here."

Denny's chest flared. *That decorator.* "The countertops were here when I bought the house. Stop."

Rosa finally looked up, her cheeks pink with effort. "Excuse me. I thought you'd want to keep it clean since it's all new."

Denny worked his lips, physically trying to keep everything inside. Anger ripped at his chest, but he couldn't take it out on his parents. It wasn't their fault. It was his. If he'd been honest from the start, if he had owned his shit, none of this would've happened.

"I'm gonna take a shower," Denny said. "We'll leave around seven for dinner, yeah? There's this really good place in town called Three Daughters."

"Why so late?" Rosa said. "We should go earlier."

Denny exhaled loudly. "Fine. Six?"

Rosa grinned. If she suspected his frustration, she didn't show it. "Sounds good."

With a headache threatening, Denny trudged upstairs into his painfully quiet bedroom and cranked the handle in the shower. *That* shower. Their shower. He had yet to take a single rinse without remembering Bee perched on the shallow ledge, legs spread and mouth open, the lines and colors of her tattoos shimmering in the hot water.

He showered and toweled off, feeling dirtier than when he walked in. Just as he considered calling her, his cordless phone rang.

"Hello?"

"Where you been, bugga?" The forced, cartoon islander voice spread over Denny's skin like hot honey.

He beamed as he ran a hand over his wet hair. "Sorry, who is this?"

"Don't make me hop a flight and give you one false crack."

"You've been saying that since I was a kid," Denny said. "I'm starting to think you'll never make good on the threat."

Coach Maiava laughed, a deep, belly chuckle that rattled the line, before dropping the cartoon voice and slipping back into his own baritone. "You know me too well."

"Listen," Denny said, "I'm so sorry I haven't emailed you back. The truth is, your grandson looks just like you and I didn't know how to tell you without insulting his mom, yeah?"

Coach Maiava laughed again. "You want me to tell Sefina you said that?"

Denny had actually been slapped on the head by Mrs. Coach more than once. She made good on her promises. "Nah, I can't afford another concussion."

"How've you been, Denny?"

Where to begin? Bee plagued his thoughts from the second he laid his head down on the pillow, throughout his breakfast, his golf game, the drive home. But Coach M. didn't call to hear about his sad crush.

Instead, Denny filled him in on his work with the high school team. He told him about the drills, the playbook, their playoff chances, Coach Parker, and the kids who'd won him over no matter how much he resisted.

"I should've known you'd end up working with kids," Coach said. "Truth be told, I thought you'd be in the league until your fortieth birthday, but we've already talked that to death."

Denny bit his bottom lip. He didn't need to defend himself to Coach. They were too close for all that. "Working with this team," Denny said, "it's all the best parts of the game without all the bullshit."

"Eh," Coach grunted. "There's bullshit in high school play, too. You'll find that out soon enough."

"Maybe not." Denny didn't want to vocalize that he'd texted Jared that morning to ask how much he thought the house would sell for with all the interiors finished. Jared wrote back that he wouldn't even consider taking the listing.

"What does that mean?" Coach said.

Denny cleared his throat. "Nothing. How's your team this season?"

"Nuh-uh," Coach said. "Tell me what you meant. You know you can't pull that with me."

Denny lowered himself to seated, perching on the edge of his bed. Coach taught him to think before he spoke. It was a skill he hadn't practiced lately.

"I don't know if I'm sticking around," Denny said.

"Oh yeah? Why's that?"

He considered lying. But where had it gotten him so far? "The truth?"

"When have I ever accepted less from you?"

"That one time I pretended like I hadn't tried beer for the first time before I showed up to practice."

Coach barked a full belly laugh, and Denny cracked a smile. "It was ninety-five degrees, and you were green before we even started. God punished you enough that day."

Denny breathed deep. "I met somebody here," he said. "It didn't end well. And now it's all tainted. This house, the lake, the whole freaking town."

"Mm," Coach hummed. "I knew there was a reason I didn't hear from you. Never suspected it was a woman."

"Not just a woman." Denny pinched the bridge of his nose. "She's . . . I don't even know how to describe her. She's like Sefina."

"Doesn't let you get away with shit?"

"Sort of," Denny said on a laugh. "She's just like, the kindest person I've ever met. Levelheaded. She's tough and stubborn, and she made me work for it."

"Lots of women have made you work for it," Coach said.

"Well, she made me feel like the work was worth it."

"Ah," Coach said. "There it is. So what happened?"

Denny exhaled through pursed lips. He didn't even really understand what had happened between them. Within the span of four hours she'd gone from loving him to shutting the door completely. And yet, she hadn't left the guest cabin yet. She didn't move into Sydney's guest room or check into Indigo Hotels Adirondack Park. She was still in Pine Ridge, on his property, hanging around his periphery and hovering in his rearview.

He gave Coach the short version of their last real conversation in the guest cabin. "She's making me pay for things that other people did to her," Denny said. "It's not fair."

Coach laughed, and Denny could see his wide, friendly face wrinkling up into a smile. He missed his friend.

"Oh, it's not fair, huh?" Coach laughed again. "You're too much, boy."

"I don't mean it like that," Denny said. "I know, you're gonna tell me life's not fair."

"You know I don't deal in clichés." Coach paused. Denny saw him, standing on the football field, staring out at his players with a smug grin on his lips. "You remember when we first met?"

Denny searched his memory. "Mm . . . I had to be about fourteen? My sophomore year?"

"Mm hm. Fourteen-year-old Denny. Annoying as shit."

Denny laughed, feeling more at ease than he had all day. "Sounds about right."

"Did you like me?"

Another shot of laughter burst out of him. "We still talk after all these years. Of course I liked you. You were the only adult I ever connected with. That I saw as a person instead of a parole officer."

"Sure, but at first. In the early days. I was tough."

It wasn't how Denny remembered it. His father was tough. Rosa was tough. Coach was caring, knowledgeable, smart. He made sure every kid on the field was properly coached whether he liked it or not.

"Eh," Denny said, "you knew what you wanted from us, but you weren't that tough."

Coach laughed, a lilting, mocking tone carrying over the miles. "Your memory's garbage, Torres. You wanted to punch my lights out for the entire first year you played for me. But I knew it was because everybody before me had demanded greatness without teaching you how to actually achieve it. You had so much talent, but your lack of patience was gonna kill that for you."

Denny thought of his parents downstairs. *Demanded greatness.* An understatement.

"I don't remember hating you, though," Denny said.

Coach huffed out a satisfied grunt. Probably had his arms crossed over his barrel chest. "Take a second. Think about what I just said."

The lesson floated around Denny's brain, settling like sand in the lake. "You're trying to tell me if anything's worth having, it's worth working for."

"Something like that." Coach cleared his throat. "You want what you want when you want it. I think this girl's trying to tell you that you have to work a little harder. Be a little more patient. I don't know every detail of what's going on with you, but I think if you pause, use your head, and really think it over, you'll figure out how to make it work."

"Thought you didn't work in clichés, old man."

Coach laughed. "Sometimes they become cliché for a reason."

Denny raked a hand through his damp hair and studied

the bedside lamp, the bronze curves of the base replicating the shape of a woman.

It's kinda sexy, isn't it? Bee had said.

She always saw the things he didn't.

"She's afraid I'm impulsive," Denny said. "That I'm gonna change my mind and go looking for my parents' approval again. That nothing about this kind of life could ever fulfill me."

"Is she right?"

He gazed around his bedroom: the dark wood bed frame; the plush, faux-fur blanket; the single wall painted faded black and highlighted by a strikingly large photo of a bison obscured by snow. Bee had managed to wrangle his love of Pine Ridge and the mountains and bring it indoors. He loved the town. He loved the house. And she saw all of it.

"No," Denny said. "She's wrong."

"Well, then," Coach said. "You have to make her see it."

Sydney pulled Sam's pickup truck to a stop at the corner of Nineteenth and Eighth and cut the engine. "God, I hate driving in the city."

"I really appreciate you driving me." Bee glanced out at the black bricks marking the entrance to Club Trade. "Saved me from having to rent a car."

Sydney hadn't blinked when Bee asked if she'd drive her into the city and back. She needed to grab some stuff from her apartment before she headed to London, but she also wasn't entirely ready to leave Pine Ridge. The thought of spending her last night before heading overseas on the couch of her old apartment—crashing with Jamie instead of in the warm bubble of the town she'd grown to love—made her heart hurt. When Sydney offered to make the unnecessary trip with her, Bee knew she didn't have to explain herself.

They climbed out of the truck into the balmy October

day, the temperature decidedly warmer than the chill of upstate. The scent of salty boiled hot dogs assaulted Bee's nose, and a woman with her face buried in her cell phone pushed past, nearly knocking Bee off the curb.

"Jesus," Bee grumbled as Sydney joined her.

"Missing small-town life already?" Syd said.

Bee glared at her friend, but Sydney's wide smile remained. "Let's just grab my stuff and go. If you're nice, I'll let you raid my makeup kit when we get up there."

Sydney's eyes lit up. "I've wanted those feather eyelashes for years!"

They brushed past the side entrance where Bee would typically enter the building in favor of the main entrance to the club. Jamie promised he'd be behind the bar for the early shift, and she wanted to say hello.

Sydney swung the door open, and Bee passed through. She made it three paces before she stopped dead in her tracks. Entering from the basement door, carrying a crate of Tito's vodka and wearing a black Club Trade T-shirt, was Isaac.

"Um, excuse me," Bee said. A smile tugged at her lips. "I must be in the wrong place."

Isaac set the crate down on the floor, a shy grin taking over his boyish face. "Go ahead. Get it all out now."

"You work here?" Sydney said, the disbelief coloring her tone. She didn't know Isaac well, but she knew him well enough to know something must've been very, very wrong.

Jamie burst from behind the stage curtain and beamed at his friends. "Is this a good surprise or what?"

Bee crept toward her brother, afraid that if she made a sudden movement he'd scamper away like a squirrel up a tree.

"Jamie said I could work here," Isaac said. "And that if I put in enough hours and proved myself, I could crash on the air mattress upstairs. So . . . here I am. Barback extraordinaire."

Bee's gaze softened, her inexperienced, woefully inept little brother looking as dazed as she'd ever seen him. "Wow," she said. "Hard work. Manual labor. The shittiest position in the club."

Isaac huffed a laugh. "Yep. It sucks."

"What else?" she said. The night at Denny's house had been a breaking point for her, a fork in the road of her life she couldn't go back to. She needed Isaac to prove himself now. A crummy bar job was a good step.

"I'm still volunteering," Isaac said. "With the Trevor Project. And your friend Marcello said if I'm interested, in a few months he might have a job opening for me."

"A paying job?" She didn't want to show him the joy surging inside her chest.

He nodded. "A paying job. They're a really incredible organization, and turns out I'm pretty good at talking to people who need help."

"Must run in the family," Sydney said.

Bee forced back tears, her eyes locked on her little brother. He looked calmer somehow. More subdued than usual. "Can I hug you?"

"Well, duh." Isaac wrapped her in a hug and squeezed. They stood clutching each other's shoulders until a tear trickled down Bee's cheek. As angry as she'd been with him, he was family. That would never change.

She sniffed back her tears and pulled away, eyes scanning his Club Trade uniform. "I'm really happy for you, Ike. Really happy."

Jamie poured them each a rum and Coke, and they settled into one of the empty tables. Club Trade at five p.m. meant they had the place to themselves.

"I talked to Mom and Dad," Isaac said. "It was good. Not world-altering, but good. I got to say what I wanted to say, and they said some things. I think eventually we'll be on good terms again."

Bee sipped her cocktail, the shock of sugar coursing across her tongue. "That's great."

"Maybe you should call them again, too," Isaac said. "When you're ready."

She tugged her hands inside the sleeves of her oversize teal cardigan. She wasn't there yet. But maybe someday she would be.

"Maybe."

He nodded slowly. "I messed up, Beè. I'm really sorry. I haven't wanted to really explore why my life is the way it is, or how I got here. I have a lot of stuff I have to figure out. But Jamie and Abe have been amazing. They hooked me up with a therapist."

Jamie raised his expertly manicured eyebrows and pursed his lips. "Sometimes it takes somebody *outside* your family to tell you what you don't want to hear. Or, you know. A professional."

"I'm so proud of you," Bee said. The tension between siblings hadn't fully dissipated yet, but she liked this new normal. It was honest.

"So . . ." Isaac's voice lowered as his eyes darted hesitantly around the group. "Why are you here? Jamie said you're grabbing some stuff before a trip?"

The joy seeped out of Bee. She'd forgotten, momentarily, about everything that had happened with Denny.

She shrugged. "I'm going to London. Saturday. I just came to grab some things."

Isaac, Sydney, and Jamie shared cock-eyed glances.

"Are we allowed to ask what happened?" Isaac said.

"Nothing happened," Bee said. "This was always the plan. I did the decorating job, I got the money, and now I'm onto the next step. Moving to the city I had always planned to move to, even if it's not under the exact same circumstances. That's it. I'm not sure why everybody expected me to fall in love and abandon everything I'd set out to do."

"Sissy," Isaac said, his eyes widening to the size of saucers. "If you fall in love, you're allowed to change your plans."

"No," Bee stammered, her heart pounding. "I meant, like . . . everyone *expected* me to fall in love. Not that I actually did. Just— Never mind."

The three people closest to her swapped another look.

"Bee," Jamie said, sliding his hand over hers. She hadn't realized she'd been trembling. "I know what I saw. You felt things for him."

Bee took another long drink of her cocktail, but no alcohol in the world had the power to calm her vibrating nerves. "I've felt things for a lot of people over the years. You're the one who loves reminding me."

Jamie raised his favorite *Oh please* eyebrow. "Then hear me when I say. I have never—and I mean *never*—seen you act like you did with Denny."

"What?" Bee said. "Dumber than usual?"

"Realer than usual."

The air around them paused as if even the atmosphere waited for an answer.

"I agree," Sydney said. "And I'm not just saying this because I want you to stay, okay? Because above all I want you to be happy. You seem really comfortable in Pine Ridge. Like professional Bee and club Bee and homebody Bee all met each other for the first time."

"Yes!" Isaac said. He nearly jumped out of his chair. "Thank you. You just articulated exactly what I've been trying to pinpoint for the past two months."

Bee's lips parted as she stared at her brother. "What does that mean?"

"You kicked me out," Isaac said, each word a bullet. "You! My softy, pushover sister. Never in a million years did I think you'd kick me out, much less kick me out late at night with a freaking boot on my foot. You didn't even call to make sure I got back to the city okay. I spent that ridiculously long train ride from Utica thinking about it, but I finally decided I was impressed. You never had those balls before."

Guilt flooded her chest. But Isaac was fine. He *had* made it to the city okay. He had a job with the prospect of a career. And no sign of the boot.

"Are you all healed up?" she said.

Isaac laughed. "Yes, Mama Bee. Old habits die hard, huh?"

"The point," Jamie said, squeezing her palm. "Is that I liked Pine Ridge Bee. I liked her a *lot*. I'm not saying it's because of Denny, but . . ."

"But why run away from the person who inspired all that?" Sydney said.

Bee's chest tightened. "I didn't run away. He . . . he wasn't showing me all of himself. You know what I mean?"

"Maybe that *was* all of him," Isaac said. "Maybe he'd never shown that person to anyone else before. Is it possible that maybe he finally discovered a place and a person that made *him* the best version of himself, too?" His eyebrows lifted clear into his forehead as he placed his hands on the table.

Three pairs of eyes lighted on Isaac, all with the same inquisitive expression.

"That was really deep," Sydney said.

"Look at you," Jamie said. "A few weeks of manual labor and you're freaking Dr. Ruth over here."

Sydney and Jamie continued to gently rib Isaac, but Bee sank into what he'd said. Sure, it seemed possible. If Bee could change—hell, if *Isaac* could begin to change—wasn't it possible that Denny had changed, too?

Sydney helped Bee grab loose ends from her apartment—her passport, packing cubes, voltage adapters, and travel hair dryer—and together they hugged Jamie and Isaac before hitting the road.

The five-hour drive did nothing to calm Bee's nerves. By the time they reached Denny's driveway, her face tingled with anxiety. She had one full day left in Pine Ridge. A deep, throbbing ache resonated inside. She missed it and she hadn't even left yet.

Sam's truck ambled up the drive, approaching the lit-up house with caution. Through the massive windows, Bee watched Denny shift on the couch, raising the TV remote and keeping his eyes trained on the screen. He knew she'd arrived home. And yet, he didn't look.

"What about tomorrow?" Syd asked. "Will it be weird to go to his housewarming party?"

"I can't go," Bee said. "How could he possibly want me there now?"

"You're just gonna camp out in the guesthouse?"

Bee turned her frustrated gaze on her friend. "Please don't make this any harder than it already is. I know you want everybody else to have the love story that you did, but I'm not you, Syd. This isn't the same."

"Definitely not the same." Sydney turned her full attention on Bee, lowering her dark eyes. "Just . . . consider coming, okay? I know you care about him, and I think he really does want you there."

Bee paused, studying Sydney's face in case she gave anything away. "Did he tell you that?"

"Sort of."

"He told Sam."

Sydney shrugged. "Guys should know better than to tell things to their friends with wives and expect them to remain secret."

As the new information settled into her chest, Bee turned back to look into the house. Denny ran a hand through his hair, sending the silky tresses into disarray. He crossed his feet on the coffee table, sipped a beer, checked his phone. He was still trying not to look at her sitting in his driveway.

She promised Sydney she'd consider attending the party

and climbed out of Sam's truck. Just before she reached the door, she heard the whir of a window lowering behind her.

"Hey," Sydney called out. "I better see you before you leave either way, okay? You owe me that much."

"Of course." Bee grinned. "I'll need some reading material for the plane, obviously."

Sydney laughed as she raised the window and pulled out of the driveway. Bee cast one more glance at Denny's house. Just in time to catch his gaze before he turned back to the TV.

chapter **twenty-one**

The sun sliced through the trees, stinging Bee's eyes and forcing her to squint. She raised the zipper on her fleece-lined jacket and breathed deep, spicy balsam and cold October breeze burning her lungs. The trail curved ahead of her, the tiny waterfall to her left.

Just past the bend, the swimming hole appeared. The water shimmered in the morning light, reminding her of the way Denny's long, lean body slipped beneath its surface on the first day she knew she was in too deep.

She lowered her backpack to the ground and picked across the slick rocks to the edge of the water. Her heart pounded in her chest, adrenaline and fear combined. The rational part of her brain told her the water was no danger, especially if she stayed a few feet back. Her nerves still sparked and flickered. When she'd told Sydney she was taking a hike behind Denny's house, Syd offered to join. But Bee needed to do this on her own.

With a deep inhale, she took another step toward the swimming hole. When she'd first arrived two months ago, she didn't understand how people connected to nature or why it drew them in. But when she woke up on her last full day in Pine Ridge, the trail and the water called to her like home. She needed to see it one last time.

She stepped gingerly over the large rocks, darkened by the powerful waterfall spray, and breathed in the crisp air. Just inches from the surface of the water, she sat down. Her pants would be damp, but she didn't care. Denny dived headfirst into everything he did. With her feet dangling over the rock's edge, she understood why.

For the past week, she'd felt numb, floating through her days and fighting against the pull of the main house. More than once, she'd approached the front door and raised a fist, ready to tell him they should give it a shot. But every time she did, she remembered how he caved to his parents and how if he didn't prove himself a changed man, it would be her heart on the line.

She thought seven days might be enough time for him to rush over to *her* door, to beg *her* back. To prove to her he really could commit. She wanted him to tell her he'd called his parents, told them all about her, all about how he wanted to stay in Pine Ridge and make this new life work for him. That he was owning his choices.

But he never showed. He never knocked.

She stared down into the swirling pond water, brown leaves caught and twisting in the bubbling current. The thought of whatever waited below the surface still stuck in her throat and choked her breath. Her legs tingled with anticipation as if urging her to jump while her brain screamed not to. But she'd turned a corner. Fear wasn't holding her back anymore. She was facing the unknown head-on, putting herself first, and diving in on her own terms.

She sat at the edge of the pond until the sun shone high

in the sky and her stomach grumbled with hunger. She inhaled, soaking up as much pine-scented air as she could, hoping it infiltrated her skin and stayed there permanently.

With weighted limbs, she retrieved her backpack and headed back to Denny's house. She rounded the curve of the lake, watching the dock and hoping against logic that he'd be sitting there with a beer, waiting for her. But his house remained silent, quiet, dark.

She climbed the slope of the hill and reached the guest cabin to find a slip of paper taped to the front door.

Really hoping I'll see you tonight. —D

Her heart turned to liquid and trickled into her stomach as she clutched the note in her feverish palm and went inside.

Bee tossed another blouse into the reject pile. At this rate, she'd have to leave the party early no matter what to repack her suitcase. At least she had a good excuse.

Her phone buzzed with a text as she yanked off a metallic T-shirt and added it to the discard pile.

Where are you?? I can see your light on. Get your ass over here. We're about to do tequila shots and we want to toast to the decorator of this INSANELY gorgeous house!

Fear clogged Bee's throat as she read Sydney's text. She yanked a big hunter-green turtleneck sweater over her high waisted jeans and shoved her feet into snakeskin slides. Better to go and get it over with regardless of her outfit. No cute top or tight jeans would make seeing Denny any easier. She checked her minimal makeup in the bathroom mirror and forced herself into the night.

She slipped through Denny's front door without knocking, the booming bass and dull roar of conversation promising to shield her from too much attention. A wall of warmth met her as she entered, bodies filling every square inch of the first floor.

"There you are!" Sydney tackled her in a one-armed hug, the other hand occupied with a can of Coors Light. Even the shitty beer made Bee's heart hurt.

Syd pulled away and glanced down at Bee's outfit with a grimace.

"What?" Bee asked.

"I dunno," Sydney said. "You couldn't have shown off a little cleavage or something?"

Bee tugged lovingly at her sweater. "Why, Syd? Who am I seducing?"

Sydney raised one eyebrow as a suggestive smile curled onto her lips. "No comment. Come on, let's get you a drink."

"Wait." Bee grabbed Sydney's wrist as she turned toward the kitchen. "I'm here, okay? I'm being mature about it. But I need you to be gentle with me. Where is he? So I can prepare myself."

"He's in the basement showing off his stupid gym." Sydney rolled her eyes. "The men in this town, I swear."

Bee breathed a momentary sigh of relief as they entered the kitchen. Mila, Nicole, and Allison stood around the kitchen island, all pink-cheeked and smiling. A shudder passed over Bee's shoulders. The kitchen where he'd made her breakfast, now occupied by the friends she'd come to love. The power of the moment nearly knocked her backward.

The women gushed over Bee and her interior design accomplishment. Each of them wanted information on sources and inspiration, asking after stores and websites. Sydney said, with a gleam in her eyes, that she'd try to get the attention of mountain magazines to come in and photograph it.

"I have a friend of a friend who used to work for *Architectural Digest*," Sydney said. "I'm gonna put feelers out just to see."

"They'd be fools not to come and shoot it," Mila agreed. "It's so different from—"

Mila's voice faded away as the group fell silent, and those on the opposite side of the island stared over Bee's head. She didn't need any additional indicators to know who had entered the room.

Her stomach tightened as she reached for the nearest beer and took a long drink before turning around. She didn't care who the booze belonged to. She needed its effects now more than ever.

A small group of men hovered just inside the archway between the basement door and the kitchen. Denny stood in front, swiping a hand over his chiseled jaw and staring down at her with wide, penetrating eyes.

The room fell silent, all eyes on them.

"Hey," he said.

"Hi."

Behind her, Sydney called for another round of shots, and gratefully, the group's noise level rose again. The boys filtered around the bubble between Denny and Bee. His stare never left hers.

"I'm glad you came," he said. He wore a buffalo plaid flannel over a V-neck T-shirt, the thin, white fabric stretching across the firm planes of his chest and drawing a drumbeat pulse from between her legs.

"Of course," she said. "I mean, all of Pine Ridge is here. How could I miss it?"

"Can we—"

"Yo!" Jared slapped Denny on the shoulder, drawing him into a hug and clapping his back. "Sick party, dude. Had I known what a perfect party house it was, I'd have thrown an event to sell it in the first place."

Denny forced a dry laugh, and Sam appeared, crowding

the doorway and forcing Bee to step back and give them some space. As she turned to grab another drink, she heard Sam say, "He's joking. Don't get any ideas. We like having you around too much, Denny. Jared's never selling this place again, no matter how much you beg him."

She couldn't help herself. She turned back in time to catch Denny's wide-eyed stare.

"Selling this place?" she said. Her voice barely made it out of her throat.

"He's not selling it." A wide smile hung on Jared's lips. "To be honest, I think he just wanted to know how much more he'd get with all your cool furniture and stuff inside. You ever considered staging homes, Bee? You'd make my job a hell of a lot easier."

The noise swelled around her, crowding her thoughts and blurring Denny's face. She suspected it, worried about it, feared it, but she never actually believed it. Until now. He was actually leaving.

"They don't know what they're talking about," Denny said. "Can we go somewhere for a second? Away from everybody?"

Bee gritted her teeth and slipped through the crowd, desperate to escape as quickly as the mass of people allowed. She wanted to disappear. She'd hide out in the guest cabin until the sun came up, and then she'd get on her train into the city and forget she'd ever met Denny Torres.

She made it as far as the front door before Sydney caught her.

"Hey," Syd said. Her face creased in concern. "You okay?"

"Fine," Bee said. "I just . . . I knew I shouldn't have come. I can't be around him. It's too hard."

"Oh God," Sydney groaned. "Was it the tattoo? It's too much, right?"

Bee paused, her hand on the front doorknob. "What tattoo?"

Sydney's face softened. "He didn't tell you?"

"Tell me what?" Her voice edged on manic.

"Just . . . talk to him. Don't leave yet."

Bee opened her mouth to protest, and Sydney held up a hand.

"Seriously," Sydney said. "Before you storm out."

With her heart in her throat, Bee waited for one more beat while Sydney challenged her friend with a raised eyebrow.

"Fine," Bee said. She steeled her nerves as she reentered the house to find Denny.

She drifted through the crowds of people in the kitchen, the living room, the study, and the basement, but Denny wasn't among any of them. She asked around if anyone had seen him, and finally, Nicole said he'd slipped out the kitchen doors.

Bee stepped out onto the deck, shivering against the frigid night air and wishing she'd worn a coat. Down the slope of the lawn and just past the pair of Adirondack chairs loomed a tall figure staring out over the lake.

Darkness enveloped her as she shuffled across the lawn, the damp grass tickling her bare ankles. A rhythmic chorus of rustling trees and buzzing insects surrounded her as if guiding her toward the water.

"Denny." His name crossed her lips on a soft breeze, and he raised his chin but didn't turn.

"I don't have it in me to have this conversation again," he said. He shoved his hands into the pockets of his fitted jeans.

She walked slowly down the dock and stood to his right, forcing herself into his view. After a few quiet moments, he lowered his gaze to look at her.

"Are you selling the house?" she asked.

"No." He didn't blink. "I texted Jared after you and I . . . talked. After the barbecue. I just wanted to cut and run like you were cutting and running."

Her chest burned. "I'm not—"

He turned toward her, intensifying his gaze and stopping her words mid-sentence. "I'm gonna say some stuff now, okay?"

All she could do was nod.

"I'm in love with you," he said. "I don't want you to leave Pine Ridge. I have never wanted to take care of anybody, to do things differently for anybody, and I wanted to do everything for you. I *want* to do everything for you. You can go to London, but I'm not gonna stop loving you. I said I lied about that, but you know what, Bee, I don't even think I have a choice."

His words melted over her skin, sinking into her flesh and stinging like nettles.

She forced back the tears. "Oh yeah?"

A short breath passed his lips. "Yeah. You're afraid I'm flighty or impulsive or that I'm gonna up and decide to disappear . . ."

"No," she said. "I was. I'm not. Anymore, I mean."

He lowered his chin. "You can be. I don't expect you to just trust me completely overnight. But I want the chance to prove it. That's all I'm asking for."

Something in her chest wobbled and wavered, threatening to break and spill. She wanted him. She wanted their life together. She wanted it so badly she could taste it.

Her two months in Pine Ridge had shifted something inside of her, the inner mechanisms of her world twisting and clicking as everything finally made sense. As everything settled. She'd been so terrified for so long that her decisions depended solely on the man in her life, while Denny had simply been the catalyst. By the time she looked up from all the plans she'd set for herself long ago, she barely recognized the life that had materialized in front of her. A life based on intuition, passion, and heart. With Denny and Pine Ridge at the center of it.

"I have a lot of walls up," she said feebly.

He gifted her with his lopsided grin. "I know."

She twisted her fingers together. "I started to feel things for you," she said. "I got scared."

"I thought you were so comfortable with love? I'm supposed to be the one who's not good at it."

She laughed. "I'm starting to think that maybe I'd never actually experienced it before."

His jaw ticked, the sharp angles of his cheeks catching the moonlight and lighting his impossibly smooth skin. He'd managed to turn her into putty, despite all the years she'd spent hardening her shell.

"Why are you leaving, Bee?"

She shrugged. "If I stay . . ."

Could she say it? She'd had a lot of time to hear the words in her head, but vocalizing them was another feat altogether.

"Yeah?"

"You could hurt me," she said. It was the truth. It was the thing she always feared in a partner. The thing she feared most in life. The reason she tried to control things.

"I'm not gonna hurt you." He paused. "I want to take care of you. I think you deserve that. I think we both do. To take care of each other."

Her chest rose and fell dramatically, her body begging to cross the barren space between them and press against his solid build. "It'll take some getting used to."

He grinned. "I can be patient."

"Can you? Mr. Impulsive?"

He bit his lip, and his eyes twinkled. "I did do something impulsive."

"What?"

Cautiously, he stepped toward her and raised his big right hand. He closed his fingers into a fist, leaving his index finger exposed to reveal a tiny, cursive word tattooed on the inside of his knuckle. She had to lean in to read it.

Be.

Her lips parted, the tension and fear leaking out of her slowly. She fought the impulse to lick that finger. "Are you freaking kidding me?"

"It's not your name," he said. "I mean, obviously it is, but it's also the reminder. To be. I got it right after I told my parents about staying in Pine Ridge and working with the high school team and committing to a life here. After I told them I'm in love with my decorator. I'm owning my shit. I'm . . . being."

His dark form turned blurry in front of her, and she blinked, sending tears spilling down her sweater. A tattoo. A word injected into his skin to remind him of her and the impact she'd had on him. She ran her thumb over her own finger tattoo as if summoning its power.

"Are you pissed?" he said, brushing the tattooed knuckle across her cheek. "Is it creepy?"

"No," she said through laughter. She looked back up at him, glittering tears turning her view sparkly and magical. "That means everything to me."

With strong fingers, he tucked a loose strand of hair behind her ear.

"Can you come here already?" he said. "You've been too far away for too long."

He tucked a hand behind her neck, drawing her into his chest as she slipped her hands around his back. She trailed her fingers under his T-shirt to the warm, soft skin below.

"You want me to add the extra 'e' to this thing?" he said, the words muffled by her hair. "Really drive it home?"

She grinned. "Let's wait for that, okay?"

"Wait? Until . . . ?"

Until we get married. She knew the words wouldn't scare him, but it was too soon. Less than an hour ago, she'd planned to get on a plane and cross the Atlantic in search of a new life. Tonight, she'd focus on settling into the life she'd already created. With him. Marriage talk could wait. They'd get there. Eventually.

He pulled back and lowered his face to hers. With one press of his lips, the familiar taste of him spread across her tongue and she melted. He held her jaw with warm palms, and she breathed him in.

Their lips parted, but she couldn't bear to be away from him. She wrapped her arms around his neck, tracing the tip of her nose across his cheekbone.

"My plane ticket," she whispered.

"I'll come with you."

She grinned, nuzzling the crook of his neck. "Oh yeah?"

"Yes." He tucked his chin enough to look straight into her eyes. "Well, after football season ends. I don't want you to give up your plan of design school."

"They have online courses, too," she said. She'd explored all options within the program, paying special attention to those that allowed her to study from anywhere.

"Oh, they do?" He grinned.

"Living in London is just one option," she said. "It's not the only option."

"I want you to do whatever it is that makes you happy," he said. "The point is, I'm not going anywhere. I'll be here. Waiting for you."

He ran his tongue across his lower lip and tightened his grip on her waist. The shadows in his gaze deepened as his hips pressed against her, removing any doubt as to what he wanted next.

"I wish you didn't have a house full of people right now," she said. Her lips brushed across his as his eyes flashed.

"Yeah?"

She closed her teeth around his bottom lip and tugged. "Yeah."

A low grunt escaped his throat. His hands slipped around her butt and tightened. "Come on."

He linked his fingers with hers and hurried up the lawn, moving swiftly toward the guest cabin. She used the key from her back pocket to open the door and barely shut it before his mouth crashed over hers.

With frantic hands, he yanked off her sweater. He trailed his tongue from her jaw down the column of her throat to the deep V of her cleavage and nipped at her flesh as fire coursed through her veins, her head floating in disbelief that she had him again. She wanted to slow everything down, but her body wouldn't let her.

"Off," she breathed, tugging at his flannel shirt. He tore the shirt off and reached behind his neck to shed the T-shirt, too. His muscles rippled in the low light, shadows creating mountain ranges out of his pecs and abs.

Everything about him soothed her, from the deep, searchlight stare he cast over her to the warm, familiar scent of his skin. She'd always thought love could ruin a person, tear her apart with reckless abandon. Denny made her feel quieter, cared for, filled up. He gave her the space to release everything she'd always tried to contain.

She made quick work of his belt, button, and zipper, and his stomach contracted as he tugged and kicked his pants off. His erection tented the fabric of his boxer briefs, and she clutched it with desperate hands. Caring for him, even in the midst of blind desire, felt like a privilege.

"God, I missed you," he said, brushing hands over her hair and sucking her tongue into his mouth. The rhythmic pulse of their mouths turned her insides to liquid.

Within seconds, her jeans, bra, and panties joined the pile of discarded clothes on the ground, and their bodies met in the middle of the tiny cabin. Her head flooded with lust, her body clamoring to be nearer to him than physical restrictions allowed.

"Come here," he said. He guided her to the bed, their mouths still tangled, and sat her on the edge. With one hand, he balanced on the mattress and leaned against her until she reclined, her feet still touching the floor.

He dragged his open mouth down her breasts, catching a nipple between gentle teeth before lighting over her tattoo. One hand massaged her breast as he licked across the script at her ribs.

"You like that one, huh?" she said.

He lifted his heavy gaze, lips parted and wet. "I like every single one."

Strong fingers slid down her body until they landed at her thighs, his attention finding the next decorated stretch of skin. His teeth grazed her hip before scraping across the lions' heads, her body vibrating head to toe with desire.

"Pride tattooed in her skin," he said, his breath hot on her flesh. "I should've known the type of tough girl I was getting involved with."

She lifted her head. "What did you say?"

"Pride," he said. He traced the word, slightly obstructed by curling leaves and branches, with the same knuckle he'd had tattooed. "Your body is like a gallery."

She melted. He saw her. He took the time to examine, to question, to dig. He wasn't content to admire her shell or the exterior she'd worked hard to decorate. He wanted it all.

Before she could respond, his attention turned inward. He settled his mouth over her clit, working his jaw up and down until ragged gasps escaped her throat. With a slow drag of his tongue, he moved back upward.

His mouth met hers, and she raised a leg to hook around his waist, wild and desperate to have him inside of her. She tasted herself on his lips.

"I need you," she said.

"God, it feels good to hear you say that."

She rolled over onto her stomach, lifting her hips as his taut, corded arms framed her on the bed. The hard length of his cock slid along her seam and teased her clit as he dragged himself back and forth between her legs.

"You have condoms in here?" He purred into her ear, clouding her thoughts until she could barely see straight.

She tried to stand up, but he placed a strong hand on her arched lower back.

"Uh-uh," he said. "I want you to stay just like this. Tell me where."

She managed to choke out "Medicine cabinet" before he removed his warm body from her and disappeared into the bathroom. Within seconds, he returned alongside the sound of crinkling plastic and heavy breaths.

His firm thighs brushed the backs of her legs as the latex-covered head slipped between her folds, pressing into her entrance and drawing a cry from her throat. He slid deeper, and her eyes squeezed shut, frantic to hold on to every moment of overwhelming pleasure.

With strong hands, he gripped her hips before lowering himself across her back. He nestled his face in the mess of hair at her neck, breathing her in and rocking against her as the pressure built.

He dragged her hair away from her neck and pressed his mouth against her flesh. One arm depressed the mattress to her left while his other hand snaked under her body, fingers pressing softly against her clit and stripping away her last shreds of control.

"Oh God," she gasped. "Don't stop. Please don't stop."

The pads of his fingers circled her sex, the tiny motions mirroring the rhythmic grinding of his hips against her until she clawed at the blankets, a mad woman in the throes of mind-melting bliss. She lost herself with him, and she didn't mind if she never came back.

Vivid colors burst behind her eyelids as she crested the wave, the release tickling her periphery as they rocked together. He sucked her earlobe into his mouth before whispering, "I love making you come."

Her body exploded from the inside out, twitching against the mattress as he cocooned on top of her. Sparks shot off in her limbs as if someone had tucked dynamite into her arms and legs, and Denny had lit the match.

With one last thrust, an expletive fell off his lips, and he shuddered and collapsed, pressing her into the bed and forcing a dazed grin to her face. The weight of his big, muscled body consumed her, and she wanted to stay in his guest cabin just like that until the sun came up.

He placed a gentle kiss on the back of her neck before standing up and disappearing into the bathroom. She tried to slow her breath. By the time he returned, she'd regained feeling in her legs and leaned against the bed, her skin damp and pebbled in the chilly night air.

With a lowered brow and a dreamy grin on his lips, he sauntered across the room and placed his hands on her hips. She couldn't keep the smile from taking over her face.

"I'm not sure how convincing I'll be at telling all those people in there we definitely *weren't* out here having sex," he said.

"I forgot about the party." She scrunched up her nose in disappointment. "If I texted Sydney we're holed up in the guesthouse getting at it, she'd clear everybody out in about four seconds."

He smiled before kissing her, slow and deep. "Let's go back in and celebrate the fact that you're staying. Then when everybody does leave, I'm gonna keep you up till dawn."

Her pulse stuttered. There was nothing she wanted more.

She smiled. "Who said I'm staying?"

The grin melted from his face.

She nuzzled his neck and wrapped her arms around his broad shoulders. "You're too easy."

In one swift move, he pinned her against the mattress, his lopsided grin reappearing as he hovered over her. He brushed the hair away from her face and gazed down lovingly.

"I kinda can't wait to see what our life together looks like," he said.

Her heart swelled, and peace settled over her shoulders. She envisioned hikes in the mountains, breakfasts at the diner, and dips in the lake, but also galleries in Paris, gelato in Italy, and bikes in Amsterdam. Her life with him would look different than the life she'd planned, but also better than she could've hoped.

"Me too," she said. She kissed him. "I think it's gonna be spectacular."

epilogue

Denny's lips curled into an evil smile, and a nervous, mottled blush spread down Bee's neck. She gripped his forearms.

"I don't trust you."

He tilted his head, waiting for her to take it back.

"When it comes to *this*," she said.

"We're not even on the water yet."

Her tanned skin showcased a brilliant white bikini, almost distracting him from the task at hand. No matter how many times he'd seen her naked, something about his tatted-up girl in a bikini sent his head spinning.

He'd set the water skis out on the lawn so she could experience the rubber foot enclosures before she got out on the lake. It had taken him weeks to convince her to set foot in the boat dealership, another week to get her to agree to the purchase, and another month to coax her on board the damned thing. When he promised to earn her trust, he'd never expected all that.

"Can't we just swim?" she said, placing her hands on her dangerously curvy hips and squinting against the summer sun. "I'm totally comfortable with that."

He sighed. "We can do whatever you want, baby. You told me you were ready to try."

Her lips worked as she stared down at the water skis. In the past year, he'd convinced her to climb four of the forty-six Adirondacks High Peaks, rent a Ferrari in Rome, and take a hot-air balloon ride over São Paulo. But she still clammed up when it came to water.

"I think . . . ," she said. "I think I'm ready to take beers out on the boat and drink while you drive us around."

"All right," he said with a grin. "Take those things off and I'll get the beer. What am I grabbing for you?"

"I think I'll try that Good Nature IPA? Sam and Mila will drink that, too. And obviously pack ten cases of Coors Light for you and Jared so you guys can catch half a buzz."

She winked. Some aspects of their personalities would never change. He'd be patient with her fear of water, and she'd be patient with his affinity for light beer. In the grand scheme of relationships, there were worse arguments to have.

Denny filled a cooler with beer, ice, and water, and ambled down the sloping lawn just as Sydney, Sam, Jared, and Mila arrived. Bee had talked him out of buying a speedboat for what he'd thought were obvious reasons, but as he watched his group of friends clamber onto the pontoon boat, he realized she may have been up to more than steering him away from danger.

Jared held Mila's hand as she pushed off the dock onto the lolling boat, and then pinched her butt after she made it on safely. Sam followed and held both of Sydney's hands as she maneuvered herself onto the boat, a big, round, seven-month belly peeking out from beneath her tank top and disrupting her balance. Every time Denny thought of Bee in a similar state, something churned deep inside his chest.

As Denny settled behind the steering wheel and turned the key, revving the boat to life, he slid his sunglasses down over his nose and pulled the vessel away from the dock.

They sped across the glassy water toward his and Bee's favorite spot, a little cove tucked away but still soaked in sunshine for most of the day. He turned the wheel slightly right as Bee slid between his legs. She leaned back, flooding his senses with her warm, spicy perfume and sending her hair whipping past his neck.

He cut the engine as they pulled into the quiet pocket of the lake, surrounded by lush green pine trees and tall grass swaying in the summer breeze. Jared dropped the anchor and snagged a beer.

"Denny, you want one?" Jared said, already holding a second can of Coors Light.

"I'm only allowed two on the boat if I'm driving," he said, "so I'll wait."

"Allowed?" Jared said. "According to who?"

"My wife."

Bee's spine stiffened, and she shot him a look as the group laughed.

He'd been hinting since January that the proposal was imminent, but she didn't take him seriously. They had agreed to take it slow, feel each other out, get all the big arguments out of the way first. But she moved into his house permanently back in October, and they'd barely spent a day apart since. He hadn't fallen in love with her slowly, and he couldn't do this slowly, either. He'd sent a jeweler in LA some ring ideas last week.

"I suddenly feel like diving headfirst into the water," Bee said.

Denny wrapped an arm around her shoulders from behind. "Ouch."

"Well, it's hot as hell," Sam said, peeling off his T-shirt. "So I actually do feel like diving headfirst into this water."

Sam and Sydney joined Mila and Jared in the cool lake,

splashing and laughing and leaving Denny and Bee alone for a moment.

Bee stood up and placed her hands on Denny's sun-warmed shoulders. "I'm just kidding, you know."

He fought back a laugh. "Nah, you can't take it back now. You don't want to marry me, I can tell."

With a smile playing on her lips, she straddled his waist, inching forward until they were hip to hip. "The things I would do to you if you were my husband . . ."

"Oh, are you holding back because I'm not?"

A flip book of their sex life skipped through his brain: upright facing the master bathroom mirror and missionary on the couch; blow jobs on the dock, and licking her until she came perched on the bathroom sink at Utz's; Christmas at her parents' house in her childhood bedroom, and the time he'd used only his fingers under a blanket to make her orgasm twice as they flew over the Atlantic toward London.

He couldn't imagine what happened after he put a ring on her finger.

She shifted her hips, a lazy smile stretching across her full lips. "Only one way to find out."

With his hands draped over her butt, he said, "You're gonna make me hard right now."

"I'm not sure our friends will be willing to plug their ears and close their eyes while we take care of that. Better wait till we get home."

She wiggled backward but not before he dragged a finger under the edge of her bikini top, his knuckle skimming her tight nipple. Her pupils dilated in a look he'd become intimately familiar with, and she pressed on his chest until she stood upright.

"That was mean," she said.

"Just something to think about until we're alone again."

With a knowing smile, she draped herself across the boat's bench seat and lifted her face to the sun. Maybe she'd swim later. She was still getting used to life on the water, but he hadn't seen her freeze up because of it since last year.

A lot had changed since then. She'd taken on dozens of house-staging jobs thanks to Jared, spruced up Denny's guest cabin, and enrolled at an interior design course in the hospitality department at Paul Smith's College a few towns over. Pine Ridge trickled into her life bit by bit, and each time they returned home from a trip, they sank into their big gray couch and gushed about how much they'd missed it.

Denny shoved himself out of the driver's seat and cannonballed into the water, the lake slapping his back and shocking the lust right out of him. When he burst free from the surface of the water, he gulped in a mouthful of fresh, clean air and flipped his hair back.

He looked up at the trees, at the sky, at his future wife. At his bright future, glittering in the sun.

In 2010, after about six months of dating my husband, he invited me to meet his family in San Diego. I packed my most respectable (yet chic) meet-the-family looks and prepared for all the standard introductory questions.

Oh, what a fool I was.

Josh's family is reading this right now and laughing. Hard.

"You wanna stop by this wedding my family is at?" Josh asked over tacos. I looked down at my T-shirt and jeans. "A wedding? No. Look at me! No way."

Fifteen minutes later, I was engulfed in a sea of Porlas's, dragged onto the dance floor, handed a drink, and officially welcomed into the family.

My husband grew up in Southern California in a Filipino Hawaiian and Portuguese Hawaiian family. I quickly learned about their penchant for absurdly delicious food like chicken long rice, lumpia, roast pig, and lomi lomi salmon. I became familiar with over-the-top first birthday parties complete with hula dancers and live entertainment that none of those babies would ever remember and holiday events that started in the morning and lasted until well past midnight. If you're lucky enough to attend one of these events, you'll hear cousins singing classic Hawaiian songs, someone will tell you about Uncle Loo's particular method of mixing up the mac salad, and Tutu might even dance

hula. Oh, who are we kidding, Tutu will definitely dance
hula.

I am beyond lucky to have married into such rich traditions, and when I started envisioning the last book in the
Forever Adirondacks series, I knew my hero would have
some of those same traditions. Denny Torres was born in
Southern California to a Filipino Hawaiian family and his
experiences mirror those I've become intimately familiar
with because of my in-laws. They are not representative of
all Hawaiians or all Filipino Hawaiians, and they are not
meant to reflect Hawaiian culture as a whole. I wanted
Denny to embody some of the wonderful qualities my in-
laws have shared with me over the years, and I hope I've
come close to making them proud.

Special thanks to my sister-in-law, Rowena Accardo, for
reading an early draft and giving your thoughts. It means a
lot to me.

And to the readers, thank you for allowing me to share
this part of myself and my family with you! They're so
special to me and I hope, through Denny and his family,
I've brought a little bit of that warmth to the page.

With love,
Lauren Accardo

ACKNOWLEDGMENTS

First and foremost, I have to thank the Porlas family, the Wright family, the Accardo family, and all the branches that stem from them. I only hope the newest addition to the ohana feels even half as much love as I have over the years from all of you.

Thank you, as always, to Eva Scalzo, who makes the difficult phone calls (always preempted by a text so I don't have a full on freak out) and has the uncanny ability to walk me through every aspect of publishing, from the most difficult to the most rewarding. May we have many more text exchanges that include mostly exclamation points and each other's names in all CAPS.

To Sarah Blumenstock: I truly can't thank you enough for taking my ideas and giving them shape and direction. I can't believe this is the last book in this series! You've taught me so much about writing, romance, and how to bring my stories to readers in the most effective way. It's been an absolute honor to work with you.

Thank you to the incomparable team at Berkley Romance, specifically Brittanie Black, Erica Ferguson, and Natalie Sellars. Your enthusiasm and excitement over this series has made every part of the process a joy. Thank you for everything.

Thank you to the Berkletes, #RChat, and specifically to Brittany Kelley and Michelle McCraw. A writer is nobody without the community around her, and I pride myself on having the best of the best. For the "Can I be petty for a second?" moments and the "Okay, I'm not supposed to say anything yet, BUT . . ." messages and everything in between—I would be a lost soul without each of you.

Thank you to Sarah Smith, who has truly gone above and beyond for a brand-new debut author! From the blurb to the sensitivity read to the uplifting messages that seem to come whenever I need them most, I am so lucky to have been introduced to you and continue to be humbled by your kindness.

To every single one of you who preordered, purchased, and posted about *Wild Love*, I seriously can't even wrap my brain around the level of support you've shown me. To my friends who sent flowers and congratulatory champagne, to the people I haven't spoken to in years who sent hopeful messages and photos of the book in stores, to those of you I've never met who felt compelled to reach out and tell me how much you liked the book, I am forever grateful.

To all the readers who posted reviews, the writers who included me in roundups and articles, and the book bloggers and podcasters who supported my debut, THANK YOU. A special shoutout to Corinne Fisher, Krystyna Hutchinson, Maureen Van Zandt, and Josh Accardo for taking a chance on someone who frequently stumbles over her words and having me on your podcasts. I am so, so grateful for the opportunities.

To my family: Mom, Dad, Christopher, and Steph, I knew you'd support me, but I had no idea you'd turn into a full on promotional team. I only hope you show the same enthusiasm for books that are not set in the Adirondacks.

And of course, to Josh. How much more can I gush? Thanks for being my real-life love story, my most vocal cheerleader, my partner, my family. You made this the most special year of my life, and I love you so much.

Don't miss

wild love

Available now

from Berkley Jove!

Biting, icy wind whistled through the open car windows, and Sydney shuddered. It had to be at least twenty degrees colder up in the mountains. She raised the windows and hunched over the steering wheel, her already tense shoulders tightening further, like a jack-in-the-box about to pop.

Hot food. She needed hot food.

What she really needed was a memory eraser. She'd gladly give up any shred of happiness from the last ten years if it meant losing the last twelve hours.

Connor and the blonde. The sting in her mouth as she realized she'd chewed her lip enough to bleed. The deeply creased pitying stare on her mother's face when she'd arrived like a lost puppy at her door.

A shaky exhale breezed past her nostrils. One thing at a time.

She pulled her BMW into the sparsely populated parking lot of Utz's, a shadowy nondescript bar with a flashing **HOT FOOD TO GO** sign in the window.

Her stomach yawning with hunger, she scurried out of the warm car and into the fresh, pine-scented air. She might have fled to Pine Ridge under desperate circumstances, but she breathed its perfumed atmosphere into her lungs like a tourist on vacation.

A bright blue flier caught the wind and stuck against the leg of her yoga pants before she snatched it up. **Bingo Night at Utz's! Door Prizes. Cheap Drinks. All U Can Eat HOT WINGZ.**

"Jesus," she muttered. "Hot *wingz*. As if they spelled it correctly, nobody would show up."

With a grimace, she tucked the flier in a nearby trash can and hugged her cashmere cardigan tighter around her body, aching for any comfort she could find. But nothing could erase the memory of that asshole's stupid face as he grunted and moaned, the random blonde perched atop his hips.

She shook off the highlight reel running in her head.

Hot food. She'd promised her mother hot food for dinner.

A tiny bell rang over the door as she entered Utz's. Two burly men at the bar in front of her turned over their hulking shoulders and, after a cursory glance, resumed watching the football game blaring from the TV set on the wall.

"Howdy," the elderly bartender greeted her. A halo of gray hair framed his head, and a friendly grin pressed into his ruddy moon-shaped face. "What can I do you for?"

"Do you have a food menu? I'm gonna get some things to go."

He slid a paper menu toward her and turned back to the football game.

Sydney scanned the offerings. **Fried clams. Burgers. Fried chicken sandwiches. Nachos. Pizza. French fries.**

Onion rings. She twisted her lips and calculated probable calorie counts. So much fat. So many carbs. Not a green vegetable in sight. Maybe just for today, while the dull ache in her chest thudded in time with *Connor and the blonde*, she'd take a cheat day.

Ha. A cheat day. Her lips curled into a bitter grin.

What would her mother like? It had been years since they'd spent any real time together. Was she a vegetarian now? Nah. Couldn't be. The last time Sydney had ventured up to Pine Ridge they'd eaten out at the "nicest place in town," and Karen had ordered the cheeseburger.

Sydney ordered two chili cheeseburgers, french fries, onion rings, and something called "mixed vegetables," which probably came from a can but might be worth the gamble.

She climbed onto a barstool to wait for her food and glanced around the space.

TV sets played the Giants game, signs advertised fried-food specials, and the heavy scent of stale beer and cleaning fluid hung in the air. On a typical Thursday evening she'd be sipping drinks with Connor at the plush NoMad bar or cooing over art she didn't understand at an opening downtown.

Since she'd been let go from her job at the law firm a year ago, she'd slipped seamlessly into the role of "Connor's girlfriend." Silk blouses appeared in her closet as her *The Future Is Female* T-shirt found its way to the donate pile. She joined a Tuesday morning book club. Instead of watching football at a dark, dingy bar on Sunday afternoons, she brunched with Connor and his finance buddies. She'd needed a break from the stress of work, but as time passed and she handed over control of her days to Connor, she'd lost little bits of herself without even noticing.

As the booming announcer's voice called the football game and pint glasses thudded dully against the worn wooden bar, Sydney rested. Her body settled into the barstool, and for the first time in a long time, the tension in her neck eased a fraction of an inch.

Maybe Connor had done her a favor by cheating on her. In their apartment. On their bed. In their sheets.

Bile rose up in her throat.

Maybe not.

She turned her attention to the TV screen as the bartender returned.

"Get you something while you wait?"

A cold hoppy beer would be heaven, but in addition to the chili cheeseburger? She'd pay for it in the gym next week. The girls in her book club seemed to survive on raw almonds and green juice.

She scanned the taps, just in case, and recognized a familiar brown logo. Raquette River Brewing. A nearby brewery whose beer she never saw in New York City. She grinned.

"She'll have a cosmopolitan." The behemoth to her right giggled, his voice a bad imitation of Minnie Mouse.

The equally large man to his right nudged him with a meaty elbow. "With extra cranberry!"

They erupted in laughter, and Sydney glared.

"How'd you know what's in a cosmopolitan?"

The laughter halted, and they stared at each other and then at her.

"He's the one who knew!" one of them called out, pointing at the other.

"No way, you're the one who said it!"

A deep, throaty chuckle interrupted the buffoons. Past them, half-hidden by the sheer size of his friends, was a third male patron. How had she overlooked him? A patch of dried mud on his left forearm spoke to outdoor work, and a dark, neatly trimmed beard covered half his face but couldn't hide a full, rosy mouth. He took a sip of beer and licked the residual froth from his lips.

"You have something to say, too?" Sydney's voice cracked midsentence.

As he turned his piercing gaze on her, the breath caught in her throat.

Well, hello, Mountain Man.

"I didn't say anything." His voice reverberated like a needle on an old jazz record.

She held his steady stare for one moment longer before he turned back to the TV.

The bartender cleared his throat, breaking the spell and dragging her attention back to him. "Anything for you, miss?"

"Oh . . . Um, yes, please. I'll have the Raquette River IPA."

The bartender pulled the pint, and the second her hands closed around the glass, a deep breath escaped her lips. As the first spicy, bitter mouthful of beer slid down her throat, her shoulders relaxed. Perhaps she had underestimated the healing powers of this sleepy mountain town.

She sipped steadily at the pint as the New York Giants moved the football down the field. On third down, Derek Tahoe let go of a wobbly pass, and a Dallas Cowboys defender snatched the interception.

"Oh, you piece of garbage!" Sydney exclaimed. "Are you freaking kidding me with that ham sandwich?" She tilted the pint glass nearly upside down as the last frothy dregs hit her tongue. Empty already.

"Another?" the bartender asked.

"Sure, why not?"

Her diet was already shot to shit for the day anyway. He placed the beer in front of her, and she took a grateful sip.

The Cowboys couldn't manage a score on the drive, and the Giants got the ball back, making good progress on the possession. Once again, on third down, Derek Tahoe scanned the field like a scared little boy in Pop Warner football camp. The ball skimmed the tips of his fingers, wobbled, and fell into the hands of the exact same Cowboys cornerback.

"Are you kidding me?!" Sydney leaped off her barstool. "You human wasteland! What do we pay you for?"

She expected the entire bar to be just as outraged as she was, but instead, a trio of blank faces stared at her. She slid back onto her barstool and gritted her teeth. "Patriots fans?"

"Who *are* you?" Mountain Man asked.

All at once she missed the anonymity of a big city. "Who are *you*?"

"Sam Kirkland. Is your identity a matter of national security?"

"No." She tugged at her cardigan. "Sydney Walsh."

"Walsh, huh? Karen Walsh's daughter?"

"Yeah. How'd you know that?"

"Everybody knows Karen's got a prissy daughter living in New York City who never comes to visit her," Behemoth #1 said. "And you look just like her."

Okay, so she didn't come up to Pine Ridge every other weekend to visit her mother, but *prissy*? Because she wasn't sporting last season's L.L.Bean and a camo baseball cap?

She licked her lips and straightened her spine. If nothing else, she could defend half his accusation. "My mother and I don't look anything alike."

"Are you kidding?" Behemoth #1 said. "Around the eyes? Plus, you can tell Karen was a dime back in the day."

Sydney blushed and clutched the cold pint glass.

"If that wasn't perfectly clear, Joe just called you a dime," Mountain Man said.

Sydney stared into his eyes again, this time noticing the depths of the deep brown irises. A baseball cap obstructed some of his brow, but his eyes were like almond-shaped searchlights, peeking out from beneath the navy-blue brim.

Okay, so maybe this town had more than spruce-scented air going for it.

The bartender reappeared and placed a paper bag on the counter in front of her. "That's everything," he said. "It'll be thirty-five seventy-four."

She winced as she handed over Connor's credit card. In a few weeks, the monthly payment on her own maxed-out card would be due, and where would she be then? How soon until Connor canceled this card? Maybe her mother could loan her some money. She shuddered.

For the moment, she brushed the thought away. She'd spend a few days hiding out in Pine Ridge and deal with real life later.

"Aw, you're leaving?" Behemoth #1 said.

"Yeah, but gosh, am I heartbroken to miss the rest of the nail-biter."

The Cowboys had scored on the turnover, and the score was a grisly 45 to 3. Despite the joke, the bar drew her in. If she had to choose between pints and football and the quiet awkwardness of her mother's apartment, there was no choice at all. But duty called.

"Have fun, guys."

She climbed into her car and rested the bag of hot, deliciously greasy food on the passenger seat. Before she turned the car on, she checked her phone. Reception was spotty in Pine Ridge, but the bar must've had Wi-Fi because a bevy of messages lit up her phone. With nausea brewing in her gut, she opened the few from Connor.

I haven't been able to move since you left. Please call me. I love you.

Her eyes glazed over as the bright light of her phone screen dimmed and then ceased. Pure inky darkness hugged her from all sides. The blackness covered her like a blanket, and for a moment, she was safe. Untouchable.

With a sharp expletive she tossed her phone into her purse and slid the car key into the ignition. She punched the gear shift into reverse, hit the gas pedal, and didn't get more than three feet before the earsplitting crunch.

Ready to find
your next great read?

Let us help.

Visit prh.com/nextread

Penguin
Random
House